Patrick Gale was born on the Isle of Wight. He spent his infancy at Wandsworth Prison, which his father governed, then grew up in Winchester before going to Oxford University. He now lives on a farm near Land's End. One of this country's best-loved novelists, his most recent works are *A Perfectly Good Man*, the Richard and Judy bestseller *Notes from an Exhibition*, and the bestselling *A Place Called Winter*.

Praise for Patrick Gale's short stories:

'Gale has long been a master of short fiction . . . the form utilises all his strengths of acute observation, gentle wit and humane acceptance of human diversity . . . Wit and wisdom, metaphor and moment constantly combine to delight' *The Times*

'Dark, witty and often obliquely moving . . . Gale is interested in power and the lack of it and his stories pull the reader in unexpected ways, offering worlds that are far from certain and where love or its absence can never be predicted' Carol Ann Duffy, *Sunday Telegraph*

'Further evidence of Gale's stylistic deftness, insight and wonderfully eclectic range of interests' *Independent*

'Vivid, believable characters . . . Gale has a light touch with social commentary but the undertones are often menacing' *TLS*

'The stories confirm Gale's ability to exploit the short story genre's capacity to deliver a caffeinated hit . . . [they] showcase his capacity for combining a light touch and a macabre sense of humour with an understated strength of human feeling' *Metro*

'A hugely enjoyable collection which proves that the short story is still very much alive . . . Gale has a distinctive sense of humour and it is not unusual for something sinister to be lurking beneath the apparently unruffled and genteel surface of his narrative' *Daily Express*

'Not one . . . very much aliv

'The pros

C33   D0547944

By Patrick Gale and available from Tinder Press

The Aerodynamics of Pork
Kansas in August
Ease
Facing the Tank
Little Bits of Baby
The Cat Sanctuary
Caesar's Wife
The Facts of Life
Dangerous Pleasures
Tree Surgery for Beginners
Rough Music
A Sweet Obscurity
Friendly Fire
Notes from an Exhibition
The Whole Day Through
Gentleman's Relish
A Perfectly Good Man
A Place Called Winter
Take Nothing With You

PATRICK GALE

THREE DECADES OF STORIES

TINDER
PRESS

Copyright © 1991, 1996, 2009 Patrick Gale

The right of Patrick Gale to be identified as the Author of
the Work has been asserted by him in accordance with the
Copyright, Designs and Patents Act 1988.

Dangerous Pleasures first published in Great Britain by Flamingo in 1996
Caeser's Wife first published in Great Britain in *Secret Lives: Three Novellas*
by Tom Wakefield, Patrick Gale and Francis King by Constable in 1991
Gentleman's Relish first published in Great Britain by Fourth Estate in 2009

First published in this paperback edition in 2018 by Tinder Press
An imprint of HEADLINE PUBLISHING GROUP

1

Cataloguing in Publication Data is available from the British Library

ISBN 978 1 4722 5808 3

Typeset in Sabon 10.5/14.55 pt by Jouve (UK), Milton Keynes

Printed and bound in Great Britain by Clays Ltd, Elcograf S.p.A.

Headline's policy is to use papers that are natural, renewable and recyclable
products and made from wood grown in well-managed forests and other
controlled sources. The logging and manufacturing processes are expected to
conform to the environmental regulations of the country of origin.

HEADLINE PUBLISHING GROUP
An Hachette UK Company
Carmelite House
50 Victoria Embankment
London EC4Y 0DZ

www.tinderpress.co.uk
www.headline.co.uk
www.hachette.co.uk

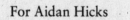
For Aidan Hicks

ON THREE DECADES OF
SHORT STORIES

Our traditional preference, as a nation, for a three-course fictional meal over a dish of protein-rich canapés is a pity. In America the story has enough high-profile outlets for gifted writers to have based whole careers on producing nothing else. In the UK, it's different, though I do vividly remember slim collections such as Ian McEwan's creepy *First Love, Last Rites* and Helen Simpson's delicious *Four Bare Legs in a Bed* being on everyone's laps or beach towels for a season or more. Happily, the conjunction of new and light reading devices and time-poor readers has led to an increase in shorter publications.

If I think back to being five or six years old and becoming an early devotee of that cunning piece of 1960s reader-recruitment, the Puffin Club, all the earliest books I remember cherishing to the point where their spines crumbled were collections of short stories. My older brother delighted in re-reading *Stig of the Dump* and *Emil and the Detectives* but my comfort books were *The Little Prince and Other Stories* and *The Puffin Book of Princesses*. From these I succumbed to the group addiction at boarding school and graduated, via a devotion held still for the Moomin novels and *The Phantom Tollbooth* to the Pan editions of ghost stories and horror stories, many from superb writers. I charted my way through the subversive tales of Saki and the unsettling stories by Daphne du Maurier and John Wyndham and came to realize, as I began to study literature seriously, that the truly great short stories by writers such as Alice Munro, Chekhov, John Cheever and

Mavis Gallant, were not simply short but were stories which managed to distil the emotional impact of a novel into a tiny space; like the moment when two minutes of overheard argument in a train carriage or a snippet from a muttered phone call in a crowded bus stop can open out in your head to reveal everything about a marriage gone sour, a life turned awry.

Having written stories throughout my school days and years as a student, it felt entirely natural, in my first year of living as an independent grown-up in Notting Hill in the mid-1980s, to write an entry for the Whitbread Short Story competition. Supported by the publisher Christopher Sinclair-Stevenson, and judged by Martin Amis, who was the epitome of literary cool, the shortlisted stories included *Borneo*, my homage to Saki, and were published in a paperback anthology. The prize vanished the following year, to be reinvented later as the Costa Short Story Prize, but that one little paperback led to my finding a deal for my first two, slender novels.

I'm lucky to have twice persuaded publishers in the UK to publish anthologies of mine. *Dangerous Pleasures* came out ten years into my writing career, *Gentleman's Relish*, a decade afterwards. Thereafter I continued to write stories alongside my novels. Some – *Dressing Up in Voices* or *In the Colony* – were intimately linked to novels I had recently finished or was about to write, but most were written as an end in themselves, to exorcise some idea smoking up my brain, and often served, during a period of agonizingly slow novel-writing, to remind myself I was still capable of completing a writing exercise. Many of them, including the shortest here, were born of commissions from the BBC for Radio 4's precious *Afternoon Story* slot. These were frequently to be written to a theme – the anniversary of *Alice in Wonderland*, for instance.

The anomaly, reprinted here for the first time, is *Caesar's Wife*. This comic novella, or long short story, is the only excursion I've ever made into first person narration. It was written for *Secret Lives*, a collection of three such stories around a theme created with my late friends Francis King and Tom Wakefield, at a time when I was briefly Tom's lodger and the three of us were forever meeting for lunch and hatching plans.

My devotion to stories, as writer and reader, is undimmed, not least because the shorter form, where there is less room for the slow revelation of character or gradual extension of sympathies that is so intrinsic to a novel's pleasure, allows me to give voice to a darker, even brutal side to my nature. There is murder here and violence, and stories of the uncanny, alongside the quieter, funnier exploration of character and family more familiar to readers of my novels.

I suspect that readers follow publishers and publishers follow prizes, so that what is needed is something with the heft of the Costa Book Award or Man Booker Prize to be devoted to a complete volume of short stories. Were that to happen, I'd cheerfully sacrifice a long summer to sitting reading in the garden as a judge; I know I'd not be the only reader to be delighted.

CONTENTS

DANGEROUS PLEASURES

Wig   3
Dressing up in Voices   31
A Slight Chill   53
Borneo   83
Paint   107
Other Men's Sweetness   135
Wheee!   167
Old Boys   183
The List   211
Choking   229
Dangerous Pleasures   249

CAESER'S WIFE

Caesar's Wife   275

GENTLEMAN'S RELISH

The Lesson   347
Cookery   363
Fourth of July, 1862   379
Saving Space   389
Petals on a Pool   399

CONTENTS

Obedience 421

In the Camp 439

The Dark Cutter 451

Making Hay 467

Brahms and Moonshine 481

The Excursion 491

Hushèd Casket 503

Dream Lover 523

Sleep Tight 533

Freedom 543

Gentleman's Relish 553

DANGEROUS
PLEASURES

WIG

for Rupert Tyler

Wanda would never have thought of buying such a thing, never have *planned* to do so. In this case, however, her thoughts and plans were immaterial. She was put upon, the object, quite literally, thrust upon her. The salesman pounced as she was waiting for a friend and as soon as she had felt the thing's slippery heaviness between her fingers, her fate was sealed.

Wanda had never mastered the art of evading the attentions of department store demonstrators and had gone through life being squirted with unwanted scents. Where other women could stride purposefully by, freezing all overtures with a glare or a scornful laugh, she would feel coerced into buying small gadgets for slicing eggs into perfect sections or recycling old bits of soap into garishly striped blocks. On the rare occasions when she heard him speak of her to his friends, she gathered that her husband's image of her was coloured by this weakness.

'She loves gadgets,' he would say. 'If she thinks it saves her time, she'll buy it. When they invent a gadget to live your life for you, she'll be first in the queue and let herself be talked into buying six.'

In her youth she had become a not terribly fervent Christian in the same way – sold the idea by a catchy sermon involving some crafty use of props – until her faith went the way of the spring-loaded cucumber dicer and the Bye-Bye Blemish foundation cream, gathering to it a kind of dusty griminess that dulled her guilt at its under-use.

'Excuse me, Madam.' It was a less vigorous approach than usual, tired and mechanical. He was evidently too drained by a long day of false charm to be mindful of his commission. 'Would you like to try a wig?'

A chip slicer she might have resisted. She had one of those already. And a hoover attachment for grooming the cat (not a great success) but the very strangeness of that little monosyllable seemed to pluck at her elbow. She paused and half-turned.

'I beg your pardon?'

He was a nondescript, sandy man; the kind of man one looked straight through. She did not imagine he could draw in much business and yet, now that he had caught her eye, she perceived something confidential in his very nothingness. She felt an immediate sense that, in talking to him, she became invisible too, temporarily shielded from critical view.

'A wig, Madam,' he repeated. 'Would you like to try one?' He did not smile. His manner was earnest, even urgent.

'Should I be insulted?' she asked, touching her own hair instinctively. 'Why me? Why didn't you ask someone else?'

'I did,' he said, with a ghost of a smile. 'I've sold several.' He considered the small rack of the things ranged on polystyrene heads on the trolley at his side like the grim evidence of an executioner's zeal, and stretched one over the backs of his simian fingers. 'I think *this* one for you,' he said. 'Not our most popular model, because it's rather expensive. To be quite frank with you, designs from the cheaper range tend to go to people looking for fancy dress or hoping to cover the short term effects of medical therapy. Try it on. I know you'll be surprised.'

She took it gingerly, expecting the cheap sweatiness of nylon but it was pleasantly cool, sending a kind of shock through her fingertips. It put her in mind of being allowed to hold a school friend's angora rabbit for the first time; now, as then, she was seized with an immoderate temptation to hold it to her cheek. It was blonde, of course. To that extent he *was* like any salesman. He had assumed, quite erroneously, that being a quiet-looking brunette with a sensible cut she could brush behind her ears or tame with an Alice band, she harboured a secret desire for Nordic bubble curls. Obedient, resigned to humiliation, she pulled out her hair slides then slid the wig over her tingling scalp. Feeling slightly dizzy, she bent her head forward – she was slightly taller than the salesman – and allowed him to tuck in any locks of her hair still showing.

For all its mass, it felt no heavier than a straw hat. She could not restrain a soft laugh; she knew she would not buy but this was amusement as harmless as raiding the dressing-up box and, smiling at her, he seemed to enter into her childish pleasure.

'Good,' he said. '*Very* good.'

'Quick,' she said. 'Let me see.'

He was stooping below his little trolley for the mirror when she saw her friend – one used the term loosely – returning from the haberdashery department with the shoulder pads and French chalk she had been seeking when they parted company. The friend was a conventional woman with a tendency to spiteful tale bearing when she caught any of her acquaintance doing anything eccentric or irrational. Wanda froze as the friend approached, suddenly aware that the salesman had frozen too, in suggestive complicity. It was too late to pull the wig off without hopelessly disordering her hair yet she could think of no plausible explanation as to why she was standing there trying it on. The friend's worst done, she would find herself receiving pitying looks as one bravely keeping a struggle with cancer or alopecia to herself or she would be scorned as the frivolous vulgarian they had long suspected her of being. The latter would be almost welcome. Her friends were merely neighbourhood women who had taken her under their wings; ambiguous controllers she would happily avoid. She could easily hide solitary days from her husband.

The friend passed her by however, without the slightest betrayal of recognition, continuing to look querulously about for her missing companion. Wanda looked after her retreating form in amazement. Had she a bolder appearance, she might have thought it miraculous. The salesman had found the mirror and was holding it out.

'See for yourself,' he said. 'Of course, it *is* beautifully styled, but the reason it's so much more expensive is that, apart from the basic skull cap, every fibre in it is human.'

She did not look directly in the mirror but, in the second before she tugged the thing free of her head in a spasm of revulsion, she seemed to catch a reflected glimpse of an angry stranger.

'Horrible,' she stammered. 'I'm so sorry. My friend's waiting for me.' And she hurried off for a reprimand from the friend and a dour, unfattening lunch.

When he first singled her out for his special attentions – fumbling trips to the cinema, long, circular drives in his car, hectoring sessions of golf tuition – her husband had praised her normality. 'The thing I really like about you,' he would say, 'is you're so normal.'

Delivered in lieu of anything more romantic, the praise warmed her heart and briefly convinced her that normality was indeed her special feature. Pressing through on his advantage, he wooed, wed and twice impregnated her. By some sleight of hand, he managed to do all four without once mentioning love. She did not love *him* – this had been one of the certainties that lent her courage in accepting his proposal – but she nonetheless hoped that he might love *her* and be holding something back out of manly reserve. This fond delusion evaporated shortly after the birth of their second child, when he passed on an infestation of pubic lice and blamed it, with neither apology nor embarrassment, on insufficient aeroplane hygiene. She had learned to live with the delusion's residue. She had a nice house, two clean, healthy children and a generous housekeeping allowance from which she could grant herself occasional treats without detection. Although she had only ever experienced orgasm by accident, her husband continued to grant her perfunctory sexual intercourse at least once a fortnight.

For most wives, that evening might have been a memorably bad one; for her it was much like any other. Their daughter, Jennifer, refused to eat supper, pleading incipient vegetarianism, and was sent to bed with no alternative. At several points during the meal, Mark, their son, imitated Wanda's way of talking, most unpleasantly, only to be rewarded with her husband's indulgent laughter. When she had seen the children off to bed, smuggling in an apple and some cheese to Jennifer, he pointedly admired a Swedish actress's breasts throughout the thriller she had not wanted to watch. After that, when she was ready to drop with exhaustion, he made her sit up and play Scrabble. Scrabble, like her normality, had been one of the things originally to bring them together. He had made her play it the first time he took her to Godalming to meet his mother.

An inveterate snob, he had learnt from his mother that most card games apart from bridge were somehow common and bridge, he swiftly gathered, lay beyond his impatient understanding. Scrabble, however, appealed to him. He assured her it was a game 'smart' people played. When challenged he would never say why and she suspected he was influenced by the game's appearance in a hackneyed advertisement for chocolate mint creams. His mother claimed it was sophisticated because it came in a dark green box and anyone knew that all the best things came in dark green – waxed jackets, cars, Wellington boots, folding TV dinner tables and so forth. The problem was that Scrabble was one of the few pastimes at which her husband seemed dim beside her. In front of his friends he pretended to boast of her cleverness, her facility for scoring forty-five with a four letter word placed slyly across the ends of two others, but in private she knew it maddened him. She learned early on in their relationship to temper her glee at triumphing over him. She avoided forming words like gnomon or philtrum which she knew he would vainly insist on challenging and she tortured herself by passing up frequent opportunities to score Scrabbles. Try as she might, however, she could not let him win. It was a game at which he could never excel. She hoped he would abandon the challenge, dismiss the skill he lacked as being feminine and therefore pointless but it was as if he wished to bludgeon the game into submission the way he did the television, or the dog. He knew he could beat her effortlessly at golf, drive faster and mow the lawn better than she ever would but he would not accept that in this one, insignificant area of their life, he had no mastery and was her inferior.

As usual, tonight, she trounced him despite her best efforts to help him win. She murmured soothingly that he had wretched luck with the letters he picked up but she knew he was seething from the way he splashed his whisky when he poured his night-cap and the entirely unnecessary fuss he made over some small item of household expense for which she had failed to obtain a receipt during that day's shopping excursion. She was weary to her very soul and knew she would have to make an early start the next morning because it was her day to drive the school run so she pointedly popped a sleeping tablet before pecking him a placid goodnight.

He ignored the hint, however. The cheap posturing of the film had left him restless and aroused and his humiliation at the Scrabble board had stirred in him a need for vengeance. She knew the warning signs of old. An unpleasant memory from when she was once laid low with gastric flu told her he would not be denied.

'You only have to lie there,' he said when she demurred and, tugging aside the pyjama bottoms she suddenly remembered she had forgotten to include in that morning's wash, he thrust his erection into her face. It bumped her nose once then she obediently took it in her mouth, remembering to keep her teeth out of the way. She had once been ambushed by an article on oral sex while waiting in the dentist's waiting room for her son to receive some fillings. It had changed her life – at least, it had changed a small part of her life – with the advice to make a yawning motion so as to widen the entry to the throat and avoid telltale, not to say unflattering, gagging. Tonight she found it difficult not to choke. As he pumped back and forth, his thighs weighty on her breasts, his grasp causing the headboard to bang against the wall, she fought back spasm upon nauseated spasm, diverting her thoughts onto undone tasks, recipe cards, the alpine perennials she had yet to plant on her rockery.

'I bet *she* never has to take this,' he said, mentioning the actress. 'I bet no one ever does this to *her*. She'd be on top. She'd call all the shots.'

He spoke in so matter of fact a manner that she feared his mind was on rockeries too and the ordeal might be prolonged much further but suddenly her cheeks were filling with his vile, familiar jelly. Never one for delicate gestures, he heaped insult on assault with a comment about helping to wash down her sleeping tablets. As he rolled off her and walked to the bathroom, she took a certain pleasure in spitting out his juices into the back pages of some golfing memoirs he had been reading.

Her children were enrolled in consecutive years of the same school and she shared the school run with mothers of three of their friends. School runs were a far cry from the easy suburban slovenliness of dropping one's husband off at the station with an overcoat flung over one's nightdress. Other children were all too often hostile emissaries of their parents, spitefully observant as only children could be. Normally she presented them with as clean and careful a version of herself as she would offer her husband's colleagues at the Christmas party. This morning, however, she had dressed in a hurry, thrown into confusion by a bad night's sleep and the discovery that her son had unplugged the tumble drier so as to recharge some batteries, and so left in a sodden heap that day's blouse which she had planned to iron before breakfast.

'You were wearing that dress yesterday,' said her daughter's best friend in a tone of friendly astonishment.

'I don't think so,' she said. 'Hurry up and belt up or we'll be late.'

'Yes you were,' said the child. 'I'm belted now so you can drive on. Yes you were. I saw you when Mummy came to pick up Mark and Jennifer.'

'Really?' Wanda replied, pretending to frown at some road

works. 'I really don't remember. Maybe I was. How funny. Now. What have you all got on your timetables today? Is it horrid maths?' Incredulously she felt herself break out in a nervous sweat. The girl had turned away, oblivious to the bright conversational gambit. 'Mummy changes at least twice a day,' she told the others. 'Three times if she's gardening or something. She says Daddy likes it.'

Wanda amused herself briefly with the image of the woman in question actually effecting regular bodily changes – new hair, new teeth, new leg lengths – with the restlessness of a dissatisfied flower arranger. Then the unnervingly self-possessed Morag, the next child they picked up, physically recoiled as Wanda laughed her hello in her face, and she realized she had forgotten, in the rush, to brush her teeth. She was caught out in her hasty rootle through the glove compartment for a packet of peppermints and, forced therefore to pass them round, had to admit to her lapse if she was to justify taking the last mint and thereby depriving Jennifer of one. Any ground gained by doling out sweets was doubly lost by this tasteless revelation. The girls shifted slightly on their seats and giggled except for poor Jennifer, who pressed her nose to the window and stared with forlorn fury at the passing houses, condemned now for a mother not only slatternly but unhygienic.

After seeing the children safely into the playground, Wanda drove directly into town, while she was still fired with humiliation and rage. Only half aware of why she was there at all, she found a parking space then half-strode, half-ran back to the department store. For a moment she froze as it seemed that the salesman and his trolley had vanished but then she saw with a start that he was only feet away, helping a woman peel a long, red creation off her own head of nondescript grey.

Instinct and a kind of warning glance from him told her to stand back until the woman had made her purchase then, as she stepped forward he greeted her with a blandly surprised, 'Ah, Madam,' and asked if she wished to try on the same model again.

'No,' she told him. 'It's perfect. I know it is. I was just being silly before. About the hair being human I mean. I don't know why. Perhaps it made me think of nuns. But now I . . .' She faltered, her mouth suddenly dry with nerves. His face briefly clouded by concern, he asked if she would like to wear it immediately.

'Oh no,' she said, scandalized. 'Wrap it up, please I . . . I'll try it on again once I get it home.'

He wrapped it in tissue then shut it into a bag so discreet it might have contained a roll of curtain-heading tape or a box of talcum powder.

Meeting the extravagant price with a handful of notes from the horde she had pared from her housekeeping budget, she experienced a dizziness that verged on the erotic and she had to hurry to the coffee bar to eat two slices of cake to recover her equilibrium. It was only as she sat there, terrible booty on the chair beside her, softly munching, reduced like the immobilized shoppers around her to a contented sugar-trance, that she noticed the bag was not one of the store's own but of a different provenance entirely. It was black with small gold lettering which boasted outlets in France, Luxemburg and Florida. *Silence*, the company appeared to be called, which put her in mind of libraries. Perhaps it was meant to be pronounced in a French accent to sound less an imperative, more a bewitching promise. In small curly letters beneath the title the bag whispered, *Your secret is our pride.* She wondered if the store's management knew the salesman was there at all or whether he slyly played on the employees' ignorance of one another's purpose and throve in their scented midst like a parasite on a sleek but cumbersome host. As if to confirm her suspicion, he had moved his trolley again when she glanced around her from the downward escalator. He had shifted his favours from foundation garments and hosiery to between costume jewellery and winter hats.

At first she only wore the wig at home, when she was safely alone, honouring it with all the ritual befitting a complex pornographic pursuit. She would lock doors and draw curtains. She took off all her too familiar clothes, the better to focus on the wig's effects, and wrapped her body Grecian-style in a sheet or bath towel, much as she had done as a slyly preening child. Every time she stretched it anew across her knuckles and tucked it around her scalp she felt afresh the near-electric sensations that had first surprised her in the store. She was fascinated by what she saw, transfixed before the unfamiliar woman she conjured up in the mirrored doors of the bedroom cupboards. If the doorbell or the telephone rang during the hours of her observances, she ignored them, although, lent courage by curls, she made a few anonymous calls to people she disliked, words slipping from her lips which the unwigged her could never have uttered. Had her husband come home unexpectedly, he would have caught her in as much guilty confusion as if he had surprised her in some rank adulterous act.

And yet with each resumption of blondeship she grew less timid. The woman in the looking glass would not be ignored, it seemed, and her influence proved cumulative. Wanda grew bolder. She began to make short daytime excursions in the wig and did things she imagined a woman with such hair would do. She drove to smarter districts than her husband's where she sat in pavement cafés and ordered a glass of red wine that brought a flush to her cheeks or a searingly bitter double espresso whose grounds she savoured on her tongue. She bought expensive magazines, flicked through them with a knowing smile as though she recognized the people within, then, casually profligate, left them behind on restaurant tables without even bothering to retrieve the small sachets of free samples glued to certain advertisements.

She had a pedicure at an elegant chiropodist's, which left her feet dangerously soft in the new black shoes she had bought herself. Then, inspired by the pleasure of watching a woman crouch below her working at her feet with little blades and chafing devices, she paid to have her toe and fingernails painted traffic light red. This last impulsive indulgence seemed a miscalculation at first since it could not be shut away in her wardrobe like the wig and the shoes or easily washed off like the new, distinguished scent, but her husband seemed to like her with claws. Or at least he did not seem actively to *dislike* her with them. A few weeks ago she would have thought them entirely out of keeping with her rather homely character and what she thought of as her 'look' but now they seemed no more than a newly exposed facet of her personality. Her fingers seemed longer and more tapering than they had before, her clothes less a necessity and more of a statement.

It was only a matter of time – two weeks, in fact, before she dared to leave the wig on when she picked the children up from school. As she waited by the gates, other mothers complimented her on her bold new style. She did not duck her head or offer bashful thanks and explanation as she might have done before but merely smiled and said, 'You think so?' for their opinions were now entirely unimportant to her wellbeing. The children, especially the other girls on the school run, usually so slack in their compliments, touched her with their enthusiasm.

'It's amazing!' they cried ingenuously. 'You look like a film star!'

She knew that children's ideas of glamour were hopelessly tawdry and overblown, that, in the undereducated estimation of little girls, anything forbidden them – lipstick, bosoms, cigarettes, false eyelashes – was of its very nature beautiful so that mere prostitutes acquired a near-royal loveliness for them. She knew she should not take their effusions as a compliment. She knew she should play along for a moment or two then expose the wig for the fraud it was. After all, she would still have shown herself to be that rare thing among mothers – a good sport with a potential for sexiness. But then she saw how her daughter was sitting, squeezed into her usual corner of the back seat, mutely glowing at the praise her mother was receiving from these all-important peers. She even received a rare gesture of affection from her son; a warm, dry hand placed on her shoulder as he boasted of the points he had received for a geography test. She imagined the disappointment, disgust even, on their faces if she suddenly tugged the wig off. They might not praise her as a good sport; they might simply declare her mad. She was not yet so far from her own childhood as to have forgotten that madness in mothers was even less forgivable than bad hats.

So she drove on. Wigged. A game, laughing lie made flesh. She laid rapid plans. If she could make it through the night undetected, she would cash in the rest of her rainy day fund, call at her usual salon the next day, throw caution to the winds and have her own hair dyed and styled to match the wig. At the thought that she would thereby become the woman in her looking glass, the stylish, effortless woman of her daylight excursions, she felt herself suffused with a warm glow that began in her scalp and ran down her neck and across her breasts and belly. She gazed at the suburban roads unfolding ahead of her and smiled in a way that might have scared the children had they been less absorbed in their own chatter by now. She dreaded her husband's return however. She dreaded his mockery or anger. Once supper was safely in the oven and the children were bathed, she locked herself in the bathroom to check with a mirror that no tell tale label or lock of her own hair were showing. The look was perfect however. She reapplied her new carmine lipstick, gave the back of her neck a squirt of scent then stood back to admire her full length reflection, stepping this way and that. He had a treat in store. He had a whole new wife.

Which were his own words exactly. At first he was perturbed. He wanted to know what had suddenly made her do it.

'You,' she said lightly. 'You said you wished I was blonde like that actress. So I am. I can always change back if you don't like it.'

'No', he said, looking at her in an uncertain, sideways fashion as he mixed his gin and tonic and poured her a sweet sherry. 'No. Don't do that. Was it very expensive?'

'Not very.'

He had no idea how much women's hair cost to fix. He naïvely thought it was maybe twice what he was charged by the barber in the station car park.

'Supper'll be about five minutes,' she said. 'I'm running a bit late. And I don't want a sherry. I want a gin.'

'But you like sherry. You always have sherry,' he insisted.

'I'd rather have what you're having,' she said. 'If there's enough that is.'

'Sure. Of course there's enough. There's always enough.' He

tipped the sherry back into its sticky lipped bottle and poured her gin. 'I dunno,' he said. 'I go to the office and when I come back I find a whole new wife.'

She simply smiled. 'Plenty of tonic,' she said girlishly. 'Or it'll go to my head.'

Over dinner he admired her nails too, apparently only noticing them for the first time now that she was blonde. He tried not to stare but she felt him watching her whenever she walked over to the cooker or the fridge.

'What are you staring at?' she asked at last, amazed that he had made no comment on the unpleasantly chemical pudding she had made by whipping milk into the brown powdered contents of a convenient packet and tossing in a few biscuits soaked in cherry brandy.

'You've killed her,' he joked. 'Haven't you? You've gone and killed her and put her outside in the deep freeze or something.'

She paused at the dishwasher with her back to him and shuddered involuntarily.

'Don't be silly,' she said as soon as she could. 'You'll give me the creeps. Coffee?'

'Please.'

'In here? Or are we playing Scrabble?'

'No games tonight,' he said, affecting a yawn. 'I thought perhaps an early night . . .'

She had always wondered how oral sex would feel when performed on her but in all the years of their marriage he had never offered and she had never thought it entirely proper to ask. Tonight, emboldened by the unprecedented interest he was showing in her hands, her feet and her borrowed hair, she realized that she needed no words to ask him. While he was giving

19

her breasts more attention than the usual cursory lick, she simply placed a hand on his head and pushed. He hesitated for a moment as though unable to believe what she was suggesting so she pushed again, quite firmly, so that her wishes should be unmistakable. The surprising pleasure he proceeded to give her had little to do with anything he was doing to her and everything to do with what she was doing to him. She had always supposed that sex was a matter of submission, patience even, but now it dawned on her that it was eight-tenths power.

She woke with a headache. She wondered if it had anything to do with the gin then thought that perhaps the wig was too tight. Could her head have expanded? *Did* heads expand? Like hot feet? The headache intensified as she dressed. She scowled as she brushed her teeth and teased the wig back into shape on her scalp. Downstairs the pain broke out as sulkiness, when she complained about being expected to polish her husband's shoes, and naked temper when she shouted at her daughter – her beloved Jennifer – for complaining that there was no fat-free milk for her cereal. Where these displays would normally have been beaten down by louder ones from the offended parties, she was amazed to see her husband mutely take up the boot polish and her daughter reach for the gold top with something like terror. Landed with the school run again by some cooked-up excuse from another mother, she thought her head would burst with the added burden of the children's chatter. She paused at some traffic lights to rifle her bag for painkillers which she gulped down without water, heedless of curious stares from behind her. Odious Morag – whose favour her children only cultivated because her parents had a swimming pool and threw vulgarly ostentatious birthday parties for her – had already riled her by insisting on sitting in the front like an adult because she said the back of the car 'had a bad smell'. She then began to tease Jennifer for having a crush on a teacher.

'That's enough,' Wanda said, wincing at the pain her own voice caused, booming behind her eyes. 'Stop being horrid.'

'But it's true,' Morag insisted. 'She always tries to sit in the front row.'

'I don't!' Jennifer protested.

'She *does*. And yesterday she stayed behind to ask him questions before break.'

'I said that's *enough*!' Wanda said and found herself slapping Morag on her soft, pink thigh.

For a moment there was stunned silence as Morag looked from thigh to driver and back again. It had been a fierce little slap; Wanda's palm still stung seconds later.

'I'll tell,' Morag said at last.

'Good,' Wanda told her, giddy with the release of uttering words she had too long swallowed. 'Then maybe you'll get another slap for being a telltale as well as an ill-bred little madam.'

Morag made as if to cry at this but Wanda silenced her.

'Stop it,' she hissed, astonished at the scorn in her tone. 'You're too *big* to play the baby.'

The euphoria of the others was palpable behind their silence as Morag stifled her petulant sniffles. Pulling up outside the school, Wanda defied the pain in her head.

'Jennifer,' she said. 'I'm *glad* you're showing an interest in your lessons. I'm *proud* of you, darling.' Jennifer shone with pleasure even as Morag seemed to shrink in significance.

Wanda tore the wig off with a gasp as soon as she was clear of the area. Glancing in the mirror to flick her own hair back to a semblance of life, she saw a livid, purplish welt where the thing's netting had been grinding into her forehead. From time to time as she drove, she would rub hard at it with her fingertips. She had a tendency to raise her eyebrows when people were talking to her, especially when she had no interest in what they were telling her. Possibly this habitual action had made the wig's chafing worse, producing this shaming record of insincerity.

Back in her house, before she had even loaded the breakfast things into the dishwasher, she hurried to the telephone and called her hairdresser's. To her dismay, no one, not even a junior, could see her for anything more than a dry-it-yourself light trim for two days. She had a deep, almost pathological sense of consumer loyalty, never being lured by a bargain rate into forsaking the tradesmen she had always patronized without a commensurate sense of guilt which she felt obliged to own when she next entered her usual shop.

'I bought half a pound of these in that other place on the parade,' she would confide in a confused salesperson. 'I never normally shop anywhere but here but, well, you know how it is. I just saw the price and in I went.'

Often as not she would add some placatory lie about the bargain goods having proved inferior to those from her usual stockist as though the thought that her dereliction had been punished would comfort them over her momentary infidelity. It was with a heavy heart, therefore, that she reached for the *Yellow Pages* and looked up the numbers of rival salons. She would not tip, she told herself, however good they proved; that way the disloyalty would seem less wounding. But neither Bernice of Bromley, Shy Locks or Louis D'Alsace could fit her in. After a few more, similarly disappointing calls, she gave up, called back her usual salon, and made a morning appointment for the next day. It was only another forty-eight hours, she told herself. If she had fooled her small world so far, she could fool it a little further.

To soothe her nerves she left the wig on the hall table for swift snatching up should there be any surprise callers then she threw herself into a satisfactory penance of housework. She scrubbed the bath, pulling a skein of matted hairs from the plughole, cleaned the nasty fluffy bit of carpet behind the loo, wiped the tops of the door surrounds and descaled the shower head with a powerful caustic she had recently heard of being used in a desperate suicide bid. Then, with no break for coffee, she set about taking every saucepan and labour-saving device from the kitchen cupboards, cleaning it, washing down its shelf, then putting it back again. She even wiped the sticky residue from jam and marmalade pots. The varnish on her new nails chipped off in places but she slaved on, taking a kind of delight in finding other unpalatable tasks to tackle. She skipped lunch, eating only aspirin because she still had the residue of her morning's headache, and forged on with polishing her husband's collection of silver plate trophies and the fiddly cake stand with matching slice which his aunt had given them on their wedding day. (Wanda had kept it in the back of a cupboard, polishing it still more rarely than she used it because it had too many little nooks and crannies and something in her rebelled at using even a discarded toothbrush to clean it.)

Suddenly she saw it was time to be picking the children up again. Cursing clothes, time, duty, she ran to the hall, tossing aside her apron and snatching up the wig. The wig no longer fitted. She glared at her pink-cheeked reflection as she stuffed her hair back behind her ears and tried again. She even checked to see if the label were the right way round. She glanced at her watch and let out a whimper. She caught herself toying with the possibility of driving into school as she was only with a head-scarf on in the vain hope that the children would prove less sharp-eyed than usual. This was ridiculous! Wigs did not shrink. It was not in their nature. And heads, healthy adult heads, did not grow. Brooking no nonsense, she tried one more time.

Never had the saying that one must suffer to be beautiful been so rigorously brought home to her. She succeeded in don-ning the wig and styling it much as before but it might have been made of cheese-wire it dug so fiercely into her. The head-ache, which had never entirely left her all day, paled by comparison with such immediate pain. Driving to the school, she felt herself multiply martyred. She was not yet so vain as to have become irrational. She wondered if she were sick. Women such as she had become, women with scarlet nails and bor-rowed splendour, were never ill. They had everything organized, and disease was not part of their plan. They vomited with tidy aggression in other women's bathrooms then partied on, lips painted afresh. They scorned hospitals. Illness bored them and the surgeon's knife filled them with selfish fears. They died vio-lently, she sensed, in a kind of anger at a world that had cheated them. Women who made love in blonde wigs and took pains to deceive their children died crushed beneath the wheels of trains or skewered by the steering columns of their lovers' cars. A trickle of warm moisture ran from under the wig across her temple. She glanced fearfully up at the mirror, half expecting to see blood, but it was merely sweat and she dabbed it away with a handkerchief.

She was one of the last of the parents to arrive but there was not a breath of complaint from the children and she remem-bered her show of strength that morning. She noticed its effect almost immediately; a change had come over the pecking order in the group. To her surprise she saw that it was her daughter who now held sway, telling people where to sit, holding power of ultimate disapproval or permission. And it was Morag, normally so haughty and spiteful who was now the po-faced wheedler and appeaser.

'Mrs Spalding, I know it's very short notice,' she began, with such soft shyness that Wanda anticipated mockery, 'but my parents are taking me to the cinema tonight and I wondered if you'd let Mark and Jennifer come too. We've all done our homework already. We did most of it in break and we finished it in the last lesson because Mr Dukes was off sick. Daddy would drop them off afterwards. So you wouldn't have to do anything.'

Wanda acquiesced so easily they seemed quite startled. Jennifer began to plead automatically before realizing her wish was already granted. Wanda could think of nothing but the cruel way their voices played upon the pain in her head. The possibility of emptying the car that little bit sooner and facing an evening of relative tranquillity was an unlooked-for blessing. Her immediate impulse on swinging clear of Morag's parents' long drive was to snatch the wig off but she checked herself with the thought that she would only have to pull it on again for her husband's benefit, possibly with even greater difficulty and pain than before.

When she reached home, she walked swiftly round drawing all the curtains and turning on a few lights to create a pleasant, welcoming atmosphere, then she kicked off her shoes and lay in the middle of the drawing room carpet, breathing gently. The scents of potpourri and cleaning products soothed her. The tang of carpet freshening powder was a reminder that she had not rested all day. She closed her eyes, concentrating on breathing

25

slower and slower, counting to herself as she drew in the fragrant air. The pain in her head began to subside and, fancying she felt the wig loosen perceptibly about her skull, she slipped into a sensuous doze.

She had given no thought all day to what they were to eat for supper. Normally it was something she did after the children had been taken from her after breakfast. She would load the dishwasher then allow herself a cup of coffee and a couple of the biscuits she kept hidden inside the drum of the electric potato peeler and she would pore over recipe books and a shopping list. Given though she might be to the blandishments of kitchen gadgets, she had never been one of those modern mothers (slatternly mothers, she thought of them, lucky, happy slatterns) who contented themselves with a hoard of frozen meals and a microwave oven. Apart from *Instant Whip*, the nearest she had ever allowed herself to fast food was a pressure cooker, and *that* she only used for steaming puddings and root vegetables. When she woke to find her husband standing over her asking if she were all right and what was for supper because he couldn't smell anything cooking, she stared up at him and felt panic in her very soul.

'I . . . I fell asleep,' she stammered, climbing to her feet and padding, shoeless, into the supperless space across the hall. 'Morag's parents have taken the children to the cinema. I had a headache when I got back and I lay down and I must have fallen asleep. Sorry.' She looked about her. The lack of lights and steam, the lack of sizzle, formed a dreadful, silent accusation. She could not pretend that the automatic oven switch had failed to come on when there was palpably nothing in there waiting to be cooked. There was not even a piece of meat. She opened the fridge door then closed it again hurriedly as he came in behind her. There was nothing. No bacon. No chicken breasts. Not even some humbly reassuring mince.

'I work my guts out all day,' he was saying, as to some invisible jury, 'and it's been a bugger of a day too, and I come back to find you fast asleep, looking like nothing on earth, and the table not even laid.' She darted a hand to her head and was relieved to find the wig still in place. 'What's got into you?' he asked.

She decided to brazen it out. 'I forgot,' she said.

'You *what*?!'

'I forgot. I've never done it before and I won't do it again. But I forgot. I spent the whole day cleaning and scrubbing and I completely forgot about supper. And I've had a terrible headache. Why don't I fix us both a nice drink? Better still, why don't we live a little and go out. The children are safe with the Hewitsons until 9.40. If we went now I'm sure we could get a table. I've had a bugger of a day too.' From somewhere deep within her she found a reserve of flirtatious gaiety. 'Come on,' she said. 'You mix us both a nice gin and put your feet up while I go and put on something pretty then we can pretend we're young and free again and you can take me out for dinner. Somewhere cosy. Somewhere French with candles!'

There was a pause, perhaps for only a second, in which she was intensely aware that the fridge had developed a louder buzz than usual, which she knew was the sign that it was reaching its point of built-in obsolescence, then he began to shout at her. He called her filthy things – filthier things than he ever did when they were having sexual intercourse. He implied she was a failure as a wife, a mother, a woman even, and then he slapped her. He had offered her many insults in his way and in his time but he had never, until this evening, touched her in violence. She fell back against the sink. Then, all at once, the shock

27

of his big bony hand against her jaw seemed the ultimate denigration and she took a knife from the wooden block beside the bread bin and pushed it into his stomach. It was a big knife, her biggest, and the block was a particularly cunning one with a discreet mechanism which sharpened each blade as it released it for use.

She had often heard of the similarities between pork and human flesh, in particular their skin structure and the thickness of their fatty deposits. After the initial resistance, which might as well have been caused by the starched cotton of his shirt as by any strength of skin and muscle, the knife slid in with appalling ease and swiftness. The sensation was not unlike slicing into a rolled pork loin. Her husband gasped and staggered backwards, then forwards, then slumped to the floor. Never having taken a first aid exam, he did not know better than to pull the knife out. She had punctured his liver. By the time he was writhing and coughing on the linoleum, his suit was turning purple with his gore. She tried to staunch the flow with tea towels, but he was beyond her help. He seemed to spit in her face as he died but perhaps he was only coughing.

She called for an ambulance and the police, telling them her husband had been stabbed but not by whom, then she looked up the relevant cinema in the local newspaper and telephoned to leave an urgent message for the Hewitsons that an emergency had arisen and they were to hang on to Mark and Jennifer until contacted by the authorities. Turning back, she saw the big red thing on the kitchen floor and was suddenly sick, just as she had imagined women with blonde wigs should be. She vomited nothing but acrid juices, having eaten nothing all day, but it ruined the parts of her clothes the blood had not already stained, and she determined to change into something cleaner before the emergency services arrived. Both hospital and police station were a good fifteen minutes' drive away. Skidding slightly, because her feet were wet, she hurried across the kitchen and up the stairs to the bathroom. She tugged her blouse over her head and stepped out of her skirt. She began to wash her bloodied hands in the sink then realized that there was so much of the stuff on her that a shower would do the job better.

Having been descaled only that afternoon, the jet was extra strong and she welcomed its buffeting. It was only as she raised her hands to her face that she remembered she was still wearing the wig. Blinking the water from her eyes, heedless now of how badly she treated the thing, she took a handful of curls and tugged. She recoiled with a gasp. Crying out as though the water were scalding her, she flung back the shower curtain and struggled to see herself in the looking glass. The mirrored surface had steamed up and her flailing hand could not reach it so she tugged once more at the curls and felt once more the unmistakable agony of her own outraged scalp refusing to yield.

DRESSING UP IN VOICES

for Jonathan Dove

'The only time I ever lost control – I mean truly lost control,' he said, 'was with someone else's wife.'

'Go on,' she said and pushed aside the carcass of the small bird she had just eaten.

'Well he was some kind of financial genius. I met them through Flavia.'

She wrinkled her brow to show that she knew no Flavia.

'You know,' he went on. 'Flavia. The broker who used to lead Edward around like a spaniel.'

'Oh yes,' she lied, keen for him to press on.

'Anyway, the genius, who incidentally was ugly as sin, had to go away to Washington for some secret advisory mission and she turned up on my doorstep and we sort of fell into bed.'

'Goodness,' she said.

'Quite. I mean, she was dead sexy and all that but ... Actually, now that I think about it she wasn't sexy at all. But that was just it, you see.'

'What was?'

'Why I lost control. It was all forbidden. She said she loved him, or at least that she had immense respect for him. There was something else too, because she forbade me to let on to anyone else what was going on.'

'So she turned up on your doorstep more than once?' she asked, for whom his doorstep was as yet no more than a dot lovingly marked on an A–Z page.

33

'God yes. Every day for a month.'

'No more?'

'A month was quite enough. Anyway, he came back. She seemed to be scared of him, terrified that he might find out. She wouldn't talk about it, but now and then there was a close shave – someone meeting her on her way to my place, that sort of thing – and I'd see the panic in her eyes. Smell it on her almost.'

'Goodness.'

'Of course, it was only the trappings I fell for; the secrecy, the air of the illicit and probably the knowledge that, all being well, I'd never have to take up any responsibility for her. Anyway, I lost control. Utterly. She would ring up at about six to ask if I was free and I would say yes, ridiculously excited, then ring whoever I was meant to be seeing and cancel. Even really good friends.'

'Didn't anyone suspect?'

'Well of course they did, but I blinded them with half-truths. There was a married woman, I said, but no one any of them had ever met. I think, when a month went by and no one had been introduced, they just assumed that I was ashamed of her.'

'Or that she was ashamed of you.'

'What?' He looked up from the napkin he had been shredding and saw that she was mocking him. He snorted. Their waiter took away his spotless plate and her bird carcass. Gus asked him to bring them both a pudding. He asked for it in fast Italian.

'What did you ask for?' she demanded, cross because she had wanted *zabaglione*.

'Oh, it's their speciality. It's a kind of ice-cream grenade, encased in white chocolate and dribbled with Benedictine.'

'Oh.'

'Sorry. Did you want something else?'

'No.'

'No, come on. Did you? 'Cause I can grab someone and change the order.'

'Well . . .' She looked across the candle into his pale green eyes. He wore the apologetic expression she had seen last night. He had been doing something delectable back and forth across her abdomen with his short, blond hair and small, pointed tongue. She had run a hand across the back of his neck, as much to feel the stubble there as to make some dumb show of gratitude, but he had stopped and looked up at her with that apologetic look on his face; a painfully proper child caught out at an impropriety. 'No. Go on,' she had told him then. Now she merely smiled and confessed to a hankering after a warm froth of egg and Marsala. He had the waiter at his side with one brief turn of the head.

'You do have *zabaglione*, don't you?' he asked.

'*Certo, ma è freddo*,' the waiter told him. '*Per i barbari americani*.'

'Oh no,' she burst out. 'Please don't bother. The ice-cream thing would be fine.' Cold *zabaglione* was like offering a virgin a bed with dirty sheets. She had wanted the world's most erotic food and they were trying to fob her off with a pornographic approximation. She loathed Benedictine, but now would suffer it meekly.

'But I'm sure they could heat it up for you,' he urged her, visibly embarrassed. 'They could use a *bain-marie*.'

'No, Gus, honestly,' she insisted and turned to send the waiter away. 'What he ordered will do beautifully,' she assured him. The waiter left them with a tinge of a sneer. Gus's ring hand lay on the table. 'Sorry about that,' she muttered and reached out to touch his fingers with her own. He let his hand lie dead beneath hers then withdrew it to effect a needless adjustment to his hair.

'How about you?' he asked.

'What about me?'

'When did *you* last lose control?'

'Oh,' she laughed. 'It's sad, but I don't believe I ever have.'

'So your books aren't autobiographical? All that rage? All those thwarted lusts?'

'Lord no,' she sighed, peeling a runnel of softened wax off the candle. 'I mean, of course I have to write about feelings I can sympathize with, but I couldn't begin to live such a violent life. The very idea!' and they both laughed. The very idea of such a sane animal running fabulously amok! How too absurd! How . . . How endearing! She felt herself grow dim before the massed jury of her heroines and continued, 'Besides, I don't think you can put real happenings into fiction. Not without toning them down.'

'Too wild?'

'Sort of. There are too many jagged, messy bits. Heaven knows, there's nothing more dead than a tidy story, but there needs to be some kind of perspective.'

'Oh look. *Perfetto*,' he pronounced as their white chocolate grenades of ice cream arrived before them. He attacked his at once with that same decorous greed she had noticed in bed. She sank a spoon into hers and watched the chocolate armour crumble into the alcoholic ooze below. She carved out a spoonful then let it lie.

'I'm not altogether sure that I've ever been in love,' she said. He failed to interrupt so she continued. 'It's not that I'm heartless, or even incapable. I've *thought* I was in love several times.'

'Tell me about it,' he said, eyeing her pudding as his own all but disappeared.

'I suppose you could call my attitude romantic insofar as I believe in the possibility of meeting someone with whom one could pass the rest of one's life and for whom one would be prepared to die.' She realized of a sudden that the man at the adjoining table was listening with keen interest so she paused to take a mouthful of her grenade and give him time to resume his conversation with the youth before him. The ice cream hurt her throat. Benedictine was as reminiscent of dry-cleaning fluid as the last time she had tasted it. Mutely she offered her plate to Gus.

'Are you sure?' he asked. She nodded. He accepted it and began to eat again.

'And each time I meet someone and they say they love me, I'm flattered, and usually for them to have got that far they have to be fairly attractive, so I'm excited as well. And, I don't know. The whole business is so very beguiling. Other people's bedrooms and breakfast. Going through a day with that mixture of smugness and light-headed exhaustion . . .'

'Bliss.'

Was he, she wondered, talking about love or the pudding?

'So I throw myself into it, fingers crossed and hoping that this time it'll be the real thing. But of course that's stupid because, as I realize each time I bring something to an end, if it *were* the real thing I shouldn't have had to cross my fingers, or hope, or crank up my indulgence. If it were the real thing, I'd have lost control. Of course writers and films exaggerate no end but there's no smoke without a fire and I just know that, if I don't feel physically sick at separation and giddy every time I hear someone's voice or find one of their odd socks at the bottom of the bed, then I'm faking. Every time, after I've started faking and got myself thoroughly involved, there comes a

37

sickening moment when some demonstration of theirs shows me that they've lost control and I'm still sitting there with fingers crossed and my spare hand firmly on the joystick.'

The man with the youth tittered. Gus quashed him silent with a sharp look. It was one of the unimportant things that made her sick at their every separation and giddy when she heard his voice. That and the wholly irrational whatever that caused her to invite him repeatedly to her bed while the furies of rationality keened a despairing no.

She had found him at an unmemorable dinner party three years ago with his pretty and seemingly vacuous girlfriend, Loulou. Gut-stabbed by lust, she had set out perversely to woo the girl rather than charm the man. Loulou proved far from vacuous, was calculating indeed, and she had been made swiftly a party to her ceaseless round of infidelities. They would ask her to supper and she would dutifully play the role of professional wit and novelist, gabbling away about nothing when she needed to take Gus by the lapels and scream about the betrayals that passed unseen beneath his patrician nose. More recently there had been a falling off in their meetings because the strain had been becoming too much for her. Also she had been busy convincing herself that she loved another man, who was yet too ghastly to trundle out for friendly inspection. Then, three weeks ago, a postcard had arrived.

'As you may have gathered from the radio silence, my life has been suffering a sea-change,' Gus wrote. 'Have severed communications with Louise and am anxious not to lose you in the ensuing drawing-up of ranks. Let's have supper. Soon.'

On one heady impulse, she sacked the horrendous man whom no one had met, and invited Gus round for supper and sympathy.

She had planned to borrow a leaf from Loulou's book. She had planned to question him mercilessly about his domestic disaster and shattered faith in love then offer a shoulder to cry on and a brave new bedfellow to help him forget. ('Poor Gus', *bang*). In the event, she sat back and watched the unfamiliar spectacle of herself losing control. After feeding him with what she knew to be his favourite dishes, shopped for and prepared with passionless care that afternoon, she started to tell the truth then could not stem the confessional tide.

'I want you,' she had told him, curled in her chair as he sprawled across her sofa. 'I've wanted you ever since I first saw you in Nadia's horrid green kitchen. And I hated Loulou because she had you and I only became her friend so as to find out more about you and get as close to you as I could. I thought she was vacuous and that you deserved better and then she started to . . . Gus, I knew everything. She told me everything and I didn't tell you because I wanted her to be as unfaithful as possible. I thought that the more she slept around, the less likely you'd be to forgive her if ever you found out. Sometimes, knowing what I knew and not telling you, was more than I could stand. But I couldn't tell you, you see, because I knew you loved her and that you'd hate whoever opened your eyes. So I couldn't come between you. I had to wait. And now you're probably wondering how best to extricate yourself from this appallingly tawdry little scene.'

But he had not left. Not until breakfast. And he had come back. Again and again.

As he drank cognac and she a small black coffee, she realized that they had made no plans for the night. Tomorrow was a bank holiday Monday, so there would be no need for him to get up early to be at his office. She had kept tomorrow free on purpose so as to share his day off but he had still said nothing. He talked about how depressing it was to watch one's friends marry off, settle down and revise their address book according to their partner's whims. She listened with half an ear, making sighed or chuckled responses where necessary, but she was thinking about that night, the next day and the following weekend. She wanted him to ask her back to the 'smallish place' in Islington that she had never seen. She wanted to wake up in his bed, feel his back beside her then fall asleep again only to have him rouse her later with coffee and a wet, late rose. (She watched the man and the youth leave. She saw the fleeting brush of his hand across the youth's own.) She wanted to explore Gus's bookshelves and record collection while he shaved. Would his flat be indescribably sordid, with a dirty frying pan on the stove and a mattress on a dusty floor, or was Gus hiding behind a landlord's furniture and non-committal colours? She drained her cup to the bitter dregs and slid her miniature macaroons across the table to his eager hands.

'Shall we, er?' he asked, when he had finished munching. She hummed assent and smiled until he had to smile back. She watched as he summoned the bill, and she reached for her wallet.

'Here,' she said, crinkling a note at him.

'No.' He waved it away, deftly handing back the bill to the waiter with a piece of plastic tucked inside it. 'You bought the tickets so this is on me.'

The tickets had cost far less, but she demurred for only an instant as his salary far outweighed her publisher's most recent advance. Proportionately, her concert tickets had cost her several of his grand meals.

'I'll wait for you outside,' she said and headed for the door.

'Your coat, *signorina*.'

'Of course. How stupid of me.' She had forgotten her coat. She stood awkwardly as the waiter insisted on helping her on with it.

'*Buona notte*,' he said and held open the door with a grin.

'Goodnight,' she replied and went out.

The pavement was nearly empty, although it was not long past eleven. She had forgotten how even the West End could become suburban on Sunday nights. Autumn was coming. The sky was cloudless and there was a chill in the air. She watched a woman dancing, drunk, with her reflection in a darkened hairdresser's window, then turned back, nervous, to see if Gus was coming. There he was, swinging into his cream mac with a frown, mildly irritated by a hovering waiter, and she knew that she would have to speak first. As he emerged on to the pavement he did not return her smile but the words were already on her lips. As good as spoken, so, '*Dove adesso?*' she asked.

'What?'

'How shall we get back?'

'Um. Look.' He drew her alongside him with an arm across her shoulders. 'We need to have a talk.'

We've talked too much already, she thought, panic clutching her from within. That's our trouble. We've talked everything to death. We should hurry home, hurry to either of our homes and make rapid, violent love without a word being spoken. Then again, slowly, still in silence. Then make ourselves over to sleep. Tomorrow all will be well. Then. For now.

'I'm all ears,' she said brightly, making as if to meet his eye but seeing no further than his coat buttons before cowardice drove her to look straight ahead. They began to walk.

'We've had a lovely time,' he said swiftly. 'A *good* time. And I'm very fond of you, but . . .'

'But,' she echoed.

Don't say another word, she meant to say. Least of all fond. Fond, with its connotations of passing folly. I'll find a taxi, leave you here and we'll never meet again. Oh Christ, Christ, Christ. This is going to hurt, whatever you say, and the least you could do is let me go without you making a little speech to make your suffering less. The least you could do would be to shut up and hurt; suffer a part of what I . . . We shall have to meet in hot Christmas sitting rooms and bray delightedly.

They came to a line of scaffolding poles ranged along a length of pavement. She slipped apart from him and walked on the pavement's edge so that the metal came between them. She was looking sternly ahead and felt that he was too. She pictured their two, pinched, white faces as an oncomer might see them. Second division terrorists trying to pass plans for an assassination without it being seen that they are known to one another. But the pavement was empty. They waited, obedient, at a crossing although there were no cars coming through the green lights.

'But I don't think we should carry on with the bed bit,' he said. She said nothing. They walked on and she could find nothing to say. 'Do you see?' he asked eventually, as they came into Trafalgar Square and waited at another crossing.

'Yes,' she said. 'It's just that I can't think of anything to say that isn't banal.'

'What a pity?'

'Yes. That would do.'

No more words. Leave me. Let me go home. I want so *much* to go home.

'How will you get home?' he asked.

'Walk in the right direction until I find a taxi, I suppose. What about you?'

'Can I walk with you until you find one?'

'If you like.'

Go away. Take your patrician nose and go away. No. No. Stay and get in the taxi with me. Come home. Unsay it all. Gainsay.

'I think the trouble was that I'd got so used to not thinking of you in, well, *that* way. With Loulou around and everything and you were so . . .'

'What?'

'So horribly clever.'

'That's *no* reason. That's a worthless thing to say.'

'Yes it is.'

'I moved too fast,' she cut in. 'I frightened you off.'

'No. Not that.'

'What, then?'

'I don't think it would have made any difference how fast you moved. I just wasn't ready. Not for you. Not for anyone. Anything.'

'I think I could tell,' she said slowly.

Of course she could tell. He had organized the entire weekend so that, while spending every hour together, they spent as many of them as possible out of doors, in public, away from any kind of bed. He had engineered the discussion over dinner. The disgusting, cold discussion. He thought he had prepared the ground so that it would be less of a shock for her. Well he made a lousy job of it.

'I suppose, if the chemistry is wrong, then no amount of good will can help,' she said, feeling cheapened by the words.

'Yup,' he said. 'And believe me,' this with an awkward little

43

tug at her shoulders that made her teeter and graze one of her ankles on a heel, 'there was plenty of it.'

They walked the length of Whitehall in total silence. Three late buses sailed past them, buses she could have taken to escape him, but she needed to hurt herself. She resolved on taking a taxi or nothing, knowing that taxis on the route she would take were rare. They reached Parliament Square and she clutched at a straw.

'Look, Gus, this is silly. There are loads of cabs going in your direction. Leave me here. I'll be fine.'

'Are you sure?'

'Yup. Easier on my own. I'll be fine. But look, there's some stuff of yours in my flat; that black jersey and some socks and things.'

'Oh God. So there are. What are you doing tomorrow?'

'Nothing much.'

'Let's meet for tea and you can give me them then.'

Success!

'Where?'

'St James's. That funny sixties cafeteria place.'

'Okay. Fourish?'

'Make it five.'

'All right. But are you sure?'

'How do you mean?'

'Well.' She paused. 'I could always post them to you.'

'Don't be stupid. I still want to see you, remember.'

'Oh yes.' Silly me, she thought, I forgot.

'Here's a cab,' he said. 'I must run.'

They tried to shake hands but she missed and ended up with a fistful of mackintosh. She waited until she heard his taxi door slam then allowed herself a brief wave as he escaped her up Whitehall.

She walked home along the North bank of the river and over Albert's fairground of a bridge. Buses only passed her when she was between stops and taxis were either busy or going the wrong way and unwilling to turn back. She toyed with the idea of climbing the low railings into the small green space known as the Pimlico Shrubbery for a good weep, or abandoning herself to showier grief on a bench facing Battersea Power Station, but she preferred to walk and punish her elegantly shod feet. If she got home too soon, she would not sleep, thanks to the coffee she had drunk and the ideas circling wildly as to how she should approach tea-time tomorrow. A middle-aged black couple were having trouble starting their car at one point and she stopped to help the husband push it. When it started, he offered her a lift home but she said no thank you, she was almost there, although she had at least a mile to go. Pushing the car, she had broken the heel of one of her shoes.

Before letting herself in, she leaned into a neighbour's skip to vomit all she had eaten in the restaurant. This was easily done; there had been gobbets of blood around the small bird's bones and she had only to think of these. Sleep came, thick and dreamless. She woke with blisters on both big toes and fresh resolution in her heart.

She rarely wrote short stories. Her novels were fat, exhaustive expositions of character and possibility that drove critics to wield terms like *sprawling* or *magisterial*, and she found the smaller form unsatisfactory. The short stories she *had* written gained most of their poignancy from the fact of their being dismembered first chapters, and could not stand comparison with the more finished work of specialists. She had spoken truly in telling Gus that her novels made no use of autobiography. She left herself alone but, unconsciously, she did use her acquaintances, transmogrified with bits and pieces of each other. Her method resembled a child's picture book whose pages were cunningly split into threes, enabling one to join head of stork with body of rhino and mermaid's tail. Thus Janet's temper might join with Edward's charity in Susan's body. Susan's body was one of a kind, but neither she nor Janet nor Edward ever recognized their contributions to the hybrid result. Hardly surprising, since even the authoress frequently failed to recognize what she had done.

Though using real people, she had never drawn on real events. Real events were too hard to transplant; each had its peculiar logic and trailed sticky strands of cause and consequence that refused to adapt to the simpler systems of fiction. This morning's material was different, however, because she would treat it in isolation with the bare minimum of adaptation. At least, that was the idea.

She was in the bath inspecting her blisters when the thought came to her, so she went straight back to bed, her head turbaned in a towel. She always worked in bed in the winter months because she suffered from the cold when immobile. She kept the computer on a hospital table that she could swing over the mattress before her as she sat cross-legged and furled in a quilt. The green letters sliding across her glasses, she worked for several hours without answering the telephone or pointed beseeching of the cat, and told the truth.

She wrote about how she had met Gus and Loulou, how she had inveigled her way into their lives and eventually into Gus's bed. (Well . . . Gus into *her* bed.) She told how they had walked around Clapham looking at hurricane damage, how she had taken him to hear her favourite pianist playing her favourite Brahms intermezzo and how he had found her ugly after feeding her on a small, bleeding bird and hateful French liqueur. Ugly as sin. She told of her walk home. She changed the facts in only a few points. She had herself accept the lift from the middle-aged black couple, whose lasting devotion she then envied until they took her home for a drink and she saw their child's wheelchair. She turned herself into a scholarly lesbian and she switched Gus and Loulou's genders. Loulou became, with perhaps wanton cruelty, a philandering estate agent called Lucian, while Gus became Rose, an uncertain blonde. Gus had many faults, one of the more endearing of which was his failure to understand why lesbians should exist, much less to sympathize with what they might do. Even if she had herself and 'her' do exactly the same things in bed, he would never recognize himself in Rose.

She stopped writing towards three because it was time to feed the cat and dress for tea but also because she could not finish the story until she knew how their own would end. As long as she had been tapping at the computer keyboard, she had kept thoughts of the night before at a bearable distance, but as she brushed her hair and chose her clothes, the hurt returned. She realized that she still had not wept. For all the fluttering in her chest and the returning tightness in her throat, she found herself yet capable of selecting clothes with an un-selected look and of lending a mournful pallor to her make-up with a pale powder she had once bought by mistake. His black jersey (surely one that Loulou had given him), a pair of very unwashed socks and a tie that was rather too wide, were in a carrier bag near the front door. She had gathered and folded them last night apparently, in a daze between vomiting dinner and brushing teeth.

She arrived at the cafeteria far too early, of course. He was nowhere in sight, so she forced herself to walk over to the crowded bridge to kill time. Several nondescript women and an elderly man with a crutch were leaning on the eastern railings staring crazily at the sparrows that clustered over their crumb-filled hands, as though this minor miracle were not something they indulged in every afternoon. A few children shouted amazement and a youth in a Chinese revolutionary cap filmed them on a Japanese camera. She walked on, past the hideous Walt Disney candelabra and crouched a while to watch the aggressive patrolling of a black swan. She should have brought it something to eat. She wondered if she could remember to return with a piece of cake when their tea was over. She held out her empty hands to it, fingers spread.

'Sorry,' she told it, then saw a woman crouched, photographing her from a few yards away. She had on a brilliant white dress that looked far too thin for the day and she wore her armfuls of almost pink red hair in a mane. The woman lowered the camera and smiled, showing her teeth, then stood to show that she was tall and built like Juno. She could not smile back so she stared. Then Gus called her name and set her free. She turned and hurried to the squat, round cafeteria where he was waiting.

'There was a dreadful queue when I got here so I got us stuff without waiting for you. Do you mind?'

'Of course not.'

'Shall we sit in or out?'

'Oh out, I think. It's cold but the sunshine is so lovely.'

She led him to an empty table. There were no free-standing chairs, only circles of wood with fixed-on arms that splayed out from each central table column. It felt as if they were sitting at either side of some chaste playground mechanism; a miniature roundabout that, with a few thrusts from their short, childish legs, would set them gently turning, very safely, always equidistant.

'While I remember,' she said, and passed him the carrier bag.

'Oh. Thanks,' he said, feigning surprise then peering inside to make sure she had held on to nothing that was his. 'My favourite,' he said, inspecting the outside to see which shop it hailed from. 'How clever of you. You got home okay?'

'Yes. But I walked, like an idiot, and now I've got blisters on my toes.'

'Now look,' he said. 'I know you like fruity teas and they had a huge choice so I brought several bags and some hot water.'

'Goodness.'

'Cherry, mandarin or . . .' He exaggerated the need to peer at the third. 'Yes, or mixed fruit.'

'Cherry sounds lovely.'

'Pop the others in your bag.'

'Are you sure?'

'Yes. Go on.'

'How absurd we both sound; like maiden aunts stealing sugar lumps from Fortnum's.'

They laughed, uproariously almost, and she saw that he was wearing the tie she had given him two years ago, at Loulou's Christmas party. He had bought a plateful of cakes and proceeded to sink his teeth into a chocolate one. His nose just cleared the icing. She decided on the vanilla one for the black swan and set it aside on a paper napkin.

'What's that for?' he asked, dabbing crumbs off his chin.

'A black swan. I teased it by crouching down with nothing to give. Made me feel guilty.'

'Wouldn't it rather have bread?'

'Would you?'

'Point taken.'

'Bread or cake; they're neither of them exactly natural fodder for a water bird.'

She took a mouthful of a rather nasty, dried-out flapjack and dunked her cherry tea bag up and down. The water did not turn pink but became a disappointing, traditional sort of brown. Suddenly she saw the statuesque camera woman approaching and turned back to Gus.

'What are you up to this evening?' she asked.

'Nothing much. Tabitha's having a drinks party.' She wrinkled her brow to show that she knew no Tabitha. 'You know. *Tabitha*. She helps run the Burden Friday Gallery. Anyway, it's a choice between her or the reprint of *La Dolce Vita*. Want to come?'

'I don't know her.'

'To the Fellini.'

'No. I can't.' He looked a question at her and she thought quickly. Why couldn't she go? Would she not love to? Sit close beside him and be bombarded by glamorous disillusion in a darkened room? She met his pale, bland gaze and thought that on reflection she would not. 'I've a story to finish.'

'I didn't know you stooped to stories.'

'Actually it's a question of aspiring; they're far harder than novels. And yes, I do sometimes. This one's for a magazine. They pay absurdly well.' She saw that he was not listening to her but was smiling politely up over her shoulder.

'Can I help?' he asked.

She turned round to a warm, brown cleavage and what, close-to, proved to be pure white cashmere.

'*I thought* it was you!' The woman's camera – a large,

professional thing – dangled from one hand. There was no time
to make any kind of face as she bowed and kissed her warmly
at the edge of each cheek. The brush of lip whispered in her ear
and a scent of ambergris hung, delicious, after she had with-
drawn. 'How *are* you? You look so *well*!' A long, smooth hand
stroked her jaw and shoulder. The stranger laughed, brushing
back tumbling hair. 'Sorry. How awful of me!' She turned to
shake Gus's hand. 'Joanna Ventura.'

'Angus Packard.'

'I must run. I'm late again, but please,' she turned back and
touched the shoulder again, 'ring me. Please?' As she vanished
into the crowd, Gus all but gaped.

'Where have you been keeping *her*?'

'Oh,' she said drily, 'Joanna's hardly ever in town so when
she is I tend to keep her all to myself.'

'She looks like Anita Ekberg.'

'Who?'

'The one in the fountain in *La Dolce Vita*.'

'Oh.'

'I didn't know you knew any Americans apart from squat
Jewish publishers.' Funny. She had not noticed the accent.

She finished the story swiftly, perched on the edge of the bed,
her coat unbuttoned but still on. Her women in love held their
last meeting over cheap Muscadet outside the National Film
Theatre. The rendezvous was ostensibly held for Gus/Rose to
return an unlikely black silk petticoat. She handed it over to
the jilted heroine, wrapped in a used, brown paper envelope,
then broke down. She begged her to forget the hasty words of
the previous night then went on to make an absurd scene when
her generosity was rebuffed. The heroine paused in her return

across Westminster Bridge to open the envelope and send the petticoat dancing down to the brown waters beneath them, then laughed wildly in the face of a man in a suit who stopped to rebuke her for littering the city.

She pressed a button that corrected her typing then set the machine to print. As the daisywheel rattled away, she felt in her coat pocket for a handkerchief and found a ticket for the next evening's showing of *La Dolce Vita*. There was writing on the back. A woman's hand. She read it, turned the ticket over to check the performance time, then turned back to reread the writing. 'I dare you,' it said and there was a telephone number.

Suddenly the printer went wrong. There was a high-pitched bleep and a grinding sound as a half-typed sheet of paper was chewed up. She threw the ticket aside and, scowling, busied herself with freeing the page and returning the cursor to the beginning of her new text. The challenge was in red ink, however, and she could see it from the corner of her eye.

A SLIGHT CHILL

for Francesca Johnson

'Careful of the paintwork, Harper!' Angel sighed. 'I said *careful*!'

'Sorry, Miss,' said the plump girl, labouring under the weight of her trunk. 'It's heavy. I slipped.'

'I know, Harper. Just go a little more slowly and you won't slip again. Girls have broken legs on these stairs before now. You might cause a serious accident.'

'Yes Miss. Sorry.'

Harper moved on down the stairs and banged the paintwork again. She did not care. Usually Angel inspired a certain sisterly respect among the girls, fear even but it was the last day of term so a spirit of barely subdued anarchy scented the air along with the usual, stouter smells of disinfectant, boiled greens and a particularly noxious *eau de toilette* the fifth formers had taken to wearing. There was no time for punishments or black house stars. Trunks had to be packed and trunk lists checked. There were beds to strip and books to return to the library. Lockers had to be swept out and inspected and there was the brief, rowdy ceremony of prize-giving to be got through along with the usual perfunctory speech and presentation to a retiring mistress.

Very few parents lived close enough to collect their girls by car – most of the school population would be evacuated to Newcastle and the London train by a convoy of buses after prize-giving – and yet girls were already drawing arrogant strength from the incipient resurgence into their lives of men.

The mere anticipation of fathers, stepfathers, older brothers and, in some unfortunate cases, mothers' flash fiancés was already rendering the female rule of term time negligible. For a few brief, dangerous hours Miss Prewett, Miss Clandage and Dr Trudeau ceased to be terrible absolute rulers and became objects of mirth, even of pity. Angel always felt that the last day of term, more than any other, reminded one that the teachers were dependent on the girls for their livelihood. Girls returned to wealthy, even distinguished households for parties, new dresses, extravagant presents, a whole world of social advantage, while the likes of Miss Clandage would be spending Christmas visiting other, similarly frugal women or burdening families to whom they were not figures of awesome learning but unweddable sisters, ridiculous aunts. Miss Prewett would be earning her Christmas keep by executing tidy watercolours of her sister's children in distant Taunton. Dr Trudeau was leading a skiing and study party in Aviemore. Angel would be visiting her parents in Hampshire but before then she would be seeing Richard.

Richard! She stood back in her corner of the landing as the girls trooped past her from the trunk store to the dormitories and looked on them with a fresh benevolence. She was one of them, she knew. She was not born to be a teacher. She was only marking time here, a kind of skivvy doubling up as assistant matron and junior school English teacher. Times arose, had arisen often during this last, long term, when she feared the isolation of the place, its undiluted femininity, might be leeching away her youth and crusting her over. Matron or one of the older teachers would assume her complicity, envelop her with a deadening first person plural, and she would feel a chill across her heart. How many of them, she would wonder, had begun as she had, with no

56

intention of staying much beyond a year or two only to give the place an entire life? At such times, however, she had only to think of Richard. His dog-eared photograph, used by her as a bookmark, was her passport to normality. She had even let some of the older girls glimpse it so they should know she was really one of them and a mere tourist in the common room.

The photograph showed him in uniform. He was a captain in the 17/21st Lancers and currently based at Sandhurst where he seemed to spend much of his time teaching mountaineering skills and planning the next expedition he would lead to the Himalayas. He had seen no active service beyond an early tour of duty in Northern Ireland but still it worried her when he wrote her letters on regimental notepaper which bore the motto *Or Glory* beneath a menacing, winged death's head. (Dr Trudeau had been on the point of leaving the school for marriage when her fiancé's plane was shot down on a bombing mission.) Richard and his solicitor brother owned a small flat in Baron's Court. The brother was away at the moment so the first precious days of Richard's Christmas leave and her school holidays were to be spent in indulgent privacy at the flat before she joined her parents in the Itchen Valley. He had pressed her to spend Christmas with him too and she was sorely tempted. She was an only child, however, so subject to extreme parental pressure at this time of year. She was lying to her parents as it was, having told them she was spending a few days with an old school friend. They knew Richard existed, approved of him, indeed, as a future son-in-law but Angel sensed that they preferred not to think of her as a sexual animal just yet. She knew, from chance remarks, that her father, especially, liked the thought of her spending her days immured in this chaste, all-female institution rather than having her gad about town with her contemporaries.

The last girls, juniors mostly, struggled past her down the stairs with their empty trunks on their backs. The smallest helped one another out, bearing their luggage between them, grimacing at how strenuous the steepness of the staircase made this. Angel walked up to check that the trunk store was empty. One remained. She stooped to read the label and saw with a shock that it belonged to Kay Flanders. Kay, a cowering creature, unpopular for no discernible reason, had died suddenly in her sleep earlier in the term. In the rush to have the whole ghastly business over as soon as possible so as to cause as little distress as possible to the other girls, no one had seen fit to empty the trunk store to uncover her suitcase. Her uniform and sports kit had been donated to the school second-hand shop, her few remaining belongings – her 'effects' as the undertakers called them – parcelled up and borne back to her family with the tiny, bloodless corpse. Angel locked the trunk store door and carried the oddly pathetic suitcase down to the sick-bay for Matron to deal with. She paused on the way to tear off the incriminating label and crumple it away in her cardigan pocket. Ghoulish stories were already circulating in the dormitories that Kay's pale shade loitered in the blue washroom humming 'I Can Sing a Rainbow' while she jabbed at her skinny limbs with a pair of carefully nametaped nail scissors. Angel wanted nothing to feed the myth. Girls would say anything to frighten one another. Girls' imaginations were flexible as the tiger in their cruelty. The suitcase always reappeared, they said, lying in wait for whichever junior was luckless enough to be last in the line to reclaim her trunk. It was neatly packed with Kay's dismembered body, they said. On quiet nights, they said, it could be heard shifting around in the crowded attic, twitching, hungry.

She found Matron taking a girl's temperature. It was Adams. Alice Adams, a wan, spiritless little thing, rarely without a runny nose or a patch of eczema. Angel found herself suddenly coy about drawing attention to the dead girl's suitcase, realizing that Alice Adams had subtly replaced Kay Flanders as the girl always on her own, in the corner, at the back, the girl nobody wanted on their team, the girl found indefinably unwholesome. Adams gazed up at Angel as Matron took back the thermometer to read it. As ever, her small eyes were dully reproachful.

'Guess who fainted,' Matron said. 'Set down her trunk on her bed then keeled over. Thank heavens she wasn't on the stairs or someone might have been hurt. Well Adams. No temperature. How do you feel?'

'A bit sick, Matron.'

'Well go and lie down in there for a bit, out of everyone's way, then we'll see how you feel in a little while. Have you fainted before?'

Adams nodded seriously. 'Last week,' she said. 'But not for long and I felt all right afterwards.'

'Hmm. Well go and lie down for now.'

Adams walked into the sickbay and closed the door behind her.

'I found Kay Flanders' trunk,' Angel said.

'Bloody hell,' said Matron. 'Stick it under the table and I'll get it sent home to the parents. Listen. I was going to come and find you anyway.'

'What?'

'You're going back to your parents for Christmas, aren't you?'

'Well yes. Eventually. I was going to spend some time in London first. With a school friend.'

'Ah.'

59

'There's a problem?'

Matron jerked her head towards the sickroom door as answer.

'She's not well. I mean, she doesn't have a temperature or any obvious symptoms but she's getting more and more weak and listless and I'm convinced she's anaemic.'

'Shades of Kay Flanders.'

'Well exactly. I don't want to start a panic about viruses or anything on the last day of term but I do want Adams checked out by the haematologist in town.'

'I could drive her in.'

'Bless you. The trouble is – God I hate to ask you this.'

'What?'

'Well there was never any question of her going home for the holidays since there's only the mother and she's out in New Zealand.'

'Ah.'

'She was going home with the Lloyds who'd offered to take her skiing with them but frankly I don't think I can allow it. She's far too weak. And I was wondering whether – I mean, I can happily take her on from about the twenty-eighth but between now and Christmas is simply impossible for me. Could you bear it? We'd all be so grateful, Angel. She's a sweet little thing really. Very quiet. Fond of books. I don't know why they're all so beastly to her.'

Angel cursed herself. If only she had told the truth from the beginning, if she had blithely admitted to looking forward to six days of uninterrupted Richard, lie-ins, romantic walks round Kensington, last minute Christmas shopping instead of repeating the virginal lie about the old school friend. Confessed now, the truth would sound like a sad, graceless little fiction, and the impatient, uniformed, mountaineering fiancé from Sandhurst, like the product of too many cheap romances read in a practical flannel nightdress.

'Yes,' she heard herself say without a trace of hesitation. 'Of course I can.'

'Count your blessings, Angel,' her mother was always telling her. '*Then* complain. There's always a bright side if you'll only look.'

Her mother would have been proud of her. Sitting at the foot of Adams' bed, explaining the change in holiday plans, she was rewarded by an enchanting smile from the child's bloodless lips. Skiing, apparently, would have been a torment to her, much less skiing with the Philistine Lloyd girls. 'Can we go to the British Museum and see the mummified cats?' she asked, excited. 'Can we go to the National Gallery, Miss?'

'Of course,' Angel told her, 'but only if you promise not to faint.' And she realized that her plans need not be wholly scuppered. Richard's brother was not there. Alice Adams could have his room and surely be bribed to say nothing to Angel's parents about the sleeping arrangements. Certainly, there could be little afternoon passion – unless, as seemed probable, the child could be exhausted sufficiently to take to her bed for an after lunch nap . . .

'Do you like animals?' she asked. 'Dogs and things?'

'Oh *yes*, Miss! My mother never let me have a pet because she thinks they make me wheeze. But they don't.'

'Well *my* mother has always preferred animals to humans,' Angel assured her. 'So you'll have a lovely time when I take you home. She has several dogs. Six I think.'

'Six?!'

'Then there are the cats and she looks after several ponies

from the village, so you'll be able to go riding if you're feeling strong enough by then.'

Alice Adams' pleasure was cheaply bought. Angel foresaw an easy transfer of duties once they were back at her parents' house. There was nothing her mother enjoyed more than an animal-mad child; she liked to exploit their weakness in a kind of indulgent slavery. Alice would soon be set to mucking out stables, mashing dog food and wielding currycombs. She would love every minute of it, regain some colour in her soap-pale cheeks and prove no trouble at all.

Before prize-giving, all the girls had to gather in their forms to be set their holiday essays and to hear how well or badly each had done in the course of the term. The clamour from these traditionally rowdy gatherings followed Angel down a corridor on her way to call Sandhurst from the pay phone under the stairs. To thwart queues, the apparatus had been meanly rigged so as not to receive incoming calls. Because of this, most of her communication with Richard was by mail, her three or four pages of chat being met by his unvarying two sides of more buttoned-up reports of barracks life. On this occasion, her stock of change had almost run out by the time he was called to the phone so she had a scant two minutes of his voice. She blurted out about Alice Adams, fearing his disappointment, but he was sweet and funny and said it would be fine and could he see the mummified cats too. 'Christ,' he said, 'I'm horny,' just before they were cut off, so she was blushing as she emerged from the phone cupboard.

Angel relaxed again. She hurriedly finished writing the reports on her English class then combed her hair, repaired her lipstick and joined the staff at the back of the hall for prize-giving. By the time she was joining in the school song, 'Fields of

Honour, Chambers of Wisdom', she had half-convinced herself that having the child tag along need be no bar to her enjoyment of time with Richard and might even enhance it. The time alone with him would be all the more precious for being the harder won. She had recalled, too, a dictum of her grandmother's that other people's children were a telling means of auditioning the prospective father of one's own. Would he play imaginatively with the girl without teasing her? Would he prove hard and impatient or would he actively enter into Alice's entertainment the better to woo Angel?

In the hour that followed, the school emptied with astonishing rapidity. Fathers and daughters carried trunks to cars. Mistresses, clutching travel bags, shepherded excited girls onto waiting buses for the trains south. There were hasty, tearful farewells on the terrace, rapidly swapped Christmas presents, a diminishing hubbub of greetings, promises, hearty invitations and sighed regret, then Angel found herself alone on the gravel, coat buttoned up against the icy moorland wind. There were no late parents, no missed trains. The evacuation was almost military in its precision.

She was not quite alone, of course. Adams, she knew, was still lying in the sick bay and the cleaning women had descended with mops, dusters, drums of bleach and carbolic and wax. She heard them chatting loudly as they worked and realized this was a last day of term for them too. Matron passed her on the stairs, jauntily got up in a lambskin jacket and vivid headscarf. She was carrying a tartan suitcase and a newspaper parcel of flowers from the garden and whistling at the pleasure of escape. Seeing Angel, she stopped whistling and modified the perkiness in her step, recalled abruptly to the responsibilities she was about to abandon.

'I've rung the haematology department and made her an

appointment for tomorrow at ten,' she said. 'And after that you'll both be free as air.'

'Oh good,' said Angel.

'Yes and I've had a word with Mrs Brack to let her know you'll be staying on the extra night or two. She's cleaning out the freezers but she'll leave you bread and milk and eggs and so on in the pantry. If you have to buy anything, keep the receipts. Oh and you'd better give me your parents' number so I can sort out about picking her up after Christmas or you'll end up with her the entire holidays!' Matron laughed gaily and Angel smelled sherry on her breath.

Approaching the sickroom door, she heard one of the cleaners chatting to Adams then realized it was another child. Hurrying in, she saw it was Lotta Wexel. She was sitting at the foot of Adams' bed and chuckling at something. Hearing Angel, she turned, a smile still bright on her rounded face. Angel felt a stab of vexation.

'Wexel? Weren't you meant to be catching the London train? All the buses have gone!'

'Oh I know. But I couldn't go with poor Alice stuck up here on her own. And anyway, my parents don't come over from Budapest until Christmas Eve so I was only going to be staying in an hotel.'

'On your *own*?'

'Oh yes.' Wexel shrugged maddeningly, as though this were perfectly usual for an eleven year old. 'So I might as well stay on too and keep Alice company. Oh please, Miss. Say I can.'

'Well . . . I hadn't really planned on staying . . .' Angel felt even her modified plans under siege.

Newly arrived this term, Lotta Wexel was officially the nearest Alice Adams had to a friend, insofar as she spent most of her free time at her side demanding confidences and forcing them on the other girl in return. The bond was inexplicable. Where Adams was thin, pale and listless, Wexel was vigorously Central European. Pink cheeked and raven haired, she made up for the want of distinction in her looks with rude good health and a superabundance of energy. 'Paprika in her *blood*!' Miss Clandage would sigh.

Born in the saddle, apparently, she was one of several girls who rode with the local hunt during term time and was entirely without fear, riding at the front and taking hedges and walls in a frenzy of excitement. Her foreignness was untraceable in her accent, she was not too clever, her parents were well connected; she should, by rights, have been one of the most popular girls in her year, a natural pack-leader. However she elected to spend most of her time with the outcast Adams. Previously her closest attachment had been poor, sinister Kay Flanders. The other teachers thought there was something commendable in this and only Angel had found something faintly repellent in the India rubber cheerfulness with which Wexel had bounced back after Kay's sudden death.

What Alice Adams gained from such a high profile protectress would be hard to say. She was so quiet and mirthless by comparison. One might almost have fancied her a kind of parasite, battening on the other girl's hale ebullience. Looking at her now, her pinched face pale even against the pillows, Angel wondered if Adams were not a little reluctant, however, at having such a playmate thrust herself upon her. Then she realized the pleading in Adams' eyes merely stemmed from fear lest this change of plan might jeopardize the promise of time with her mother's menagerie. Angel mustered a reassuring smile.

'Well of course you can stay on, Wexel. I have to take Adams into the hospital tomorrow for a blood test. We can make a trip of it. Maybe go to the cinema in the afternoon. How would that be?'

'Oh *yes*!' Lotta enthused and slapped the mattress beneath her.

'But you're not to tire poor Adams out. She's not very strong at the moment.'

'I know. *Poor* Alice.' Wexel turned a sickly smile on her stricken friend.

Angel realized, bitterly, she would have to call Richard again. One juvenile invalid might not have changed their plans so very much but her tireless companion certainly would.

'Don't you need to tell your parents, Wexel?' she asked, clutching at straws. 'Won't they worry if they call the hotel and find you're not there?'

'Oh no,' Wexel insisted coolly. 'They never worry. They won't ring anyway. They're far too busy travelling around. My father's reclaiming some old estates of my grandmother's which the Communists stole. One was turned into a loony bin. Just imagine! And another one was turned into a horrid collective farm. They'll be fine, Miss. Don't worry.'

As Angel turned from the room, Adams went into a spasm of panic.

'Please, Miss. Where are you going, Miss?'

'It's all right, Adams. I just have to telephone my friend in London. To say we won't be coming to stay there now. I'm afraid we'll have to see the museums another time.'

'Museums are boring anyway, Alice,' said Wexel. 'We can play hide and seek. We can climb up on the roof and pretend it's a castle.'

'You most certainly may not,' Angel insisted.

'Please, Miss.'

'What, Adams?'

'Can't you call us by our Christian names now that it's the holidays?'

Angel sighed. 'Yes, yes,' she said. 'We'll have supper at six as usual then you can come up to the staff sitting room where it's cosier and we can watch television. How's that?'

'Brilliant, Miss. Thank you, Miss.'

'Lotta?'

'Yes, Miss?'

'Have you got change for a fiver?'

As Angel walked back to the pay phone, change bulging her cardigan pocket, she heard Wexel's laughter again and her low, insistent gossiping tone. She wondered what such inexperienced girls could possibly find to discuss at such length.

Richard was disappointed, of course, even a little angry. Why could she not just send this other girl packing, he asked. Why could she not assert herself for once. The questions were rhetorical, however. He knew Angel was not assertive. He suggested instead that he apply for a change of leave so they could meet up after Christmas instead. She could still see her parents, still maintain the fib about the school friend in town and that way they would enjoy time alone as planned, unchaperoned by sick children. His patience lent her heart and she unpacked her things again with a sadness on the sweeter side of bleak.

Wexel saddled up her pony and galloped off onto the moor for two hours before supper. Perhaps Angel only imagined Adams' relief, but the child certainly revived a little when left alone and came downstairs to nestle quietly in a window seat reading Edith Sitwell's life of Elizabeth I. The last of the cleaners left. Disinfected and aired, whole sections of the school were now closed off. As the afternoon drew swiftly on and rain clouds scudded across the moor, Angel busied herself writing letters and tried not to dwell on the acreage of dark and empty rooms stretching out around them. The temperature plummeted and they retreated early to the staff sitting room where Angel lit the gas fire and wound the clock. Darkness fell before Wexel returned. Hearing the clatter of hooves in the stable yard, Angel realized, with a guilty start, that she had quite forgotten about the other girl and should, by rights, have been worrying about her. Adams, too, showed a trace of surprise, starting from her book and hastening to draw the curtains against the night.

Wexel had evidently thrived on her ride. She had ridden miles, she claimed, taken several walls at a gallop, seen a fox and hawks and had great fun being chased by some young beef cattle. Her green eyes shone and her cheeks were scarlet from the cold. She was wet through but not even shivering.

Glad of an excuse to take charge again, Angel hurried her off to a hot bath and a change of clothes while she and Adams whisked up mushroom omelettes and a mountain of buttered toast for supper. The meal over, she sent Adams up for her bath and sent Wexel to watch the television and plan their evening's viewing.

When she followed Wexel up, she found the television playing to an empty room. Happy of solitude, however brief, she watched ten minutes of the news then began to feel uneasy and climbed the dark stair to the dormitory wing to check on them, feeling the chill from the great, black windows she passed on the way. The fluorescent light from the washrooms spilled out across the newly waxed boards of the upper corridor. A small cloud of steam was gathering outside the open door. She could hear a bath filling. One of the great advantages of institutional life was the quantity of hot water the furnaces churned out. Baths here filled in moments.

At first, all Angel could hear above the gushing water was whimpering. Then someone turned the taps off and she heard, with a shock, that it was a thin, pallid, girlish voice singing.

'. . . pink and purple and blue.
I can sing a rainbow, sing a rainbow.
Sing a rainbow too!'

The voice was weirdly magnified by the washroom acoustic. Angel froze for a moment, thinking, despite herself, of Kay Flanders' trunk waiting below the table in Matron's consulting room. Then she pulled herself together and strode into the washroom where Wexel was crouched behind a bank of wash-basins, singing into the steam overhead. Adams was huddled in her dressing gown in a chair beside one of the baths, wash bag clutched in her lap.

'Lotta, stop that nonsense at once and go downstairs to the television.'

Wexel stood grinning.

'Sorry, Miss. Were you scared?'

'Not a bit. Go on. Let poor Adams – I mean Alice – take her bath.'

Wexel came out and, with a parting grin at Adams, slapped down the stairs in her slippers. Adams slipped off her dressing gown, which she had held so tightly about her, and slid into the bath.

69

'I wasn't a bit scared,' she said wearily. 'I don't know why she bothers.'

She began soaping herself, briskly unselfconscious. Angel was shocked at how skinny she was. Her ribs stood out and her veins showed grey-blue against her translucent skin. She put Angel in mind of some eerily transparent fish she had kept briefly as a child, their visible internal organs in constant fluttering motion.

'Don't be too long,' she said, then paused. 'What's that under your arm?' There was a reddish patch in the girl's left armpit.

'Nothing.' Suddenly modest, Adams slapped a hand over the strange welt to hide it from view. 'It's just some eczema. Nothing serious. I often get it.'

Angel remembered seeing Adams adjust her shirt repeatedly at the supper table and realized the fabric must have been chafing her. Recurrent or not, the eczema was serious enough to have been scratched to the raw. She had glimpsed fresh blood, livid on its surface.

'I'll make us some cocoa if you like,' she said. 'Don't be too long.'

She made a mental note to have a word with the doctor about it the next day. When she returned downstairs, she found Wexel merrily making cocoa already, singing innocently to herself as she whisked the milk.

The remainder of the evening passed quietly enough once she had put the girls to bed in their dormitory. At one point she thought she heard weeping but when she stepped out onto the stairs to listen, found it to be only giggling. The school was a red brick Victorian monstrosity, surrounded by uninhabited moorland and windswept hills – the folly of a long since bankrupt mining baron. Even with all girls and staff present, there was room to spare. Left alone there, the three of them were preposterously isolated. As rain lashed the windows and draughts moaned in the chimneys and caused distant doors to slam, she had antici-pated bedtime fears but found Wexel and Adams apparently fearless and herself far more disturbed than they at the prospect of sleeping adrift on such a remote raft of bricks. The girls at least had each other for company. She was alone at the other end of a long corridor and a flight of stairs. Aware of her own absurd-ity, she found herself going to bed with a light left on outside her door for comfort and even then she tossed and turned, watching the racing of moonlit clouds through a gap in her curtains and trying in vain to wrestle her thoughts into quiet moderation.

When she slept at last she dreamed, not of ghoulies and ghosties but, in exaggerated technicolour, of Richard. Nothing happened in the dream. He just sat on a rug in dappled shade and becoming battledress, talking contentedly in a language she could not understand and breaking off his monologue occasionally to smile at her and touch the side of her face with a roughly bandaged hand.

In the morning she realized she was not the only one to sleep badly. Wexel was up before any of them, taking her pony for a dawn canter, but Angel found Adams still paler and weaker than on the previous day. When she offered to drive into town and see if she could persuade the doctor back with her, how-ever, the possibility of being left behind seemed to galvanize the child into action. Wexel returned before long, noisily full of the joys of the winter landscape and soon the three of them were crossing the moor in Angel's Morris Traveller.

They caught the haematology department on a miraculously quiet day. Samples were taken and Angel told that if she cared to return after three, results would be ready by then. In the

71

interim, she took the girls for an improving walk around the castle ruins, followed by an indulgent trip to watch a deeply sentimental cartoon film at the cinema.

As they took their seats, Adams made a sudden apologetic darting movement past Angel so as to sit on the other side of her from Wexel. Angel was concerned that Wexel's feelings would be hurt but the girl said nothing of it, merely enthusing about how excited she was to be seeing the film, having heard so much about it from the others. Having made such protestations, it was strange therefore how often Angel looked about her during the film to find Wexel's stare fixed not on the screen but across Angel on Adams' obediently attentive face. Caught out a second time, Wexel turned hastily back to the film but now it was Angel who turned to stare at Adams, struck again by her air of mute parasitism, her excessive emotional hunger. The way she devoured the mawkish events on the screen was of a part with the way she had darted through to another seat so as to have unlimited access to an adult. Watching her, Angel felt two waves of revulsion, the first at the child, the second at herself for so easily joining the ranks of despisers and bullies.

The junior haematologist confessed herself confused.

'Could I have a word in private?' she asked.

'Of course. Alice, go and see what Lotta's up to in the waiting room. We won't be a minute.'

Adams left the room. The haematologist watched the closing door then turned back.

'I have to say that if Dr Murchison were still here we'd have sorted this out in a minute; she's the expert on things like this. Are you sure all these details are correct? Her blood type and so on?'

'Well . . .' Angel shrugged. 'I didn't take them myself. The parents supply most of them to Matron and each girl has a medical at the beginning of the academic year. Why?'

'Has she . . .' The young doctor frowned, picking at the rubber on her pencil then looked up. 'Has she been abroad recently? To the Tropics, perhaps? India?'

'Not to my knowledge. Her mother lives in New Zealand. I don't know if that counts. Why?'

'Well . . .' The doctor tried to laugh. 'You'll think I'm awfully stupid but we took two samples and I looked at them over and over and got a colleague to check and, well . . . There's something not quite right.'

'Does she have a virus?'

'Not that I could recognize. It's more as though she has a whole new blood type. Now listen. There's probably no need to worry. She *is* very anaemic and that can be dealt with at once. I'll give you an iron prescription for her and you can make sure she eats plenty of iron-rich food. Meanwhile I'm going to send these samples on to London for a second opinion.'

It was agreed that Matron, who lived in Sussex, would drive Adams into London for a further examination after Christmas. Shopping for dinner on the way back to the car, Angel collected the prescription and bought spinach and steak. Wexel chattered all the way home about the film, about other films, about the Christmas lights in the department stores. Deaf to her prattle, Angel caught glimpses of Adams' listless face watching her in the rear view mirror and caught herself thinking that, far from being sick, the child was not even human.

'Look!' Wexel shouted in her ear as they pulled up the school drive. 'There's a man in the window!'

'Nonsense,' Angel said. 'It was probably just a shadow or a curtain.'

'There's a man. There. Look!'

Sure enough, as they pulled closer a man came out of the front door to greet them and she saw that it was Richard.

'It's a friend of mine,' she told them rapidly, suppressing a sudden urge to leave them locked in the car and lead him into the house. 'A good friend. He must have come to stay.' She felt herself beaming as she opened the car door. 'How on earth did you get here?' she asked him, aching to give him more than the perfunctory hug and a peck she allowed.

'Taxi from the station,' he told her. 'Emptied my wallet so I hope you're not going to turn me away. I found a back door unlocked and let myself in. What an old barn! So. Who's this?'

She introduced him to the girls who were staring, then led the way to the kitchen and food.

It had proved impossible to take his leave after Christmas instead because officers with children apparently took priority. Faced with the options of moping alone in Baron's Court or visiting his parents, he had decided to surprise her. While the girls took their baths, she showed him around and had the pleasure of defiling the tiny, old maid's bedroom that had been her cell these last months. They were both indecently excited at making love with the sounds of the girls singing and splashing in the washroom below, and at having to be quiet and quick. She bathed her cheeks with a flannel soaked in freezing water in an effort to still their burning while he watched from the bed, smug and smoking. The room smelled frankly male of a sudden. She tidied her clothes and hair and, fighting off further advances, slipped downstairs again to make supper and prepare the way.

Wexel was first down, cheeks even pinker than usual from her bath, and took an unsqueamish pleasure in slicing the three bloody steaks into pieces for a pie that would serve four. When some blood splashed onto her dressing gown she merely giggled. Angel had planned on bribing her, buying her discretion with treats, but found the girls' connivance offered without asking.

'Is Richard your boyfriend, Miss?'

'Yes. He's my fiancé.'

'He's very handsome.'

'Thank you, Lotta.'

'You needn't worry. We won't tell anyone he was here. Alice says she'll feel safer tonight having a man about the house.' Wexel laughed again at the smutty innuendo of what she had just said, or possibly at the absurdity of Adams' girlish confidence.

As auditions for fatherhood went, Richard's was a success. As if responding to careful gender programming, the girls took to him the moment they learned he was a cavalry officer. They teased him like an older brother, swung on his big hands as if they had known him all their lives and, it seemed, accorded Angel new respect by association. Richard appeared genuinely to enjoy their company – he had always had an immature streak – and could hardly wait until supper was over so as to play hide and seek and murder in the dark around the cavernous, empty classrooms. In this, however, he had the ulterior motive of ensuring they were thoroughly exhausted by nine o'clock and begging for bed so as to leave him the more adult pleasure of exhausting his appetite for Angel.

The next morning, conditioned by Sandhurst, he was up early and left Angel for a lie in while he thrilled 'the chubby Hungarian thing' by taking her riding. The weather was clear, even thinly sunny, by the time they returned so the rest of the day was spent in taking a long ramble across the moor, broken by a pub lunch and several stops for thermos coffee and custard creams. He tested their map reading, their knowledge of birds and geology and – supreme nobility – gave Adams a piggyback ride when she grew too tired to walk any further. Angel began to feel slightly left out of the fun and found herself planning that, as and when she *did* marry him, she would bring forth men children only. She reminded herself, however, that it was important to keep the girls sweet. One word of this escapade when they returned next term and she would be job hunting without a reference. Announcing that it was important to Adams' iron levels, she let Richard serve the girls red wine with their supper and knew their discretion was purchased for another night at least.

Letting him read them a bedtime ghost story was not such a good idea, however. Wine-doped, they seemed on the brink of sleep when Angel left them, but she and Richard had not progressed far beyond the slow unbuttoning stage, when the night was rent with distant screams. Cursing, buttoning her blouse up again, Angel hurried down her bedroom stairs and along the dormitory corridor to find Adams almost frenzied with terror and Wexel watching her with the same calm cheerfulness she had brought to the slicing of steak and rolling of pie crust. She calmed Adams but could not break her insistence that she sleep with Angel and Wexel sleep elsewhere. Angel was secretly furious but sensed the child's implacability and knew the night would be interrupted repeatedly until she gave in. Wexel was curiously compliant.

'Poor Alice,' she said. 'If it helps you sleep. But honestly, it was only a silly story. It's all right, Miss. You sleep here and I'll go in the sick bay. There's still a bed made up.'

'Very well,' Angel sighed. 'This is incredibly irritating of you, Adams. I hope you realize that.'

'Sorry, Miss.'

'I'll just settle Wexel in over there and I'll be back. Don't worry. I'll leave all the lights on.'

'Sorry,' she told Richard, with a kiss. 'I think she's a bit drunk actually. You'll just have to watch TV if you can't sleep. There's a portable next door in Matron's room and she keeps her sherry in the cupboard in her bathroom. Adams will fall asleep soon. I'll probably be able to slip back to you during the night.'

'You'd better,' he growled and playfully nibbled the side of her neck, 'or I'll get restless and come and find you and who knows whose bed I might stumble into.'

Sadly, she proved as deeply affected by wine and fresh air as her nervous charge and after five or so minutes of lying in the dormitory listening to Adams' adenoidal breathing, Angel fell into a slumber deep as the darkness around her. When she awoke, with a start, the clock over the stable yard gate was striking seven. For a while she lay there, assessing how her need for sleep weighed against the pleasure of tip-toeing back along the corridor and up to Richard's musky bed. He would stir slightly in his sleep, mumble faintly. She would rouse him slowly with small, nuzzling kisses and the judicious touch of her dawn-chilled fingers . . .

She rose and pulled her dressing gown about her. Adams was snoring, far from fear. Climbing the stairs to her bedroom, carefully avoiding the stair that creaked, Angel reflected that this was probably far more fun than Baron's Court. She opened the door as softly as she could, eager to surprise him by touch rather than sound. Then she froze, unable to believe what she thought she saw in the grey dawn light.

He lay spreadeagled on the bed on his back, one arm trailing over the mattress' side. His eyes were open but fixed dreamily on the ceiling. Lotta Wexel was crouched over his naked body, her back to the door, eagerly chewing at the bridge of muscle across his armpit. As Angel darted back from the doorway, he let out a helpless groan of desire.

Mind reeling through scenario after nightmare scenario, Angel walked swiftly then ran back to the dormitory. Adams showed no sign of waking at her approach. Angel lay on the bed without taking off her dressing gown. This was absurd. Ridiculous. It was unthinkable that he should do such a thing and unlikely that Wexel, for all her insufferable bumptiousness, would prove so pliable to his will. After five, maybe six, minutes of indignant soul-searching, Angel sat up and walked back along the corridor. Either she was seeing things, delusions brought on by too much rat-trap cheese at dinner and his flirtatious references to impatient bed-hopping, or she was compelled to act, however compromised her professional position already was.

Checking first on the sick bay, she almost laughed aloud with relief. Wexel was fast asleep there, one of her pillows tumbled onto the floor, one chubby foot protruding from the bedclothes. Vowing to say nothing to him for fear he should think her quite mad, Angel passed on to Richard, who was also deep in dreams, and woke him with teasing slowness, rousing him delectably as planned.

Angel was the last to wake in the morning, finding herself sprawled in bed alone and naked with a pleasantly bruised feeling in her groin to remind her she had not been alone for long. She packed swiftly and came down to find Richard frying up a hearty farewell breakfast for the girls. He led them in singing songs and playing games most of the way home, although Alice

Adams soon retreated into a doze in her corner of the back seat. Angel dropped him off at his parents' house on the way, pausing for a lingering kiss in their shrubbery and a promise that he would ring her at her own parents' house that night.

It was already dark when she pulled the Morris up at a meter outside the Wexels' Mayfair hotel. Leaving Alice to sleep beneath a blanket, she ushered Lotta into the lobby while a porter unfastened the trunk from the roof-rack. She was surprised to find she had grown almost fond of the girl, intensely irritating as she was. The parents proved surprisingly elegant. The mother was sparely chic, with dark hair tied back and fat pearls glistening at her neck. Mr Wexel was taller and broader even than Richard, with bright eyes and a closely clipped beard. It was hard to imagine that boisterous Lotta could have anything to do with them. Then they kissed the child and Angel saw a strong family resemblance in the mother's profile and the father's busy glance.

'And this is Miss Voysey. She's given us *such* a good time.'

'*Enchanté.*'

Mr Wexel did not quite kiss Angel's hand but he bowed over it minutely and held it a fraction too long for comfort, raising his black eyes to hers and causing her a spasm of erotic perturbation. Mrs Wexel and Lotta had slipped outside to check on the trunk and say goodbye to Adams.

'Such a sweet child,' Mrs Wexel told Angel. 'But so thin and pale one could see moonlight through her,' and she laughed a well-bred phantom of Lotta's red-blooded guffaw.

Returning to the car, eager to make headway because snow had been forecast, Angel found Adams awake and trembling. She had locked all the doors from the inside.

'Let me in, Alice. Quickly. That's it.'

'Can we go now, Miss?'

'Of course. We'll be there in an hour. Really, what a performance! Did you take your iron pill?'

'Yes, Miss.'

'Good girl.'

Before they had reached the motorway out of Chiswick, Adams was already fast asleep again, her legs drawn up so that she was lying the width of the back seat. Angel reached back to pull the travel rug over her for warmth. It began to snow, just as Mr Wexel had prophesied. The flurries fell thicker and faster until Angel was half-blinded by the conical glare they made before the headlamps and was reduced to driving at a crawl. Desperate for coffee and something sweet to fortify her, and anxious to ring ahead to her parents and tell them not to worry if she was late, she pulled off into the motorway services at Fleet.

Turning round as she unfastened her seat belt, she tried to stir Adams gently and found that she couldn't wake her.

'Adams? Adams!' Fear made her reach instinctively to the formality of term time. 'Adams, wake up.'

She grasped at the girl's skinny wrist, felt the sides of her neck. There was a pulse, only a faint one but she was alive. Terrified that the child she thought was sleeping peacefully had slid into a coma, she locked the car and sprinted across to a bank of telephones outside a fast food restaurant to summon an ambulance. She was about to return to the car when a certain apprehension made her fumble in her bag for Richard's number at his parent's house. His mother answered and chided her for not having come in for tea when she dropped him off.

'Sorry,' Angel said. 'I'd have loved to but I was so late and I had some children to drop off too. Is he there? Could I have a word?'

'I'm sorry, dear.'

'Has he gone out?'

'Oh no. He's taken to his bed and he's only just managed to fall asleep. Nothing much wrong with him but he came over all weak and dizzy so I tucked him up with some hot whisky and lemon and the electric blanket. He's just caught a slight chill, I expect, walking on those moors.'

The ambulance was held up in the snow. Alice Adams was dead on arrival at the hospital. Angel arrived at her parents hours later, after a terrible blur of forms to be signed, calls to be made and statements to be given. Climbing from the Morris in her parents' garage, numb from cold and emotional exhaustion, she saw she had the girl's redundant trunk still strapped to the roof rack. The leather label flapped in the breeze that was flinging snow through the open doors and, watching its feeble motions, Angel thought of Kay Flanders and how she had died, as the letter to parents put it, quietly, in her sleep.

BORNEO

for Nick Hay

Bee took a sandwich, doing her best to fill the gap left behind, and opened the French windows onto the garden. She stood on the steps for a moment then saw that the whirligig clothesline was still out, laden with knickers and bras. Stuffing the sandwich into her mouth, she strode out to remove the wretched thing from disapproving view.

Tony had died on a draughty Sunday in late autumn. They had some friends to lunch after Eucharist, then the two of them had gone up on the downs to walk off the blackberry and apple crumble. The wind had been so strong that they played games, leaning into it, yelling to make themselves heard. Tony's deputy, Mike, was playing at Evensong so there had been no rush. When they came home, he had sat down to watch the new Trollope serial while she made a pot of tea. She had walked in with the tray to find him lying on the floor, his face twisted, dribbling at the pain. His hands had pressed at his temples as if his head were trying to burst. When the nurse had let her in to kiss her husband goodbye, Bee had seen bruises from the pressure of his own fingertips.

'Coo-eee.'

Bee spun around with a handful of knickers. Mrs de Vere was standing there in a tea cosy hat and second-hand coat. Sturdy, black NHS specs glinting in the sun.

85

'Mrs de Vere. How lovely.'

Mrs de Vere was not meant to be here. Thursday mornings were usually the time for Bee's Afghanistan bandage parties. She would pour out coffee for a collection of the more lonely or immobile women of the area (picking them up by car, where necessary) while they cut up old sheets into bandages for her to send to refugee camps. In fact, Bee had not got around to sending any bandages for months, and was stockpiling the things in a fertilizer bag in the basement. She thought she had put off all her regulars. Evidently this one had slipped through the diplomatic net. A pronounced outcast, on account of her thick Dutch accent, disgusting mothbally smell and jealous obsession with the Bishop (whom she was rumoured to have followed from post to post since his ordination), Mrs de Vere was not coffee morning material.

'I was not going to come this morning, on account of my arthritis you see, but I heard that you were having a coffee morning next week so I thought today I make a special effort for the little Afghans, yes?' she burbled.

'Of course. How kind. Actually, I'm giving a coffee morning today as well,' said Bee, hoping that her breathing through her mouth was not too evident. 'So I thought I could find you a chair near the fire and give you a sheet and let you get on with it. There'll be all your friends here. Let's go in, shall we, and find you a cup of coffee. You like it made with milk, don't you?'

Dinah had yet to appear with the rest of the cups and saucers. Bee prayed that the guests would not arrive in a rush. She ensconced her unexpected visitor in the gloomier corner by the dining room fire and found her a pair of scissors and an old sheet. Mrs de Vere would insist on humming Lutheran hymns as she worked. Perhaps the spitting of the logs would cover it.

*

Everyone had been marvellous, of course. They had all heard within hours, without her breathing a word, and for the next month she was surrounded by a cushioned wall of comfort. Bee had seen this in operation on others, been a press-ganged accessory to it herself. She had imagined she would react angrily, stifled by the crushing affection. Her submission, in the event, surprised her. The house had reeked of flowers. Every hour brought another fistful of cards and letters. She was honoured with gifts, as one miraculous; packets of home-made fudge, the solace of chocolate cakes, deep-frozen cassoulets for one, books of poetry with the relevant pages kindly earmarked. There was a small bunch of friends who had sent or brought something every day; a token of love. Once she started to venture out, she could subside into tears in the most unsuitable places, like the public library, secure in the knowledge that someone in the vicinity who *knew* would rush over with hugs and murmurings. She had never realized before how many of them had suffered. Tony's hideous death brought such a quantity of pain and doubt to the surface that the community had seemed irrevocably altered. Her affection for it was not increased, but she approached it with new-found respect. That they had all felt the agony of bereavement at first-hand was only natural, far more interesting was the chemistry in death that caused so many of them to lay bare the poverty of their faith. Not a batch of consolations arrived but contained one astonishing recognition of the insane cruelty of existence, of the seeming impossibility of any but a psychopathic deity. The strongest of the latter were written on diocesan notepaper. Bee was an atheist. It was her best kept secret. Only Reuben knew. She had meant to confess to Tony, but his cheerful faith had disarmed her, and then he had died. The spate of avowals in the wake of his death had implicated her in the community. This was the first cord that bound her in. The second had been their guilt.

The house in the cathedral close was a traditional perk of the post of Organist. Mike took over Tony's job. He had five children as well as a wife. Gently, shamefacedly, Bee was evicted. She had finished her teacher's training after meeting Tony, but had done no work since their marriage. The task of teaching the Baby Form at the choir school had recently fallen vacant and it came with a half-share in a pretty, Regency house just outside the Close gates. It was widely known that Bee got on well with children, probably because she was unable to have any of her own, poor thing, so the headmaster's wife was approached to approach the headmaster, who subsequently approached Bee who, to everyone's relief, accepted his kind offer. As the sole woman on the teaching staff, Baby Mistress shared number eight, Chaplain's Walk with the Assistant Matron. Jennifer was a cheery, horsy type, who lived happily alongside Bee for two years before following the custom of her post, getting herself impregnated by Stephen Simkins (PE) after being seen swimming with him in the moonlight and the buff. They were still on their honeymoon and Bee had the house to herself until Jennifer's replacement arrived.

She handed Mrs de Vere her coffee, then retraced the smell of hot lemon and spices to the kitchen. Her twenty-three-year-old brother, Reuben, was using a fish slice to slide some newly baked biscuits onto a wire tray. The frown of concentration and faint baker's flush only enhanced his vulpine charm.

'That's the last batch,' he said. 'How many d'you think'll come?'

'Oh, Christ. It could be forty. There are fifty local members. Twenty of them are in homes or bed-ridden, but the others all promised to bring friends. Oh Christ.'

'Have a gulp of my gin.'

'Rube, it's only ten-thirty!'

'So? Have a gulp of my gin.'

'Thanks.'

She took the flour-dusty glass, perched on the kitchen stool and gulped. He had descended on her five days ago, tanned, penniless and suggesting, by his echoing want of a future tense, that the stay was indefinite. The tan was Indian. He had been out there for nearly a year, making a small, shady fortune as a jewel dealer.

'I still don't understand why,' he said, arranging cupcakes in rings of alternating colours on a vast, borrowed plate.

'Because it's usually run by Miranda Cotterel, but she fell off her bike and did in her hip.'

He had woken one morning to find himself relieved of every worldly possession, save the sleeping bag around him and a quantity of Marks and Spencer underwear. His copy of *India on a Dollar a Day* had also been left behind, apparently on a whim of superstitious benevolence. His escape involved a Foreign Office ex of his from school, then a certain amount of murkiness in Bangkok. Dear Rube was nothing if not resourceful.

'You're not on the committee, are you, though?'

'No. But Miranda Cotterel has some very persuasive friends who are.'

'An offer you couldn't refuse?'

'Sort of, only they think they do it to give me something to occupy my poor, bereaved soul. Rube, you're a saint. Can I do anything?'

'Don't you dare.'

He had dropped out of school at seventeen to enrol in life's university as, variously, masseur, waiter, singing telegram and escort; all activities pursued under the generic carapace of travel writer.

'Bee, do you even know where Borneo is?'

'No. But then, neither do they.'

'Have you read the charity's magazine?'

'Lot of smiley black nuns, isn't it? Look, let me take those through. I hate feeling spare.'

'Don't drop them.'

'I'm not incapable.'

She bent forward to kiss his gilded cheek and brushed her twinset on a plate of sieved icing sugar.

'Dolt.' He dusted her down and pushed her gently from the room.

The clock on the dining room mantelpiece struck eleven. In the kitchen, Reuben had two kettles, a preserving pan and a pressure cooker full of steaming water at the ready. The two thirty-cup teapots on loan from the WI had been scrubbed and contained equal heaps of Gold Blend. He poured himself another generous gin. Interleaved biscuits and radiating rings of small cakes waited on the sideboard.

'Will you have a biscuit, Mrs de Vere? Those ones are lemon. Very good. Freshly baked.'

Mrs de Vere lowered her busy hands to her lap and gave Bee a stare. Her lenses were thick, full of milky eye.

'I must not be eating biscuits or cake neither. They cause me to choke. I had an unpleasant experience as a child and have been prone to choking ever since. But you must have one, thank you all the same.'

'Oh dear. Yes. I think I shall.'

Bee bit off a piece of biscuit. It was still faintly warm and crumbled delightfully on her tongue, but the doorbell rang and she had to swallow the rest in a rush.

'Bee. Anyone here?'

'Dinah.' Dinah Stapleton, friend with cups and saucers. 'Thank God. No. They're all late.'

Dinah was the school secretary. Urbane and discreetly pagan, she survived on an illusory sense that her every pleasure was illicit. She conducted her friendship along conspiratorial lines, making a point of arriving among the first, whenever Bee was entertaining, so as to enjoy a snatched conversation, sotto voce, in the hall. She heaved her basket-on-wheels up the steps, scowling at each clatter of the school crockery within, then stopped dead and pointed at the alien coat hanging on a hook.

She mouthed her enquiry: 'Whose is that?'

Bee grinned and beckoned her into the kitchen.

'Hello, Dinah.'

'I say. Home is the sailor. Hello, Reuben. Have you been terribly busy? Don't answer that. Bee, who?'

'Mrs de Vere.'

'What? Why?'

'Quite. She's not meant to be here, but she didn't realize that the Bandage Girls were cancelled for this week, and she lives right up on Priory Hill so I couldn't very well turn her away.'

'Well no. Of course not.'

'Bless you for bringing all that.'

'Yes. We must shove it on trays for you. Come on. No rush, though; they'll be at least another ten minutes. Oh yes. I've got something horrid for the Bring and Buy –'

'Damn! The stall. I still haven't –'

'It's all right,' soothed Reuben, placing a slightly unsteady hand on her shoulder. 'I did it while you were boiling Dame Vermeer's milk.'

'Thanks.'

Dinah was clattering out a third trayload.

'Your stalls are always so well stocked, Bee,' she said. 'I don't know where you manage to find so many unwanted Christmas presents. Don't you ever get any you want to keep?'

'Not often. What did you mean about ten minutes?'

'They're all at the Deanery.'

'Why the hell? They know they're meant to be here.'

'Didn't anyone tell you? You picked an appalling day. *She* invited everyone to a rival do about a week before you did. Boat People.'

'Why didn't she invite me?'

'The crib gaffe.'

'I only gave it a bit of a dust and changed the dead flowers. You'd think she made the thing by hand, she's so prickly about it.'

'She did.'

'It was one of those plaster-cast kits.'

'Well, she made the manger.'

'Excuse my butting in,' said Reuben, 'But they're here.'

He had seen them walking up the drive. Bee hurried into the hall and opened the door as Mrs Clutterbuck reached for the bell-push.

'Daphne, how lovely.'

'Hello, Bee. You know Mrs Thomas. And this is my cousin, Jane.'

'Hello.'

'How d'you do.'

'Come in.'

'Hello, Dinah.'

'You've been terribly busy.'

'Is that the errant brother out there?'

'Look at all the biscuits.'

'Marvellous spread, Bee.'

'Oh. Mrs de Vere. How nice.'

'What are you doing with that sheet?'

'Rag-rugs? Oh I see. It's bandages. Lovely.'

'Milk, no shug. Perfect.'

'Wonderful bikkies, Bee.'

'Reuben's actually. Coming! Hello. Come in. I'm Bridget Martin,' said Bee.

'Hello.'

'Hello.'

Miss Trott. Miss Deakin. Mrs and the Misses Hewlings. Penny Friston. Marge Brill. Reverend and the Mrs Pyke. Reverend Yeats. Sister Veronica and Mother Lucy from that strange community at Perton Bagshawe. Rapidly the dining room filled and the temperature rose. The hooks were laden with tweed and scarves and a pile of coats began to form at the foot of the stairs. Bee stopped answering the door and left it propped open with the umbrella stand. She realized that she should have served coffee from a table in the hall for the dining room, and by degrees the drawing room as well, were becoming so crowded that it was difficult to manoeuvre a coffee pot, cream jug and sugar bowl simultaneously. Dinah had manned the Bring and Buy stall and was therefore cut off at the far end of the room. Bee stood, helpless, outside the dining room door, tray in hand, and made explanatory faces at Miss Wodding and Mrs Lloyd-Mogg who were staring mournfully at their empty cups.

93

'Could you? Excuse me . . . er . . . Could you . . .?' she tried a few times, but went unheeded by the stockade of rounded backs.

Reuben appeared at her elbow. 'You'll have to shout,' he said. 'They won't mind.'

'I can't'

'Coward.' He faced into the room and called out, 'Ladies. Ladies.' The din in both rooms dissolved at once into mildly indignant question mark noises. A score of puffy faces turned and stared. He was quite unabashed. 'It's rather hard for us to get to you, so if you'd like some more coffee – and there is plenty – would you like to step out into the hall?'

They stepped out with a vengeance. Reuben set up a pouring station at the hall table, as a queue formed, thrusting the second jug onto Bee. She toured the drawing room, seeing to the less mobile. These sat on sofas and chairs, sticks at their sides, offending wrists or legs laid, ostentatious, before them. Miss Coley. Barbie Sears. Miss Rossington and Miss Pidsley. They showed no sign of enjoying themselves or guilt at being waited on. The room was just large enough for each to stare without encountering the eyes of the others. Bee exchanged a few words with each in turn, asking after their health and less healthy friends, checking that each had secured a copy of the magazine, watchful for any anxiety about where they could *powder their noses*. Then she crossed the hall, with muttered thanks to Reuben en route, and endeavoured to teeter through the suffocating room to Dinah.

The latter was counting a wad of notes into a shortbread tin.

'Dinah, are you all right?'

'Fine.'

'You've taken loads.'

'Always the same. You do a roaring trade in the first ten minutes. Everyone brings a thing, buys a thing, dumps it, and there an end.'

'Yes.' Bee recognized a jar of rhubarb chutney she had made two years ago, which had evidently been doing the benevolent rounds ever since. All her original horrors had been sold, and replaced with not dissimilar fare. There were a dry-looking sponge with thin pink icing, two tins of lychees and some elderly paperbacks. There were also some quite passable lavender bags, which she would pocket if no one else did. 'How's Mrs de Vere?' she went on. 'I couldn't reach her.'

'Oh, she's okay. Ripping and rolling away. There was a lull after Reuben summoned them into the hall, and I managed to get over and have a chat. Someone had given her a collection of those heavenly biscuits, and she was quite cheerful for once.'

'But she's not allowed biscuits. She said so!'

'Well she was munching away. Said how good they were. Hang on. The cake, Mrs Friston? Oh, I dunno. What do you think for the cake, Bee? I haven't had time to price it.'

'How about fifty pence?'

'Fifty pence it is.'

'But is it fresh?' asked Mrs Friston, giving the article a sharp poke.

'Oh I should think so, wouldn't you?' Dinah used her school dinners tone, and took the customer's uncertainly proffered coin. 'Thanks. There we are. Have a good tea.' She dropped the takings into the tin with a clatter. 'Her Nibs won't be pleased.'

'Why not? They all went to her first.'

'But that's just it. You always go first to the thing you're going to leave. I think the old trouts are here to stay.'

'Now now. We'll be among them before long.'

'Don't,' said Dinah, who was several years her senior. She looked across the bobbing tussocks of grey hairs and blue much as she would survey the field at the boys' football matches. She addressed Bee in an undertone without turning. 'Is *he* coming, then?'

'Dick Greville? Yes, but he'll be late.'

'Not him, you ass. You know. *Him*. Is he?'

'Teddy?'

Bee smiled involuntarily as she spoke the name and Dinah laughed aloud. 'Well,' Bee felt herself redden. 'He said he'd try. Now I must go and help Reuben.'

Teddy Gardiner had kissed her all over her sofa. Over six foot, with dark, leonine hair and eyes of unexpected blue, he had arrived on the teaching staff the year before she did. He was a lay clerk in the cathedral, singing bass, taught English and coached the first fifteen. His body might have devastated were it not for the sense that it was the unconscious creation of wholesome pleasure, not an effortless endowment of birth. She had noticed him at once, but had stilled her interest with the reflection that, while no great beauty, Tony was blessedly indolent. Dinah had taken an immediate shine to him, but had passed unnoticed and so recovered. Just three weeks into Bee's widowhood, he had come, grave of face, to express his sympathy. He had said how sorry he was to hear, she had said not at all, then they had sat side by side on the sofa talking about the Dean's latest sermon and the tummy bug epidemic. The talk had flagged and, after a finger-itching silence, they had slid into a wild embrace. Things would certainly have progressed had he not kicked over the sherry bottle. Jennifer had come home in the middle of the mopping-up and he had fled in confusion to supervise the boys' prep. Over the twenty-four months that ensued, his sporadic courtship had not gone unremarked.

Bee made her way back to the kitchen, pausing only long enough to be told that the rival do at the Deanery had been the usual dour affair and that most, if not all, of the guests had come on to hers. She found Reuben sitting on the draining board swinging his legs. He was not alone. He was nose to nose with the young Precentor.

'Hello, Dick.'

'Bee. How splendid.'

Did she fancy that guilty start?

'I had no idea you two knew each other,' she said. Dick Greville, who sang like an angel, was teaching the choristers plainsong technique and was rumoured to be a favourite at Clarence House, coughed and said, 'Well . . . er . . . yes.'

'Mrs Hewlings just introduced us,' said Reuben sharply. 'But actually we'd met once before at the Brills'. How is everything?'

'Oh, fine. Fine. Nothing left to do now but chat. Reuben's been a wonder, Dick. He took over all the baking for me.'

'Oh really? How splendid.'

'Yes, well, I was just saying I'd show our Precentor the old wasps' nest in the summer house.' So saying, Reuben opened the kitchen door and stepped out into the back yard. Dick, who had a reputation for purity, hovered on the doormat, wrinkling his brow.

'Are you . . . er?' he asked Bee.

'No thanks. I'd better take the jug again.' She beamed.

'Oh. Right. Bye.'

He shut the door behind him. Bee leaned on the kitchen stool and heard Reuben's laugh around the corner. Then she watched the two of them cross the lawn and, after a hasty look round, vanish into the gloom of the summer house. She had found a dried-out wasps' nest in there, glued to the rafters. Reuben had never seemed particularly interested.

She made a fresh jug of coffee and set out to refill cups. Everyone said how much they were enjoying themselves. No one had left, although a few had deserted the main body to go upstairs on an *explore*. Sister Veronica's stout-booted form was trotting across the half-way landing as Bee crossed the hall. She saw Bee in a mirror and stopped, turning with a twitter, a smile and a sparrow flap of her hand. A deeper voice barked from further up, 'Come on, Knickers. You'll get left behind,' at which Veronica hesitated minutely before scampering round the corner, out of sight. Bee saw Dinah surreptitiously collecting cups and saucers from behind drinkers' backs. Her friend caught her eye and gave her a wink. She turned into the drawing room.

'More coffee, girls?' she called, feeling suddenly tired.

'Rather. White and two shugs. Isn't that naughty of me?'

'Oh but no, I think there comes a time when . . .'

'Black, please. Yes. That's lovely.'

'Whichever's easiest . . . Oh, well, darkish brown, then, please.'

She met the chorus with bland smiles. She reached Miss Rossington, whose leg was stretched out on a pile of cushions and a footstool and found that she was fast asleep. Slowly she lifted the cup and saucer from off the woman's lap and slid them onto her tray. She turned and saw Teddy. Everyone else saw her seeing Teddy, too, and carried on chatting with eyes and minds in suspension.

'Hello,' he said. 'I'm late, aren't I?'

'Yes, but it's sweet of you to come at all.'

'Oh nonsense. I mean . . . Borneo and things are . . . Well. Let me help you with that. Are you going to the kitchen with it?'

'Yes.'

He took the tray in his great hands and swung out the way she had come. She watched his shoulder blades beneath the Harris tweed and wished again that he were not quite so sporty. In the kitchen she took the tray from him and opened the basement door.

'In there. Quickly.'

He obeyed. She glanced into the hall to see that she was unobserved, then darted in behind him, closing the door. She shot the bolt and turned on the steps.

His thick arms grabbed her in the dark and pushed her back against the floor polisher and some pampas grass she was drying for the harvest festival. She sought his mouth and pulled his rugger thighs against her. He smelled faintly of Old Spice. She ran her fingers into his tough hair and pulled his head back so that she could take a series of rapid bites around his Adam's apple. With a moan he broke free and thrust himself hard against her, making the shoe-cleaning things rattle in their box.

'Now,' he said.

'No.'

'Yes.'

'I say *no*.'

'Mrs Martin? Mrs Martin, are you there?'

'Blast. Her Nibs. Get down there and count to a hundred and fifty before you come out.'

He lurched down the stairs, kicking over a fertilizer bag as he went. Bee flicked on the light, smoothed out her skirt and twinset, then slid back the bolt without a sound.

The Dean's wife was standing on the kitchen doormat. She was a tall, ugly woman and strained her goldfish eyes to see over Bee's emerging shoulder. Bee shut the door behind her.

'Mrs Crewe. I'm so glad you could make it.'

'Well I'm not really making it, you know,' she snapped. 'I'm looking for Mr Gardiner. I gather he's here.'

'Yes. He is. Why do you need him?'

Bee set out firmly for the hall again, forcing Mrs Crewe to follow her. She glanced out of the window as they went, noting that the summer house door was still shut.

'I gave a coffee morning today as well, as you probably heard, and he promised he'd come and help move my trestle tables when it was all over, but it finished a little earlier than planned and the Dean wants the room free for his heraldry class tonight. Mrs Friston said Mr Gardiner was here, so I wonder . . .'

'Yes he is, as I say. I'm not sure where. He followed me out to the kitchen then said something about going around the garden to take a look at my leaning wall for me.'

'Oh really? Well, perhaps I can find him there.'

'Mrs Crewe?'

Teddy walked in through the open front door, his hands thrust deep in his pockets. Bee flashed her praise.

'Ah, Teddy, there you are.' Her Nibs threw a glance at her hostess. 'I'm afraid I'm going to kidnap you a little early.' Without a word of thanks she stalked him from the house. Once again Bee faced a ring of enquiring faces.

'Has anyone seen the Precentor?'

'I thought I saw him earlier on.'

'I wanted to ask him about that dreadful Series Three.'

'Oh yes. King James is so much more . . . well . . . it feels more *right* somehow, doesn't it?'

'Of course, poor Mrs Crewe does have an awful lot on her plate.'

'Sixty-two, isn't she now? I must say, it's lasting rather a long time.'

'Bee, quick.' Dinah's face was colourless. 'In the dining room. It's Mrs de Vere!'

'Mrs de *Vere*? Is she here?'

'Well, perhaps she's just joined. There was something about new members.'

'I thought perhaps the committee . . .'

Ignoring the chatter around her, Bee ran into the dining room. The grey-haired sea parted before her. In her chair by the fire, Mrs de Vere was writhing. One hand flailed before her, where it had dropped a coffee cup, the other plucked at her throat. Her vein-strung legs, bandaged at the ankles, twisted and kicked in their sensible, brown walking shoes, and her old wool skirt was riding up over a greyish petticoat.

'God, she's choking!' Bee exclaimed, rushing forward. 'Dinah, could you ring for an ambulance?'

With little or no idea what to do, Bee reached the old woman and unbuttoned the top of her blouse. The lapels of her cardigan were studded with crude costume jewellery. A gold chain hung around her neck, tinkling with good luck charms.

'Mrs de Vere! Mrs de Vere!' she shouted, and banged her furiously on the back.

'Yes, ambulance, and quickly please. We have an old woman choking on a biscuit here.' Dinah's voice rang out in the stunned near-silence of the hall. 'What? Oh yes. Number eight, Chaplain's Walk. But it's one-way, so you'll have to approach it from Bridge Street, at the other end.'

Halfway onto the floor now, Mrs de Vere was turning

grey-blue. Her glasses had fallen off and her milky eyes were wide with pain and terror. Her breath came in deep agonized sucks that made her teeth whistle. The other guests kept outside a neat four foot radius. Some stared blankly, others touched their mouths with listless fingers or picked unthinkingly at their clothes. Reverend Pyke was among them. His wife turned on him.

'Jack, darling. What did you do to Kathy Roach that time? Quickly. Try to remember.'

'Well I . . . I punched her. You always have to punch them hard on the solar plexus.'

'Well do it.'

Breathless from belabouring the gasping woman's back, Bee looked up in despair.

'Oh yes. Please. Try anything you know. She's going to pass out any second.' He dithered, finding a place to set down his cup and saucer and she felt her anger rise. 'Well come on, then! She's dying!'

He darted forward, rolling up a shirt sleeve.

'Hold her back so I can get at her,' he said. Getting behind the armchair, Bee took Mrs de Vere under the arms and hauled her upright. 'Steady. Steady.' His voice was quavering. Bee noticed how black the hair was on his fist. 'Now!'

With a grunt of effort, he punched hard at the top of her ribs. Mrs de Vere's hooting cry was hidden by the gasp from the onlookers. Her sucking whistles continued, only fainter.

'Upside down,' called Dinah. 'We'll have to get her upside down, as if it was a fish bone or something.'

'Yes. That's right.'

'Upside down.' There was a suggestion of hilarity in the rejoinders. Swing the old trout upside down.

'I'll take her legs,' announced Reverend Pyke.

He took her by the ankles and walked round, almost ponderously it seemed to Bee. With her feet over the back of the chair, the choking woman's skirt flopped down onto her waist.

'No. Jiggle her up and down a bit,' called Miss Coley, who, chronic disabilities notwithstanding, had found her way onto a dining chair at the back of the crowd.

'You'll have to be quite fierce, though, Jack, if we're to shake it loose.'

Urged on by the well-wishers, Jack Pyke jiggled her up and down quite fiercely. Her tongue lolled outside her bloodless lips and her straggly hair began to swing against the carpet. Somebody laughed.

Bee could stand it no longer. She bent down and cradled the woman's jerking shoulders in her arm.

'Stop. Stop. For God's sake, stop! I think she's dead.'

But Reverend Pyke appeared not to have heard. Sweat streaming down his scarlet face, indignant from the fire, he continued to jolt his patient.

'Just a few more. I think we're nearly there,' he gasped.

'No, Jack,' his wife called. 'Stop. Stop.'

She ran forward and laid a hand on his arm. He looked at her, then down to where Bee, near tears, was trying to lift Mrs de Vere back to dignity. He let go of the ankles and followed his wife from the room. With Dinah's help, Bee turned the old woman round so that her feet were on the ground once more. The crinkled head dangled to one side. Dinah listened to her heart.

'She's dead,' she said.

A sigh – half apology, half disgust – ran through the crowd. Behind Bee's back, they began to find their coats, telling each other that perhaps the most useful thing they could do was to get out of the way and let the ambulance men deal with it.

'Where's the Precentor?' asked Mrs Brill. 'I did so want to ask him . . .'

'Perhaps tomorrow,' hushed her daughter.

The ambulance men duly arrived. As the two of them rolled Mrs de Vere onto a stretcher and covered her in a royal blue blanket, a nurse who was with them assured Bee that there was nothing more she could have done.

'Looks as though she had a good run for her money, though, doesn't it? At least she went out enjoying herself,' she said. 'Better than for it to happen alone.'

'Yes,' agreed Dinah. 'There's always something worse. Look, Bee, I'll ride up to the hospital in the ambulance to see if they need any details or anything like that. She won't have any next of kin that we know of. I'll get back as soon as I can.'

'Bless you,' said Bee. 'I'll cope.'

She stood in the porch and watched the forlorn little procession wend its way down the drive. Dinah was chatting to the nurse in the stretcher's wake. The coats had all gone except for Mrs de Vere's. Bee walked with a tray around the drawing room gathering cups and saucers, then did the same in the dining room. She plumped out a few cushions, rearranged the armchairs and walked over to the Bring and Buy stall. The lavender bags were still there. She slipped them into her pocket, then took a half-eaten biscuit out of the shortbread tin and counted the money. They had taken twenty-five pounds. Without the float that was nineteen. The remaining issues of the quarterly magazine had been knocked onto the carpet in the excitement. She gathered them up, threw them on top of the glowing logs, watched them flare up, then carried the dirty cups and saucers through to the kitchen.

There was still no trace of Reuben or the Precentor. She

assumed that they had discovered a shared interest in Kashmir or something, and had gone for a walk. She stood at the sink, squirted some washing-up liquid into the bowl and turned on the hot tap. As the foam rose, she picked up the rubber gloves and blew into them to turn the fingers the right way out. As she pulled them on, someone pressed up behind her. She jumped, then realized who it was.

'She let you go early,' she said, leaning her head back onto his shoulder as his hands ensnared her waist.

'I heard what had happened and thought you might need a hand.'

'Oh Teddy, Teddy,' she murmured as he licked one of her ears, somewhat clumsily. 'I want you to put me in your little red car and drive me fast, anywhere else, for several hours.'

'Actually the big end's gone,' he apologized. 'I've only got the bicycle at the moment.'

Over the browning leaves of the geranium on the window-sill, she watched the summer house door open. Reuben emerged with a delicate yawn.

'There's a drying-up cloth on the back of the door,' she said.

PAINT

for Paul Luke

Andrew was moving an overgrown shrub when he heard the telephone. It was a lavatera which had outstayed its welcome in what had only ever been intended as a temporary resting place. The roots were huge now, and deep. He had abandoned the fork and was having to scrabble in the earth with sore fingers, heaving at the obscene growths with all his weight to free them from the moist, unyielding clay. He was not altogether sure this was the time of year to be moving plants. The thing would probably die, traumatized by such rough handling. He ignored the ringing at first, then realized the answering machine was off and hurried, swearing, back to the house, rubbing earth off his hands and onto his jeans. The telephone fell silent just as he reached it, causing his head to spin briefly with sad possibilities of who he might have disappointed. Just as he was turning back to the door, it rang again, causing him to jump.

'Hello?'

'Don't sound so uncertain,' his mother was always teasing him. 'You answer it as if it wasn't your phone and you were taking some awful liberty.'

'Hello?' he said again, more forcefully.

There was a clatter at the other end, as if the caller were doing several things at once.

'Hello, Andy. It's Dad.'

'Dad. Hi. Is there some problem with tomorrow?'

'No. No. Unless you want to cancel or something.'

'Of course not. No.'

The brief exchange was so typical of their relations; hesitant, uncommunicative, fraught with embarrassment at the very possibility of complications.

'You see,' his father went on, 'it's just that I wondered if you'd made any plans for our evening together.'

'Er . . . No. Not really.' Andrew wondered again whether he should have invited people, thrown his father a supper party. But he knew no people. Or no one he could comfortably seat at the same table as his father.

'Because I thought we might drop in on some friends. For tea or something. I don't think you know them. They're doing a job on a house down there. Somewhere called Saint Vaisey.'

'That's not far from here.'

'I know. We . . . er . . . I looked it up. They're nice people. You'd like them. But I don't want to mess up your plans.'

'I don't have any plans, Dad. I already said.'

'Fine then. You can pick me up at Truro okay? I could always cab it.'

'Course I can. Two-ten.'

'Want a word with your mother? She's hitting something on the kitchen table but I can get her.'

'Better not,' Andrew said, thinking of the lavatera roots drying above ground. 'It's an expensive time to be calling. Give her my love.'

'Will do.'

As he hung up he felt a stab of irritation that his father, who was coming West to visit Andrew's home for the first time in the ten years he had lived there, should already be diluting the bare twenty-four hours they would have together with an addition of strangers. Then, as he returned to do battle with the lavatera, irritation was joined by the apprehension he always felt at having to meet new people. There was a shaft of relief too. After thirty years of having nothing to say to his father, the sudden prospect of having the man to stay on his own had been daunting. Andrew had bravely determined that this was a heaven-sent opportunity, a chance to meet as independent adults, to view one another without the deflecting mist of his mother's nervous chatter. It was only twenty-four hours, after all. An afternoon, a night and a morning. As the days passed, however, those twenty-four hours had begun to loom over his pleasingly unsociable routine like an inescapable thundercloud. Having extra people to involve would relieve the tension. They might even have the makings of friends. Andrew lived alone and would not have had it any other way but he liked the idea, at least, of friendship.

Looked at with apprehensive eyes, the little house seemed too basic, under furnished, poorly decorated. The few antiques he had inherited from his grandmother – a longcase clock, a rocking chair, a uselessly delicate chaise longue and a dingy oil painting of a woodland cottage – clustered in a corner of the sitting room. There they seemed to form an unintentional shrine to his parents' effortless good taste, and sat awkwardly alongside the shabby but serviceable armchairs and once-amusing junk he had found in village jumble sales. His father had not noticed Andrew's small attacks of chronic depression, attacks which Andrew always felt never quite amounted to a respectably full-blown nervous breakdown, but he had disapproved strongly of their immediate effect – a decision to abandon a legal training to *run away* to Cornwall.

'It's not the sixties any more, you know,' his father jeered. 'Only idiots drop out now. Idiots and ignorant, ungrateful fools.'

Ironically, however, the spirit of the sixties, or at least selected

111

highlights of the era, seemed to be creeping back into the nation's consciousness. After six years Andrew found that his untroubled existence, living in a small village, working as a National Trust warden on the county's beaches and coastal paths, was more in vogue than any city solicitor's could ever be. In her occasional, faintly surreptitious letters, his mother claimed that his father had discovered he could now speak of Andrew's *mad decision* with a note of pride and was describing him, absurdly, as *living on the land*.

'He couldn't help being a bit disappointed, darling,' she explained. 'You must see that. I suppose it's my fault really, for not having had more children. Big families leave more room for lovely eccentricity but only children like you have to play the be-all and end-all. I could have had more and I should have. But I didn't. So there it is. Now, about those bulbs you said you'd find me . . .'

The following morning he rose early as always and drove over to a large local supermarket he rarely visited. He laid in stocks of the sort of things he remembered his father liked to eat and drink – whisky, steak, potatoes, chocolate-ripple ice cream, Stilton, claret. It was an expensive basketful – on his own he tended to live off vegetables, brown bread and tea – but the expenditure calmed him, lending him a kind of irreproachability in the face of anticipated criticism. On the way home he stopped at a garage to give the Land Rover a rare wash and take an industrial-power hoover to its filthy interior. Then he cleaned the house from top to bottom – an habitual Saturday chore performed with fresh vigour in his father's honour. He made up the spare room bed and even arranged a jam jar of spring flowers on the bedside table before he decided this was somehow too soft and diligent a welcome and relegated the posy to the kitchen windowsill.

He arrived at the station far too early and was forced to sit in the car park, poring over the road atlas, needlessly checking on the route to Saint Vaisey. When the train, which was late, of course, pulled in, a bewildering crowd of passengers disembarked from doors all along its length. For a few minutes Andrew had to stand on tiptoe and crane his head this way and that for fear of missing him. And then there he was, jauntily swinging a small overnight bag and clutching, in his other hand, an herbaceous geranium from Andrew's mother. Andrew tried to relieve his father of both or either and, after the fuss, it was suddenly too late to shake hands naturally, so they did not touch at all. Claiming to be ravenous despite his sandwiches, his father insisted on stopping to buy some chocolate from a machine. He munched his way swiftly through two bars as they drove away, eyes bright with satisfied greed, snapping off pieces between his teeth rather than using his fingers.

'Sure you don't want any?' he asked, offering the last inch of the second bar.

'No thanks,' Andrew said and could not help smiling.

'What's so funny?' his father asked, munching.

'I'd forgotten how hungry you get.'

'Bloody sandwiches were an absolute rip-off. I'd have made some decent thick ones before I set off, but you know how late your mother leaves things and we ended up in a god awful rush. You look well.'

'So do you.'

He did. Andrew was surprised how young his father looked, even vigorous. He was fifty-three but could have passed for a prematurely greying forty-two. His hands, clutching the battered leather case on his lap, were thick but sinewy – not at all the soft, pink things one would expect on a barrister.

113

He asked Andrew questions on the way home. He asked about his work, about problems with pollution, footpath maintenance, erosion. He asked about the local population, unemployment and politics. To a stranger it might have sounded like genuine fatherly interest but to Andrew, it was like polite questioning from a visiting dignitary, benefiting from advance briefing at the hands of diplomats. Still, the impersonal questions and answers smoothed their way. He retorted in kind, with questions about his father's work and was surprised to hear him paying lip service, at least, to the importance of encouraging racial and sexual equality at the Bar and of introducing certain radical reforms in the Law. Like his father's youthful appearance, it made Andrew realize the extent to which he had coped with their unspoken estrangement by distorting his remembered image of the man into something older, more ogreishly hidebound.

Back at the house, his father continued to make appropriate noises, asking with surprising tact about any plans Andrew might have to redecorate. And yet, behind all the diplomacy, a restless energy seemed to be simmering that had nothing whatever to do with his son's life. He was keyed up, and not with any tension about meeting Andrew again. Andrew wondered whether he had some grim announcement to make. His father plainly was not ill. Perhaps his mother was? Returning to the kitchen after the necessarily brief tour of a small domain, his father seized the telephone and was already tapping out a number before he remembered to ask permission to use the thing.

'Just thought I'd –' he began to explain then was cut short when someone answered. 'Hi,' he told them. 'It's Kenneth . . . Hmm. Not bad . . . Soon I should think.' He turned to Andrew. 'We could drive over there pretty soon, couldn't we?' Andrew nodded and watched his father turn eagerly back to the mouth-piece. 'Yup. We'll be over in a bit . . . Yes. He knows the way . . . See you.'

They set out immediately. Andrew did not even bother to offer coffee. The hospitable gesture would have been entirely redundant and coffee was never hotter than when unwanted. Before they left, however, his father dug in his bag and retrieved an envelope which he handed over.

'I would have brought wine or something but I thought you might prefer these. It's two tickets to San Francisco.' He gave some complicated explanation about business traveller's perks.

'But don't you and Mum want to use them?'

'Not really. She hates America and I haven't got time. You can change the date quite easily if that doesn't suit. Just ring the number in the corner. Do you good to get away.'

As Andrew tucked the two tickets carefully behind a vase on the dresser, it struck him that they were probably now the most valuable objects in the house, after the longcase clock, inappropri-ate to the place as a whirlpool bath or sophisticated dishwasher.

'Well, thank you,' he said, and laughed. 'Thanks, Dad.'

Locking the door behind them, he wondered who he could take. He had a brief, heady fantasy of approaching the exceed-ingly pretty girl who always gave him a kind smile in the fruit shop but sensed, even as the fantasy evaporated, that he would probably give both tickets away and see his own surprise repro-duced on another's face.

In the car, it struck him as strange that his father offered no information about the people they were visiting but had to be asked.

'They're friends of your mother's as well,' he was told.

115

'They're decorators. Muralists. Things like that. Holly and Clifford. Dreadful names, really; like a couple of hairdressers. Still. I'm sure you'll like them.'

'How did you come to know them?' Andrew laughed at the implausibility of the connection.

'They worked next door – for the Nicholsons. Cheered up that gloomy dining room of theirs by turning it into a sort of, well, I dunno, sort of Pompeian pavilion. But all with paint. Very clever. If you like that sort of thing. Actually, I reckon she could survive on her own as a proper painter but she supports him. I mean, he's clever, and a pretty interesting bloke once you get him talking – especially about Africa – but not really gifted like her. Or *I* don't think so. Now, she said to turn left after the church and keep on going straight towards the sea.'

And he channelled a now sporadic conversation into a series of non sequential exchanges about signposts, wild flowers and the extraordinarily good condition of Cornish roads after the potholed stretches of the London borough *where your mother still insists on living.*

The house was a sprawling Edwardian one, tucked deep in a thickly wooded valley running down to an inhospitably rocky cove. If there were any other houses in the area, they were hidden entirely in greenery. Even half a mile away, Andrew could hear the furious booming of spring tide waves and he climbed down from the Land Rover. A beautiful lurcher, its shaggy grey fur streaming in the wind, bounded frantically from its nest in the long grass beneath a tree, circled the two of them, panting as it went, then raced into the house announcing their arrival with no sound beyond the swift clattering of its feet on the weedy gravel path. As they drew near the front door, it emerged again, leading a slight, boyish man with very short, black hair. He wore paint-spattered dungarees over bare skin and no shoes on his small, dusty feet. He reassured the dog then greeted Andrew's father like an old friend, with no hint of respect, as though they were of an age. Then he held his hand out to Andrew with a sweet smile.

'And you must be Andrew. I'm Clifford. Come in. Holly's got to finish what she's started as the paint's mixed, but she hasn't got long to go. I'll get us all some tea. She's through there, at the end of the corridor.' He turned to the dog and pointed. 'Show the way, Fingal. Show the way.'

The lurcher did indeed show the way, pacing gracefully before them down the high, sunny corridor towards a half-open door and the sound of piano music. The building was filled with a strong smell of paint and solvents. Everywhere windows had been tugged open in an effort to drive the smells away and the air was lively with sudden gusts of sea breeze which fluttered papers and banged doors. The lurcher pushed into the room, barging the door wide open to reveal a small, blonde woman perched on the top of a ladder to decorate a high, windowless wall. She had covered most of the wall with thickly painted foliage and the branches of laden fruit trees but the focal point of the 'illusion' was a man and a woman bathing and embracing in an ornamental fountain.

'Coming,' she said, not turning. 'Any second. This wretched colour's a bugger to mix right.'

'Hi,' said Andrew's father. 'Take your time.'

'Just one more peach. There!'

She picked her way daintily down the ladder – she too was in bare feet – dropped her brush into a jam jar of white spirit, flicked off the radio with a big toe, then came across an expanse of rumpled dustsheet to shake hands.

117

'Kenneth!'

They kissed one another's cheeks – again like old friends. And again it was a fresh shock to hear his father called by his Christian name – his mother always called him 'darling'. His father's hand lingered for a moment on the shoulder of her rugger shirt as she turned to Andrew. She flicked a strand of ash blonde hair off her face and examined her other visitor with humorous, grey eyes. She could not have been more than thirty. Her handshake was firm as a man's, her small, heart-shaped face so lovely, so hand-cuppable, that the fruit shop girl was eclipsed in a callous instant.

'Hello,' he told her. 'I'm Andrew.'

'I know,' she said, and gave him a conspiratorial smile. Just then Clifford appeared with a tray and she exclaimed, 'Tea! I'm parched. Let's go out on the terrace. I know it's a bit windy but the air's *poisonous* in here. Down, Fingal! Yes. I love you too.'

Sensing she was briefly released from the constraints of work, the lurcher had jumped up to flex his paws against her breasts. She hugged him affectionately and kissed his nose before pushing him gently from her. As they walked out through some French windows, the dog stayed close beside her, constantly glancing up at her face, plainly an abject slave.

She handed round tea, Clifford lavishly buttered scones, while Andrew drove from his mind a seductive image of her in Golden Gate Park, reflecting how unfair it was that two such attractive people should have found each other. They exuded cheerful self-sufficiency. He felt they enjoyed this temporary interruption of their exclusivity, were amused by it, but that it was precisely that: a *temporary* interruption.

Perhaps to compensate for his comments in the car, his father gave most of his attention to Clifford, asking about the house and its absent owners. Just occasionally his eyes were drawn back to Holly. Feet tucked up onto the bench beneath her, she drew Andrew out on his Cornish life and her wide-eyed fascination and frequent little pouts of concern imbued his account of his solitary tasks with a windswept romance. Suddenly she seemed struck with an idea and laughed, running a paint-spotted hand through her hair.

'Would you mind? Clifford do you think he'd mind? Kenneth?'

'Mind what?' Andrew asked her, quite sure that he wouldn't.

'Posing. I've suddenly realized you'd be perfect. I need a shepherd to peer through the undergrowth at my couple in the fountain in there.'

'Well I'm not sure I'd be very good at sitting still.'

'You wouldn't have to. You don't even have to take off your clothes. Not unless you wanted to.' She laughed. 'Go on. It would be fun.'

'Go on, Andy,' his father urged.

'All right,' said Andrew.

'Brilliant,' Holly enthused and winked at him. 'We were going to invent someone or use a photograph but real people are so much better. And Kenneth, I want you to come and see the beach. You're looking all grey and Londonish and in need of fresh air. You can manage, can't you Clifford?'

'I can manage,' said Clifford, stroking her arm as she passed his chair.

The tea things were abandoned where they lay as Holly led his father off beneath the trees and Andrew followed Clifford back into the house. He was peeved that it was not Holly he would pose for, but Clifford seemed to read his thoughts.

'I'll just do some sketches,' he explained, seating Andrew halfway up the ladder and setting to work with charcoal and a pad. 'The artist will do her stuff later.'

The sky was clouding over rapidly. Shadows hurtled across the lawn. A gust of wind billowed the thin curtains away from the French windows. Fingal trotted in.

'Got bored, did you?' Clifford muttered under his breath. 'Settle down, then.'

The lovely dog performed a quick, enquiring circuit of the room, turned a few, nest-making circles on the spot then settled with a low grumble on a heap of dirty overalls, watching his master at work.

'Could you just pull a bit of your hair down?' Clifford asked. 'No. Like this. Hang on.' He stepped forward and, reaching up, pushed Andrew's hair back off his forehead with thin fingers before teasing down a single lock. Andrew must have stiffened unconsciously at the contact. 'It's okay,' Clifford assured him. 'I don't bite. None of us does.'

Andrew tried to relax but the cool draught had chilled him.

'Amazing place,' he said, for something to say.

'Yes. It's surprisingly noisy at night. There are owls and a fox and the house is full of creaks and bangs. Like a ship. We've tried sleeping in different rooms too. It's fun waking to new views. There! Look at yourself!' He held up a startlingly truthful sketch then almost immediately started on another one. 'Here,' he said, 'let's try you with this on,' and he crowned Andrew with a wreath of plastic leaves sprayed gold. 'Ah. *That*'s better! Holly wore that to a fancy dress party once. She said men kept reaching out to touch it then blushing. Did Kenneth let you have a dressing-up box when you were small?'

'Er . . . no,' Andrew confessed, thinking back. All he could remember was a train set with a realistic steam effect. And a neglected stamp collection. 'I was an only child,' he added, for some reason.

'We dressed up all the time. Even when it wasn't a fancy dress party we'd go as pirates or witches.'

'Did you have many brothers and sisters.'

'No. Just Holly.'

'Oh,' said Andrew. 'Oh.'

Clifford laughed.

'You didn't . . .?'

'Fraid so. Dad didn't explain anything.'

'She's my twin.'

'Oh yes.' Andrew saw it. 'You've got the same eyebrows.'

'Yes. Among other things.'

'But you share a room?'

Clifford frowned momentarily, glancing up at Andrew then back at the paper.

'Holly hates to sleep alone,' he said at last. 'One more sketch, then we're done and you're immortal. Let's have you the other way this time. Ah yes. That's much your strongest profile but you always show the other. I wonder why that is. Head up. That's it. Hold that for a bit if you can. So. Tell me. When you're out on your warden duty do you have to wear a uniform?'

'Yes. It's sort of khaki and brown. Not very interesting,' Andrew told him then wished he had kept quiet as he saw Clifford's interest quicken. Various facts about this rootless ménage were slipping into place. He was not entirely innocent, having had some embarrassing encounters when collecting litter in the more remote sand dunes by the military zone at Perranporth. A certain kind of male sunbather, he had discovered, became excited at the very idea of a coastal warden.

121

'Holly's extraordinarily attractive,' he said, in clumsy self-defence.

'Hmm,' said her brother, 'and sometimes fatally unaware of the effect she has.'

The sketches finished, Clifford took Andrew on a tour of the building. The owner was the grandchild of a famous artistic hostess and the place was littered with paintings and memorabilia. Ordinarily it might have interested Andrew but his thoughts were half a mile away, under the trees, on the beach. After the tour, he retreated into a bathroom and stole some poison-green mouthwash in case he had a chance to stand near Holly before he left. Fingal was waiting outside the door when he emerged and shepherded him along another, darker corridor cooled by a floor of great slate slabs, to the kitchen, where Clifford was absorbed in rapidly filling a cryptic crossword. Andrew peered through an overgrown window, straining to see across the daisied lawn.

'They're taking a long time,' he said at last. 'The weather's turning with a vengeance. I hope everything's all right.'

'She's probably making him go for a *proper* walk along the cliff path. They'll be fine. Anyway, you'll stay for supper, won't you?'

'Oh I think Dad's quite tired after his journey. And I hate to stop you both working. We ought to get back,' Andrew said hastily, thinking of the steak he would never eat on his own.

'Holly wouldn't like that.' Clifford tossed aside the finished crossword. 'Can you cook?'

'Not much. I can chop.'

'Come on, then. You can chop veggies while I'm creative. Have some wine.' Clifford pulled open the fridge and splashed the contents of a half-drunk bottle into two mugs. Pushing one across the kitchen worktop, he looked assessingly over Andrew's face and laughed at him again. 'You're really worried about your dad, aren't you?'

'No, I . . . No,' Andrew assured him and gulped some wine, but the mere denial brought nightmare scenarios to mind. How could he explain to his mother that Dad had broken his neck while exploring cliff tops alone with some absentmindedly seductive, shoeless blonde?

Holly brought his father back after another twenty minutes, by which time Andrew was thoroughly involved in preparing supper. The clouds had burst minutes before and the two of them were soaked. Clifford poured them brandies while Holly towelled her hair and then Andrew's father's. Andrew watched her pick pieces of fern off his father's back.

'How was the beach, Dad?' he asked.

'Wonderful,' his father enthused, shivering over his brandy but contriving to look even less fifty-three than he had on leaving the train. 'All my cobwebs thoroughly blown.' He raised his glass in a toast. 'Don't know how you ever get any work done, Clifford.'

'Easy.' Clifford slid a tray into the oven. 'We work with our backs to the windows.'

'Are we staying for dinner, Andy?' his father asked.

'Of course you are,' said Holly.

His father raised his eyebrows enquiringly.

'Andy?'

Andrew was torn. A part of him, a tight, celibate part, wanted everything to go ahead as he had originally planned, wanted his father to eat steak and ice cream, wanted to take him away from these dangerous people. Another part, frightened yet eager for carelessness, was glad that his stuffy father had not been afraid to cultivate these sexy friends so much younger than himself.

'Well I did buy us food,' he admitted, 'but it can keep. And look at the time! It's half past seven already.'

'That's settled then,' said Holly.

'It already was,' her brother murmured.

Andrew's father only replied by offering Andrew a strangely crestfallen smile. Or perhaps he imagined the crestfallen bit and his father was merely pleased to be promised a better meal than he knew his son could cook him.

'This shirt's soaked,' Holly said. 'I'm going to change.'

Before Andrew had time to control his expression or at least pretend to look elsewhere, she had tugged her rugger shirt over her head and walked, pertly topless, to the door, tossing the shirt onto a heap by the washing machine on her way. In her absence, Clifford asked after 'Margery', Andrew's mother. This conversation, in Holly's absence, made the evening feel slightly more ordinary and yet even now, something in the way the men discussed his mother made her sound perturbingly not herself. She was a dry-humoured chatterbox, a frustrated writer, yet on Clifford's tongue she became someone slightly wild and unpredictable, a creature dignified by strong emotion, a character in an unwritten novel. This new evocation was so strong that, when Holly returned, in dark blue leggings and a teal-blue man's jersey that hung just below her bum, it was briefly as though there were two women in the room.

'Put this on, Kenneth. You're still soaked,' she said and held out a dry shirt. This time Clifford as well as Andrew seemed momentarily abstracted from bibulous chatter as Andrew's father stood to pull off his wet things, revealing an expanse of hairy chest that was broader and more muscular than in Andrew's seaside holiday recollections.

The meal – chicken roast in a crust of herbs, salt and garlic, then salad, cheese and fruit – was one of the best Andrew had eaten in months. Holly sat at one end of the table, between him and his father. She smelled faintly of turpentine and white spirit and sometimes, when she leaned forward to laugh, he could feel her breath warm on his cheek. She had slipped on long earrings which ended in large balls of some dark wood which kept bouncing softly against her neck. Once or twice, emphasizing a point, she laid a hand on his forearm but then she did the same to his father, so he knew it signified nothing. Slightly giddy with the insinuating comfort of it all, Andrew drank more glasses of wine than he could count. When Holly produced dope from a small Elastoplast tin and rolled an expertly tidy joint, he waited, astonished, to see his father take three deep lungfuls of it then felt honour-bound to do the same. The drug, as always, made Andrew talk, recounting minutely various strands of village gossip which seemed to amuse the others, who encouraged him. He chattered all the more wildly when his father laid one of his huge hands over Holly's and squeezed it and he was plunged into sudden, stunned silence when, on the way to make coffee, she no less unmistakably caressed the back of his father's neck.

If these were unguarded indiscretions, his father showed no panic, flashed no warning message across the table. All was easy. All was warm. His father's smiles to him were warm. Clifford's passing touch to his shoulder was warm. At one point, Holly actually picked up Andrew's hand and gave it a warm kiss; he forgot exactly why. Candles were produced when the electric light grew too hard to bear. Coffee was drunk, another joint smoked.

Clifford lit a candelabra and drifted into a room across the way where he began to play Chopin preludes rather well. For the crazy symmetry of the evening to be complete, Andrew should have followed him; he was so stoned, he would have been putty in anyone's hands, man or woman. He stayed obstinately put, however, fiddling with candle wax and singeing pieces of orange peel.

'Do you want us to go?' his father asked at last.

Andrew could not believe his ears. The night had been allowed to progress this far and now his father seemed to be asking his permission to let it continue.

'Would you mind?' Andrew asked Holly and she merely smiled. 'I'm not sure I'm in any state to drive,' he added.

His father asked the same question three times in the woozy, elastic hours which followed. Nothing had been clearly spoken. His father and Holly were, by now, sitting on opposite sides of a fireplace, yards apart, and yet with each reiteration of Andrew's consent, he felt himself implicated more deeply in whatever was afoot. One moment they made him feel an innocent child, the next, a paterfamilias, whose permission must be sought at every stage.

At last, driven by a mounting tension between the two of them and dimly aware that Clifford had stopped playing the piano and slipped upstairs, Andrew rose uncertainly to his feet and asked where he should sleep.

'Well if, like me, you hate to sleep alone, Clifford's in the blue room – third on the left.' Holly came forward from the fireplace and stood on tiptoe to kiss his forehead.

'I . . . er . . . I don't think so,' he stammered.

'Then I should go right to the end of the upstairs corridor. That one's got a nice bathroom and a heavenly view when you wake up.'

'Night, Dad.'

'Sleep well, Andy.'

As he mounted the long stairs, Fingal skittering protectively upwards ahead of him, he could hear their low voices and his father's chuckle. He used the loo, splashed water on his face then found his bed in the darkness. The sheets were chilly and slightly damp, which sobered him briefly. For a few minutes he lay, the bed seeming to float beneath him, trying to make sense of the evening, but found that the sentences of his logic crumbled at their beginnings before he succeeded in forming their ends. Then a quilt of sleep enveloped him.

He dreamed he was alone on a huge, palm-fringed beach with Holly. He dreamed she was utterly available to him. She held him firmly by the wrists and rubbed a cut lemon over each of his arms in turn then encouraged him to taste his own, freshly citric skin. For some reason this was intensely exciting, like discovering one had a spectacular hidden talent. Then she held out the other half of the lemon to him and threw back her head while he squeezed the fruit's juice over her deeply tanned breasts. He lowered his mouth to lick then suckle at one of her sun-warmed nipples. It was slightly crunchy with sand and tasted, not of lemon, but sea water. Once he had tasted her nipple he was afraid to meet her gaze. He dreamed she sensed this and, lying back on the baking sand, pushed his face further down, so that his nose nestled by her belly button, where a lemon pip had stuck. She stroked his hair and encouraged him to sleep. Which he dreamed that he did.

He woke when Fingal, whom he had unwittingly shut in the room with him, pushed his muzzle across the pillows, eager to be let out. The sun was up and dazzled his sleep-sore eyes. He was momentarily disorientated by the huge, unfamiliar room with its ornate, canopied bed and (indeed astonishing) view across treetops to the sea. Moving slowly, because he found that as well as having a furry mouth, his head was beginning to throb, he let the dog out, wandered into the bathroom to pee copiously then pulled on the rest of his clothes. (He appeared to have fallen into bed while still half-dressed.) He walked to the bay window. Fingal had evidently found an open door or window downstairs for Andrew saw him racing away across the garden like a thin, black shadow, a long, pink tongue trailing back from the corner of his jaws. Overcome with a wave of exhaustion, he sank onto the window seat and closed his eyes.

Now the night before began to make perfect sense. With a spasm of remorse, he saw that his nocturnal suspicions were foolish paranoia. Swayed by dope, wine, his attraction to his hostess and the pathetic sexual envy of an overgrown adolescent, he had imagined the unimaginable. Evidently he had been single too long.

He pulled open the window and, closing his eyes once more, took deep breaths of cool morning air. The threat of a headache receded a fraction. He wished that his mortification might follow it. Suppressing the ignoble impulse to slip down to the Land Rover and beat a shy retreat, leaving his father to cadge a lift, he forced himself to retrace the events of the night in humiliating search of any behaviour on his part, any words, that might have betrayed the teenage imaginings that had so tormented him. He remembered pieces of gaucherie, bumpkin cack-handedness, but nothing worse than his perfectly innocent blunder in assuming brother and sister to be husband and wife. Perhaps, after all, he could face them without alarm. Fantasy followed hard on the heels of this comforting discovery. He reminded himself that Holly and Clifford would be working down here long after his father's departure.

Andrew would invite them over for supper. Perhaps Holly might even visit on her own. He might even, in the subtlest way possible, and only on a third or fourth encounter, trail beneath her prettily uptilted nose the possibility of her using his second ticket to San Francisco. Just to see what she said, of course; it was most unlikely that she would accept.

He shivered, closed the window and went to find his shoes. Halfway through tying the second lace, he heard a strange thumping noise. Thinking it might be Fingal, returned and pushing at the door, he stood and walked out onto the landing. There was no dog and the noise stopped before he could trace it. A delicious smell of fresh coffee and toast was curling up from below. He remembered it was a Sunday. Perhaps there would be papers, a rare luxury in which he could lose himself. He started along the corridor for the stairs then froze. The thumping had begun again and with it, voices, coming from behind a door to his right. The door had been left open a little and the few inches of darkness it revealed were dense at once with privacy and suggestion. The thumping, as was clear from the faint squeaking of springs which provided its rhythmical underlay, was the headboard of a bed knocking against the other side of the wall. Someone was gasping, sucking in thin breaths after each thump of oak on plaster. Louder than them, his voice distorted with painful urgency, his father was keeping up a stream of forbidden words.

Unable to walk on, unable to return to his room, Andrew sank slowly to the top step, one hand fingering the banisters beside him. Long ago, as a boy, he had learned to listen for the sound of his parents making love – usually on a Sunday morning – learned to associate its rare occurrences with the ensuing twenty-four hours of unusual, secretive smiles on his

129

mother's face and uncharacteristic generosities practised by his father. His parents had made love in silence, however – doubtless unaware of the sympathetic squeaking their muffled exertions produced in the neighbouring bathroom. This new, graphic voicing of his father's deepest appetite, which now pinned Andrew to the spot, laid waste whole decades of boyish certainty. For a few seconds Andrew entertained the repellently hopeful possibility that sweet, beguiling Holly was downstairs brewing coffee and that it was Clifford who was so efficiently lancing his father's festered desire. Then the sighs swelled in volume and became unmistakably female and Andrew found himself watching tears splash off his cheeks onto the dusty step below his knees. He remained rooted to the spot until the yelps in the bedroom turned to laughter, then he wiped his eyes and carried on downstairs, heedless of whether the couple heard him blow his nose so close to its door.

Clifford had begun work in another room. He had washed a wall with a watery, terracotta paint and was rubbing it around with a rag, so that a paler colour below showed through here and there. Sensing that Andrew needed occupation, he brought him strong coffee then tied an apron round his waist, placed a brush in his hand and set him to washing colour over another section of wall. He was kind enough to sustain a pretence that nothing untoward had occurred overnight. At least, Andrew took it for kindness but on reflection it might have been a kind of moral delinquency in him. The work was calming, as, curiously, was Clifford's rich supply of scandalous erotic anecdotes. At last, when Holly called from the kitchen that she was frying bacon and eggs, Andrew felt able to face her and his father with equanimity, if not insouciance.

Predictably his father was all joviality, full of enthusiasm for the effects of the country and a good night's sleep. He gave even less sign than Clifford that anything out of the ordinary had happened, unless his cheerfully electing to wash up the remains of the previous night's meal was symptomatic of a need for expiation, which Andrew doubted. Holly kissed Andrew's cheek and earnestly asked him if he slept well.

'I hope I didn't wake you,' she went on before he could answer. 'I came up long after everyone – even poor old Kenneth. I suddenly felt this desperate need to get on and paint.'

She was interrupted by a sudden commotion. Pursued by Clifford's laughter, Fingal burst into the kitchen clutching a lifeless lamb in his jaws and evidently hugely pleased with himself. Andrew was horrified. He exclaimed that if a farmer caught him the dog would be shot. But Holly was utterly untroubled, as though this happened all the time.

'But he wasn't caught, was he?' she said, easing the lamb from Fingal's jaws and laying it on the *Observer* business section. 'How delicious. Get busy, Clifford, and we can have it for lunch.' She stooped to kiss Fingal. 'Clever boy. *Clever* boy!'

'Oh don't be such a prig, Andy!' his father exclaimed, seeing Andrew's expression at her rank encouragement of crime. 'Get her to show you the painting. She's caught you exactly. Even that expression. Go on, Holly. I'll watch the bacon.'

As Clifford began to sharpen a knife for skinning and butchering the lamb, Holly took Andrew's hand. He was sweating and might have slipped from her grasp but her fingers were relentless. She pulled him back to the big, dust-sheeted saloon, pulled aside the ladder and pointed.

Andrew stared and could not restrain a guffaw of recognition. There he was, wreathed in golden laurels, peering through

131

the parted branches of a peach tree. It was not mere imagination which made him see Holly in the girlish figure in the fountain – she had Holly's hair and dark eyebrows. The broad-backed male figure, so keen to enjoy her, had his face turned away into the painting but his identity now seemed immaterial. It was Andrew she had recorded on plaster, pinned down, fingered, as the police would say.

They ate the lamb for lunch, with rosemary and new potatoes purloined from the owner's garden. It was quite delicious. Andrew's father was forced to catch a slightly later train than planned because they did not start eating until mid afternoon.

'Come again,' Holly called, waving as Andrew drove back up the drive. 'Now that you've found us, come again.'

He wound down the window but did not know what to say so merely smiled and pressed on the accelerator. While they drove to the station, his father's one-sided conversation began to assume a London gravity as his thoughts returned to the heavy load of long-winded commercial briefs and the tedious day of interviewing candidates for pupillage which awaited him. Having made no mention of the strangeness of arranging to make a long-postponed visit to one's son, only to use him as a pretext for receiving the hospitality of another, his parting words were a casual request that Andrew ring his mother to warn of his later arrival.

'Andrew?' Her voice was rich with the evening's first drink. 'How lovely. How did it go?'

'Fine,' he told her. 'Thanks for the geranium. Dad seems very well.'

'He is.'

'And we visited some friends of yours. Those decorators.'

'Holly and Clifford? What fun. They're *so* nice.'

'Yes. Er. Mum?' Dialling her number, Andrew had steeled himself to risk sounding prudish. She ought to know. He was sure of it. But first he found himself picturing the needless pain he might cause her, then he felt obscurely guilty for the passive role he had just played in his father's off-hand infidelity. Mouthing silently into the mouthpiece, aware afresh of the tickets to California winking at him from their hiding place on the dresser, he found he could go no further. 'How was *your* weekend?' he asked instead.

'Fine. You know I'd have loved to have come too – Cornwall's such heaven at this time of year – but I did think it was important for Dad to spend a little time alone with you for once. Anyway, I had a friend of my own visiting. James Bedford.'

'Who?'

'Oh you *know*. That nice academic I met when poor Kate and I went to Florence last year. He's *so* nice. He's still here in fact, so I better let you go. I promised to let him cast an eye over some of my silly bits and pieces before he goes.' She giggled. 'Bye darling. Don't work too hard. Bye.'

As he soaked in the bath, preparing for an early night, it struck him that his mother's nice academic might be her lover. She might be well aware of his father's involvement, or whatever one called it, with Holly. It was his mother, after all, who had first so unexpectedly posited the idea of his father's coming to stay. If the business of his coming were no more than an elaborate charade for the adulterer, forcing his son to play alibi, then might it not also have proved an erotic convenience for the adulterer's wife?

Andrew reached out a soapy arm to turn up the volume on the radio, resolving to push the matter from his mind by an effort to focus on a laconic discussion of the Islamic Question. He must learn to avoid fantasizing. That way, as his mother was always saying, lay madness. He wiped away a tear and returned to scrubbing at the terracotta paint which clung so persistently to his fingernails.

OTHER MEN'S SWEETNESS

for Tom Wakefield

'Sarah-Jane? Sarah-Jane? Wake up. We're nearly there!'

Jane opened her small, green eyes, yawned and focused on her mother from the back of the overloaded car. From as early as she could remember, she had loathed the name Sarah and the hyphen that accompanied it. People who really loved her, like her dolls and the sweetshop lady, called her Jane. Her mother smiled and turned back to face the road. Jane shifted and winced crossly. The rear of the car was hot and stuffy and she had outgrown her safety seat.

'I'm too big for it now,' she had complained as her father strapped her in.

'Nonsense,' he said. 'It's meant for ages three to five. You can have a new one on your birthday.'

She looked down at Jones, the only doll she had been allowed to bring. ('Quickly, Sarah-Jane! Choose one quickly! We don't have all day.') Jones's eyes clicked open to reveal a baby-blue stare. Jane tugged Jones's red nylon hair and felt a little more cheerful. Then she looked out of the window. They were in the flattest place she had ever seen. On either side of the slightly raised road, fields flat as carpets stretched out as far as the eye could see. Here and there was a line of sickly trees or a sinister stream straight as a ruler. The road was straight too and seemed to stretch as far as the horizon.

'Where are we?' she asked.

'Cambridgeshire,' her father said.

'We're about to cross the border into Norfolk,' her mother added.

'Where?'

'Any . . . minute . . . *now*! Here! Now we're in Norfolk.'

They passed a sign. The road looked just the same, as did the countryside. Flat. Flat. Flat.

'Where's Norfolk?'

'East Anglia. On the East coast.'

'And why did we have to get a cottage *here*?'

'Your mum liked the idea.'

'And your dad found the perfect place.'

'And we got it at a bargain price,' her father went on. 'Can't think why no one else has discovered this bit. I mean, it was a bit grim having to drive out through the East End, but I suppose, if one were to keep clear of the rush hours and so forth, it wouldn't be so bad . . .'

Her parents lapsed back into one of their usual, incredibly tedious conversations, cobwebbed with adult impenetrables like *Hangar Lane Gyratory System* and *Miles Per Gallon* and *Post War Architecture*. They were not nearly there. Her mother had lied again. Sometimes she seemed to resent Jane's falling asleep in the car and wake her for the hell of it. Jane fell to pulling Jones's hair again then tried to push out one of the doll's eyes with its own, miniature thumb.

She had twenty-nine other dolls at home and a hammock and an exercise bicycle and her own fridge for cold drinks and her own colour television and a child size portable video camera and her own stereo system with compact disc player and remote control facility. She had her own bathroom, with a bidet and an extensive menagerie of clockwork bathroom toys and a whole wall of fitted cupboards to house the dress collection she planned to amass over the years to come. She had piano lessons and ballet classes and went to the cinema often and had only been refused a pet because her mother said she was too young to look after one. They had a lovely house in Islington, with two garages and a gym and both her parents seemed happy with their jobs. Why then had they seen fit to buy – another adult impenetrable – *a Little Place in the Country*?

'Sarah-Jane? Sarah-Jane? Look! We're here! There it is!'

Jane looked up from her ponderings. They were pulling up on the outskirts of a village. There was a farmhouse in a cluster of outbuildings overgrown with creepers and long grass. To their left crouched a small, red-brick building not unlike a rather cheap doll's house, set near the road in a patch of wind-swept garden.

'Oh,' said Jane.

'Well you could show a little more enthusiasm,' her mother snapped.

'Don't bully her,' her father said. 'She'll like it when she looks around. Come on. We can unpack later.'

He unstrapped Jane's harness and lifted her down to the grass verge. She followed as he walked arm in arm with her mother up the garden path. A dead rat glistened with flies under a rose bush but Jane said nothing. She would save it to come back to later.

The house was quite nice inside. It smelled of wet paint and there was only one bathroom, but her bedroom under the eaves was so tiny and had such a small window that it reminded her of the houses she liked to build under her mother's dressing table or inside the airing cupboard. She began to understand her parents' enthusiasm. It was all a game.

'Do you like it, then?' her father asked her.

Jane bounced on her bed to make it squeak.

'When are we having lunch?' she asked.

'She likes it,' her mother said. 'Thank Christ for that.'

And Jane had to watch while her parents kissed exaggerat-edly like a couple in a cartoon.

They were busy with suitcases and spice racks after lunch and Jane found herself repeatedly in their way. So, responding to their impatient suggestions, she slipped out to play by herself in the garden. At the back of the house was a cluster of tired fruit trees. An old tyre hung from one and she amused herself for a while by swinging on it until she felt dizzy. She tried an apple or two but they were hard and their sour juice made her tongue curl. Then she found a congregation of slugs glistening in the rhubarb patch and had fun squashing it with a stone. She needed to pee suddenly and felt pangs of hunger (lunch had been olives and salad) so she started back towards the house. Her parents were shouting at each other however, and she was frightened to go in. Instead, she relieved herself in some bushes below one of the windows. Crouching on the dry earth she gradually became aware of a delicious smell; warm, sweet, spicy. It was coming from the shabby farmhouse next door. She followed it across the garden as far as a broken part of the fence and stopped there to sniff again. The smell curled around in her head and made her stomach gurgle. The gap in the fence was not wide and she had to squeeze and shove to force her belly through.

Once she was on the other side it seemed impossible to go back the way she had come. So she went on. She was enchanted to find a small zoo at large in the yard. A cat was dozing on a bale of hay. Another was draped across a sack of fertilizer, swishing its tabby tail. An old sheepdog rose from his place by the back door to sniff and lick her face. There were ducks on a greenish pond and hens scratching in the earth. A donkey brayed and wheezed in a paddock where a huge black horse watched her from the shadow of a tree. A goat, safely tethered, paused in its munching to fix her with reptile eyes and she counted three cows grazing in the field beyond the paddock. She stopped to pat the dog and pet the cats, then she followed the delicious scent – which was making her quite ravenous now – to the open back door.

A batch of sugary Chelsea buns and two seed-dusted loaves were steaming on a wire rack below the window. Further into the room, in the shadows, a woman and a man were seated, one behind the other. She was gently combing out his black hair, which was nearly as long as hers. They were both beautiful. Not like her mother and father, who were beautiful and handsome respectively of course, but beautiful in a new, unsettling way. They didn't look altogether clean and the woman wore no make-up, but they had a kind of glow. It brought Jane to a sudden, hurtful realization that her parents might not be the most attractive people she would ever meet. The man had been working on the farm. He had no shirt on and there were streaks of mud among the black hairs which formed whorls on his chest where her father's was pink and smooth. His eyes were shut with pleasure but the woman saw Jane and smiled without stopping her combing.

'Hello,' she said, in a faintly mocking, low voice. 'Who are you?'

The man opened his eyes briefly but did not move.

'I'm Jane,' said Jane. 'We live next door now. Can I take a bun?'

141

'Sure,' the woman said and, as Jane carefully picked the bun nearest her and sank her teeth into its sticky crust, she twisted the man's hair into a glossy braid and kissed the nape of his neck. The dough was still warm and one or two currants tumbled from its torn surface to the floor, where the sheepdog licked them up and sat, with a barely discernible whine, to wait for more. The man opened his eyes again then pushed back his chair and stood. He winked at Jane and walked out across the yard to the barn, where he started using a noisy machine.

'Like your bun?' asked the woman, grinning now.

Jane nodded vigorously. She would have liked another but knew this was best left for a sort of going-home present.

'I'm Jeanette,' the woman said. 'And that was Dougal. Do your parents know you're here?'

'No,' Jane told her. 'They're busy.'

'Well,' Jeanette winced, 'so am I, in a way. But you can watch if you like.'

'Yes please.'

'Come and sit on a chair, then, instead of standing there like a pudding.'

Jane came forward and clambered onto a kitchen chair. The woman, Jeanette, in whose honour she had already resolved to rechristen one of her better-favoured dolls, had switched on a light in a corner of the big, low-ceilinged room, and was turning her attention to a chest of drawers. It was painted dusky blue all over and someone had started to decorate it further with little clumps of painted leaves.

'Are you a farmer's wife?' Jane asked.

Jeanette chuckled.

'No. The animals are just pets and the field and paddock are all the land we've got really. This is how we make our living.

Well. Our sort-of living. We buy old bits of bashed up wooden furniture at auctions. Dougal mends them and does the base coat and I paint on the twiddly pretty bits.' She shook her yard of blonde hair away from her face and tied it impatiently in a handkerchief, then she reached for a saucer of paint and a brush.

'What are you doing now?'

'Pull that chair closer and I'll show you.'

Jane moved closer and watched Jeanette paint leaves and buds and tendrils. She had a smell that was almost as good as the buns – Jane's mother never wore scent and stopped Jane's father wearing it either because it made her sneeze. There were other good smells in the room besides Jeanette and the buns. Bunches of pungent leaves were hanging from the beams to dry and there was a fragrant mound of orange peel and a pot of cooling coffee on the table. Jane watched, fascinated, as Jeanette's long, dirty fingers made deft twists this way and that with the brush. Dougal stopped using the machine and began to make gentle taps with a hammer. He sang to himself as he worked. Jane pulled her feet up onto the chair beside her. The good smells, the bun and the pleasing sense of doing nothing while adults laboured, conspired to bring a delicious drowsiness over her. For a few lucid seconds before she nodded off, she wondered why her life was not always like this, why this sense of well-fed contentment was so unfamiliar.

When she awoke, the cupboard was all painted and her parents were in the room making clucking, apologetic noises to Jeanette.

'She's been no trouble, honestly,' Jeanette was saying.

'We had no idea. I'm so *sorry*!' Jane's mother exclaimed.

'No bother at all,' Dougal added. He winked again as her

father swung her up against his shoulder and followed her mother outside. He winked privately, so that no one else noticed.

'Come again,' Jeanette murmured, with her discreet smile. 'Pop round.'

Her parents rarely came again however. In the weekends that followed, they were preoccupied with adult impenetrables – *Hand Blocked Paper*, *Damp Course*, the demise of a *Feature Fireplace* and some lengthy and bad-tempered dealings with someone called *Artex Removal*. But Jane came. She could barely wait for each weekend to begin in order to squeeze through the gap in the fence and visit her new friends. Dougal let her stir paint and showed her how to milk the cows and goat. Jeanette taught her to plait her own hair (which seemed to make her mother cross). She gave her handfuls of bread dough to knead into shapes and bake and she used to stretch a sheet of yellowed lining paper across the kitchen table for Jane to paint on while she worked at her grown-up painting along-side her.

Jane's parents were perturbed at first, in case Jane were proving an embarrassment, then they seemed to accept the idea that Jane had adopted a second family. They chuckled, in her hearing, about the *Hippies* and pounced on any small infelici-ties that crept from their neighbours' speech into their daughter's. (Jane, uncomprehending, told Jeanette that her mother said that Jeanette had a *terrible Norfolk burr* and Jeanette laughed and fed her some cooking chocolate.) That Jeanette could be handy as a child-minder was swiftly appreciated. Jane's mother was often unable to come to the cottage for more than two weekends in a row. On these occasions, Jane's father would bring work with him and closet himself with the portable computer in the dining room while Jane went to play with the animals she now thought of as hers. It was not unheard of for Jeanette to invite him to come over with Jane for long, boozy meals in the farmhouse but Jane preferred it when he stayed on his side of the fence. She was not above keeping a proffered invitation to herself and passing back some fabricated apology so as to keep her friends to herself.

When her nursery school began its holidays she was even left behind one weekend to spend seven glorious days as Jeanette and Dougal's guest. She fitted quite easily into their routines, rising and retiring when she felt like it, washing as little as they did and eating whatever pleasantly meatless meals Jeanette placed before her. Two things set the seal on the week's pleasure for her: lying awake listening to the loud sighs and open laughter that came from their bedroom – a far cry from the embarrassed coughs and inexplicable creaks that came from her parents' well-appointed own – and being woken by Dougal at the dead of night to watch one of the cats giving birth.

Her parents joined her for a fortnight's holiday after that and brought with them bad weather, bitterness and altercation. While Jane sheltered, bored, from the rain, they argued. Jeanette's name was raised as was that of a young Frenchman who lived with their neighbours in London. Adult impenetrables to do with *Planning Permission*, *Fraud*, *Silk Purses* and *Sows' Ears* crackled on the air over Jane's head and when she tried to slope off to Jeanette and Dougal, as had become her habit, she was faced with an inexplicable edict.

'You are *not* to go round there any more, Sarah-Jane,' her father commanded. 'You are not to see them. Do you understand?'

Stunned, Jane retreated both to her room and to the

temporarily abandoned solace of her dolls and their unstinting fidelity. She sat them in elegant half-circles around her on the bedroom floor, trying not to listen too closely to the angry phrases that followed her up the stairs.

'I've a good mind to go round there and have it out with him.'

'*Him?* You think *he*'s behind it? Oh no. It was her. Her name was on that form. It was her application for planning permission that had so carefully been allowed to lapse until we'd had the searches done. She's the one that took you for a ride. Simple, unworldly hippies my arse. She saw you coming a mile off and if you hadn't been blinded by lust –'

'Well if we're talking lust, I hardly think last week's sordid little revelation leaves you in *any* position to –'

Jane quietly shut the door to keep out the sounds of their anger and climbed on the bed with a pad of paper and some crayons. She drew the perfect house where she and the more attractive of her dolls would live. They had a gym and a swimming pool and a bathroom apiece and there were dogs and kittens and a cow and a donkey and a place for Jeanette and Dougal to make her buns. Her parents, perhaps, might live next door. In a slightly smaller house because their needs were simpler and their natures undeserving.

Her mother came upstairs after a while, her hair newly tidy and lips newly red, to announce that the three of them were going to drive to the seaside for tea. For the rest of the week an unnatural parade of normality was mounted. Where they would formerly have amused themselves, they now did everything as a closely bound trio, or, rather, as a pair with Jane a necessary buffer zone. They had picnics and a boat trip. They made apple chutney and visited *historic* buildings where Jane was rewarded for her boredom with cake or ice cream. There were no more arguments apart from quickly stifled bickering about road directions and timetables. Jane saw nothing of Jeanette and Dougal – there was no time and the ceaseless activities left her whimpering only for sleep.

On the last evening of the holiday, Jane's mother delivered a startling piece of news. Jane's father had returned in high excitement from taking a phone call and a bottle of champagne had been opened. Jane could smell it on her mother's breath as she bathed her.

'Sarah-Jane, you do realize, don't you, that we're going back to London tomorrow and we won't be coming back here?'

'No.'

'Well we won't, you see. We've just managed to sell the cottage.'

'But why?'

'We had to. It turns out the naughty woman who sold it to your dad kept lots of bad things secret.'

'What bad things?'

'Oh. Well. That there are going to be a lot of horrid new houses on all the land around here. Things like that.'

'Oh.'

'So it was very important to sell quickly and get a good price before anyone else found out. Daddy's found a buyer today and we've accepted the offer. It's a shame but there it is. Now. Let's wash your hair so it's as shiny as a little doll's. You *are* getting plump, darling! We'll have to put you back on salads for a while. Whatever can that Jeanette have been feeding you?'

Jane started to ask why her father had kept bad things secret too but her mother had turned the shower on and her eyes and mouth threatened to fill with water. She cried while her hair was washed and grizzled as her mother rubbed her dry. But she quietened down when allowed a dusting of Chanel talcum powder and by the time she was tucked up in bed in her tiny room for the last time, she was utterly calm. She had forged a plan.

'Do you want me to read you a story?' asked her mother, who had unthinkingly ascribed her tears to a surfeit of tiring pleasures during the day.

'No,' Jane told her and enjoyed her mother's *moue* of disappointment at the small rejection. Left alone with the eerie reflection of her night-light in her dolls' eyes, Jane dwelt on her simple plan. She had tried for a while to share herself with two households. Now thoughtless decisions from adults left her no option but to choose. She had already transferred her loyalties from the household and parents she was born with to those she coveted. Now she had merely to follow through with a bodily transfer. She would swap families. Like any nicely brought-up girl faced with a plate of cakes, she would reach for the sweetness that lay closest to her.

In such familiar territory, the defection was easily performed. As Jane had suspected, the next day was taken up with frantic preparations for removal men. Many boxes of books had remained packed all summer for want of shelves but there were china and glass to wrap and linen to sort and pictures to protect. When she slipped out of the house after a perfunctory late lunch and squeezed through the gap in the fence, she was not missed therefore. She hid at the side of the barn and watched until she was certain that both Jeanette and Dougal were in the house, then she darted around the corner and through the barn door. Jules, the dog, stood and wagged his tail to see her but he was still tethered by the back door to keep him from bothering the kittens so he could not give away her whereabouts.

On one side of the barn, bales of fresh straw were stacked up high over Jane's head. She had played for hours on these, drunk with their heady smell, until Dougal frightened her off with a warning that children could easily slip out of reach, deep between the bales, and die for lack of air. Against the other walls clustered a collection of wooden wardrobes, chests of drawers, looking glasses and trunks in various stages of restoration and dismemberment. Jane walked over to a dusty looking glass to stare at her reflection nose to nose. Then she heard Dougal talking as he left the house. She knew he would be happy to learn she was adopting him, but sensed that it was wisest not to confront him until her former parents had safely given her up for lost. She glanced around and chose a huge wardrobe to the back of the barn. She slithered over the chest of drawers in front, tugged open the door and slid inside. She scrabbled the door almost shut again with her fingernails, put an eye to the crack and waited. Suddenly her mother's voice rang out, crystal clear, from the garden.

'Sarah-Jane? Sarah-Jane?' There was a muttered curse and she called back to the cottage. 'She's nowhere in sight, Brian. Are you sure she wasn't upstairs? . . . Well look again, could you?'

Dougal appeared, walking towards the barn entrance with a painted bathroom cabinet under one arm.

'Oh, er, Dougal?' her mother called out. He stopped, then walked out of view, towards the fence.

'Hello?'

'You, er, you haven't seen Sarah-Jane, have you?'

'Jane? Have you lost her?'

'Well. Not exactly. I just wondered if she'd come over.'

'Sorry.'

'Send her back if you see her, would you? We're meant to be leaving soon.'

'No problem.'

'Thanks.'

Dougal came on into the barn, set down the cabinet and gathered up some electric cable which he tidied lazily into loops over his arm. As he left again, Jane suppressed an urge to jump out shouting boo as she had done several times before. She leaned against the back of the wardrobe and listened to her mother's fretful, now slightly irritated cries.

'Sarah-Jane? Sarah-Jane? Where *are* you?'

Jane smiled to herself. She would miss her dolls and her party frocks but at least, after today, she would never again be called Sarah or given a hyphen. Her mother's cries stopped and for a while there was silence except for the clucking of two hens which had appeared to scratch at the earth and wood shavings in the doorway. Jane's stomach gurgled and she rubbed it reassuringly. Then she heard her mother's voice again and her father's, followed by a knock at the back door of the farmhouse. Jeanette answered. Jane couldn't make out the words but she heard the one woman's anxiety being passed on to the other and soon her parents and Jeanette were walking towards the barn. Her mother's face looked tight and cold, despite the warm remains of the day. Her father strode on ahead.

As he walked in he seemed momentarily subdued by the barn's looming shadows.

'Sarah-Jane?' he asked quietly. 'Sarah-Jane?'

Jane bit her lip and stared out at him, her fingertips holding the door in place before her. Her mother appeared in the doorway with Jeanette.

'Sarah-Jane?' she called out. 'Don't be silly, darling. Game's over now.'

She came forward and opened a large chest then let the lid shut with a bang. Suddenly both Jane's parents were galvanized into action. They hurried here and there, in and out of Jane's narrow range of vision, tugging open drawers and wardrobes and shifting things to peer into the shadows. Jeanette stood, hands on hips, and watched them.

'The hay!' Jane's mother shouted. 'She might have slipped down inside the hay!' The air filled with straw dust as, grunting, she had Jane's father set about tugging down bales.

'She isn't here,' Jeanette said softly. Jane's father came into view again. He started clambering over the chest of drawers to reach the wardrobe where she was hiding. Jane slid into the farthest corner and held her breath as he stretched out a hand towards the doorknob. Then Jeanette shouted, causing him to turn around. 'Look, I said she isn't here! Now would you both please get out?'

'Listen, you,' Jane's mother began then seemed to run out of words. Jane heard her panting.

'Come on, Christine. She isn't here,' Jeanette said, reaching out an arm. Jane's mother gave a little whimper and ran forward in tears. Jeanette led her gently out into the fading light. Jane's father lingered a moment. He had picked up a small carved box and turned it over in his hands, evidently admiring it. He glanced around, saw no one was looking and, to Jane's astonishment, slipped it into the deep poacher's pocket of his waxed jacket. Aimlessly he then opened a few more doors and slammed them shut again. Dougal walked across the yard.

'Come on, Brian,' he called. 'It's no use. We've called the police for you.'

In a sudden burst of anger, Jane's father turned and shoved hard on the chest of drawers in front of her hiding place. It slid back with a complaint of old wood and banged hard into the wardrobe, slamming the door firmly shut in his daughter's face. Jane waited a moment, rubbing her forehead where the wood had struck it and wondering whether to cry, then she pushed and found the door stuck fast. She couldn't shout out to Dougal yet. Not with her father still there. She looked frantically about her in the increasingly musty space and saw light coming through a tiny crack by the hinges. She shifted her position as quietly as she could and thrust an eye to the space. Squinting, she just made out her father's silhouette as he walked into the yard. Dougal was still there, looking around at the furniture. She would wait just long enough for her parents to get clear then she would call. Or perhaps she would wait until after the police had been? Perhaps she should call out now? She wanted to pee and she was getting hungry, but if the police caught her they might punish her. She might be punished anyway.

She hesitated a moment too long. Dougal turned on his heel, strode out into the yard and swung the barn doors shut with a terrific bang then shot the bolts on the outside. Cars and voices came and went in the hour that followed but through two great thicknesses of wood they might have been two fields away. Jane shouted herself hoarse, then slumped, exhausted and tearful, to the cramped wardrobe floor. She had no coat on and the evening was turning cold. A hen emerged from its roosting place in the straw. Losing consciousness, Jane heard its clucking as it scratched for beetles.

*

As Brian drove out through Hackney and Stratford, his mood gradually lightened. He had been angry at Chrissie's refusal to join him on the house-hunting trip since it had been her idea in the first place and he had taken a day off valuable work to make it. Her refusal had been of the kind that, left unheeded, would have poisoned the entire day, however, and there was nothing he disliked more than driving anywhere with her being monosyllabic and hurt in the passenger seat. It might have been fun to have brought Sarah-Jane along at least – they so rarely spent time alone together – but she was coming increasingly to mimic her mother's every gesture and mood and would only have been monosyllabic and hurt and squeaky.

A trio of Bengali women passed chattering over a zebra cross-ing before him, the sun catching on flecks of synthetic gold in their swirling, rainbow drapes and Brian reiterated his vow to spend one Sunday soon exploring rather more of the East End than the Whitechapel Gallery and Blooms. Chrissie had bought him a glossy book on Hawksmoor churches but it had gone unread. He drove on towards the motorway, accelerating as the traffic thinned out, and his irritation evaporated. He pressed a button and the car's roof folded away. It was the latest German convertible, with an engine so quiet one was said to be able to balance a fifty pence piece on it while driving at fifty miles an hour. Brian would have felt absurd testing this claim under his family's critical eye. It was a pleasure to have the car, as well as an excursion, to himself for once. He was on holiday. He would take his pleasure where he found it. He might try the fifty pence piece test on a quiet side road. He slipped on to the motorway and smiled to himself as the speedometer registered ninety with no discernible increase in noise level.

He stopped at Wisbech to pick up details from estate agents.

153

He admired the prettiness of Georgian houses and enjoyed the bustle in the market square – such a far cry from the anger and desolation of shopping in London. Whenever he came to places like Wisbech or Salisbury he bemoaned the fact that he was not a GP or a solicitor or even a dentist – someone who could work equally profitably in a quiet provincial backwater where there was less tension, less overt competition and more time for the good things in life. Chrissie tended to be sharp with him when he mentioned this.

'You'd be bored,' she would say. 'You know you would. You're a very competitive man. You always have been. You'd wither without the cut and thrust. And there wouldn't be any good schools for Sarah-Jane. And anyway, what about me?'

Chrissie had a good job too. She travelled so much for it that there was no reason why she should not live in the country, provided she was within easy driving distance of an international airport. All she would need would be a telephone and a fax machine. But when he suggested this, she sighed, impatient but longsuffering.

'Brian,' she said, 'you *know* what I mean.'

'What? You mean parties and things?'

'And things. Yes.'

Brian looked at five cottages recommended by the agents. They were all fairly pretty, certainly, although the austere fenland landscape did not lend itself to a snug village atmosphere in the manner of rolling Cotswold hillsides or burbling Hampshire water meadows. But Hampshire and Gloucestershire were fast becoming part of the retirement belt boom whereas prices in East Anglia could only go up. There was something wrong with each of the cottages he saw, however. They were all close to the road, but that, the agents had explained, was a fenland phenomenon dictated by the very gradual process by which the need for land had triumphed over the usefulness of water. They had gardens, they were in good condition, they were clearly loved and they were within his price range. The trouble was that too much money had been lavished on them, some of it tastelessly so. *Feature* fireplaces had been installed, an owner's pride and joy, as were neo-Victorian garage doors, obtrusively modern fitted kitchens and driveways of pulsatingly orange gravel. Even this would not have been a problem usually. In London, where comfortable convenience was of paramount importance in their hectic lives, he and Chrissie had been grateful to buy a modern house with every efficient luxury already installed, a house needing only the addition of a couple, a child, and their groaning pantechnicon of possessions. Yet Brian sensed that his needs – their needs – in a weekend cottage would be different. They did not want convenience – for that, all his friends would agree, one kept a single house in London and spent one's surplus on country hotels. They wanted distraction and difficulty. Brian wanted a challenge. He wanted somewhere he could make his own, a place where he could mark out individual territory. (In his weekly work, all-powerful market forces had him exploiting originality in others, and scarcely fostered it in himself.)

He fell to perusing a copy of the *Wisbech and District Chronicle*. There, amid ragged columns of classified advertisements for land auctions and lawnmower sales, he found what he was looking for.

Fenland cottage in need of loving care, he read. *Brick-built, pantiled roof, c.1850. 1 acre. Mature fruit trees. Suit young couple with small child and vision. 35,000 ono.*

155

He called the owners on the car phone and drew up outside their ramshackle farmstead twenty minutes later. He had spoken to a man but it was a woman who emerged as he shut the car door. She had long, straight, blonde hair and was, he guessed, about his age and height. She wore a loose, scarlet dress of rough cotton that clung about her full and braless breasts and swished about her long thighs as she advanced. When she took his hand in hers and said, 'Hi. I'm Jeanette. I assume you're the intrepid house-hunter,' a twinge of lust stirred his loins. 'Sorry,' she went on, brushing her palms together, 'I've probably got flour on you. It's baking day.'

Brian smiled and assured her it was quite all right. There was a streak of flour on her forehead, running into her hair like grey.

'Normally I get Dougal to show people round,' she said, leading him across the grass at the roadside. 'He knows more about building and joists and so on than I do. But he's getting ready for an auction in Cambridge so you'll just have to make do with me.'

'Oh. Well. I'm sure you'll do very nicely,' Brian said automatically, then coughed to cover his embarrassment. She merely smiled to herself and passed on.

The cottage for sale was immediately next door, set a short garden's distance from the road, with a gnarled, flower-strewn orchard behind it. Jeanette explained that she had inherited it from her mother but could not afford to keep it on. She drew his attention to the interesting brickwork then led him around the inside. Their proximity in the tiny rooms was intoxicating. She gave off a heavy scent, composed of baking spices, yeast and another, sweeter odour he could not place. He was vaguely aware of peeling paintwork and the sour taint of damp but found that he was concentrating on her lips more than on what she was showing him. Her eyes were grey and the kohl pressed thickly round their edges and the slight wateriness it had induced, summoned louche memories of earlier, freer days, before Sarah-Jane, before Chrissie. She showed him a stained bath with chipped enamel then followed him into a minute bedroom under the eaves.

'Now this would do for . . . Do you have kids?'

'Yes,' he told her. 'One. Sarah-Jane.'

'Ah. Sweet.'

'Yes. She'd love it up here.' Brian crouched to peer out of the small, low window at the dyke that lay, a still, dark mirror, along the other side of the road. 'Do you have children?' he asked, turning back to her. 'You and . . .?'

'Dougal. No. We've tried, but no. Sometimes I catch myself peering into pushchairs at the supermarket and just, well, lusting. I catch myself planning how I could just reach in and take one.' She had to pass close by him to reach the landing again. She paused, looked deep into his eyes and pressed his erection frankly with her wrist and fingertips. 'Believe me,' she said, 'I'm tempted.'

Brian felt himself blush hotly. She released him and moved on just before he made a move so that he lunged at nothing. He followed downstairs, watching the swishing of her skirt and wondering how it would be if he seized a handful of her hair and bit into her lips. Was it other people's babies who tempted her or his all too visible lust? She had blurred the distinctions. His head was full of her scent and the cottage suddenly felt as though it had been designed for smaller, surer-footed creatures.

She stopped in the hall and swung her hair behind her shoulders as she waited for him to come down.

'Well?' she asked. 'What do you think?' Her Norfolk accent would have been comical had it not been so intensely erotic.

'I like it,' he stammered. 'I like it very much. I think it's a good idea.'

'Are you making an offer, then?'

'I'll give you twenty-eight for it.'

'Thirty-two.'

'Thirty.'

'Done.' She held out her hand. As he shook it, a sly corner of his brain, unimpeded by lust, told him he had done her out of a bargain. 'I'll put you in touch with my solicitors,' she said. Then, rather than let go, she lifted his hand and rubbed its palm across her breasts then down to where, he could tell at a touch, she was knickerless.

'Oh God,' he groaned.

'Yes?' she teased, smiling.

'Your husband . . .'

'Dougal's off to Cambridge,' she sighed. 'Don't mind Dougal.'

The red dress came off over her head in one liquid movement. He forgot, in his haste, to take his shoes off first, so he was caught with his jeans locked around his ankles and had difficulty keeping his balance. Surprisingly strong, she lowered him to the foot of the stairs and sat astride him but he became fearful of splinters and they tried leaning in the doorway then moved to the kitchen table.

'Yes,' she cried. 'Yes! Yes!' and she struck him hard on the buttocks with her boot heels.

At that moment, Brian looked up to see an extremely handsome, pigtailed man swing over the farmstead fence and stride through the orchard towards the cottage. Seeing what they were at, the man stopped, raised a hand and threw them a dazzling smile.

'Er,' Brian said.

'Don't stop,' Jeanette ordered.

'Your husband.'

'Yes.'

'Oh God.'

'Yes!' Letting her head hang back off the table's end, she returned her husband's smile and, laughing, scaled a peak of pleasure on her own as Brian withered inside her.

*

'Why don't *we* get a little place in the country?'

Chrissie, who had shortened her name when she first perceived it to be a feminization for Jesus's, had always been driven by things. As a child, she learnt to charm toys from hateful relatives. She had worked hard at school because she liked prizes. Love of things dictated her career, on the sales team of a firm of clothing chain stores. It dictated her choice of husband; Brian earned far more at his record company than her other candidates did in the city. He was also more generous. He would buy her more things. The danger of materialism, as her credit card statements reminded her with cruel regularity, was its infinitude. Love of things was a black hole, a ravenous virus, a galloping soul-cancer. Since to acquire was a compulsive pleasure in itself, quite unrelated to the individual attraction of the things acquired, each acquisition could only leave her hungry for more. A friend of hers, Nicci, had a similar compulsion where the telephone was concerned. Nicci used to spend hours, literally, ringing up friends, acquaintance, even near strangers on expensive services like *Dial-a-Pal*, *Chat-a-Lot* and the infamous *Hunk Junkie*. Eventually, when Nicci's bank refused to extend her overdraft any further, her mother had declined to bail her out unless she visited a hypnotist. The latter successfully induced an acute jabbing sensation in her ear whenever she held a receiver to it unnecessarily. He also offered a red-hot credit card service, but Chrissie scorned to approach him. She recognized her habit for what it was and made sure she earned enough to stop it turning ugly. She gained an ironic distance on it and, thereby, a measure of control. At a conference in Houston, she bought a Barbara Kruger tee-shirt which proclaimed with witty frankness: *I Shop Therefore I Am.*

In her youth, she had despised her parent's suburban rivalry with their neighbours; the race to the first Flymo, the first double garage, the first conservatory, the first retirement, the first brush with death. When she became pregnant, however, several years into her marriage to Brian, and the two of them decided it was time to exchange their sexy flat in Soho for something larger, cheaper and further out, she was brought to a fuller understanding. She and Brian had neighbours on either side in Islington; the Kilmers and the Pengs. The Pengs were Chinese and industrious and their house was council-owned. Not that Chrissie had anything against people in council housing – far from it – but the Pengs were somehow unapproachable. She always said hello and stopped to admire their (really very sweet) children, but she found it hard to understand why they continued to throw money away on rent when they could be investing it in an endowment mortgage. The Kilmers on the other hand became firm friends soon after the delivery of Brian's first BMW convertible.

Everything Chrissie wanted, Jade and Ian bought. Or maybe it was the other way around. They took midwinter holidays in Phuket, booked boxes at the opera, sent a son to Hill House and *had him down for a place* at Westminster. Ian played expensive, perilous sports while Jade belonged to a chic women-only health club and probably wore hand-sewn underwear beneath her kaleidoscopic array of designer clothing. These blessings of existence scarcely needed parading when the two couples got together; their abundance made them unmissable. As the younger, less wealthy pair, Chrissie and Brian could only fawn and coo. And envy. That Jade was *old* enough to have a son at prep school was small consolation to her maso-chistically observant neighbour and that her figure failed to justify so much expenditure was, if anything, a goad.

Then, after five cosy, neighbourly years, three things hap-pened to change the course of Chrissie's life. She was promoted to marketing manager for her company's expansion into Europe, Brian came to fit less and less with her image of the life she felt she should be living and the Kilmers took delivery of an *au pair* boy from a *good* Bordelais family.

'Laurent has beautiful manners, he cooks like a dream and actually likes it *and* he's doing wonders for Sebastian's French,' Jade had exclaimed as Laurent, tall, tanned and twenty-three, set warm duck salad before them and went to open another bottle of wine. 'Besides, what would I want with some sulky girl around the house? I mean, Chrissie, can you picture it? Lisa had that Marie-Paulette all last summer. She almost had a breakdown, she and Vaughan barely speak now and Sharon still managed to fail her GCSE. Ask anyone. *Au pair* girls are torture, but *au pair boys* . . . well!'

'What do you do all day?' Chrissie asked Laurent, once he was seated before her and had pouted becomingly in response to the compliments on his *salade tiède*.

'Oh. Not much. I take the little ones to school, I tidy the

house, I do some shopping and then perhaps I go swimming or play tennis.'

'The answer to every maiden's prayer,' laughed Ian and returned to some lecture he was giving Brian on market research and demographics.

'Quite,' said Chrissie. 'Actually, if you get bored, and if Jade can spare you, of course, I'm going to need to draw up five or six French documents for some presentations in Paris and Toulouse next month and you could be a huge help. The company would pay you, naturally.'

'Of course I can spare him,' Jade laughed. 'So long as you promise not to cook for her too, Laurent.'

'*Mais bien sûr*,' Laurent said, with a smile that revealed his dimples. 'I'd be delighted,' and Chrissie, who had the figure if not the clothing account, was not surprised to feel his shoeless foot unmistakably caressing her calf.

In the fortnight that followed, it caressed her again, as adventurously as an inquisitive typist and the glass partition walls of an open plan office would allow. Chrissie found herself stirred up to an uncharacteristic fever pitch of desire and frustration. She ached for a bed, for any discreetly situated horizontal even, but Jade could only spare Laurent on weekday mornings, times when Chrissie's employers could rarely spare her.

As usual, her love of things or, more properly, her love of other people's, brought her a solution. Jade and Ian owned a farmhouse a little north of Banbury, where they retreated most weekends and where they had often invited Chrissie, Brian and Sarah-Jane. Whenever he was there, Brian became soft and sentimental about his country childhood (spent in a red-brick suburb of Reading) and exerted pressure on Chrissie.

'It would be a good place to bring up children,' was a typical opening. 'Sarah-Jane loves animals.'

'What about schools?' she would retort. 'She'd have to board. She wouldn't love that. And if you think I'm commuting, you've another thing coming, Brian Warner.'

But later she noticed that Ian occasionally let Jade take the children to the farmhouse while he stayed behind to work, which seemed to involve his dressing in his smartest casuals and leaving the house on Saturday afternoon, reeking of after-shave (a waft of it blew through the trellis as he slammed the car door) to return in the early hours of Sunday afternoon. Brian typically failed to notice this dereliction. Chrissie, a childhood subscriber to *Look and Learn*, was extra kind to Jade and kept her observations to herself.

Another weekend was spent in Oxfordshire with their neighbours and Laurent's unbearably stimulating foot. Chrissie made a big effort. She cajoled them all to a nearby church fête. She taught Sarah-Jane to make daisy-chains and Laurent how to make scones. ('No, rub the butter in like this.' 'Like this?' 'Oh. Laurent. Yes. *Exactement*.') Leaning her head on Brian's shoulder as he drove them home, she asked, with just a hint of a knowing smile, 'Why don't *we* get a little place in the country?'

'So you want one now?'

'Why not? I mean, nothing large. Not like Jade and Ian's. That's too much hard work and, well, frankly I think they've made it rather common.'

'Mmm. All those paint effects.'

'And those fussy curtains. No. I was thinking of a cottage. A real cottage. A contrast to London.'

'Somewhere quite run down that we could do up?'

'Exactly. Everyone's going on exotic holidays nowadays. I

163

think it might be rather smart to spend some time in England for a change. A cottage would be the perfect excuse.'

'When shall we start looking?'

'Oh God. Brian, you *know* how I hate house-hunting.'

'Do you?'

'You remember what I was like over Islington. I can never picture how things will look. I just see squalor and naff things that people have done everywhere. And I get so tired. Couldn't you go on your own. I trust your judgement implicitly.'

'Well that wouldn't be so much fun. Why don't you take a Friday off and we can make a weekend of it?'

'Not a weekend. Sarah-Jane's got her ballet classes on Saturdays until the twenty-fourth. Let's take off a day midweek. The roads will be clearer then. We could get a babysitter for Sarah-Jane after school and come home late. How about Wednesday? There was going to be a sales briefing but Janine had to cancel.'

'Okay.'

Their Wednesdays were taken off accordingly, a babysitter arranged and Laurent was informed by a message slipped across Chrissie's desk on the previous Friday: '*Jettes-toi les chausettes – mercredi on aura un lit!*' Then, on Tuesday night, she returned just in time for supper and announced, with a passable show of irritation, that Janine was now available again and the sales briefing was back on for the next day.

'But you've taken tomorrow off. They can't make you go in.'

'They can't *make* me, Brian,' she agreed, 'but I can hardly stay away. Now can I? You wouldn't in my position.'

They argued the question from every angle. Then, for several awful minutes, Brian threatened to spend his day off working at his accounts instead. Chrissie found herself, watched across the dining table by Sarah-Jane's pinched and questioning gaze, protesting that of course he should go ahead. He knew so much better than she what houses would suit them and which would not.

'It was your idea after all,' she added.

'It was yours!'

'Hardly. You've been suggesting we get a place in the country ever since Ian and Jade had us to the farmhouse for the first time. You know how envious you were of them. Besides, it would be fun to have a day off. The weather's going to be great.'

'More fun with two.'

'Now don't start.'

Suddenly Sarah-Jane interrupted them with the unfamiliar sound of weeping. She hardly ever cried. She was a sensible, well-ordered little girl; her mother's child. Tears coursed down her sweet, fat cheeks at an alarming rate and she screwed her fists back and forth on her eyelids.

'Don't,' she sobbed, 'Don't don't don't!'

Brian lifted her into his arms and walked up and down, rubbing her back and stilling her cries.

The subject was dropped until the next morning, when he made one last abortive effort to dissuade Chrissie from work. She had put on her smartest blue linen suit with a deep purple blouse and jet black accessories. Sarah-Jane complimented her enchantingly as they left the house together. It was a pity she was getting so fat. Even her ballet teacher had commented on it. The Fultons' little girl was so lithe and pretty.

Laurent was loading his charges into Jade's other car for the school run. As he pulled out alongside Chrissie and the children waved and called frantically to each other, he smiled at her through the racket and showed his dimples.

'*A bientôt*,' she mouthed through the glass and smiled.

'What did you tell him?' Sarah-Jane piped up as they waited at the junction with Caledonian Road.

'I've a hard day ahead of me this morning,' Chrissie told her crisply. 'Try to be good.'

WHEEE!

for Anna Gale

It was not, she reflected, the way one imagined one's mother going. Elderly mothers were meant to slide peacefully to their death in a snoreless doze in lemon-yellow rooms scented with barley sugars and fresh lavender with wheeling seagulls beyond an open window and a distant sound of waves dragging through shingle. At best, they died in their own beds after a brief and painless illness, at worst, in hospital, after a harsh but still seemly medical crisis. They did not wantonly make spectacles of themselves. They did not leap to their deaths from cliff tops in bald daylight and high season. If they did commit suicide – and Matilda still saw no reason why *her* mother should have done so – they contained the urge until the wetter, greyer months, so as to do the deed unobserved. It was a wonder, she considered, that no holiday makers had been wounded or even killed by the body flying so suddenly onto the rocks in their midst. Retaining a shamingly sweet tooth to the bitter end, her mother had not been a small woman. No unworldly old bird she.

In her brief interview with the police, foul play was immediately ruled out. Not only was there no discernible motive – the old woman had little to leave her only heir and, however irritating, could hardly be believed to have goaded anyone into murdering her out of pure malice – but it was accepted that a person pushed from so great a height would let out a scream, or at least an audible gasp. The sound widely reported to have emerged from Matilda's plummeting mother was a full-bodied laugh. Either from tact or apathy, the old woman was allowed to have lost her footing.

'The grass can be slippery up there,' the policeman explained, 'even in summer. And there's a deceptive overhang. Could happen to anybody.'

The possibility of self-murder dangled between them unacknowledged. Matilda had been brought up to trust in policemen and was happy not to question their wisdom now.

The funeral had been excruciatingly embarrassing. The sole surviving relative, she had assumed she could slip quietly down for the day and see the whole business conducted swiftly and with no fuss. The matron of the home had greeted her tearfully, of course, but one expected some of that; a good show of solicitude was one of the things one paid her for. But then the wretched woman announced that so many *friends* had been telephoning and calling round since the *unhappy event* that she had felt obliged to lay on a small spread of sandwiches, cakes and tea. Matilda's mother, it appeared, had actually made herself popular. Very popular. In her discussion with the recommended local undertaker, Matilda had booked the smaller of the two crematorium chapels, not wishing to have a grim event made grimmer by having to preside over the coffin as sole mourner in a grotesquely large space. There were already some thirty people waiting eagerly in their pews when she drew up behind the hearse, however. By the time the priest was intoning the opening sentences – again she had requested the smallest possible rite, with no fuss and no hymns – so many mourners had arrived that a crowd of them was forced to remain outside the open doors, craning their necks and discreetly jockeying for a better view. Young, aged, men, women, smart and down-at-heel, white, brown, swarthy and even Oriental; they were so heterogenous a crowd, so entirely not the kind of friends she might have expected a woman of her mother's age and background to have acquired, that she actually wondered if she had followed the wrong hearse and attended the wrong funeral. They all pressed around to wring her by the hand afterwards, however, and pursued her back across the town to the rest home for a funeral tea that was little short of riotous. Few of them were wearing black so she felt herself conspicuous in their colourful midst as a raven caught up in a chattering flock of budgerigars. This, like the ruling out of suicide, was some consolation in such a crisis; her status as chief mourner and sole next of kin was apparent for all to see.

The token servings of milky tea were soon superseded by alcohol as bottles of wine, and even stronger stuff, were smilingly presented and thirstily splashed into disposable cups. In her anxiety to have the ordeal done with as soon as possible, Matilda had fondly assumed that, once the small rafts of sandwiches, Battenburg and Jaffa Cake mis-shapes had been swept away, the guests would show some sense of decorum and take their leave. Rather, bags of crisps and small boxes of sausage rolls began to materialize. One ridiculous woman even broke merrily into what appeared to be her week's supply of grocery shopping, brought along to the funeral in several plastic bags.

'Plenty more where this came from,' she said and gaily offered Matilda a selection of lurid fondant fancies. Matilda flinched but found herself taking the nearest one, in a kind of desperation. It was pink. It tasted pink. Impulsively she snatched a second before a man in a turban and medals could whisk them out of reach. Someone took away her teacup and thrust a beaker of warm Chardonnay into her unwary hand. She glanced at her watch, saw with alarm that it was nearly six, and drank.

She had not once felt tempted to tears during the funeral.

Ritual and the iron laws of good behaviour had saved her from that. As this unstructured, seemingly endless celebration continued, however, she repeatedly felt her nose-tip tingle and her tear ducts burn. Guest after guest came to pay their respects. Several, deeply moved, did so more than once. Some described themselves as friends of her mother's – women who played her at gin rummy, who knew her from her watercolour class – but many freely confessed to only a slight acquaintance but a strong impression of her character. There was a man from the library she had regularly dealt with, who recalled her taste for the most challenging modem fiction. A Hindu couple who often met her walking on the cliff paths cherished vivid recollections of a long conversation she had begun on the subject of the afterlife.

'We don't understand it,' she was told repeatedly. 'She seemed so happy-go-lucky', 'So bursting with vim', 'So audacious', 'So funny'.

She told the first few that the police had diagnosed an accident but she felt crushed by their sad, understanding little smiles of reply and, refusing to give them further opportunity to humour her with simpers, made no further allusion to suicide and let them infer what they pleased.

The picture they built up of her mother could not have been further from the woman she knew. Her mother was independent certainly – it had been she who insisted on entering a rest home after her second hip replacement, waving aside Matilda's (admittedly half-hearted) offer of a new base in her spare room – but she was hardly merry. She had always struck her daughter as the quietly humourless sort, the kind of woman who works years in the corner of an office only to be distinguished by her eventual absence. They saw each other rarely. Matilda had followed her husband to the other side of the country and remained there alone on his death. They rarely spoke – each hated the telephone – but Matilda had been a dutiful correspondent, firing off a tidy three-and-a-half sides on blue Basildon Bond once a month. Her mother's replies were erratic, which Matilda put down to a lack of news in her life, and largely composed of dry comment on the gossip Matilda had passed on. She wondered if, were she to read them again, she would detect a note of vigorous, even cruel merriment in them.

The possibility that she had misjudged or underestimated her mother's character did not occur to her. Instead she felt wounded to the quick that her mother had felt the need to mute her natural exuberance when Matilda was around. Matilda was not partial to excessive display of any kind, even as a child, but she appreciated vivacity in its place. The thought that her mother had suppressed such a side to herself, had been on dully good behaviour in her daughter's presence, awakened at once a sensation of profound regret at losing a companion whose company she might, after all, have enjoyed and of shock at the bitter possibility that here was an older woman who had not *liked* her.

'Don't be silly', she was fond of telling her more yielding friends when family matters were discussed. 'Like or not like doesn't come into it. They're your family. They're what you're born to. They're the only people in your life you don't get to choose.'

But she had always spoken, however bracingly, from the secure belief that her mother had loved her with unquestioning loyalty, however vague or erratic its expression. Admittedly her feelings towards her mother had long since cooled to the merely dutiful, but she allowed herself the odd crisis of sentimental warmth at birthdays and Christmas, and soothed any pangs of conscience with the thought that the love of the young for the

173

old was, by its very nature, a less vigorous growth than the helpless bond between mother and child.

At last she could bear it no longer. The matron was tearfully recounting the happy evenings she and Matilda's mother – 'more like a pal than a resident really' – had spent at the cinema on the sea front and how very up-to-date her mother's taste in films had become, when Matilda felt a great surge of childish envy pass over her, a wave of bilious heat. How *dared* this woman, any of these people, lay such tender claim to her mother? *Hers!*

Leaning against the hostess trolley in which the matron had seen fit, in view of the hour and the lingering guests, to warm up some individual meat pies, she cried tears of outrage, hot on cheeks tired from smiling. The matron was kindness itself, quite prepared to break up *the little party* but Matilda, who hated scenes, seized the opportunity of escape and, with a quick moan about the sudden need for solitude and fresh air, hurried out through the gathering crowd to the front door. Her first thought was only of peace, which was swiftly found in such a quiet neighbourhood, but a natural momentum seemed to drive her down the garden path, out of the gate and along the road towards the sea.

The house was on the genteel side of town, in a district of large, outmoded Victorian mansions on streets named after long forgotten Bavarian resorts. The sea was clearly visible at intervals between cedars or over shrubberies, and the air was bracing, but the houses nestled a safe distance from the palmy turmoil of the esplanade. Golf links lay close to hand (inexplicably her mother had refused to take up the sport despite the benefit the exercise would have done her figure) and helped preserve the area's tranquillity. Rosenheim Avenue ended abruptly with the golf course club house beside which lay the beginning of a cliff top footpath.

The grass was mown, there was a sign enforcing a pooper-scoop bylaw and, here and there, wooden benches had been constructed a little higher than usual to make them easier for less flexible citizens to vacate. Thus tempted, Matilda walked on for some ten minutes, recovering her composure and admiring the first hints of a sunset. A few last golfers were striding about the links in pastels but apart from a young man with an old dog she met no one on the path. Relishing the sense of being quite alone again, she sat on a bench with a fine view out to sea and back towards the esplanade. Seagulls wheeled and dropped, cackling, into their colonies on the cliff face below her. Occasionally she heard a shout or a burst of laughter from the beach. As a girl she had loved heights. She used to stand right on the edge, whooping into the wind, until her mother called her back. At some stage, puberty probably, she acquired a fear of them, however. She grew taller and wiser and learned geological dread and social embarrassment as if by the same hormonal process. Her husband could not understand this. He made her ride lifts to the top of towers to teeter out on pigeon-haunted platforms. He convinced her that if she lay on her belly to peer over a cliff edge it was less dizzying but she found it all the more so, like some film effect where an actor was meant to be hanging from a window ledge and one knew they were lying on their belly in front of a back projection. Once she was doing this, at his insistence, when he lifted her feet off the ground *for a joke*. It was the cause of their first major argument and caused her to fall out of love with him.

Matilda closed her eyes and basked. There was still some heat in the sun. This was where her mother had walked. This, or somewhere near it, was where she had brought her watercolours and talked with the young Asian couple. This was where she had jumped.

She opened her eyes again abruptly. Had her mother walked calmly to the edge or made her way gingerly? Had she perhaps sat on the precipice first then bounced off as one might from a low wall? Had she made herself drunk beforehand? That would, at least, explain her reported laughter. The bench was some forty feet from where the grass began its gentle slope down to the void but Matilda shuddered and glanced instinctively over her shoulder and grasped tight on the bench wood as though some malevolent stranger were about to give her a murderous shove from behind. There was no one there of course. The sunset was beginning in earnest, dyeing some clouds an unpleasant shade of salmon pink not unlike the curtains in her late mother's room.

'I should be getting back,' she said aloud, surprising herself with the sound of her own voice. Mutely she wondered if a single plastic cup of wine could have been enough to inebriate her.

In the distance she made out a small boy running along the path towards her. He could not have been more than eight, although, childless, she considered herself a poor judge of age in the young. He was solidly built, his little legs pounding like pistons. His head was down, his small arms pumping. She sat back to watch him, remembering the childish pleasure of following a narrow path with the blind obedience of a train. If anyone were to meet him walking in the other direction, she had no doubt that they would have to stand aside to let him pass. As he drew closer, she saw that he was in school uniform: grey shorts, a short-sleeved grey shirt and a purple tie. At least, she assumed they must be uniform. No modern mother would dress her child so formally. One saw so few children in uniform now. It was something she missed. Children now seemed barely to touch upon a childish phase before they were hanging around on buses and street corners like so many vengeful unemployed. Children had become insolent, even intimidating. She was glad she had not become a teacher. Her youthful ambition had been based on recent memories of a school where girls wore elegant brown gymslips over cream blouses and where teachers called Miss This or Mrs That were regarded with a respect approaching adoration.

She rose to go but as she returned to the path she glanced back along it. The boy's face was red with the effort of running and as he drew closer she saw that he was crying. She avoided addressing children as a rule but something in his uniform and pitiful state inspired confidence. She stood until he approached her, his run slowing to a panting walk. He was rather chubby. There was a deep cut on his knee which needed a mother's attention; a dab of iodine and perhaps a bandage to make him feel a hero. She mustered her kindest smile.

'Hello? Is something the matter?'

He glanced around him, at the sea, at the grass, bashful in his tears.

'I . . . I've lost my mother.'

So few children called their mothers that any more. He was nicely spoken too. Like a child from an old film.

'Oh. Oh dear. Where did you see her last?'

'I . . . I'm not sure. Here somewhere. I've been looking for simply ages.' As a slightly cross note entered his voice, he looked at her, his small, black eyes searching her face as if only just noticing her.

'Well why don't you blow your nose, first, then you can tell me all about it and I'll see what I can do. Have you got a handkerchief?'

177

He searched his pockets, producing string, some shells and a quantity of what looked like seaweed.

'Lost it,' he said and seemed about to cry again.

'Here,' she told him and passed him hers. 'It's quite clean.'

'Thank you,' he said. He gave his nose and eyes a perfunctory wipe before handing it back to her. He looked calmer now, almost distinguished. She thought back to her girlhood, to the panic of losing her mother while shopping, to the constant, trustless fear of being wilfully left behind at the swings and slides, in a hospital, on a beach . . . Mothers nowadays were so slatternly.

'Where do you live?' she asked.

'I . . . I can't remember.'

'Oh. Well. What's your name?'

'Tom.'

'I'm Matilda.'

'Hello.'

'Well it's going to get dark in about an hour so I suggest I take you to a telephone and we call a nice policeman to help us out.'

'Thank you.'

Entirely trusting, he put his hand in hers. Despite the run he had just taken, it felt cool. She wondered if he was in shock. She glanced at his knee. Blood was trickling down to the rim of his sock and soaking in. Perhaps there had been an accident. Perhaps the poor thing's mother had slipped and fallen and he was too traumatized to recall anything. Welcoming the diversion from her own, sad affairs as she did any opportunity to take responsible charge of a situation, she began to lead him back towards the town. There was nobody else in sight. The club house was further than she remembered.

'Are you on holiday?' she asked.

'No,' he said. 'Are you?'

'No I was . . . visiting a friend.'

As she said this the weight of her mother's death and that afternoon's grim rituals seemed to slip away from her and she received a fleeting intuition that her mother was a good age and had spared herself the indignity of senility. She had also, in a curious way, set Matilda free from an implicit burden of guilt and frustrated duty. Matilda had no ties. No husband. No mother. She was free as air. She could emigrate. She could dye her hair. She could run a little wild. She had been at liberty to do all these things for some time, of course, ever since her widowing, but the knowledge that she still had a mother, albeit a fiercely independent one, had placed a check on her.

They were reaching an upward slope in the path. Strangely elated, almost gay, she squeezed the boy's hand and began to sing to cheer him up.

'The grand old Duke of York,
He had ten thousand men . . .'

She stamped in time to the tune.

'He marched them up to the top of the hill . . . Do you know this?' she asked him, breaking off.

By way of answer the boy swung her hand in his and sang back,

'And he marched them down again.
The grand old Duke of . . .'

Together they marched and sang to the top of the gentle incline. The club house seemed so far away still she could almost believe they had been walking in circles, or on the spot, were that not patently absurd. She sighed to herself, foreseeing a visit to a police station, time-consuming giving of statements, a reunion with some unsuitable, probably unmarried mother

179

and a delayed journey home to her London friends, perhaps even an enforced night in some bleak hotel full of pensioners and friendless sales reps.

'Can you skip?' the boy asked cheerfully.

'Of course,' she said.

He began to skip, tugging her along so that she was obliged to skip too to keep in step.

'He marched them up to the top of the hill
And he marched them down . . .'

What did it matter? What did anything matter? There was no one to see her behaving so inanely and what if there were? She had no plans to return. She had forgotten what fun skipping was; the lilting step, its surprising, elegant swiftness. And the view was delightful from this point. Small boats on the water, a row of palms on the promenade, a grand hotel, creamy pink in the setting sun. She laughed as she sang, growing quite breathless, and glanced down at the boy, happy that she should have raised his spirits so effortlessly and her own in the process. He glanced back at her, black eyes shining like a small bird's, sharp little teeth clenched in a grin.

Quite suddenly they swerved off the path and were skipping across the grass towards the dangerous slope. Taking this for youthful high spirits, she tried to tug him back towards safety, but he yanked her along with him.

'Stop,' she cried, imperious now. 'Tom, stop it. This is silly. Tom!'

He ignored her. His fingers had imperceptibly changed their position so that instead of enlacing with hers they were now grasping her by the wrist. His grasp, like the force in his fat little arm, seemed steely as a grown man's.

'Stop it! You'll make me fall. Stop!'

She swung her hand out at a last passing bench but missed her grip on it, succeeding only in grazing her wrist painfully as she flew by.

He had stopped the ridiculous song and stopped skipping. Now he was running, with that same pistoning movement she had seen him use in the distance, pulling her with him towards the brink. As he ran he let out a piercing, incongruous whoop of delight, as though he were merely about to jump a ha-ha or vault a fallen tree. One of her shoes came off and, hobbling, she cried out as she stamped on a thistle mat. Then her stockinged foot slipped into a rabbit hole bringing her flat on her face mere inches from the cliff. To her horror, the dreadful, crazed child seemed to fly onwards, still whooping. His hand wrenched from her, sending a spasm of agony through her wrist. Perhaps it was the Chardonnay taking effect on her imagination but she fancied his triumphant cry was tinged with fury in the seconds before it stopped.

For a full minute she lay face downwards, winded, snatching pained breaths, assuring herself that she was still safe and that her ankle and wrist were unbroken, then she clumsily hauled herself to her knees and lurched abruptly backwards, sickened at the dazzling void before her. Impelled, dreading what she was about to see, she inched forward on her hands and knees to the very edge. Perhaps there was a grassy ledge only feet below. Perhaps the little wretch knew about it and played this trick regularly by way of tasteless sport. She steeled herself for his hideous 'boo' of surprise.

There was no ledge. She saw, quite clearly, that there was no trace of him. The seagulls were crowding over a dawdling beach refuse cart, not the freshly pulped corpse of a stout little boy. He must have tricked her, jumped sideways and sprinted back across the grass as she fell. Doubtless he was watching her indignity and fear from behind a bush and giggling.

To her horror a middle-aged couple out walking had spotted her and hurried with their dog across the grass.

'Are you all right?' the man asked.

'The grass gets so slippery. You should be careful,' his wife added accusingly.

'I'm fine, thank you,' Matilda told them gruffly as they helped her up. 'I wanted to look over the edge, at the nesting birds, and my foot went in a rabbit hole.'

'Your other shoe.' The man returned it with a ridiculous, caring expression on his insipid face.

'Thanks,' she told him. 'I'll be fine. Honestly. Thank you.'

She dismissed them. They were treating her like some old thing escaped from a residential hotel.

As they continued their walk, talking, she slipped her shoe back on and made her own way back to the path, shaking the grass and mud from her clothes as best she could and determined to appear as untroubled as possible. She glowered at the nearest clumps of gorse and thornbush. She would not give the little bastard the satisfaction of seeing her upset.

Pausing to blow her nose and make a few repairs to her appearance on the corner before the rest home, she reached into her pocket for her handkerchief and was revolted to find it quite wet. She drew it from her pocket. He had scarcely dabbed his eyes and nose with it yet it was soaked, almost dripping. With a spasm of revulsion, she thrust it into a neatly clipped hedge and walked on. Dabbing at her nose with the back of her hand, she frowned to discover that even a brief contact with the wet linen had left her fingers as pungently briny as a fishmonger's.

OLD BOYS

for Susanna Martelli

The last verse of the school hymn was stirring stuff about strapping on breastplates, guarding imperilled shores and standing shoulder to shoulder against some unidentified foe. Foreigners presumably, or Sin. Boys in the gallery, spared the embarrassment of sitting with family, bellowed the familiar words with the clannish fervour of a rugby crowd. Below them, the fourteen diminutive choristers piped a descant, barely audible above the efforts of the heartier element. Wives, fragrant and carefully dressed for a long, summer day, faces raised over hymnals, delighted in the relative fragility of their own voices.

'But of course it's sexy. It's *desperately* sexy,' Elsa had insisted as they were dressing that morning. 'You can't imagine. Standing there surrounded by all that young masculinity. The odour of testosterone is quite overpowering. I'd *love* to be a headmaster's wife. I'd be a tremendous tease, wearing lots of scent and rustly silk things.'

The chaplain commanded them to prayer and the chapel filled briefly with the sounds of thumping knees, dropped hymn books and skittering leather cushions. Colin glanced across at Elsa, her lovely face partly shaded by a hat brim, subtly painted lips barely parted, eyes obediently closed. He could imagine her here, as a master's wife, jet black hair shaken out over a tumbled silk headscarf, hugging herself against the cold on a playing field touchline, calling out, 'Come on House!' with a fine show of loyalty then catching the eye of a nearby prefect and making him blush. She would be bewitching and shameless and boys would jostle to sit by her at lunch so as to admire her cleavage. On the whole, he decided, she was safer cloistered in her cubby hole at the World Service; left too long in an environment like this one, she would become more than ever like the young Elizabeth Taylor and prove the catalyst for some drama of horrific erotic violence.

Between them Harry clasped his hands tightly together and recited the Lord's Prayer slightly too loud. He had a summer cold and had just started confirmation classes. Elsa looked first at him then at Colin, smiling mischievously over their son's head.

This, of course, had been her idea. She had often said that she thought Harry should follow in his father's footsteps and he had only recently seen that she meant it seriously. He had promised himself that no child of his would be sent away to boarding school but already Elsa had persuaded him to parcel Harry off to an eminently respectable prep school in the South Downs where, apparently, the small boy thrived on pre-breakfast Latin. Enjoying lazy Saturday mornings in bed at an age when most of his contemporaries were woken at nine o'clock sharp and dragged off to fly kites and throw rugger balls, Colin was coming to understand the terms of the similar betrayal his parents had practised on him at the same age. Public school, however, was different. He had always sworn he would draw the line there, that Harry would attend an excellent day school, with girls in every year, not just the sixth form. Somewhere he could drop Latin for Spanish or Italian. And yet here he was attending an old boys' day for the first time since leaving the place eighteen years ago with a view to *casing the joint*, as Elsa put it, for Harry.

'If he doesn't like it, mind you,' he had stipulated, 'if he has the slightest reservation –'

'Then he doesn't have to go,' Elsa broke in, reassuring him with a soft touch on the back of his fist.

And Harry adored her. Colin remembered loathing his mother at that age, never forgiving her for sending him away. Yet Harry still seemed to drink Elsa in with his eyes. She handled him so well, Colin reflected. She knew when to be sweet, when to be boyishly joshing, when to be sexy. And she *was* sexy with him. Colin had watched the care with which she chose clothes for the boy's Sundays out of school. She tended to wear firmer bras for him and clinging cashmere.

'Little boys like tits, silly,' she explained. 'Haven't you noticed? All the popular boys have mums who are a bit, well . . .' and she smoothed down her jersey in explanation, smiling to herself.

'Well?' she asked as they left the chapel and headed out into a flagstoned quadrangle where swallows swooped through the sunshine in search of flies. 'Are the happy memories flooding back?'

'Not really,' he said. 'Thank God most of my teachers seem to have left.'

'Probably dead,' Harry piped up.

'Thank you, Harry,' Colin told him.

'What about friends? Surely you recognize somebody?'

'No,' Colin said, faintly relieved. 'Not yet. Let's go and find some lunch.'

'Sherry with the housemaster first,' she reminded him.

'Oh fuck.'

'Harry!' Elsa seemed genuinely surprised but could not help smile at the evident pride on Harry's face at having produced an adult expletive in adult company. 'Darling!' she added and chuckled, patting his shoulder.

They drifted with the noisy crowd out of the quadrangle and Harry expressed a wish to piss.

'I'll wait here,' Elsa said, arranging herself on a bench below a towering horse chestnut. 'Don't be long. I'm thirsty.'

Following a line of instinctive memory, Colin led his son along a corridor, across another quadrangle and into a dingy, green-tiled lavatory where they peed side by side at a urinal and then, only because each had the other with them, laboriously washed their hands.

The old swathes of graffiti had been painted over and the roller towels had been replaced with hot air hand driers but the room retained an inexpungable dankness and a threatening quality. For the first time that day, Colin was assailed by memories, none of them sunny ones. He flinched instinctively when three tall boys burst noisily in through the swing door. He panicked that Harry was taking so long over drying his hands, then remembered that he was forty-one and these hulking bullies had become children. The boys fell respectfully silent and went seriously about their business as he shepherded Harry back into the sunlight.

'How do people know if it's a ladies or a gents?' Harry asked. 'There's no sign on the door.'

'There aren't any ladies,' Colin told him. 'And when there are I suppose they just hold on until they find somewhere safe.'

Elsa came smiling from beneath the tree to meet them.

'I just met Keith Bedford,' she said.

'Who?'

'He's a newscaster,' Harry explained patiently.

'You never told me he was here with you,' she went on.

'He wasn't.'

'Well he said he was.'

'Must be younger than me, then. You never remember the

188

younger ones because they were so unimportant. They didn't count.'

'You boys are so hard and peculiar.'

Elsa took his arm as they cut back across the first quadrangle and headed out onto a broad stone path that lay along one side of a huge lawn studded with old plane trees and bounded by a high flint wall. Colin was surprised that Harry forsook his habitual place on Elsa's other side and came to walk beside his father, touched perhaps by the exclusive maleness of the place. Again she caught Colin's eye and gave him a discreet smile. At such times, when some parents would be saddened at their impotence in the face of nature, she seemed soothed, taking little reminders of biological determination as signs of a covenant that, having produced a perfectly adjusted male, she could soon relinquish all responsibility for him. Colin sighed.

'What is it?' she asked.

'I'd forgotten it was so beautiful. It's idyllic, really. Do you like it, Harry?'

'It's okay,' said Harry. 'It's very big. Isn't there a playground?'

'All this,' Colin said gesturing at the trees tall as cathedrals, the old wrought iron benches, the distant cloisters. 'This is the playground.'

With perfect timing, a troop of boys in military uniform jogged out from behind the rifle range and went puffing pinkly by, in tight formation. Harry turned to stare openly.

'Would I have to do that?' he asked.

'Only if you wanted to. Well, actually, everyone has to do it for a year then you can give it up and do social work instead if you prefer.'

'Social work?'

'Doing gardening for old ladies, clearing weeds from the

189

river, helping out at a school for the handicapped, that sort of thing. There was even a group that helped build houses on a sort of estate for the unfortunate somewhere.'

'You're joking, of course,' Elsa said.

'God's own truth.'

They walked on past the art gallery, the theatre workshop, the music school, the serried tablets to the loyal fallen in the War Cloisters and the house famous for having produced a prominent fascist, two trade union leaders and at least three Russian spies amongst its boys.

'Those were just the ones that got caught,' chuckled Elsa. 'Perhaps Harry could be a spy? His languages are getting so good.'

'There it is,' said Colin and pointed.

They were out on a public street now, but every plot of land and building in sight was still school property. Up ahead loomed Colin's old house. It was a towering red brick affair with turrets, curious flint teeth around each window and such a mess of fire escapes and extensions added on that it was hard to tell which was the front and which the back. A bevy of well-upholstered female servants, fraudulently got up in black and white for the occasion instead of their usual nylon housecoats, were variously directing guests to the cloakrooms, handing them sherry or waving them on out to join the crowd in the garden where their sisters circulated with trays of canapés.

'Look, darling. That was Daddy's house. You could go there.'

'Why?' asked Harry, singularly unimpressed.

'It's no beauty,' Colin confessed. 'If you want to live in the really old bit by the chapel as well as having your lessons there, you'll have to go in for the scholarship exam.'

'You must be joking,' said Harry and Colin abandoned the

briefly dangled possibility of annual holidays somewhere hot which a scholarship would have afforded them. Elsa demonstrated her frightening ability to read his mind.

'We can start borrowing mummy's cottage in Devon,' she said with a quick smile into the air before her. 'Oh look, Harry, they've put out a trampoline in the garden. Do you want to have a go?'

At last, just when he was congratulating himself on their absence, Colin began to meet contemporaries from his days at the school. They were none of them friends – sex, geography, money and, in one case, death, had dismantled all his schoolboy friendships. The thickening silhouettes before him were merely those of old acquaintance. In every case he found himself remembering not only a name but a nickname and at least one cruel fact to which they would be vulnerable; an armoury of psychological stings – flat feet, ginger pubic hair, a tendency to stutter, dead fathers, alcoholic mothers – which he reached for out of a long dormant instinct to wound before he was wounded. They stood around on the lawn holding their careers against each other's to compare them for size, inspecting one another's wives and mustering a chortling *bonhomie* which in seven out of eight cases Colin estimated to be entirely phoney. Acute discomfort drove them all to assume the speech patterns of men twenty years their senior, of their fathers, in fact.

'You called that man *old chap*,' Elsa said, appalled, as they were herded in through an entrance hall as drab as Colin remembered, to the sludge green dining room where a *fork luncheon* awaited them. 'You never talk like that.'

'I know,' he said. 'I'm sorry. It just slipped out. I think it's infectious.'

'The housemaster's a darling.'

'Really? We haven't spoken.'

'Oh really, Colin, that's what we're here for. Go and introduce yourself. He's the one by the fireplace with the toddler on his hip and the smile.'

'But he looks about twenty-five.'

'He is. Much healthier than the crusty types you had in your day. And the wife's no battleaxe either.'

Colin did as he was told and spoke with the housemaster who was, indeed, a darling. There was something of Peter Pan about him and Colin realized that this was why he was good at his job. A part of his development seemed to have been arrested. He had failed to acquire the calloused outer layer that marked every other man in the room. He spoke to boys with the authority of a gentle older brother and to fathers with the cheerful respectfulness of their ideal son. He was enthusiastic about everything from crab vol-au-vents to the school viol consort. His irony was confected from natural wit rather than harsh experience. He was entirely unsuited to life in an adult community. Colin was surprised, after introducing Harry then having a chat that seemed to be about nothing of any consequence, to hear the man say, 'Well we'd be delighted to have him in the house, provided he passes the exams, of course . . .'

'Oh,' Colin said. 'Well, then. Thanks very much. I'll tell Elsa the good news.'

They shook hands and Harry's small fate was sealed. Colin glanced out of the window and saw his son sitting on a low wall crumbily munching a meringue and watching some comparatively huge boys kick a football about a caged-in yard. He was disturbed at how the boy was finding his place as swiftly and naturally as a newly weaned addition to some fiercely hierarchical animal society.

Elsa was one of those rare women with a genuine interest in cricket. She came from a long line of cricketers and, being an only child, had received the full benefit of her father's instruction. She liked knowledge, particularly when it had so little practical application. It pleased Colin to watch her sweep aside the patronage of cricketing men with the breadth of her understanding, not least because he had not a sporting bone in his body. When he took her a cup of coffee, he found her arguing a fine point of test match history with a tall, mop-headed youth who wore the kind of cricketing jersey only permitted to members of the school's first team; a deity, in schoolboy terms, yet she was winning the argument.

'But then,' she sighed, gently tapping the youth's broad chest with one long finger, having pressed home her triumphant point, 'I can see you're an expert. What do *I* know? I've never even played the game.'

The youth flushed as Elsa turned to Colin. 'Coffee. How lovely. Darling, this is Hargraves.'

Hargraves offered Colin a hand. 'How do you do, sir.'

'Marvellous to be called sir,' Elsa said. 'Madam always sounds supercilious and shopkeepery.'

'He's offered Harry a place,' Colin told her. 'Subject to exams, of course.'

'But of course he did.'

'I thought I'd take a look round. See how things have changed. Want to come?'

Elsa wrinkled her nose.

'Changing rooms and things? Do we have to? I was going to catch the start of the match. Hargraves can show me the way.'

'Of course I can,' said Hargraves.

Glad to have a chance to explore on his own, Colin took a

second coffee and wandered off. The house was on its best behaviour, the presence of parents neutering its habitual rowdiness but here and there its true nature pierced the skin of decorum with a reassuringly rude noise. Colin inspected the changing room, rank with sweat and sweet shampoo, the pitifully stocked library, the day room, and a new study block, where, from the momentarily hostile glances, he sensed he had interrupted something and retreated. Here and there, boys unhampered by family were engaged in small acts of vandalism or self-improvement. One little older than Harry pored over a surprisingly undistinguished newspaper, frowning at a pouting model's breasts as though checking through a page of algebraic calculations. Uncertain of what he was looking for – some confirmation perhaps that these familiar scenes were not so irrelevant as they now felt – Colin walked back to the staircase and made for the dormitories. Here, too, little had changed. There were still no radiators or curtains but the old, thin mattresses which dipped in the middle had been replaced. He sat on a bed and was happy to find that it still betrayed the slightest movement with a creak. He walked to one of the big windows, merciless in cold weather, and saw a crowd of visitors trailing over the athletics track below towards the cricket fields nearer the river. A woman turned and called out. It was Elsa. He saw Harry sprinting to catch up with her. The boy looked up to chatter to her as they walked. If he liked the place, did Colin have the right to deprive him of the experience?

Thinking he should join them, he left his coffee cup on a chest of drawers and started back along the dormitory corridor. He passed an open door and looked in just long enough to recognize the face of a large man peering up at the beams. He moved swiftly on, halted when he heard people on the stairs and doubled back to dart into the linen room. He sat on a bench where he would not be visible from the door. He needed to recover. His heart pounded as though he had just run up the stairs. Sweat beaded on his forehead and he swept it away with a handkerchief. It was him, unmistakably him. The black hair had grown grizzled, the rangy frame become slightly leaner but the thick eyebrows and large, once-broken nose had been instantly recognizable. Colin touched the handkerchief to his upper lip recalling how the man's eyes dropped to meet his for a fraction of a second before Colin hurried on.

*

The day room was where all but the eldest boys spent their free time and evenings. It was high-ceilinged and L-shaped. Around the walls huddled wooden cubicles. Each boy had a cubicle. It comprised a desk, a cupboard, a bench and an electric light, all of them ancient. This cramped territory – sizes varied and the less cramped ones were highly sought after – was the only space in the entire school wherein one could be moderately private. The new boy had to make a mental adjustment in which the cluster of rooms, garden, pets and family he called home was compressed into a space a Victorian street urchin would have scorned. Here his individuality could be expressed in postcards, ornaments, toys, a choice of curtain and cushion cover, a store of food and even a corrugated plastic roof. Here, too, he would learn his first brutal lessons in the danger of expressing individuality of the wrong sort.

Colin and, crucially, Colin's mother, had been drilled in these matters by an older cousin. The cousin was still at the school but would be prevented, on his honour, from coming to

Colin's assistance or in any way singling him out, once Colin joined him there. Colin had been scrupulous. His curtain and cushion were of a wholly unremarkable green fabric. He had no photographs of his parents but, at his sudden insistence, had brought along one of his older sister looking sulky in a bathing costume. This he pinned up alongside a calendar with a different dog breed pictured every month. He brought no toys, nothing whatever of especial monetary or sentimental value beyond a tinny transistor radio. Yet somehow, obscurely, he was found wanting.

At first insignificant violence was offered him, daring him to react and so give an excuse for fiercer reprisals. Boys would trip him from behind – *ankle-walking* it was called – as he passed along the corridor from the dining room. He was flicked with wet towel-corners when queuing for a washbasin. They made small verbal attacks, too, mocking, relying on the support of those around them.

'Hey!' they would call. 'Hey, you!'

'Yes?' he would ask, turning.

'Nothing,' came the smirking reply. 'Nothing.'

And by common consent, Nothing, then Nuts became his nickname, until long after anyone could remember the reason why.

'Above all you must learn not to react,' his cousin had insisted. Everyone, it seemed, went through a period of being picked upon but the brief spell of initiation could be prolonged into indefinite persecution if the would-be initiate gave the wrong sort of encouragement. So Colin met whips, trippings and mockery with polite equanimity, if not quite gratitude.

He wrote home saying how much he was enjoying himself, and there *were* things to enjoy. He enjoyed singing, with no great finesse, in the school choral society. He took up pottery and made an ashtray for his father. He won a small measure of popularity among his immediate peers as cox of the first year rowing team – even if this did mean being tossed into freezing river water whenever they lost a race. But as well as being designed to transfer all one's respect from the adults – who vanished from view and consequently power soon after six o'clock – to the prefects, the school's social system induced a tantalizing sense that there were unspeakably grown-up pleasures to be tasted, if only one could chance on some secret password.

He was kept from despair by the salutary spectacle of other boys, often well into their second year, who had been cast forever beyond acceptance and were fair game even for *new bugs* like himself to tease. There was one with grotesquely protuberant ears who appeared to have given up washing, one who could easily be provoked to spectacular tantrums in which he actually stamped his feet and cried and a third, called Bollocks, because his balls had still not dropped, who babbled in a high-pitched voice about the consolations of Christianity even as one tore his essays and scattered his textbooks into muddy puddles. The one with the ears and sour smell was later diagnosed as a schizophrenic, but only once exposed to a society with marginally less appetite for aberration, in his first year at university.

Colin's initiation came six weeks into his first term, on a Sunday night. Sundays were always a dangerous time. Envy was in the air, because some boys had been whisked out to lunch by their parents and a bogus holiday mood tended to curdle without warning. A few boys were still trying to finish their Saturday night essays but most were idle, bored and fractious, their dissatisfaction fuelled by a thorough perusal of that other world of luxuries and freedom paraded so unfeelingly through the Sunday colour supplements. It was the housemaster's night off, which meant he was more thoroughly absent than usual, being inter-ruptible only *in extremis*. A boy had once been blinded with a fencing foil on a Sunday night. Only last Sunday evening, the day room had taken on a nightmarish air when someone produced a set of darts stolen from the pub and began throwing them at people's ankles for a laugh. Colin's cousin had warned him about Sunday nights. Colin was duly lying low in his cubicle behind his irreproachable curtain, reading Balzac and trying not to be noticed. A fight with cartons of gone-off milk had flared and died. A game of table tennis was threatening to turn nasty. Some-one was playing *Dark Side of the Moon* yet again, with the usual cluster of boys gathered religiously to mouth the lyrics and strum imaginary guitars. Any minute the youngest *new bug* would be called on to ring the bell for evening prayers. Only minutes lay between Balzac and the relative safety of a frosty bed.

It was a rogue attack, begun by Bollocks in an extravagant bid for acceptance by the crowd. Colin was startled as the other boy whisked back the curtain and yelped, 'Do you accept Jesus as your personal saviour?'

A few boys jeered out of habit, mocking the squeaky voice and stutter but others simply gathered to watch.

'I'm not sure,' Colin admitted.

'Do you accept Jesus as your personal saviour?' Bollocks repeated and Colin decided to gamble on his superior status, as would-be initiate over pariah.

'Why should I?' he jeered. 'Sp-sp-spastic features!'

For a moment it was uncertain which way the scene would turn, as Bollocks groped in his sports jacket for something, then he produced a can of lighter fuel, liberally anointed the curtain and pronounced, 'Then, heretic, you fry.'

And he struck a match. Colin swore and shrank back into his cubicle as the air filled with the smoke and the irreproachable green was engulfed in flames. Then one of the third years, secure in his status as a useful football player and twenty-a-day smoker, decided that Bollocks was going too far. To loud cheers, he set off a fire extinguisher, dowsing the flames then turning the jet on the pariah. Seizing the moment, Colin dashed out to land a vigorous kick on Bollocks's backside but he had misjudged the feelings of the crowd.

He was grabbed. His trousers and underpants were gleefully tugged down around his ankles and he was bent over the ping-pong table while his arse was given a stinging *douche* from what remained in the fire extinguisher. When that was no longer deemed amusing, hot, bony hands hoisted him into one of the large plastic dustbins and a saucer of meatily rancid butter was pressed down on his hair. When he tried to clear it off it was followed by a faceful of long-forgotten milk and something wet and nameless down the back of his shirt. Blinded and fighting back the urge to retch, Colin flailed out wildly in his effort to keep his balance, as his tormentors lifted the dustbin into the air. Once his eyes were sufficiently clear to see where they were carrying him, he froze and swore again. The walls above the cubicles were clad in handsome wooden panelling which reached twelve feet or more. The panelling was very thick – built like that, perhaps, to disguise pipe work – and it was possible to clamber around the room on the top of it. Colin and his dustbin were hoisted overhead and, with much cheering, balanced precariously where two sections of the panel pathway formed a corner. Then the bell rang for evening prayers and the room emptied as everyone raced up the corridor to kneel at their chairs in the dining room. Apathetic sixth-formers drifted through from their studies to follow them. Most ignored him. One blew a gobbet of chewing gum at him and another shouted some witticism in German which raised a knowing laugh.

Then he was alone. Gingerly he tried to stand but the dustbin rocked sickeningly and he dropped back to crouching in the garbage. If he fell he had no doubt he would break his neck, or at best crack his skull, on the grimy parquet floor. He pictured his funeral. There would be white lilies and the headmaster would speak damningly and at length, summoning his murderers by name and making them pray around the coffin. There would be mass expulsions, reported in the national press and a new, fiercely disciplinarian regime would be instituted. First-years would keep Colin's name alive with tears of gratitude.

For the first time since his father had left him sitting on a trunk in Waterloo station six weeks before, Colin lowered his guard and allowed himself the luxury of homesick tears.

'Oh for fuck's sake!'

He blinked and looked over the rim of the dustbin. It was Hardy, one of the prefects and a senior officer in the school army corps. Tall, dark, terrifying, Hardy rarely spoke to his juniors, keeping discipline by the sheer authority of his presence. When he did speak, it tended to be with withering sarcasm.

'Sorry, Hardy,' Colin stammered, expecting to be punished for the wrongs done to him, which was the usual way.

'Can't you get down?'

'I . . . I don't think so.'

'Well in Christ's name stay still then.'

Hardy tossed the novel he had been carrying onto the ping-pong table then clambered over the cubicles below Colin and steadied the dustbin for him. 'Go on. Get out.'

Hastily tugging up his underwear and trousers, Colin clambered out onto the ledge. Hardy dropped the dustbin to the floor, magnificently impervious to the mess he created. He jumped down after it. Colin followed more carefully. Hardy looked at him and wrinkled his nose.

'You stink. Christ!'

'Sorry, Hardy.'

'Not your fault. What's your name?'

'Cowper.'

'Well take a shower, Cowper. Now.'

'But what about evening prayers?'

'Oh sod those. Come on.'

Hardy led the way to the changing room and through it to the showers, where the air was still ripe with cigarette smoke. While Colin hastily undressed, Hardy set a shower running. As Colin slipped in past him, he shut the door behind them then he lent against the wall casually smoking while Colin washed himself in the blast of hot water. Rubbing his pale skin with soap, he became aware of bits of him that had been scraped or bruised in the attack. He looked around for a bottle of shampoo and began to wash the butter out of his hair.

'It'll need more than that,' Hardy told him, tossing his cigarette stub into a puddle where it fizzled. 'Here. Let me.' He came to stand so close that the shower splashed onto his jeans and linen jacket leaving dark stains. Colin wondered if he was drunk.

'Give,' Hardy said and Colin passed him the shampoo. Hardy filled his palm with the dark green liquid and began to rub it into Colin's scalp, brow furrowed with concentration.

At prep school, the assistant matrons – bored daughters of good families, marking time – used to let themselves into the bathrooms to wash one's hair. They were breezily teasing about his coyness and it was all acutely embarrassing. This was quite different. Hardy had been at the pub and his breath was sour-sweet with beer and tobacco. Their hands had scratched busily at his scalp as though conquering an itch but Hardy's hands moved slowly. His touch was no less firm but he used his fingertips instead of his nails. He reached round to the back of Colin's head, while working fiercely at his temples with his thumbs. He was getting soaked. Colin felt wet denim against one of his thighs. He felt an overwhelming urge to pee and found, to his horror, that he was getting an erection. Desperate that Hardy shouldn't see it, he tried his usual technique of taking deep breaths and imagining his hand being cut off with a breadknife.

Outside the bell rang again, calling first years to bed. There was a stampede of boys out in the corridor. Any minute someone might come in for a smoke. Smiling faintly, as at some private joke, Hardy pushed Colin's head back into the water and began to comb away the lather with his fingers. Nothing would get rid of the erection. Panic seemed to be making things worse. Colin felt his cock actually brush against Hardy's jeans. Hardy spotted it and chuckled.

'What's this, eh?' He tapped at it experimentally with a huge, wet hand. Colin was mortified. He shut his eyes.

'I . . . I'm sorry, Hardy.'

He tried to turn away but the older boy still had a hand on the back of his neck. Pummelling his back, the water seemed to be getting hotter.

'For fuck's sake, stop apologizing,' Hardy told him. 'Look at me.'

Colin opened his eyes just in time to find Hardy bending

down to kiss him. He gave a little yelp then was silenced by a rough mouth against his and the extraordinary sensation of a tongue plunging between his lips to seek out his own. The hand that was on the back of his neck slipped down until an arm grasped him across the shoulder blades while another hand slipped between his legs and began to wank him, vigorously.

Colin had only learnt to toss himself off a few weeks before. The age at which such knowledge was acquired depended entirely on the company into which chance threw a boy. He had risen swiftly through his prep school hierarchy and so found himself, at the age when he might have learned, captain of a comparatively prepubescent dormitory and thus deprived of exemplary demonstrations. He was haunted by painful erections, and the occasional wet dream, and forced to join in the smutty bragging of his peers in the hope that many were as ignorant as he. It was inconceivable that one might ask even a close friend how to masturbate, so he suffered in silence. On graduating to public school, he was placed at last in a mixed-age dormitory and had to wait only weeks before being made a party to a guffawing discussion of comparative techniques. Left hand, right hand, underwater, upside down against a sheet – suddenly he had not only knowledge, but choice. His experience of induced orgasm was still novel, so experiencing it at the hands of another was, literally, staggering. After freezing with his hands at his sides for a few seconds, he found his knees buckling and flung his arms around Hardy as though teetering on a cliff edge. He wanted to piss. He wanted to come. He wanted to cry out and he wasn't entirely sure he had not done all three by the time Hardy had done with him. Hardy took one last, long kiss then turned off the shower and held Colin's sobbing face to his chest.

'Well!' he said softly, as though the whole thing had surprised him too. 'Well, well.'

There were footsteps and chatter suddenly in the changing room and the door to the showers was flung open. Two fifth formers stood in the doorway, laughter dying in their throats. They stared for a moment. Colin tried to pull away but Hardy held him close.

'Fuck off,' he told them.

'Sorry, Hardy,' one of them said. 'The lights were off and we didn't –'

'Just fuck off.'

'Sorry, Hardy.' They turned to go. Hardy called after them. 'Gilks?'

'Yes?' One turned.

'Leave your cigarettes on the step and we'll say no more about it.'

'Of course. Sorry, Hardy.' Gilks left his cigarettes and closed the door quietly behind him.

'Ignorant, *nouveau-riche* wankers,' Hardy muttered and started to chuckle. Colin looked up at him uncertainly, as his chuckle turned to full-chested laughter. How could he take this crisis so lightly? Surely they were doomed now? Hardy ruffled his hair.

'What did you say your name was?' he asked.

'Cowper, Hardy.'

'This isn't quite a death camp. I meant your *Christian* name.' He lent a sour emphasis to the epithet, as to an obscenity.

'Oh. Sorry. It's Colin.'

'Colin,' Hardy murmured to himself as though trying the name out. He tugged someone's towel down off the hot pipes. 'Colin Cowper.' He wrapped it around Colin's shoulders. 'Well mine's Lucas.' He held out a hand and Colin obediently shook it. In the gloom he saw Hardy smile.

'Um. Hello,' Colin said.

'Know how to cook scrambled eggs?'

'Yes.'

'Good. You can make me some tomorrow.'

So saying, Hardy sloped out of the shower room, his soaked clothes leaving a trail of water. He tugged another towel down in passing and walked out, rubbing roughly at his hair.

The next day there was no scandal. Although Gilks and his friend would certainly have told everyone about what they had seen there was no allusion either to the dustbin episode or to Colin having been found in Hardy's embrace. Far from finding his initiation into house society compromised, Colin found himself suddenly, cosily in the ranks of the accepted. He was never teased or bullied again and, if any outsider threatened him, his elders in the house drew ranks to protect him. An intellectual as well as a sportsman, extravagantly hip yet not so rebellious as to damage the system he knocked, Hardy was a house hero. As his implicitly acknowledged *little man*, Colin attained an unofficial official position overnight, not unlike the pretty convict singled out as his cell mate by a respected murderer serving life. Awed, Bollocks paid for a new cubicle curtain in suitably pagan red velvet.

Hardy called Colin regularly to his bedsit in the prefect's wing where, behind a locked door, their gasps and cries smothered by the guitars and serious lyrics of the latest concept albums, they had sex. Perhaps, even, made love. In retrospect, their bedplay was unadvanced, innocent even, consisting of no more than hour upon cheek-pinking hour of kissing culminating

205

occasionally in rushed mutual masturbation. As the weeks progressed, however, the crude lovemaking was punctuated by moments of unbridled romance which, for Colin at least, would never be matched. Hardy acquired someone's car for the evening and drove him to London for dinner. He borrowed a punt and took him for picnics on the river. He summoned him to deliciously transgressive moonlit trysts in the cricket pavilion – during one of which they took great pleasure in defiling the sacred grass of the cricket square. He introduced him to port, read him Cavafy, and once, when they were both drunk with regret at it being the last night of term, stole a key and led Colin up a spiral staircase to the roof of the chapel tower where they lay shivering, gazing up at the stars.

Looking back, from the years when he began a painful education in the difficult wooing of women, Colin realized that similar scenes could never be re-enacted with as much pleasure, however delicious his female partner, because with Lucas he had played the part of a girl; an old fashioned, politically incorrect, all-demanding girl. Within the ritualized, hermetic environment of the school, Lucas, too, had been able to play a role – that of the all-powerful hero – which would be ridiculously unsustainable in the world beyond the institution's venerable confines.

As it was, the relationship had no reality beyond the school terms. In the holidays, each returned to his family which, in Lucas's case, meant Iran, where his father worked for an oil company. Neither would have dreamed of corresponding. They saw each other for the last time a little over a year since their first encounter. Lucas won a scholarship to Cambridge and vanished into the glamour of a year off, honouring Colin with a brief succession of postcards from the Mediterranean, which petered out somewhere in the Peloponnese. After that, Colin's only sexual experiences at school were with his fist. He snubbed all approaches that were made. Lucas had lent him stature, protected him from the system. He had worried that, with Lucas gone, he would be vulnerable again but his fears were groundless. He remained safe, coloured by boys' respect for the one who had gone, protected *in absentia*.

*

'Colin? It is Colin, isn't it?'

He had found him. Oh God, he had found him! Colin stood hurriedly, brushing his palms on his trousers before shaking hands.

'Lucas!'

He felt fourteen again. Lucas still towered over him. His grip was firm as ever. His forearms were now wreathed in black hairs. He wore a chunky gold watch. He smelled of money.

'What were you doing in *here* for fuck's sake?'

'I was just, er –'

Lucas grinned.

'You were hiding. That's okay. I was hiding too.'

They laughed. Lucas slapped him on the shoulder and held open the door to the corridor. His accent had acquired a touch of American, like a suntan. It suited him.

'The old boys are a pretty grim bunch, huh?'

'Yes,' Colin agreed as, by unspoken assent, they headed for the stairs and the sunlight. 'Ghastly.'

'So what are you doing here?'

'Casing the joint for Harry. My son. He's nearly thirteen. I wasn't sure. I'm still not, but Elsa's been on at me. My wife.'

Grinning, Lucas nodded, showing a wing of fine lines around each eye.

'I know.'

'You met her?'

'No. I mean I knew you'd got married. I saw it in the papers.'

'Ah.'

Lucas held open the door to the yard and Colin could not help but notice that he too wore a plain gold band.

'You're settled too?' he asked, unsure how he felt about this.

'And how. Ten years now. Funnily enough, we're sniffing around for a place to send Willy.'

'Could do worse.'

'Could do better. Christ, this place still has tin baths! I know America's spoiled me but even by English standards the plumbing here is medieval.'

'Ah but the academic standards . . .'

'Yes. I know I know. I've heard it. It's always the ones who didn't come to these places who fight to perpetuate the whole thing. Left to us it would turn co-ed and be handed over to the state, right? I tell you, Colin, night after night I've had nothing but *academic excellence*, *valuable networking*, *cultural heritage*. I had to agree to come just to get some peace. Where's – Elsa, did you say her name was?'

'Watching cricket. She's a fanatic.'

'That's where I left my lot too. We brought a picnic. Seeing the alma mater was one thing, but I baulked at sherry with the housemaster. So. It's been a long time.'

'It certainly has.'

Again Colin felt Lucas's great hand on his back only this time it moved up to his shoulder and rested there. What the hell? No one was staring. They were two married men now.

Two very obviously married men. He fought back a disturbing desire to kiss him full on the lips then and there and forced himself to talk personal history. By the time the cricket match was in sight, and its dense band of brightly coloured spectators gathered around the drinks marquee, he had told Lucas everything. The year off teaching in the Sudan. Oxford. Law school. The Bar. His mother's death. Elsa. Harry.

'There they are,' he said, raising a manly hand in reply to Elsa's languorous wave from a deck chair. 'But what about you? You've been to America?'

'Ever since Cambridge. I studied film at UCLA and wasted some time directing budgetless art, then I got into scripts and hit lucky. Sucked into Hollywood. A living hell but obscenely well paid. But that's where Fran came along so it was worth every minute.'

'Your wife.'

'My *man*, Colin, my *man*.' Lucas laughed, giving Colin a playful punch in the ribs. 'Jesus. There he is now, the impossibly cute one chatting up your wife. He was married, of course, but she's a wild thing and very understanding, so she let us have custody of the kid. Fran had always spent more time with him in any case. Anyway, I've gotten into production now and Fran's company are transferring him to London so –' he shrugged and gestured around them with his spare hand, 'here we are sorting out Willy's future. Christ but I hope he can pass the exams. American schools are so *backward*, you have no idea.'

'Darling!' Elsa raised a hand, which she clearly intended Colin to kiss. He merely clutched it, masking his panic with a sort of benevolent leer. She was drinking Pimms. The questionably blond American at her side stood to introduce her.

'Elsa, this is Lucas.'

'How do you do?'

'Hello.'

They shook hands.

'And this is *my* one!' Elsa laughed. 'Darling, meet Fran. It's such fun. They're moving to England and I've promised to help them find a lovely house. I've been telling Fran about that nice one for sale near us. You know? With the pretty old conservatory? Lucas, do sit here. I don't think those old trouts will dare come back. Darling? Can you see if the boys are all right? I gave Harry his pocket money and I think he might be trying to buy them both Pimms.'

Colin walked into the mouth of the tent. The air inside was baking, heavy with alcohol, flowers and the smell of hot, damp grass. He spotted Harry buying innocuous enough ice cream for himself and a boy with snowy blond hair, jeans and a baseball cap. In his suit and tie, Harry looked like a bank manager beside him. Suddenly thirsty, Colin turned back to ask the others what they wanted. Mid-anecdote, Elsa was tapping a hand on one of Lucas's knees as he sprawled in his deck chair. His – Colin sought a usable word – friend was laughing uproariously. Contenting himself with a more elegant chuckle, Lucas flicked a glance over Elsa's head to meet Colin's gaze and Colin felt a huge, threatening alteration in the scene, as though the ground had changed its angle or all the trees had suddenly grown another yard. Perhaps it was just the heat.

THE LIST

for Suzy Eva

'Mother will have a fit,' I told her.

'Polly,' she said, taking my hand in hers beneath our discarded coats. 'Calm down. It'll be okay. It's not as though it will be any great surprise for her. She knows about us and everything.'

'Yes,' I said. 'At least she should do by now – she can be evasive. But I'm her baby. Her littlest.'

'Even littlests have to fly the nest some time. You're twenty-six for Christ's sake.'

'Twenty-five.'

'Is that *all*?'

'Twenty-six next birthday.' I smiled. The taxi pulled over. Mother's street. Holy Mary, Mother of God.

'You make me feel so old,' Claudia complained.

'Mother will think you're a cradle-snatcher.'

'She won't, will she?' A moment of panic from Claudia.

'Just teasing.'

Now it was her hand's turn to be pressed.

'Anyway,' she went on, 'with you having lived it up in Rome for the last year, she can scarcely accuse me of ripping you untimely from the maternal nest.'

'Mmm,' I said, thinking of Rome, of Claudia's enormous bed in Rome, of the old pewter plate of figs and nectarines on the bedside table and the buzz of afternoon scooters beneath the shuttered window. 'But that didn't count. Abroad doesn't count as long as your mother has a room full of your things.'

'What things?' She withdrew her hand to push some hair back, exposing a silver earring in the shape of a shell. She saw me look at it. Renaissance silver. I had the other one but was not wearing it today. Mother had superstitions about wearing odd earrings. Like so many younger habits, she found it spiritually unhygienic.

'Oh. Just things,' I said. 'Books. Boxes of letters. Clothes I never wear. Winter coats. My bears.'

'Bears?'

'Teddy bears. You know. Toys. I have several. They were my grandmother's. They get passed down.'

She smiled and looked out of the window.

'We must adopt a baby *subito*,' she said.

The cab driver was counting the numbers on the white-painted porticos. Forty-six. Forty-eight. Now and at the hour of our death.

'Just stop right here.' I tugged his little window open. Claudia had shut it earlier to give our conversation privacy.

'But I thought she lived at eighty-something,' she protested.

'Yup. Right here's just fine. Thanks,' I told the driver. 'I want to walk a little,' I told her. 'Fresh air will do us good.'

'Sorry we're in the dark,' Mother said. 'Mrs Sopwith's polishing silver.'

All the thick downstairs curtains were drawn. The dining room table had been opened out and covered with several old flannel sheets. The family silver, which was kept in a broken twin-tub in the basement, was spread out on it, its variety of impractical or impenetrable shapes glistening in the light of a single, low-wattage lamp. Mrs Sopwith was hunched over a coffee pot, scrubbing at it with the brush my late father had used on his false teeth.

'Come up, come up,' sang Mother, mounting the stairs, 'and let me have a good look at you. Both of you.'

Claudia slipped a hand between my legs as we followed. Mrs Sopwith saw. I know she did.

Mother led us into the morning room. It was full of things. Even without her silver knick-knacks (which Mrs Sopwith was polishing along with the bulkier stuff) its table tops were cluttered. Family photographs smiled equably over one another's shoulders. Potpourri mouldered in assorted Chinese containers. African violets and small begonias thrived on several surfaces and a vase of lilies sent out scarves of scent from the mantel shelf. New, unread novels, freshly delivered on account, caught the autumn sunlight on her desk-top. A sheaf of well-thumbed magazines had been painstakingly fanned out on the low, rectangular table between the sofas. A coffee table in any other house, it had always remained nameless in ours, scorned by Mother for its blameless lack of antique charm. I wished myself in Rome, furled in Claudia's matchless bed linen.

'I do wish Mrs Sopwith wouldn't do that,' said Mother, sweeping the magazines back into a vertical pile. 'Makes the place look like a chiropodist's waiting room.' With a few soft pats to the sofa cushion, she gestured to Claudia to sit beside her. I sat on the sofa before them and saw with a shock that they looked almost the same age, although Mother was the older by at least ten years.

Mother was what I had always thought of as a Chelsea Blonde. I was blonde too, but to qualify for Chelsea Blondedom one's hair had to be dead straight, hanging just to the shoulder, and preferably with the subtlest hint of who-gives-a-damn silver. Seen at its best oiled sleek on a beach or revealed, *après ski* by the removal of an unflattering woolly hat, it was worn around town as occasion demanded. The severity of the look could be (and usually was) offset with all manner of frills and flounces down below and had the advantage over the dowdier Mayfair Perm of conveying an unerring purity and youthful vigour rather than mere respectability.

'So,' Mother said, fatuously, 'you must be Claudia.'

Thoughtlessly I corrected her pronunciation.

'Thank you, dear. Claudia. *Claudia*.' She turned to Claudia for confirmation, smiling girlishly. '*Claudia* to rhyme with *rowdier*?'

'That's right.' Claudia gave her a slow smile.

'*Claudia*.' Mother tried it again. 'But it sounds so much more attractive that way; quite fresh!' She laughed. I slipped off my shoes and drew my feet up onto the sofa, retreating. 'Polly's told me so much about you in her letters: Claudia this and Claudia that.'

'I hope she didn't bore you too much.'

'On the contrary. What an enchanting earring that is.'

'Thank you.'

'May I?'

'Of course.'

Mother was actually lifting Claudia's hair for a closer look. How *dared* she? Her liver-spotted digits on Claudia's silky darkness! She would never have shown such intimate interest in the few boys I had ever brought home. Smiling at the thought of her stooping to fondle Jeremy's belt buckle or Simon's latest loafer, I feigned interest in some new photographs of my cousins.

'I've given the other one to Polly,' said Claudia. 'They're pretty, aren't they? Mamma always swore they were seventeenth century, but fakes are so clever nowadays, it's almost impossible to tell.'

'Good Lord! Polly, have you got yours on now?'

'No. It's . . . It's back with my things.'

'Well I hope your things are somewhere safe.'

'Oh yes.'

'My brother's flat has more security than Fort Knox,' put in Claudia. 'Quite absurd because Enzo seems to spend his every daylight hour at the bank and has nothing to steal.'

'Is he married?'

'Enzo? No. Only to his bonds and his little screens. He does drive an absurdly powerful car, though, so I suspect he may yet surprise us all.'

'Like our Polly,' said Mother and giggled. 'But you won't be living at his place indefinitely, surely?'

'We're flat-hunting already,' I broke in.

'We?' Mother queried.

'Claudia and I.' I crossed my fingers. 'We're going to live together.'

'But surely you have to get back to Rome for your studies, darling?'

'The course is over. I must have told you several times in my letters. It finished in June. I was thinking of staying on for a bit but then Claudia's partner had this idea of opening a London office so we decided to come and set up house over here.'

In the space of a few, sunlit seconds, a miniature drama of reaction and snatched understanding was played out across Mother's greyhound features.

'Oh!' she said. '*Oh*,' (this with an undermining smile of self-mockery), 'I see.' She stood quickly and came to sit beside me. 'Darling, I hadn't realized. You must think me so stupid. It'll be so lovely having you back for good. It is for good, isn't it?'

'Fairly good,' I said. 'Yes.'

She kissed me then pushed back my hair to reveal where the other earring should have glistened. She was showing all manner of unfamiliar emotions and I was not sure I was altogether happy with any of them. She kissed me again.

'I'm so glad for you,' she said, then turned to Claudia. 'And Claudia, too,' she said, holding out her hand which Claudia, bemused but smiling, took. 'I'm so glad. We must have a party.'

'Why?' I asked.

She prodded me in the ribs and scoffed.

'You're so like your father, darling. *Why?* To celebrate. To welcome you back, to introduce everyone to Claudia and to *celebrate*! Have you found somewhere to live yet?'

'Well, as a matter of fact,' Claudia admitted, 'we looked over somewhere yesterday which was perfect. Right on the park, with a roof terrace and some good-sized rooms which would be convenient for showing off pieces to clients and a quite extraordinary bathroom . . .'

'But they were asking the earth for it,' I said. 'It was fairly huge.'

'. . . and I wasn't going to tell Polly until I'd had some confirmation, but I rang them this morning and made an offer which they accepted.'

'Claudia!'

'Are you cross?'

'No. I'm thrilled. But . . . you didn't tell me.'

I was thrilled. I was very, very happy. The flat was indeed perfect for us. Somehow the whole treat had been spoilt, however, by being revealed in Mother's presence. Our new love-nest was twenty minutes' or more drive from where we sat but suddenly I felt as though its newly painted, spectacularly empty spaces were merely a previously undisclosed adjunct to Mother's

overfurnished domain. No sooner was the precious territory
offered me than it was annexed by the Kingdom of Knick-
Knack.

Excited, Mother clapped her hands. 'Now you mustn't say
no. As my only daughter you can't escape a proper send-off.
Your father set aside a tidy sum for just such an eventuality –
well, maybe this wasn't *quite* the eventuality he had in mind
but still – so it won't cost you a thing. By rights I feel we should
put an announcement in *The Times*.'

'Mother!'

She pointed at my face and laughed at its expression.

'*Just* like your father! Don't worry. No announcements. I'm
not utterly grotesque. But I do insist on giving you both a
proper reception with invitations and I'm damned if I see why
all your dreary brothers should have got married and had lists
and you shouldn't.'

'But I'm not getting married.'

'Well you're not going to marry anyone else are you?'

'No, but . . .' She was breaking every rule. She was quite
mad. I looked to Claudia for help but she was sitting back,
stroking her gentle smile with the back of a forefinger and
looking to see what Mother would say next. She was charmed.
I could tell.

'There we are then. Why don't we go round there now? It
would be such fun.' Mother uncurled herself from the sofa and
stood, giving her Chelsea blondeness a quick flick as she
glanced in the looking glass. 'Have you got much to do this
morning?'

'No. Not really,' said Claudia, still smiling to herself. 'But
tell me, Mrs Reith . . .'

'Prudie, please.'

219

'Prudie.' Claudia's pronunciation was right first time, although the pout it lent her lips was perhaps unnecessarily seductive. 'I don't quite understand. What is this *list*?'

'When you set up house together . . .'

'Get married,' I broke in.

'Same thing,' Mother snapped.

'But it's meant to be a reward,' I said, astonished. 'For doing the right thing.'

'Just like her father,' she told Claudia again, shaking her head in mock sorrow. 'Such a shame you never met him. Anyway, when you set up house together – or marry,' she added, with a bow in my direction, 'you run up a list at your favourite shop of all the things you need to make domestic bliss complete and your friends and well-wishers call in there and buy them for you. If you get your timing right and don't go living in sin for too long beforehand, you don't have to buy a thing. You'd be amazed at people's generosity. You shall be.'

We drank a quick, celebratory gin while Claudia met Mrs Sopwith and was asked to cast a charitably professional eye over some of the more outlandish family silver. The few excuses I could drum up were quickly quashed by both Mother and Claudia and soon the three of us were walking down the road to Sloane Square.

'It's an inexplicably dull shop,' Mother explained as I held open a swing door for them both, 'but utterly trustworthy. You could leave a child in its care. I quite often did.'

The *Bride's Book* was still appropriately close to the department selling prams and pushchairs. The only apparent concession to modern living was the computer on which its lists were now maintained. Twisted with mortification, I dawdled by a shelf of soft toys and succeeded in making Claudia drop back to find me.

'What's wrong, Polly?' she asked. 'You look quite grey. Do you want to go back into the fresh air?'

'Quite right I do. She's only doing this to embarrass us. She wants to punish me for not bringing home some dull man she can approve of and tease.' I snatched a donkey and pulled on its pink felt ears. 'She's going to make a huge scene, I warn you. And so will the shop. They only do lists for nice young girls with fiancés. Not . . .' I hesitated.

'Not what?'

'Not not-so-nice young girls with elegant, titled but undeniably female partners.'

'So?' Claudia purred, setting the donkey back on its shelf and taking my hands in hers. 'Let Prudie have her joke. Let her show her feelings. Maybe it's easier for her this way. After all, it's only a shop, not the *Castello* Windsor.'

The precision of her pronunciation of Windsor made me smile through my discomfort. I called to mind the beauty of the flat she was buying us. I let her lead me forward.

The woman behind the counter was old enough to have grand-daughters. Unable to meet her eye, I fell to examining her uniform, wondering how something so ill-tailored could convey such irreproachability in the wearer. She would be scandalized.

'Good morning,' she said.

'Hello,' said Mother.

'Have you come to choose something from a list?'

'Not exactly,' said Mother. That was my cue. She was smiling at me and the woman behind the counter was waiting with her head at a politely enquiring angle.

'We've come to make one of our own,' I confessed.

'Lovely,' said the woman, her face impassive the while. 'Congratulations. I'll just open a file for you.' She tapped away at the computer keyboard. 'Your name, please.' Now she smiled at me briefly.

'Polly Reith,' I told her. 'Miss Polly Reith.'

'And the gentleman's name?'

'Er . . .' I faltered and looked to Mother for help.

'Not a gentleman,' Mother told her. 'Not a male, that is. Is there a problem?'

I noticed that the woman wore an unusual jet ring. She turned it briefly on her finger.

'Not at all,' she assured us. 'The lady's name?'

'Claudia Carafontana,' said Claudia. 'Contessa.'

I saw Mother's eyes glitter with vulgar pride. The woman behind the counter tapped in Claudia's title.

'Contessa,' she repeated under her breath. 'And will you be wanting the gifts delivered as they are bought,' she asked, 'or would you rather arrange for collection at a later date?'

'Oh, delivery would be better, I think,' said Claudia, evidently entering into the spirit of the occasion. 'Don't you think so, darling? Of course, the address is not quite certain as yet.'

'That's not a problem. If I could just have a phone number in case of queries.'

'Of course,' I said, anxious not to be quite passed over, and I gave her Lorenzo's number and address.

'Fine,' we were told. 'Walk around the store at your leisure and when you see things you'd like, just write their details on this form. Here, I'll fix it on a clipboard to make writing easier.'

'Not a perambulator,' said Claudia as we headed towards the household appliances department. 'Not just yet.'

Claudia's solicitors and those of the property developers who sold her – who sold us – the flat, worked fast. We were able to take possession within a month of her offer being accepted. In the interim, I discovered Claudia to be far richer than I had imagined. In Rome she had existed within a *mise-en-scène* completed long before my arrival. Her chests, mirrors and portraits, her rugs, pewter plates, even her vast bed with its carved headboard, were so encrusted with Carafontana family history that they seemed an extension of her personality, barely material and certainly nothing one could buy. It was something of a shock, therefore, to see her cut adrift from her historical moorings. Free to create a new setting of her very own. Of our very own. She dedicated her mornings to setting up the new branch of her antique business. Claudia and her cousin Maurizio, did nothing so sordid as buy and sell. Rather, they found antiques for clients too busy to shop themselves, discreetly arranging purchase and well-insured delivery for a large commission. She swiftly found a clutch of London clients who were either eager to buy the kind of Italian antiques that rarely found their way into auction houses or keen to sell their English furniture for the inflated prices Claudia could easily persuade her Italian clients to pay. I spent my mornings sustaining the illusion that I was searching for gainful employment.

Claudia devoted her afternoons to Mammon and Mother in equal proportions. Trailing me, astonished, in her wake, she bought paintings, looking glasses, Bokhara carpets, candelabra and vases. We pored over whole epics of fabric samples and she ordered curtains and drapes of a luxury that rounded even Mother's bridge-table eyes. She was dissatisfied with much that the property developers had done and painstaking hours were spent planning the undoing of their costly work and choosing replacement doorknobs, window catches and taps. Until then I had no idea that taps could be so expensive. This booty was stored in what had once been my bedroom, which was, as Mother pointed out, only twenty minutes' drive from the new flat. Mother would admire each new purchase judiciously, robbing it, as she did so, of the charms that had briefly seemed to distinguish it from others of its kind. She would then invariably take Claudia on some social excursion.

'You don't mind my borrowing her, do you, darling?' she asked the first few times, making it plain that I was surplus to her requirements. 'Just silly old friends who bore you rigid, but they will insist on laying eyes, if not hands, on dear Claudia before the reception.'

Claudia's capacity for such socializing astounded me. In Rome she had only met people in the evenings and then only in strictly monitored doses. She regarded her own mother and her fustian social rounds with undisguised contempt, which made her unlooked-for charity towards Prudie and her no more interesting bridge cronies doubly curious.

Left to my own devices, I indulged in cinema matinées, enjoying the excuse some of the more far-flung repertory houses gave for lengthy taxi rides. A cinema in Hampstead was showing *Rosemary's Baby*. I had missed it first time around and found the plot oddly compelling. I saw it three times in one week. Like *Othello* (which Claudia claimed had one of the theatre's richest histories of audience interruption), the more one saw it the more maddening it became.

'Open your eyes!' I wanted to scream at Mia Farrow. 'Put down that milk shake, pack your bags and run!'

But I never did.

We moved into the flat only two days before the reception was to be held there but the process was remarkably unstressful.

Claudia and Mother between them had scheduled the delivery of her larger purchases with the precision of a military campaign. Unfortunately, my half-hearted trail through the job market had proved successful and I found myself committed to a mornings-only post as a researcher.

'Never mind, *cara*,' Claudia told me. 'You can come for lunch and have a lovely surprise.'

So I set off to work from Enzo's flat as usual then came home to our own, for lunch.

Two men had been to remove taps, knobs and window catches and Claudia's choices were now in place, as were her rugs, the booty stored in my childhood bedroom and a Jacobean bed that was almost as big as the one we had shared in Rome. I stood in the doorway looking around me over the wall of cardboard boxes. Claudia shut the door, stooped to remove my shoes, kissed each of my stockinged feet then led me to the bed.

'And so,' she said, unbuttoning my suit, 'begins our new life together.' She made her habitually subtle love to me on new matchless bed linen after which she fed me champagne and, in memoriam, figs. 'Mmm,' she sighed contentedly, 'Prudie was right to have the bed delivered first. I was all for concentrating on the pictures.'

'This was *her* idea?!'

Claudia laughed nervously at my tone.

'Well, only the bed. I thought of the figs myself.'

'Glad to hear it.'

'Polly, don't sulk. It's childish.'

'Well maybe, but spending so much time with old women is unnatural.'

'Unnatural?'

'Yes.' I sat up and swung my legs off the side of the bed. 'Anyway, they're only interested because you're a countess.'

'Hardly,' Claudia snorted. 'Prudie's circle is a lot more sophisticated than you seem to realize. They haven't batted an eyelid about you and I living together and if the way that wedding list is being ticked off is any indication, they're giving us a substantial blessing.' She rubbed my shoulder. '*Cara*.' She hesitated. 'You really don't see it, do you?'

'See what?'

'When did your father die?'

'When I was about three.'

'And how many boyfriends has Prudie had since then?'

'I don't know. She's always been very discreet. Several, I should think.'

'None, Polly. She's had none. And she's still an attractive woman. Does she cherish his memory?'

'Not exactly. He was much older than her. There's a photograph of them somewhere.'

I turned at last. Claudia was leaning on one elbow, dark hair swept back to reveal her silver earring. She raised her glass to drink and her ivory bracelets slid with a clatter to her elbow. She smiled slowly.

'*No!*' I breathed.

I dressed fast, left the flat and caught a taxi to Sloane Square. My mind was filled, as in some Satanic slide show, with images of Mother and her *nearest and dearest* – Heidi Kleinstock, Tricia Rokeby, Daphne Wain, the Crane Sisters (about whom I had always had my suspicions) and even Mrs Sopwith, in a fast changing line of sexual arrangements. The editrix of the *Bride's Book* greeted me with a knowing smile and twiddled her ring. I realized why it had first caught my eye. Daphne Wain had a jet ring too, though larger, of course, and so did Heidi Kleinstock and, when blowsy peasant fashions had held

226

sway, even Mother had sported one, with large jet earrings to match.

'Good afternoon, Miss Reith,' said the woman. 'Come to make a progress check? I'll do you a print-out to take away with you.'

She pressed a button then, somewhere beneath her desk, a printer hummed into action. When it came to a rest, she handed me a sheet of paper. There were all the plates, bowls, cutlery, glasses, salad bowls and napkin sets chosen, as I had then supposed, merely to humour Mother's fantastic game the other day. And there, beside most of them, were women's names. Numerous women's names. Many of them were quite unfamiliar and all of those I recognized were single by death, solicitors or choice. Half in jest, Mother had suggested I set down the name of a highly-developed dishwasher. A chronic exhibitionist, Tricia Rokeby had bought it for us. I pictured it being delivered in a large, jet-black bow with a card attached, swirled over with her jet-black greetings and unwanted solidarity.

I drank a cup of strong tea, not because I wanted it but because the store's top floor café, The Coffee Bean, carried unfailing associations with the well-buttoned certainties of childhood. I drank a second cup because I had begun to realize that I was, perhaps, a little disorientated from drinking champagne with nothing more substantial than a few figs. Two walls of the café were taken up with windows onto the square and one of the bustling roads that fed it, a third, which I was facing, was panelled with mirrors. I stared at myself long and hard, stared at the long, un-Chelsea curls of my hair, at the unmade-up face which Mother had once called *quiet* in my hearing, at my small, ringless hands. I had bought my navy coat on a trip to Milan and it had done its best to look too big for me ever since, dissociating itself from my neck and shoulders at the least opportunity. I sat up straight and tugged slightly at the lapels. Obediently, it fitted me once more. I had taken shelter from a downpour – unprepared as usual – although Claudia was waiting for me in a restaurant on the other side of the piazza. It was the only important garment I had bought on my own since meeting her. Normally she was at my elbow, purring, 'Or this, perhaps?'

I paid for my teas and hurried down the stairs to street level. There was a hair salon a few doors away, far too fashion-conscious and young for Mother, whatever her proclivities. I let myself in. Its atmosphere was stridently chemical; bubble gum and bleach. The music was loud – Claudia tended to listen to Baroque productions performed *authentically* – and gave me back the strength the mirrors had sapped. I would have my hair cut to within an inch of my scalp and dyed red. Traffic light red. It was what my coat had always needed. Mother too, perhaps.

'Hello, there. What can we do for you, then,' asked a stylist, picking incuriously at my hair. The words sounded like a challenge but her mind was plainly on other things.

'Oh,' I said. 'Just a trim, please. And a wash.' I offered her my quietest smile.

CHOKING

for Barry Goodman

'I thought, perhaps, sardines,' Charlie said, after pecking her cheek, patting her shoulder and casting an automatically assessing eye over what she was wearing. 'I know they're a bit cheap and cheerful but we've discovered they're delicious bar-becued with a bit of lettuce and some new potato salad and cooking them outside means you don't get that awful stink hanging around the house for days afterwards.'

'How lovely,' she said. 'I love sardines.'

'I remember.'

Now that he was no longer her husband, Charlie was Maud's best friend. Not that one excluded the other – he had been her best friend all along, which was one of the things that scup-pered their marriage – but he was *still* her best friend despite now being her ex-husband. This was something other people found hard to understand. It was also, for her, a source of quiet pride.

His garden was a strenuous demonstration against what was expected behind a North London terraced cottage. There were no mundane flowers, no vegetables and no lawn. Instead Charlie had created a small jungle of big leaved foliage plants – gunnera, rhus, palms and other things too exotic for her to recognize. Water trickled over a pile of attractive rocks and striped pebbles into a square pool whose sides he had painted a nocturnal blue.

'It's a jungle!' she laughed. 'Your neighbours must think

you're mad.' She could tell from the way their windows were dressed that his neighbours grew vegetables, dahlias and hideous Blue Moon and Cheerfulness roses.

'I don't speak to my neighbours,' he said quietly.

A small table and chairs stood in a kind of clearing beyond the first swath of glossy greenery. The fish were already sizzling on a small barbecue to one side, a mute reproach to Maud for her lateness. As she sat, slipping off her jacket to enjoy the early autumn sun, Charlie wiped the drips off a bottle that had been cooling in the pond and poured them both some wine.

'So,' he said, sitting too. 'How's LA?'

'I told you before,' she laughed. 'It's not *really* LA. We're so far down Sunset Boulevard, we can see the sunsets. Amazing sunsets. And if I stand on the balcony and lean out a bit, I can see the Pacific.'

'Nice.'

'You should come. Both of you.'

'Yes. Well . . .' he sighed, allowing the impossible optimism of her suggestion to settle on the table between them. 'The tan suits you,' he added.

'You call this a tan?' she exclaimed. 'I went this colour by staying *out* of the sun and wearing total block. There are people there with necks like old shoes but they persist in lying by their pools and *baking*. For a culture so founded on vanity, it's inexplicable. Mmm. Lovely wine.'

'It's nothing special,' Charlie shrugged. 'Something Portuguese Kobo picked up.'

'How is Kobo?'

'Fine. He's with a client in Moscow; one of his German property developers. He'll be sorry he's missed you.'

*

232

Their marriage had foundered when Charlie spent some time in therapy because he was worried that he kept losing his temper over insignificant things. Guided by the therapist, he came to see that he was not a cowardly bisexual, as he had always claimed, but a homosexual liar who should never have married. They did their best to adapt – they loved each other dearly, after all, and he had no desire to hurt her – but their attempt at an *open relationship* was doomed once his safaris into the realms of uncomplicated sex caused him to stumble into love with someone else. Maud had given him up with tears but little struggle, since he was still her best friend, and she knew when she was weaker than the competition. There had been a flurry of lovers since then, and more therapy, but then Charlie met Kobo, a Japanese lighting consultant, who brought him stability and a second marriage, longer and doubtless more fulfilling than his first. Kobo was handsome and clever and Maud had little difficulty in befriending him, but he made her nervous. She felt that her manner and appearance were too untidy for him, that he must be forever rearranging her in his mind. His poise, too, could madden her. Passing through his workroom during a drinks party she had once, in pure malice, unzipped his little black rubber pencil case and shaken the contents across his immaculate desktop.

'Why are you here for such a little while?' Charlie asked, helping her to two sardines, flakes of whose charred skin fell into her helping of potato salad.

'It's not a proper trip,' she explained. 'I hitched a ride with Alvaro. The company was sending him over for a couple of meetings and he'd clocked up enough miles on his frequent flier card to bring me along for nothing. He lives in airports. It was only an economy ticket but when the stewardess saw he was in club, she upgraded me to join him. He always flies with the same airline and I think they must have his name on their computer for extra nice treatment or something. Sorry, I'm gabbling. It's jet lag.'

'Lettuce?'

'Please. Thanks.' She could tell from Charlie's abrupt change of tack that he was not about to ask about her boyfriend, even after she had asked after Kobo. She decided to tell him anyway.

'He's fine, by the way. Only he works so hard it's quite scary,' she said. 'He went straight from the airport to a meeting in Wardour Street when the most I could do was brush my teeth and crawl into bed.'

Charlie merely snorted and lifted a tab of flesh off a sardine skeleton. 'Have you got a job out there?' he asked.

'Not really. I wanted to take time out and get some painting done again. The light is wonderful, even in a flat. There's a nice bit out at the back where the kitchen is, with a glass roof and I paint in there when I can. But I've been doing a lot of childminding for Clara – that's his sister. She's so nice, and Enrique – that's the kid – is adorable. She pays me quite well. Cash in hand. But it does make it a bit hard to get on and paint sometimes because he keeps getting in the way or wanting me to play with him. Anyway for the moment it's strictly cash jobs or letting Alvaro pay for everything, because I haven't got a green card. I shouldn't even be living there. We're probably going to have trouble from immigration on the way back in.' She laughed at the memory. 'Alvaro's asked me to marry him,' she said. 'While we're over here. He proposed in the departure lounge.'

Charlie paused a moment then frowned so that she wondered if the news had hurt him.

234

'Just so you can get a permit?' he asked.

'I . . . er . . . I think there'd be more to it than that. He wants to make an honest woman of me.'

'And I suppose he wants you to have his babies too.'

'Yes, actually. I think he probably does. I should give it some thought. I'm not getting any younger.'

'Then you'll never get a job again. You know what your family are like; you'll be permanently pregnant or breast-feeding.'

'I'm not sure I want a job,' she said defiantly. 'I hate work. I'd quite like to lie back and have babies. I might write a book. I could write a book while they were sleeping.'

His pager bleeped, interrupting her. He apologized and went to call his surgery on a portable telephone. She ate on, watching him pace about in the far end of the garden as he talked. His voice was curt, slightly hectoring, the way she remembered it. It reminded her of disagreements they had suffered in the past and of the little things that made him that much easier to divorce. He used to correct her stories at dinner parties. He used to curb her drinking even when he was the one that was driving them home. When he returned, she was ready for a skirmish.

'You knew Alvaro was over here with me,' she said. 'Why didn't you ask him over too?'

'He was busy. You said he had meetings all day.'

'That's beside the point. You didn't ask him.'

'But I didn't want to see him,' he laughed, exasperated. 'I wanted to see you.'

'He noticed.'

'Good. Maybe next time we meet he'll be a bit more polite.'

'What do you mean?'

'Maud, we had you both to dinner last time, at very short notice. And he barely addressed three words to Kobo – and those were only questions. Then he dismissed my work on the NHS as a waste of resources and spent the rest of the evening banging on about market forces and the power of the almighty dollar. He's right wing.'

'No he's not. He's American. They have a different system to ours.'

Charlie dismissed this with a snort, adding, 'And he belittles you.'

'He does not.'

'He squired you around all evening. He always had a great hand clamped on your elbow or your arse. Treating you like a piece of property. It's so *Latin*.'

'Of course he's Latin. He's a Cuban. Anyway he loves me. He's very physical. He likes to touch me in public. I like to touch him. You never touched me.'

Charlie froze for a moment in passing her the last sardine. She didn't want it – the taste was turning acrid in her mouth – but she could not break in to say no in case her voice trembled.

'Yes. Well,' he said. 'If you say so, but that night I think there was more to it. He was using you as protection. You probably couldn't see it – why should you – but we both noticed it. Kobo's especially sensitive.'

'You're going to say he's uncomfortable around gays.'

'Homophobic. He's homophobic. His skin was crawling. He hardly ate a thing –'

'He was getting over food poisoning.'

'And his relief when he saw there was another straight couple – he practically congratulated them.'

'I don't see how you can say this. He works in an office surrounded by gay men. The place is *run* by Marys. He works for an entertainment corporation, for Christ's sake!'

'Precisely. And I bet not a day goes by when he doesn't wish it wasn't.'

'How can you judge him like this?' she exclaimed. 'You don't even know him. You've only met a few times. How do you know he wasn't just nervous? You're always underestimating how scary people can find you. You're a very intimidating man. And when Alvaro's nervous he can get kind of aggressive and give a bad impression.'

'So! His skin *was* crawling!'

'Oh *honestly*!' She gestured as though to brush his words off the air. 'There's no dealing with you when you're being like this. Let's just let it go and talk about something else. You don't like him. Fine. The two of you will hardly ever meet in any case. It was naïve of me to expect you to get on. I mean, the only thing you have in common is me, which is hardly grounds for a beautiful friendship.'

Indignant, she took a last, large mouthful of fish and chewed it vigorously by way of a full stop. Charlie collected a forkful of potato, dipped it in a pool of dressing then left it on his plate. He topped up the wine instead, his eyes lowered, his mouth pinched in a way she knew of old to bode only ill.

This was not part of her plan. She was barely across his threshold and they were arguing already. She had woken, dressed and travelled up here from the hotel with such high expectations, longing to see Charlie again with a true fondness, innocent of an ex-lover's spite or insecurity. Since her spur-of-the-moment dash out to California the previous year, she had written to him regularly and he wrote back; they sent each other distillations of their mood and witty accounts of recent adventures. She noticed, however, that they avoided the less spontaneous intimacy of the telephone and judiciously edited their accounts

237

of any material pertaining too closely to their respective lovers. Perhaps she was guilty of having sustained a fiction, withholding the whole business of Alvaro from his attention, the longer to sustain his old support.

The brutal truth was that Alvaro was the first lover since her divorce who had eclipsed Charlie, the first to have proved more than a divertissement, the first she loved more than she liked. She had met him while working briefly in the graphics department of his corporation's London office. Wooing her with single-minded charm, seducing her with a kind of boyish greed, he had proudly overstepped her broken marriage rather than be intimidated by it. Divorce, her enduring love of Charlie and the overly protective eye her ex-husband kept on her had left her in an unromantic limbo, locked in a glass tower whence it took Alvaro's forceful passion and, dare to whisper it, machismo to wrest her.

'What do you want?' she asked.

'How do you mean?' Charlie said, setting two small fruit brulées before them.

'Because I'm not going to give him up just because you want me to.'

'I never said I wanted you to give him up,' he protested.

'You didn't need to. I could tell it was what you were hoping.'

'I can't pretend he and I have much in common.'

'Evidently. But you can't let that be a reason for me to give him up, any more than I'd expect you to give up Kobo.'

'But you *like* Kobo.' Charlie's statement was half a plea for reassurance, allowing her anger to pass its peak.

'Only because I went out of my way to get in a position where liking him would be possible,' she said.

'You make it sound hard.'

'It wasn't. Not really. Kobo's easy to like. Kobo's a charmer. Alvaro isn't. Not with men. He's Latin, as you say, and he tends to view men – gay men included – as rivals until they prove themselves not to be. This is delicious.'

'You don't think I burnt the sugar too much?'

'No. It's perfect.'

'Kobo bought one of those little kitchen blow torches for me on a trip to Brussels.'

'As I say, he's a charmer. Is this sour cream?'

'Crème fraîche.'

'Heaven.'

'The beauty of it is the speed.'

The flawless puddings, caramel carapaces giving way to miniature marshes of raspberry, peach and ratafia, seemed to dispel the discord the smoking sardines had unconsciously unleashed. Obese for several years of her childhood before hormones taught her vanity, Maud had always laid herself open to the voodoo of food. The fizz of ripe mango on her tongue, the yeasty elasticity of warm white bread could improve her mood in seconds. Telling juxtapositions of taste – tender anchovies *au vinaigrette* laid across a waxy new potato, tay-berries bleeding rich juice over a bittersweet island of chocolate parfait – could arrest her thoughts in their tracks, leaving her staring in speechless wonder at her plate. Some people were at their most vulnerable behind the wheel of a car or dandling a child on their knee. Those who understood Maud well knew that favours were best asked while she was eating. She emptied her ramekin in contented concentration then looked up at Charlie with refreshed affection.

'I'm sorry,' she said at last. 'It's the younger child in me, always wanting everyone I love to love one another. My mother was just the same – always trying to maintain a sort of umbrella of men about her. I'm always pathetically bewildered when it doesn't happen, which is daft since there's no earthly reason why it ever should. I mean, if Alvaro lived in London, all this would be more of a problem. You'd *have* to get on because I'd be forever bringing you together. As it is, you need never meet till my funeral. And even then, one of you can send apologies. But it's sad if it means I see less of you. Do you mind? Can you face being kept in separate boxes?'

'All I mind is his taking you away from us.' Charlie muttered, lighting a cigarette from the barbecue. 'I miss you. Especially when Kobo's away. And he's away so much nowadays.'

'Darling.' She squeezed his free hand then poured them the last of the bottle. 'But I had to go. Even if you don't like him, you *must* see that. I couldn't have stayed here trailing after you two forever. It wouldn't have been fair on Kobo, and it certainly wouldn't have been fair on me. Fairies' godmother is a thankless role.'

'No one said anything about trailing. You could just have found yourself a bloke in London.'

'Someone you approved of.'

'Yes,' he said then shrugged, crossly exhaling smoke as he saw the futility of his wishes.

'I don't think,' she said carefully, 'you'd have approved of *anyone* I fell in love with.'

'I would,' he insisted. 'Michael Manners was all right. And I liked the one from that magazine. The one with the streak in his hair.'

'Terry. Hmm. Yes.' She smiled wistfully, recalling Michael's statuesque legs and the little, childish sun tattooed around one of Terry's nut brown nipples. Then she cleared her throat. 'But neither of those was love.'

'It looked like it at the time.'

'Well believe me, it wasn't. It was lust. Lust on the rebound. Great fun, very good for my morale but –'

'Not love.'

'No.'

She was not meeting Alvaro until early evening so Charlie disguised his medical bag in a rucksack and they took a walk. They headed up Highgate Hill to look in an antique shop then strolled around Waterlow Park admiring the warmth of the autumn colours and berating the dullness of the council's planting schemes. Something was tickling the back of her throat and she kept pausing to cough into a handkerchief. He patted her on the back in an effort to relieve her discomfort then left his hand comfortably across her shoulder as they moved on beneath the trees. They talked of other things as they walked, chiefly of old friends and distant enemies, of books they had read and films they had missed. They stopped for a cup of tea in the park refreshment rooms before she caught a train back into town.

He said, 'All right. We'll give him one more chance if you like. But let him know he's on parole.'

'We could meet in a restaurant,' she suggested, more relieved than she cared to show. 'Neutral territory.'

'Good idea.'

'Should we invite some camouflage along?'

'No point. He's the one I should be talking to.'

'Thanks,' she said. 'I *so* want you two to get on. Just a bit. You don't have to become best friends or anything but he's so clever and funny once he relaxes and he loves talking about films and exhibitions. He's a very keen gardener too –'

'Don't push it,' he warned her. 'I said he's on parole. We can dress down, go Dutch and steer clear of private medicine. But I'm only doing it for you, remember.'

'I know.'

'I know I should be happy you're happy and I *am* trying to be, believe me, but if I don't like him, I don't like him.'

'I know.'

Something – the staleness of the bun they were half-heartedly sharing, the long shadows on the grass outside or the too familiar sound of the waitresses squirting jets of scalding water into metal teapots – something began to cause her an ache of nostalgic regret. Possibly it was the unexpected sound of him backing down after taking a stand, touching in its way as the first time she noticed her father having to lever himself from an armchair or caught herself smiling encouragement as her mother unwittingly told her a piece of news for the second time. His pager bleeped again. He called his answering service on the pay phone then announced that he had an urgent house call to make and would have to leave her. He kissed her briskly on the lips and was gone, running off after a slowing taxi.

Gathering her things about her and walking out through the park and down to Archway tube station, she realized he had omitted to ask her response to Alvaro's proposal. Promptly she felt her nostalgia sharpen into homesickness. This was where she belonged. She had missed autumn leaves, missed the sensation of a coat furled about her, missed living in a city with regular rain, where walking for the sake of walking and taking public transport were not regarded as little short of social dereliction. Now that she was emerging from her jet lag, she felt a bizarre sense of dislocation at staying in an hotel in what still felt like her home town. She needed to hurry back to Alvaro, reground herself in reality after spending a day so pointlessly rubbing her nose in the now irrelevant past.

She had thought that the tea had driven away the tickle in her throat but, coughing again, she found the irritating sensation had returned. It was not painful, not sharp. She knew from experience the little jabs a trapped fish bone inflicted, and the instinctive panic they induced. This was less intrusive. It felt as though something were lightly resting just beyond the back of her tongue. She coughed once more, standing to one side of the pavement to let people pass by. She swallowed. She felt it there again. She bought a packet of toffees at the station entrance. She sucked them, one after another, on the train back to the hotel, thinking to induce a little rush of saliva that would wash whatever it was into her stomach and safely away from the mouth of her windpipe, but whenever she swallowed, she felt whatever it was still there and, try as she might to concentrate on her paperback, her thoughts twitched back to the irritation like fingers to an itch.

By the time she returned to the hotel, she felt petulantly in need of comfort. However luxurious, the hotel room was desolately impersonal, not a place to linger on one's own in a state of poignant indecision. Luckily Alvaro was already there, and he had missed her. His kisses tasted of coffee and beef. After Charlie, he seemed delightfully big and invasive; a great lunk of a man, her mother would have called him.

'I missed you too,' she said softly. 'Hold me.' He took her head in his hands and kissed her then she backed onto the bed and drew him about her like a human quilt. 'That's better,' she said. 'That's nice. How was your day?'

'Cruddy,' he said. 'Men in suits talking too much. It looked so great out. I wanted to be out sightseeing with you.'

'We had a nice walk around Highgate.'

'Yeah? And how was lunch?'

'Lunch was fine.'

She had promised herself there would be no more pretence now, no more dressing up the facts, no more telling them, 'He said to say hi,' or 'He was *really* sorry he missed you.' Some vestigial caution however prompted her to turn the carefully planned, too intimate sardine barbecue into something else. Barbecues, she had learnt, were the American equivalent of mowing the lawn. Barbecues, for American men, carried daddish, male, territory-marking, Labour Day connotations.

'Bread and cheese and some soup and salad,' she said and saw the corners of his mouth twitch downwards at the thought of so emasculate, meatless a meal.

He had made them a reservation for dinner and she had planned to lead him somewhere amusingly old fashioned for drinks first. It was time to shower and dress up but for one reason or another, because he was tense and she was cold and perhaps because they both needed some reassurance, they began to make love instead.

Alvaro was on the neanderthal side of hirsute. Charlie's skin was pale and marble smooth, unambiguously Saxon, so she had been surprised, amused indeed, that the contrast already so evident in their natures should be extended to the nature of their flesh. 'Oh. So my brother is a hairy man,' she had murmured when she first unbuttoned Alvaro's shirt; making the first of many literary references he failed to pick up.

While covertly regarding his hairiness as the mark of true manhood, just as he saw large breasts and fecundity as badges of womanly splendour, he treated it with a certain coyness. He liked Maud to shave the back of his neck to leave his nape boyishly naked and he habitually wore modest tee shirts beneath his unbuttoned shirt front, their whiteness enriching his golden skin. In bed, he was peculiarly sensitive to finding hairs in his mouth. Used to the vagaries of male taste, conditioned, in particular, by Charlie's squeamishness, she offered to shave herself. He was horrified at the suggestion. He often did not wait for her to undress before burying his face in her bush and claimed that picking her hairs from his teeth was one of the few free pleasures left him. Rather, it was his *own* hairs that caused him trouble, as though finding them in his mouth were deadly proof of narcissism or a species of autoerotic cannibalism. Tonight he abruptly broke off in the middle of making love to her, picked briefly at his tongue, tried to continue but broke off again with an angry sigh.

'Uh-oh,' she chuckled, familiar with the signs. 'Pube patrol.'

She watched him paw and scratch at his tongue. Aroused as she was, she was impatient for him to find the hair and get on with the matter in hand but then she realized, with a pang of relief that her own throat was no longer itchy.

'Shit,' he muttered. 'Sorry. If I can just –'

She watched guiltily as he climbed off the bed and padded through the shadows to the bathroom. She heard him curse, heard him try gargling, heard him curse again then heard the sound of a wash-bag being unzipped after which he made a series of unappetizing gagging and coughing sounds. Chafed to a pink of passion, her body was rapidly cooling in the breeze of conditioned air. She pulled the bedding up around her and stretched across the pillows to turn on her bedside light. She glanced at her little travelling alarm and saw that they were going to be late for their dinner reservation unless she started dressing now. Suddenly she felt a consuming thirst, brought on by wine at lunch and the undiluted succession of toffees.

'Look,' he was saying. 'Look at this! What the hell . . .?' He emerged from the bathroom triumphantly parading a cotton wool bud. He thrust it into the pool of light.

'Come back to bed,' she said, not looking. 'I want you. Let's eat somewhere else. Let's order room service.'

'Look,' he said again.

She looked. There was a fish scale on the tip of the bud; a sardine scale, translucent, charred at one end.

'Did you have fish for lunch?' she asked. Alvaro rarely touched fish, certainly not if it had skin on it still.

'I had steak,' he said indignantly. He glowered at the scale more closely, as though it provided some crucial piece of circumstantial evidence whose significance would be revealed to him if only he stared at it long enough.

'These British restaurants,' she said. 'They probably gave you a dirty plate.'

'I could have choked,' he said. 'I should sue. You didn't have fish, did you?'

'I told you,' she sighed. 'Charlie gave me soup. Carrot soup. And bread and cheese and some salad.'

She pulled back out of the light because she could feel her cheeks warming at the lie. She took the cotton wool bud from him and laid it on the bedside table then coaxed him back into bed. After kissing and pawing her absentmindedly for a while, however, he fell to wondering about the fish scale again. He lost his erection entirely and, when they arrived at the restaurant too late for their table, lost his temper as well. Their evening was ruined.

Lying in bed beside him – Alvaro had fallen asleep abruptly after complaining of a headache – Maud felt increasingly stifled. His heavy arm pinioned her on her back; a position in which she could never sleep for fear of snoring. The hotel bedding was at once too heavy and too short. Worst of all, Alvaro was obsessed with the mechanics of air conditioning, insisting that the windows be left hermetically sealed while the unit below them sighed its chilled, second-hand exhalations into layers of motionless net curtain. Maud could have coped if the machinery had gone about its business in silence but its constant, mournful whisper put her in mind of the sterile preservation of meat until she suffered a kind of panic attack and had to slip into her dressing gown and flee the room.

She wandered the corridors, growing close to tears in her frustrated search for a balcony or an opening window. She fell in, at last, with two Colombian chambermaids who laughed at her, ushered her onto a blissfully windy fire escape beyond their tiny kitchen then soothed her with sweet tea and biscuits. They had been admiring Alvaro from afar but laughed when Maud told them he was sound asleep.

'I love it when they sleep,' one told her. 'It's the only time they leave you free to *think*!'

There was no question but she must marry him, they said, divining the turmoil of indecision in which she found herself. He had the kind of good looks which would only improve with age, he would work hard to keep her in comfort and he would give her beautiful children. One of them read her palm and clicked her tongue at the happiness she saw there.

Reassured by their envious certainty, just as she was calmed by their tea, Maud returned to her room, switched off the air conditioning and wrapped Alvaro's sleeping arm about her like a valuable fur.

DANGEROUS PLEASURES

for Audrey Williams

The breath was now coming so slowly from Shuna's mouth that Shirley found herself beginning to count in between each painful, creaking exhalation.

'Not long now,' she thought and found she had said it aloud. She shook out her hanky and pressed it gently to her daughter's sweating temples, first one, then the other. If there was any feeling left in the poor child's body, she thought she might enjoy the cool sensation of the well-ironed cotton on her fevered skin.

'Go on,' she added, as Shuna took another spasmodic breath. She might have been encouraging her to jump into a swimming pool or let go at the top of a playground slide. 'Go on. I'm here.'

And then she found she was counting past thirty, past fifty. She allowed herself a little cry. Shuna's eyes were already closed – Shirley had not seen them open in the four days since the phone call – but she reached out and gently closed Shuna's mouth. The lips were cracked and looked sore. She took the jar of Vaseline from the bedside cupboard and rubbed a little on them with her forefinger. Then she opened the window and walked back along the corridor to the visitors' room, the crepe soles of her light summer shoes squeaking on the vinyl floor.

Karl, the nice boy from the charity, with the earring, had finally persuaded Arthur to stop pacing, sit down and drink a cup of tea. He sprang up as Shirley came in. Arthur merely raised frightened eyes.

251

'It's over,' she told them. 'She's gone.'

'Christ,' said Arthur.

Karl came over and gave Shirley a hug, which was nice. She had not been hugged in years. He was a polite, clean boy and probably good to his mother.

'Arthur, do you want to go in for a bit? Say goodbye?' she asked. Arthur merely shook his head, swallowing the tears that had begun to mist his eyes.

'Need a fag,' he muttered and pushed out of the swing door and onto the balcony.

'Do you mind if I do?' Karl asked.

'Be my guest,' Shirley told him. 'She'd have liked that.'

'Have you told the staff yet?'

'No,' she told him. 'Would . . . Would you mind, Karl?'

'Course not,' he said.

As he padded sadly out, she admired again his leather boots with the funny little chains and rings round the heels. She sighed, made herself a cup of tea at the hospitality table and joined Arthur on the balcony. He too, she could tell, had indulged in a little cry. She was glad. Men could be so bottled up.

Shirley stood beside him in companionable silence for a while, admiring the view of Chelsea stretching away from them. She could see the pumping station in the distance and, beyond that, just before the view melted into summer haze, Westminster Cathedral.

'She picked a beautiful day to go,' she said. It was a thin, silly thing to say, she knew, but it was true and she felt it needed saying. The remark slipped into the silence between them which absorbed it like dark water about a stone. When Arthur finally turned to her, it was with a face like thunder.

'Why'd she have to get such a dirty disease? As if what she was wasn't bad enough.'

'Now Arthur, you remember what Karl told us: it's not dirty, it's just a –'

'What's a pansy like that know?'

'I think he knows rather a lot, actually. I think he's already lost several of his friends.'

But Arthur was not listening.

'Why'd she have to do it to us?'

'She didn't *do* anything to *us*, Arthur. She caught a virus and she died. If anything happened to us, we did it ourselves, as well you know.'

He rounded on her, his face suddenly tight with fury.

'Shut your fucking hole,' he hissed.

Shirley turned away, angry in turn. He knew how she disliked unnecessary language. He was not really angry. He was upset. Perhaps he had not had a little cry after all. Not a proper one. He would tell it all to Bonnie when they got home; he had always told his Jack Russell the things he could not tell his wife, mostly things to do with the mysterious workings of his heart and a few others besides. She would send the two of them out to the allotment, say she needed the house to herself while she organized funeral cakes and sandwiches and so on. Death always made people want to stuff their faces. And drink. Juno at the Conservative Club could probably find her way to slipping her a case of that nice sherry cut-price.

'When do you think we can go?' Arthur asked her in a softer tone – the nearest he would come to an apology.

'There'll be forms to sign, probably,' she told him. 'That's all. And she'll have some things for us to take away or throw out or whatever.'

'Well, let's get it over with then we can catch the three-thirty before the rush hour starts.'

'No, Arthur.'

'What?'

'We've got to sort out her flat.'

'Are you mad?'

'It's Shuna's flat.'

'She only rented it. Anyway, it sounds like more of a bedsit.'

'Yes, but she lived there for eight years and I've never seen it and there'll be things to be sorted out there.'

'Leave it, Shirley. Leave it all. She didn't have anything valuable. You can be sure of that. And what there is the landlord can have in case she was behind with the rent.'

'Shuna was always meticulous about debts. That nice friend of hers said so that visited yesterday.'

'That mangy tart, you mean.'

'Arthur!'

He snorted, holding open the door for her into the visitors' room. Ordinarily Shirley would have sighed and acquiesced, but not today. Her mind was made up.

'Well you can do as you please,' she said. 'She's our daughter and I'm going to do right by her. Honour her.'

'Honour?'

'You catch the three-thirty. I'll come home when I'm ready. I might even have to spend the night.'

'You'll do no such thing.'

'I'll do what I have to do. There's food in the fridge. You know how to work the microwave. You'll survive. You're a cold bastard, Arthur, and one day it'll catch up with you.'

'Shirley!'

'You can sign all the forms for me and bring back her

overnight bag and whatever. You've done nothing else of use these last few days.' Shirley was utterly calm in her rightful fury. Karl was waiting for them at the nurses' station. 'Shall we be off, Karl? I need some fresh air.'

'Of course, Mrs Gilbert.'

She turned as they waited for the lift and took a short, hard look at her husband. She would never leave him. They fitted together now like two old shoes and divorce was grotesque in a couple over fifty. There were times, however, when she blithely contemplated murder.

She had taken the keys earlier. They were lying in the bedside locker beside an unopened carton of long life fruit juice and a bottle of Chanel No. 5, which may have suited Shuna, but which Shirley had never greatly cared for. Keys were important, personal things, unlocking secrets, disclosing treasures. She had picked these ones up instinctively to distract her while Shuna was having a long needle pushed into her arm and had forgotten to replace them. They had an interesting fob – a big, silver hoop, like an outsize curtain ring – which felt pleasingly heavy and cool in the hand. Now, as they travelled down in the lift, Shirley's fingers clasped on the bunch of metal as on a talisman.

'Shall I give you both a lift to the station?' Karl asked when they reached the lobby.

'Mr Gilbert's going to the station,' she told him. 'I'm not. I want to see her flat. Would you take me?'

'Of course. But I haven't got keys.'

'I've got keys,' she said and he gave her a quiet but twinkly little smile and she knew at once how his young life was probably rooted in small, harmless deceits and acts of sly kindness. 'Thanks,' she added. 'You're a good boy, Karl. Are you going steady with someone?'

'Yes,' he said and blushed a bit. 'Three years, now, but he's in the army, so I haven't seen much of him lately. He's out in Bosnia.'

'Ah,' she said, adding, 'that's nice,' foolishly, because she was uncertain what to say.

Karl's car was a Mini, black as sin with zebra-striped fur covers on the seat.

'It's okay,' he assured her when he saw her hesitate at the open door. 'They're ironic.'

Shuna had run away from home after one flaming row too many with her father. It had been time for her to leave anyway – she was eighteen – but Shirley was not ready to be left alone with Arthur and the girl departed in anger with no plans and no future, so it *was* a kind of running away. For three weeks they heard nothing. Then a postcard came, pointedly addressed only to Shirley. It showed a guardsman in his busby (Karl's friend had a busby, apparently), and said she was alive and well and living in London now. She asked that they do what they liked with the things she had left in her room. Arthur threw most of them out and made a great, purgative bonfire at the bottom of the garden from the rest. Shirley had retained a few things, however, retrieved from the dustbin bags without his knowledge; Shuna's old school cap, purple with yellow piping, a photograph of her as a sheep in a nativity play and a Saint Christopher medallion. Finding the medallion casually abandoned along with all the ragbag litter of youth, Shirley had felt a momentary panic that her child should be braving the big city unprotected and she had put it on herself at once, shielding Shuna by proxy. She had worn it constantly ever after, hidden from her husband's incurious gaze under slip or nightdress.

Glimpsing its cheap silver plate the previous night as she gave herself an unrefreshing top-and-tail in an overheated hospital bathroom, she reflected that she had picked quite the wrong patron saint for the girl, as redundant in Shuna's life as a cake slice at a witches' Sabbath.

More postcards followed the first, all addressed to Shirley, which pleased her hugely, though she said nothing. Shuna found a job as a waitress then as a secretary. She found a flat. She only paid one visit home, two Christmases after she left, and Shirley knew at once what her daughter had become. Shuna brought them champagne and absurdly generous presents and wore clothes she could never have afforded on a typist's income. This in itself would not have signified much – her daughter might simply have fallen in with a louche crowd or acquired a lover with criminal connections. There was no talk of boyfriends, only the constant if hazy implication of a *gang* of nameless, party-loving friends. What clinched it for Shirley was that something had died behind Shuna's eyes. The old, girlish desire to please men in general and her father in particular, had withered. Correspondingly, as if answering some age-old, unconscious stimulus, Arthur spent the festive season following Shuna around, looking at her with a new, indecently saucy brightness in his eye and he talked incessantly of how *well* she was turning out after all.

'Yes,' Shirley had thought, 'after all. After all your sarcasm, your slaps and put-downs, your relentless, stunting prohibitions, your liberty-pruning.' She had said nothing to him of what she had noticed. He, needless to say, was too dense to draw conclusions. She held her counsel, accepted the presents with embarrassment and forced herself to be glad, at least, that Shuna had found a way of making ends meet, was proving more resourceful than her father ever had. Subsequently, when

Shuna refused to return home for either his fiftieth birthday or silver wedding parties, he turned against her memory again, calling her a whore, but it was only at her deathbed that he came to see the truth in his words.

They received a phone call from the lad, Karl. That was the first they knew of it.

'Hello,' he said. 'You don't know me and officially I shouldn't be contacting you, not without her permission, but she's too sick to talk now and I know she'd want to see you. And I think you've a right to see her too before it's over. She doesn't have long, you see.'

They could not stay at an hotel because neither of them liked being away from home and now, more than ever, they needed the comfort of a nightly return to the familiar, so they came in on the train every day at some expense. They had spent the night this last night, however, marking out the long vigil with cups of watery tea from a vending machine and mournful bars of chocolate. Karl had done all the talking. Arthur was struck dumb, first with grief at the sudden *fait accompli* of her terrible condition, her wasted skin hanging on her protruding bones, her death's head eyes, and then with his understanding of what she had become.

Karl was diplomacy itself. He spoke strictly in terms of the disease and how it was only a disease and not a moral judgement. He illustrated from the depressing scrapbook of his recent memories the deadly impartiality of its appetite. He encouraged Shirley to talk too, asking her about Shuna's youth.

'There's so much she never told me,' he said. 'So much I'd love to know.' He was skilful, well-trained at drawing people out. He was a volunteer assigned months before to befriend Shuna. Shirley thought it strange and rather sad that her daughter had so few friends that new ones had to be trained and assigned to her.

The revelation for Arthur, confirmation of what Shirley had known all along, came on the second day at the hospital, when a woman called in on the ward to see Shuna. She was unnaturally tall, with an astonishingly unlifelike red wig and thigh-length, leopardette, high-heeled boots. And she wore a perfume which lingered, cutting through the hospital smells long after her brief, tearful appearance, and spoke to father and mother alike of moist, unspeakable things. After she left, Arthur, staggered, finally found his tongue.

'Who in Christ's name was *that*?' he asked Karl as she slunk away up the ward, for all the world like some pagan goddess bestowing dubious blessings. Karl had seemed utterly unfazed, kissing the woman tenderly on the cheek and leading her to the bedside with a kind of courtesy.

'Oh, that was Ange. Angela. She and Shuna work together. Used to, I mean.'

'But she's a . . .! You mean *my* daughter was . . .?' Arthur had a rich vocabulary of insulting terms, especially for women, but for once in his life he seemed unable to name names. Karl helped him out.

'Yes, Mr Gilbert. Shuna was a sex worker.'

And Arthur must have believed him because he was too crushed to pick a fight.

It was funny how names changed the way one looked at things. *Sex Worker* had an utter rightness in Shirley's mind. It was truthful, unadorned; a woman's description. Sex was work, hard work where Arthur was concerned, a strenuous matter of puffing and panting and getting hot and flushed and sticky and trying hard to concentrate and not let one's mind make that fatal drift onto wallpaper choice and obstinate claret stains. She had been not a little relieved when he granted her an early retirement about the same time he had his degrading little fling with Mary Dewhurst at the golf club. Shirley was sure that Arthur was more appalled at his late discovery of how his daughter had paid for her generous Christmas presents and fancy imitation fur coat than at her cruel and senseless early death. Sure of it. But she did not greatly care. As her mother used to say: it did not signify.

It took them a long while to drive the short distance across the park and even longer to find a parking space. London had been taken over by cars; smelly, useless things.

'It gets worse every week,' Karl told her as he failed a second time to snatch a parking space and Shirley imagined car upon car clogging the already scarcely mobile queues until a day was reached when no more cars could get in or out of the place. It would become known as the Great Standstill or Smoggy Tuesday. People would die from the poor air quality, children preferably, and finally something would be done, something sensible like persuading men it would not hurt their sexual prowess to ride a bus occasionally.

Shuna's flat was in an unexpectedly leafy square with big plane trees, a well-kept residents' garden and glossy front doors. As she clambered up out of Karl's Mini she realized she had expected something sordid; wailing children in rags, women drunk at noon, surly menfolk with too many rings. This amused her and she laughed softly.

'What?' Karl asked.

'Nothing,' she said. 'Just being silly. Is this hers?' She pointed down to a basement with a tub of flowers outside the door.

'Yes.'

'I should know the address,' she said, 'but she didn't like me to write. I rang sometimes, when Mr Gilbert was out, but I always seemed to get other people – that Angela probably – and I don't think they passed on my messages. Here.' She pulled out the keys. 'You do it.'

Karl took the key ring, looked at the fob, and smiled sadly. 'I bought her this,' he said. 'In San Francisco.'

'Where the bridge is?'

'That's right. It's not really a key ring.'

'Oh? It makes a very good one. Is it for napkins or something?'

'No. No, it's a . . . a . . .' Karl seemed uncharacteristically bashful.

'Is it something rude, Karl?' Shirley helped him out.

'Yes,' he said, grinning. 'Very.'

'Well that's nice,' she told him. 'She must have liked that.'

'She did.'

As Karl turned to unlock the door, Shirley looked at the swinging hoop again, unable to stop herself wondering what on earth such a thing could be used for that would not be extremely painful. He opened the door and she followed him in.

'Good carpet,' she noticed aloud. Shuna had liked carpets as a child, had spent hours rolling around on them as she read or watched television.

'The rent's paid until the end of the month. We've been paying it for her while she was too sick to work. So it's not a problem.'

'You and your guardsman friend?'

'No, no.' He smiled. 'The charity.'

She nodded, beginning to take in her surroundings, the calm

261

colours, the lack of pictures or ornaments, the single, big potted palm behind the sofa. Arthur had been right – it was little more than a bedsit – but it was a very comfortable, well decorated one. Shirley now felt the presence of her grown-up daughter intensely and was shy before it.

'It's very tidy,' she told Karl in a stage whisper, as if Shuna were just around the corner. 'She never used to be tidy.'

'Oh, er, I've been cleaning for her.'

'That's kind of you.'

'Not really. I like to clean.'

'You're very good at it. Shall I make us both a cup of tea?'

'Yes. No. You sit down. I'll do it. Oh God.'

He had paused, his hand on the kettle lid, and quite suddenly was overcome, hunched over the fridge. Shirley touched his shoulder gently. He turned and she drew him to her.

'I'm sorry,' he stammered. 'It suddenly hit me.'

'Don't,' she said. 'It's all right.'

He cried heavily for about ten minutes. It came over him in waves, little surges of grief that she could feel in the tightening of his arms about her. He smelled of leather, soap and man; she liked that. Apart from his brief hug in the hospital, she had not held anyone in years. She did not think she had ever held someone in a leather jacket. She let her fingers stray over its rich, studded surface and stroked the back of his head, where his hair was cut so short she had glimpsed a little strawberry mark underneath it. When he felt better and pulled gently away from her to blow his nose, she felt as relieved as if she had wept too.

'Sorry about that,' he said. 'I should go.'

'Must you?'

'I ought to pop into work, just to check on the mail and things . . . Can I pick you up later?'

'It's okay,' she said. 'I'll probably find my own way to the station when I'm ready.'

'My number's by the phone there, in case,' he said. 'You can take it with you and ring me from home, if you've a mind to.' He kissed her softly on the cheek and left. Nice boy.

She made herself a cup of tea. She explored the flat. She lay on Shuna's bed, even slipped between the sheets for a few minutes. She ate some chocolate biscuits from a tin and played a tape of strange music that was in the machine by the bath. Then, feeling she should do what bereaved relatives do, she reluctantly opened the big fitted cupboard, found a suitcase, and began folding clothes to take to the local charity shop. Shuna had developed a good eye for clothes, that much was swiftly evident, a good eye and expensive taste. They were of a size, and Shirley tried on a jacket and coat or two, wondering whether she would ever dare wear something with a famous Italian label and run the risk of Arthur's guessing where it had come from. Then she took out a hanger with the strangest garment on it she had ever seen.

It was black, and so glistening that Shirley thought at first it was a black plastic dustbin liner draped to protect something precious. Then she realized that the black plastic was the thing itself; the dress, garment, whatever. It was quite thick, almost like leather, and shiny as a taxicab in the rain. It appeared to be a kind of all-in-one or catsuit, not unlike the things she had seen ice-skating men wear on championships televized from Norway. It had long sleeves and long legs. It was shaped with reinforcements to form a pointy bosom and, strangest of all, had built-in pointy boots and long-fingered gloves. Shirley could not resist putting one of her hands into a sleeve and into the empty finger pieces. It was extraordinary. The plastic clung to her, seeming to become an extra skin. There was not a breath of air inside. It fitted her arm exactly and shone so, even in the dim light from the window on to the area steps, that it was a surprise not to feel wet. She turned to look in the mirror, fascinated as she flexed and turned her fingers and forearm this way and that. Then, as she pulled her arm out, the garment gave off a sudden scent that might have been Shuna's very essence. With a little gasp, Shirley dropped it on the bed as though it had stung her. She stared at it for a moment, then tried to resume her packing, but its gleaming blackness burned a hole in the corner of her vision. It *would* not be ignored. At last, it proved too inviting and she found herself stripping entirely naked. One could see at a glance that this was *not* a garment for sensible underwear.

Shivering with anticipation, she slipped first one foot then the other into the leg pieces and down into the boots, happy that she and Shuna had shared a shoe size, then her arms, then her shoulders were encased in the sinuous, clammy stuff. She slowly fastened the big, black zipper that ran up its front from groin to neck, marvelling at the way it caused the contours of the thing to reshape her own. She had always been proud of her trim figure but no one could withstand age and gravity entirely. As the zip reached her chest, she let out a sigh, feeling her breasts first clasped then lifted upwards and outwards by the curiously pointed cones. Something was stuck in the neck, though, forming an unflattering bulge at the back. Wincing, she reached in over her shoulder and tweaked out a thing that looked like a cross between a matronly black bathing cap and the balaclava helmet she had once knitted Shuna. She hesitated for a moment then saw herself in the mirror, saw how her body had been taken over, transformed and her head left grotesquely unaltered on top. Taking a deep breath, she pulled on the headpiece, grimacing at the queer pull of the plastic on her cheeks and she tucked in the loose strands of her short, grey hair.

Now she looked back in the full length mirror and was afraid at how easily she had become something else. 'Oh, Shuna,' she breathed. 'Shuna, my dear.' But she was exhilarated too. The leg pieces squeezed and caressed her thighs in a way Arthur had never done. The new silhouette it gave her was entirely flattering. Astounded, she drew nearer for a closer, more critical look and saw how the mask had hidden her lines, emphasizing instead the best features that remained, her deep blue eyes, her strong little nose, her still full lips. Lipstick. It needed lipstick. She sat at Shuna's dressing table, pulled open the drawer and found some expensive French stuff and smeared a rich, true crimson about her mouth. Then she stood up, wandered around the flat a little and wondered, sadly, why time could not be frozen for a while, to postpone the mournful necessity of packing up and hurrying for a train.

Exhausted by her sleepless night, her grief and her confusion, she sank onto the sofa and, almost at once, fell into a deep sleep. When the telephone rang, she jumped up from the cushions like a surprised thief. She hesitated then, deciding it would be either Arthur or Karl, answered.

'Hello?'

It was a woman's voice. Cultured. Like a voice announcing symphonies on the radio. 'Time to work, my pet?' it asked.

'Er. No. Sorry. I think you've got the wrong number.'

The woman sighed. 'Come on, darling. Wake up. Are you free to play?'

'Oh,' Shirley stammered, confused. She wondered how much she should tell. Any caller who still knew nothing could

265

hardly be counted an intimate. 'Shuna isn't here. This is her mother.'

The woman laughed. 'Oh *come* on, lovey! I haven't got all day.'

'No, honestly. It really is.'

'Listen. He's a really easy number. One of our regulars. The Wimp. Straight up and down for you. Whang, whang, no bang and you're laughing.' The coarse words sounded doubly suggestive in such a plummy mouth.

'No, you don't seem to understand. Shuna is ... Well, she's ... This really is her mother.'

The reply came quick as a blade. 'You're wearing the suit, aren't you?'

'I ... I ...' How could she deny it? 'Yes,' she boldly confessed. 'I am. It's lovely.'

'He'll be up in a couple of minutes, darling. It never takes long. Then we can talk.'

The woman hung up. Shirley stared at the telephone receiver for a moment then began to panic. She hurried over to the wardrobe and continued throwing things into bags. This was insanity. She had not slept. She was in shock. She was hearing things. The telephone probably had not rung at all. She would finish packing, catch the train home and make herself a nice cup of hot, frothy malted milk.

The doorbell sounded. Shirley choked a cry then stifled her fear with common sense. There was nothing for it but to be totally honest. She would answer the door and tell the man it was all some grotesque clerical error. He would take one look at her in any case and *see* she was only somebody's mother. It was only when Shirley tugged wide the door and saw the immediate look of terror on the face of the burly, balding man before her that she remembered she had not changed back into her own, reassuringly motherly clothes.

'I'm sorry,' he said at once.

'What?' she asked. 'No. Honestly. Please listen. I'm the one who should apologize.'

'It's not safe out here, love,' he muttered in an undertone and darted past her in to the flat.'

'Now, please! Look here,' she began. A woman was pushing a pram past on the pavement, leading a little girl who peered down into each basement as she passed it. Horrified, Shirley swiftly shut the door and turned to find her caller cringing on the carpet before her.

'Please, no,' he said. 'Please don't hurt me! I'll do anything. Anything!'

'Get out,' she said, deciding that firmness was the only way to handle such an impossible situation. 'Get up and get out.'

'I'll try to be good next time. I promise. Please.' Grovelling he reached out towards one of her shinily booted feet and grasped the ankle. Without thinking, she kicked out and struck him on the chin in self-defence.

'Oh. I'm so terribly sorry,' she began but he was reaching out for her feet again and she stamped on his hand. He gasped then cried out with what she now realized was pleasure. So she stopped apologizing. To her disgust she saw that, though still on all fours, he had reached down and was rubbing a hand between his legs.

'Stop that,' she said. 'Stop it at once!'

He looked up, his face pink and as unappealing as Arthur's when he had been drinking and began to tell off-colour jokes.

'Make me,' he said, and the challenge was half a plea. He was still playing with himself. Shirley felt sick and slightly faint. The suit was becoming intolerably hot. It was out of the question for her to run out into the street asking for help dressed as she was.

Then it struck her. She did not need to run because she was not afraid. The man was pathetic. The suit itself seemed to lend her power. She smelled again her daughter's scent in her nostrils and her mind cleared. She knew, with a sigh, what she had to do. It was laughably simple. Letting the man's piggish grunts and whimpers feed a clean anger that had begun to burn in her clutched and moulded bosom, she strode back to the cupboard, picked up the thick, black riding crop she had noticed hanging in there and turned to face him. His face lit up with pleasure.

'Please,' he begged her. 'Please, no!'

'Oh shut up,' she said, and smacked him across the back, very hard. He yelled.

'Don't make so much noise,' she spat. 'What will people say, you disgusting little man?' and she hit him again. He was a big man, like Arthur, and could have killed her quite easily with his fat, hairless hands had he wanted to, but he cringed and whimpered, utterly in her thrall as she struck out again and again. She hit him for the years of white Crimplene cardigans, for the decades of watching Arthur mow the lawn, for her wasted bloom and her vanished joys, hit him for Mary Dewhurst, hit him, hardest of all, for the way he and Arthur and stupid men like them had taken away from her the only person she had ever really loved.

It took only two minutes, three at the most. In the brief span from her first smack across his back to his subsiding in muffled ecstasy – 'Don't you dare dirty the carpet!' she hissed – Shirley Gilbert travelled further from the certainties of 66 Hollybush Drive than Saint Christopher could ever have safely carried her. By the last smack, she had stopped being angry and begun to enjoy herself.

Tired with her effort, she sat on the sofa arm, watching her visitor closely. He slowly lurched to his knees, and onto his feet. His face had cleared. He no longer looked beseeching, merely drained of necessity and she realized with a shock that she had made him comfortable. She was obscurely proud.

'Thank you,' he muttered. 'Thank you so much.' His voice was no longer wheedling but almost manly and she felt a pang of apology rising in her breast. Then he reached into his wallet, took out several bank notes, put them on the table and left without another word. No sooner was the door shut than she ran after him, shot the bolt on it and set about feverishly tugging off the catsuit. She washed her face and hands, patted herself dry with a fluffy white towel, then finished packing the suitcase. She repaired her face and hair, dabbed on some scent and tried to ignore the riding crop and mound of sweaty black plastic at the foot of the bed.

Then the doorbell rang again.

'Who is it?' she called out, querulous.

'It's all right,' said the plummy voice she had heard on the telephone. 'It's me. Ange.'

There was a spyhole in the door. Frowning, Shirley peered through it and saw it was the towering siren who had visited the hospital. She opened the door. Angela was dressed almost quietly, in a beautifully tailored linen suit and scarlet blouse.

'Hello,' she said. 'You'd better come in.'

'Thanks,' said Angela, poised as an air stewardess. 'Mind if I sit? My dogs are killing me.' She coiled her impressive length onto the armchair and kicked off her bright red court shoes.

'Well?' she asked.

'Well what?' Shirley asked her back.

Angela languidly gestured towards the heap of notes. 'What did he leave you?'

Shirley counted the notes and was astounded. 'But . . .' she stuttered. 'He must have made a mistake!'

'No mistake, darling,' Angela said, eyeing the money. 'You must have been good. Now listen. I'm sorry I was short with you earlier but his need was pressing and –'

'How did you know I was in that –'

'Mind if I smoke?' Angela cut in.

'Not at all.'

'Shuna smoked all the time. Even on the job. Sorry.'

'That's all right.'

'Anyway. The choice is yours.'

'I'm sorry?'

'The choice. You have a choice. Either you take that suitcase, leave the suit of course, and disappear off to the remainder of your quiet little life and are never heard of again, or . . . or you take that suitcase – if the suit fitted you, her other things will – *and* you take the suit then you come with me and start your new life. Either way, you get to keep the money. You earned it, after all.'

'I don't quite –'

Angela seemed oblivious to Shirley's confusion, holding her cigarette between the long, wonderfully manicured fingers of one hand and patting at her chic blonde chignon with the others. The woman was a mistress of disguise.

'You'll have to leave the flat, of course,' Angela went on. 'I'll have one of the girls torch it, make it look like a dreadful accident, to cover your traces. You'll get a new place, somewhere a little more gracious than this for you, I think, lovey. And a new ID. Car, too, if you want one. I could tell you'd be good the moment I laid eyes on you. Just like her. A natural. Have you ever worn riding stuff? Jodhpurs and so on? The strict, tight-little-hacking jacket look?'

'I'm fifty-five, for God's sake.'

'Age, as you've just so admirably demonstrated, is no bar to a perfect technique and a satisfied clientele. Did you enjoy it? Just a little bit towards the end maybe?'

Shirley froze for a moment then nodded, purse-lipped. Angela smiled lazily.

'Thought so,' she said. 'Easiest money in the world in that case. And they never even touch you. Whatever, darling, I don't have much time so what's it to be? Suburban Slavery, Arthur and *Gardeners' Question Time* or power, liberty and danger?'

Angela stood, towering over Shirley, and seemed to be waiting. She batted her thick eyelids slowly and it struck Shirley that she might not be altogether female.

Shirley felt she was standing on the brink of a precipice but had just been told she was free to fly if she wanted to.

'The other?' she whispered, and bit her lower lip.

'Sorry?' Angela asked.

'The other. The . . . The second thing you said.'

Angela smiled a huge, generous smile. 'Good,' she said and reached into her crocodile clutch bag for a gold fountain pen and what looked like a piece of parchment. 'I sign here.' She scrawled a large A with a flourish and a little x. 'And you,' she placed the pen in Shirley's trembling fingers. It was heavy, good quality. 'You sign there.'

Shirley scanned the old-fashioned manuscript. The words swam. They might as well have been Latin. Perhaps they were.

'Shouldn't I sign this in blood?' she asked.

Angela playfully slapped the back of her wrist.

'Naughty!' she said. 'I can see *you*'re going to be fun.'

271

CAESAR'S
WIFE

CAESAR'S WIFE

I

I should not have been there. The mistress should not as a rule be present at the wife's funeral, unless under such extraordinary circumstances as her being the wife's bosom friend. I was no friend of Rachel's bosom. She never addressed a single word to me. In fact, I believe to this day that she had no idea of my existence and its crucial bearing upon her own, save perhaps in some dark pouch of her shrivelled libido where she might have nursed gratitude for whoever was relieving her of the pressure of her husband's lust.

I had toyed with the charming idea of wearing my thickest veil but rejected it as being too theatrical and attention-seeking. I settled instead upon my least penetrable dark glasses, the ones with the serious tortoiseshell frames. I wore my very best black coat, the one with the delicious rustle, and my best black shoes, which have a solid gold clip about each heel. I resisted the temptation to don scarlet leather gloves, although I had a pair, bought on a macabre whim for just such an occasion. Over a silk blouse in petrol blue – she was not, after all, a bosom friend – I hung my fattest pearls. A vulgar touch perhaps, since they were the ones Tom had given me and weightier, I knew, than any bibelots in her possession, but I was nervous and they always lent me strength.

I need not have worried. As one of Europe's captains of

industry, Tom commanded a horde of acquaintance in his grief. Jewish cemetery chapels are built on the excessive side of generous but even this one was filled to capacity. A fine young man I guessed to be a nephew met me at the door. He had Tom's nose. In answer to his polite enquiry I breathed, 'Oh, Rachel and I went back a *very* long way.' Impressed, he led me to a reserved seat in a side aisle. I had a good view of the Chairman of the Bank of England, the Secretary for Trade and Industry and Rachel's coffin. The flowers were banked about it so thickly that I could smell them from several feet away.

Tom of course had no idea that I was coming. He would have found it deeply offensive. I would not go so far as to say he looked right through me when he took his place but he was not a man to notice things and he did not fail me on this occasion. His silvery-blond hair had been cut that morning, slightly too short, so that he looked cumbersome and vulnerable.

Josh came down the aisle behind his father, in his wheelchair, a black blanket tucked across his lap. I had warned him I was coming, so that he would not betray my presence with his surprise. He could not resist looking for me. Recognizing me without hesitation, he smiled broadly to himself, then remembered where he was, redirected his smile towards the ceiling to stifle it, then bowed his head in sad reflection. Dear Josh.

I had expected to feel bad – the Scarlet Woman – but I didn't. I felt like family. This was unsettling so I slipped away as soon as I could after Rachel's coffin was borne outside. I thought it best not to follow the crowd to the graveside.

II

I should explain.

My involvement with Tom took up only one seventh of my time. Every Wednesday evening he came to the flat he had bought for me in Belsize Village some seventeen years before. Occasionally there was an extra visit, a bonus, on an afternoon perhaps, but he had only ever spent the night on Wednesdays. The rest of my time I passed with total success for a single woman. I had an editorial post at one of the few remaining publishing houses still in the hands of its founding family. I took on no new authors any more, contenting myself with a respectable handful who, like me, had reached the age where nobody cared for them to do anything too surprising.

I had a meeting with one of these, an unlikely bestseller called Polly Brookes, on the afternoon of the funeral. I kept on my good clothes to go into the office, to cause a stir. I normally appeared in nothing stronger than a serviceable wool suit. Kirsty, my secretary, noticed. 'You look smart,' she said, as I walked past her desk to my office.

'Death in the family,' I told her. 'No one close, though.'

'I'll bring you a coffee,' she said.

Polly Brookes was not herself. As a rule she was composed, even to a fault, like a slightly superior librarian. Normally she was the better dressed of us two, wearing her expensive togs with a pained, distressed-gentlefolk air which intensified if one paid them too fulsome a compliment. Today she had met her match but I sensed that my clothes were not the problem. We drank tea together and mulled over possible designs for her latest book-jacket. It was only when I opened a bottle of wine from my little office fridge and let her drain her first glass that she came out with the source of her anxiety. Another author had written an article which accused her books of lacking gumption.

I turned my most reassuring gaze into her doe-eyes as she perched on the sofa's edge. 'Polly, that's nonsense. Who would say a thing like that?'

'Kathy Curry.' Miss Brookes looked up from her wine glass, rekindled anguish in her voice. 'She wrote that my writing had no balls.'

'Well of course it doesn't.'

'Doesn't it?'

I topped up both our glasses. Kathy Curry was another of my authors. She was not in Polly's league but her sales figures were on the way up.

'No. I would be most alarmed if it did, Polly. People don't buy you for balls any more than they'd think of buying Kathy for the quality of her prose. You have a following, Polly, a large following, even in translation, drawn by your flawless prose style and the insights you offer into the human situations people like Kathy neglect.'

'Tales of sad old girls in Kensington?'

'No. Not "sad old girls", nothing so patronizing. The lonely. The passed-over. And not just women. Think of Pierre in *The Good Bachelor*.' I snatched a surreptitious glance at my watch as Miss Brookes drained her third glass.

'You've taken a definite and brave artistic decision', I went on, 'to write about people who don't live happily ever after, whose prince doesn't come and who are to all intents and purposes unremarkable. You take those people and force us to see that, within the narrow confines of their lives, they *are* remarkable. Their lives have drama.' God, I was good!

'Yes, well, you would say that,' she snapped. Then she set down her glass and opened and refastened her bag in the manner, I trusted, of one on the point of leaving.

'Because I'm your editor?' I asked.

'No, because you're, well,' Polly hesitated, 'because you're one of us.'

'Who?'

'The single women, Mary. The lonely, the passed-over and all that.' She actually patted my hand as she stood. Her fingers were dry as her smile. I froze for a moment.

'Yes,' I said and smiled back, gamely. 'Yes. I suppose I am.'

'Sorry. That was uncalled for. It was the wine.'

'No. Quite all right. Anyway, it isn't just me saying that – the *New York Times* said it for over half a bloody page last month. Kathy Curry doesn't even make it into their short reviews section. Forget her.' I touched *her* hand this time. '*Forget* her, Polly. Now,' I drew her attention back to the jackets. 'You think the one with the basket of fruit is the best?'

'Yes.' She pointed. 'With the Roman typeface in that nice green.'

III

This happened all the time. People – including old acquaintances – mistook me for a spinster. A game spinster, of course, because women had to be game in publishing – fond of their food and drink, partial to gossip and smut, one of the lads – but a spinster none the less. It was my fault of course. A sexual reputation is established in one's first twenty-five years and I was a late starter. I had lost my virginity, of course, around the time when everybody else did and, like many girls, I kept quiet about this so that I could please boys and lose it several times over. I spent most of my university years in the library and sitting-rooms of an all-women college. I took a first class degree then spent a year touring Europe with my mother. She waited until Athens to tell me she was dying and we had to hurry home soon after that because her pain became too intense. I was an only child and had never known my father, just as he, I suspected, had scarcely known the woman who later called herself his widow. When she died, a month after our return, I was quite alone and fairly poor.

I joined the family publishing firm thanks to a recommendation from my tutor, whom it published. I joined as a secretary: it being a family firm, women were still expected to work their way up. Before long I was taken firmly under the wings of another secretary and her friend in the foreign rights department – confirmed spinsters both – who somehow manoeuvred me into renting a room in their Maida Vale flat. They entertained royally and often, so a steady stream of interesting Londoners passed through. Every man they allowed to come my way, however, seemed to be either gay or thoroughly involved elsewhere.

Then I met Tom. He was involved elsewhere too, of course, but we came to an immediate unspoken understanding that he could spare a part of himself for me. I was an editor by now, as recompense for having brought two authoress friends into the firm's fiction list, and I was travelling to a book fair in Lisbon. A cookery writer of ours was to give demonstrations there as part of a promotion. As the lone female on the editorial staff I was deemed the most suitable to hold her hand and keep her from the bottle. The one task was unnecessary and the other unfeasible but I held my peace because I had a fondness for Lisbon and was long overdue for a holiday. No less overdue for a rise in salary, I ensured that neither my plane ticket nor my hotel reservation spared the company's coffers.

As I fastened my safety-belt and opened the manuscript I would work on during the flight, a hostess handed me a glass of champagne. I was probably one of the only people in the first class section not to recognize Tom as he walked in and stowed his hand-luggage. His company built the engines that would hurtle us along the runway. It also built the limousines that brought him and several of our travelling companions to the airport and even the elongated shuttle buses that would ferry us across the tarmac in Portugal. His face, I would later learn, appeared regularly in the financial pages and sometimes in the social ones. Rachel's face was unknown outside the charity she chaired – industrialists' wives enjoy luxurious anonymity – but his had become public property. People could not always put a name to it but they remembered it from television interviews and articles on the economy. However relaxed his dress, the less fortunate took one look at his fading blond hair and arrogant features and smelled immense wealth. He had so often been accused of gross injustices or harassed for loans by total strangers that first class air travel was, by then, the nearest he came to public transport.

The seat beside me was meant to remain empty. This was one of the pleasures we were paying for. He should have sat two seats away. He did not smell like a smoker, however, or look like the sort of man who would prattle foolishly while I was trying to work, so I said nothing. He was the one who raised the subject.

'Oh, I'm so sorry,' he said after a few minutes. 'I should have

283

asked you first. Do you mind terribly if I sit here instead of there? It's just that I use the empty seat as a sort of desk and, being left-handed, it's more comfortable to have it on my left-hand side. Do you mind?'

'Not at all.'

'Sure?'

'Quite,' I said.

'We could always swap sides,' he suggested after a pause. I merely smiled and shook my head. Then I turned back to the manuscript on my lap, to stifle the conversation in its infancy.

Fortunately for the course of true love, it was the second novel by Polly Brookes, who was in those days one of my 'discoveries'. Whatever I might say to her face, I always found the air of poised depression in her writing unengaging. The intelligent silence of her characters' suffering was alien to my nature. (Now, perhaps, I understand it a little better although, as you see, I still do not keep silence.)

As I say, it was an early Brookes novel. My eyes strayed easily therefore and noticed his hands. Large hands with spatulate fingers, close-cut nails and a bright dusting of golden hairs. I watched them raise his champagne glass and saw how the hair grew thickly in the shadow of his shirt-cuff and around the thick gold strap of his thick gold watch.

However hard I try, I have never managed to keep reading at the moment when an aeroplane lurches off the runway and soars on a sickening diagonal towards the sky. I'm no Christian and I'm not a nervous person, but it's one of the few times when I pray. I lower my book, stare at the aisle climbing ahead of me or, if I'm feeling less brave, shut my eyes. Then I let my mind's mouth mutter some hasty travel insurance like:

Oh God, keep us safe this flight,
Secure from all our fears.
May angels guard us as we soar,
Till green earth reappears.

I have no shame, you see. I'm only human.

On this instance I kept my eyes open. I let the manuscript sink to my lap and glanced again at his hands. While he scrutinized the contents of a file, they had been playing with his fountain pen, nervously pulling off and clicking on its large black cap. The noise had been threatening to irritate me. Now I saw that his hands were shaking so violently that his aim was not sufficiently accurate to replace the cap. I looked at his face and saw a sheen of sweat on his brow and under his eyes. I reached out and firmly refastened pen and cap for him.

'Thanks,' he said, then dropped it. 'Sorry,' he added. He remained frozen with fear rather than stoop forward, so I retrieved it for him.

'We'll stop climbing any second,' I told him. 'When we level out it doesn't seem so terrible.'

'It seems bloody awful to me.'

'Is it that bad?'

He looked full at me and I saw that his eyes were a true, Cambridge blue. My own eyes are cow brown so I never fail to be disarmed by any intensity of blueness in others.

'You won't tell anyone?'

'I feel sure we know no one in common,' I replied. 'We'd have met by now if we did.'

The aeroplane took away his smile by dipping suddenly through an air pocket. He winced, clutching his knees.

'How on earth do you manage crossing the Atlantic?' I demanded.

'I never have,' he confessed.

'You mean you take a *boat* over?'

'No. I mean I've never been. I send someone else.' I laughed.

'Sorry,' I said. 'I shouldn't laugh, but it seems so unlikely.'

'How do *you* manage?'

'Me? Well, I just give myself up to despair,' I told him. He looked puzzled so I explained. 'Look. We're hurtling along at hundreds of miles an hour, thousands of feet in the air with only a fragile metal box between us and the infinite. We're defying every sensible physical law and every code for survival. If anything goes wrong, we die. We'll have deserved it for doing something so stupid.'

'Well that's a *lot* of help.'

'But it is. It really is. Once you admit that you are utterly powerless, fear becomes a waste of time. Give yourself up. Have another drink. Do your work and be grateful if and when we land. That rigmarole the stewardesses go through with the life-jackets and all the pointing makes things much worse, because it fosters the illusion that an emergency would give one anything to do but die as quickly as possible.'

'Thanks,' he said. 'I'll try.'

I wasn't sure if he was being sarcastic, but he did try. He opened his file and spent the flight alternately frowning and making notes in it. Occasionally the plane would dip or rise dramatically and I would catch him flinching. We smiled at such moments but we didn't speak.

As the minutes passed I became involved, willy-nilly, in the Brookes novel. It was only as we began to dive down through the clouds towards Lisbon and the plane made a series of stalling downward lurches that I thought to look round at him again. The poor man was quite bloodless with terror so I reached out and laid a hand on his to calm him. It seemed the natural thing to do. I left it there until we landed, at which point he heaved a sigh of relief and turned his hand so that our fingers meshed.

'Are you staying here long?'

'Just the weekend. Until Monday afternoon,' I told him.

'Which hotel?' he asked.

'The same as yours, I'd imagine.'

'How perceptive of you.'

'Mary Marlowe.'

'Tom Spellman.' He paused and frowned slightly. 'I should explain that I'm . . .'

'It's all right,' I said. 'I saw the ring before you spoke to me.'

This behaviour was utterly out of character for me but there was no point in my telling him that, for I had given him no reason to believe a word I said. Anyway, violins soar, the screen clouds up and the sordid pleasures of the next few hours are discreetly glossed over. The narrator clears her throat.

We only had to work on our first day. Tom disappeared to power-lunch somebody while I braved the book fair. The cookery writer had barely a sober moment but was a great success. Tom didn't know the city. He thought I spent the weekend parading it for his approval when actually I was posing him a test which he had to pass. I made him leave his car at the hotel so that we could ride trams. I took him on a grimy ferry across the harbour to a clutch of unpretentious cafés where the Lusitanians gorged their well-dressed children on seafood. I walked him around the Gulbenkian with my mouth shut so as to gauge his true reactions and made him eat too much lobster with me so that we could enjoy simultaneous nightmares. I only let him use his car once, on the Sunday evening, to drive us out to Sintra. I described a precise route to the chauffeur then we sat in silence while he steered us round the miniature castles and overgrown villas beneath a lowering sky. The publishers paid for a single room where I did no more than take baths and hang my clothes.

We held hands throughout the flight home and parted without a kiss before we passed through customs. I had expected no more. I had smelt his wealth, after all, and imagined his wife; I knew my place. It took him a week to track me down. I arrived at work one morning to find a great box on my desk packed with arum lilies, like the ones we had admired in a Lisbon courtyard. (I told my colleagues these had come from the cookery writer, which the fools readily believed.) Tom and I spent five or so lunchtimes, a rash Friday afternoon – I pleaded trouble with wisdom teeth – and the first of our countless Wednesday evenings, in an hotel beside the British Museum.

Honesty has never rated as highly as invention in my pantheon of virtues but I now place a hand on my powdered breast to swear that the manner of our meeting and the glorious weekend that followed were precisely as I have described: unexpected, uncharacteristic, unrepeatable. If our brief encounter in Lisbon bore all the trappings of an unfingered paperback romance, our London assignations hailed from a second-rate *film noir* with Tom and I a cut-price imitation of Fred MacMurray and Barbara Stanwyck. Whereas Tom had been relaxed and alert in Portugal, now I saw him tense and exhausted. The need for secrecy prevented our being seen to leave or arrive together and the lack of time meant that our conversation – one of my chief pleasures before – was restricted to a minimum. The room was ugly, leaving no pleasure to our eyes but one another's bodies, which it displayed in the least flattering light. Tom seemed older and thicker-waisted than he had before and I – shorn of antiquities and culture – less worldly, less assured. These were early tutorials in an uneasy sexual education. Occasionally Tom bored, hurt or disgusted me. Frequently the glance of the hotel receptionist withered my self-esteem. Flattered by his need for me, surprised at my continuing appetite for him, I questioned, whenever we were apart, the common sense in keeping our next appointment. Then Tom sent me a note bearing an address in Belsize Park Gardens. A bunch of keys followed, under separate cover.

The flat was carved out of half the ground floor of a mid-Victorian building. It was a recent conversion, with a brand new kitchen and – height of decadence – a bath with taps in the middle. The street was not of the smartest (it has since come up in the world) and the house was in some need of repair, but the flat was newly decorated. It had few rooms – only one bedroom – but one of these was a vast affair with high ceilings, a bay window overlooking the garden and a riot of *faux* rococo plasterwork. Standing in there, on the old parquet floor, with the rain lashing the horse-chestnut trees outside, and little fish cavorting with acanthus leaves about the ceiling, I could imagine myself in a house on the Bois de Boulogne. Even unfurnished, it felt like an interior described by Proust.

There was a pile of typed pages on the blush-pink marble mantelpiece. Beside them was a note from Tom.

Mary darling,

Herewith the papers making this place yours for the next 999 years. All you have to do is sign on the line I've marked on page five and post these to the solicitor whose name appears on page one. There's no mortgage or anything and the bills will be paid by standing order. I've opened an account for you because I thought you'd probably rather buy your own furniture and paintings and so on. You know things can't be any other way but if all this disgusts you, I quite understand. All you need do is return the key to the solicitor with the unsigned papers and I'll never bother you again. If I don't hear anything to the contrary, I'll drop by on Wednesday at seven. This place is yours and yours alone, my darling. The locks have just been changed and you have the only keys.

Tom

Naturally I had to read the note through several times. Then I read back and forth through every opaque sentence of the legal document. I walked around the flat. I opened and closed the silent doors of fitted wardrobes and peered into the glistening maws of fridge and oven. I tried lying on the king-size bed and even christened the lavatory. Then I returned to the great, Proustian sitting-room and took a pen from my bag to sign on the dotted line. I imagined my reflection in a high gilded mirror over the mantelshelf, lit by twin candelabra, in emerald silk with my hair up, and I thought to myself, '*Maîtresse.*'

IV

I took shameless advantage of there having been a death in the family to leave work a little early. I wanted to cook something for Tom – a custom I had rather let slide lately, having discovered a French restaurant which delivered. (Tom would sit up in bed like a mischievous invalid while I waited on him from covered dishes in the manner, I fancied, of Grace Kelly in *Rear Window*.)

Tonight, having drunk too much after the funeral, he would need bulky, unsubtle food in primary colours. I bought him fillet steak (I would grill myself a chicken breast), green peppercorns for the sauce and vivid French beans, which I would steam then toss, still hot, in a walnut vinaigrette. I covered a large plate with scarlet, weeping cross-sections of beef tomatoes, nestled a few naked garlic cloves among them, tossed on a pinch of coarse sea-salt and drizzled the whole with the headily fragrant olive oil Tom bought me from a specialist near Spitalfields. And then? Only coffee. No pudding. As he liked to point out, I was his 'just dessert'. If ever I made a pudding, if ever I reached for egg yolks, vanilla sugar and bitter cooking-chocolate, it was for their anaphrodisiac properties. In the code of our erotic conversation, puddings were my red camellias.

I laid out the pink cashmere dress (his favourite), shook sweet almond oil into the steaming bath-water and lay down for a soak, to soften my callouses and still my mind. He had not visited me for three weeks, not since the dismal evening when he had told me about Rachel's stroke and paced up and down the flat saying, 'What am I going to do? I don't know what to do.' He had wept like a child then and I had felt helpless since anything I said emerged, inevitably, weighted with seventeen years of envious bias.

You must understand, I had never wished Rachel dead.

The statement hangs before you, golden, pure, plump with conviction. It's a lie, of course; a slack pear of dishonesty. Watch closely and you see the first brown saggings of its skin.

I had wished Rachel dead many times. At first, in the first two

291

years, when I ached for his touch and found the wait from Wednesday to Wednesday intolerable, I used to fantasize to myself about her being knocked efficiently to oblivion by a jack-knifing lorry or being overcome by paint-fumes (she was forever redecorating their house) or drowning, inexpertly drunk, in her swimming pool. In Tom's presence, I merely fantasized, kitten-ish, that she might fall in love with someone else. If she left Tom, he would appear the injured party and we two could neatly side-step blame. As time wore on, however, I ceased to resent Rachel and found myself almost in her debt. I was not exactly on a perpetual honeymoon but my experience of Tom was inevitably more romantic and flattering than hers. I had never washed his underwear or ironed his shirts, never had to like his friends or enchant his colleagues. I had another life elsewhere. She, unless Tom had grossly underestimated her powers of deception and initiative, had not. When her husband and I clinked glasses, I mutely wished her a long and healthy life. While I reaped the benefits, she shouldered the burden. Until now.

Tom had indeed had too much to drink. He all but threw me over his shoulder on arrival and bore me to the bedroom for sex so swift that it was over for him before I had even begun to enjoy myself. Most definitely sex rather than lovemaking. I was forbearing, grateful that he was still capable in his late fifties of demonstrating such urgent, pubescent lust. I made him take a shower, however, to wake himself up and when I fed him his peppered steak at the fireside it took the desired effect. We made achingly slow love on the carpet. My way.

He was such a bear compared to me that we could sit quite comfortably on the floor with me between his thighs, leaning against his chest. We sat like that afterwards, wrapped in dressing gowns, and ate the remaining beans in our fingers. It was a favourite posture of mine because while he leaned back against the sofa, I could hug his calves to my sides, stroking their thick hair, and feel utterly safe. I always wondered what my colleagues would say, or Polly Brookes, if they saw me in such unspinsterly *déshabillé* and abandon, wrapped in such a poundage of important male.

'How was it?' I asked at last. 'The funeral.'

'Bearable,' he said. 'Massive turn-out, of course.'

'Would Rachel have been flattered?'

'No.' He sighed. 'Poor Rachel was too cynical. She'd have said they only turned up in such numbers because of her bank balance and my name.'

'Did she have many friends?'

'Oh yes. She preferred to play several off against each other than to single out one or two to be, you know, really close.'

'She met them through her charity work?'

'Some, yes. She got out a lot, you know.'

'She wasn't totally in your shadow?'

'No,' he said, and rubbed the backs of my ears with his nose. 'You know she wasn't.'

I passed him the last bean and reached for the plate of tomatoes.

'How's Josh?' I asked.

'Exhausted. He left pretty early. He'll be coming into work tomorrow, I expect. You can ask him about it then.'

'He hates crowded parties,' I said. 'In fact I think he hates parties full stop. I can see why. If you're stuck in a wheelchair, you can't slip away from ghastly people. And even if you could, you couldn't see where the more interesting people were who you wanted to reach. Dear Josh.'

'You've got very fond of him, haven't you?'

'Of course I have. He's my best friend. And no,' I continued, hearing his cynical snort, 'his being your son had nothing to do with it. If anything, that made me steer clear of him to start with.'

'Hmm.'

We fell silent for a few minutes, listening to the hissing of gas jets in the fake coal fire. Tom straightened his legs and leaned forward to slip a cushion to the base of his spine, then he brought them in more closely about me. I knew in an instant what was coming next. I toyed with diversionary tactics but dismissed them as cowardly.

'Just think,' he said then stopped.

'What?' I asked. A droplet of sweat tickled the underside of one of my arms.

'I mean, it's awful to bring it up so soon . . .'

'What?' I asked again, knowing perfectly well.

'I could start seeing you on other nights now,' he went on finally. 'Not just on Wednesdays.'

'Yes,' I said, hugging his legs. 'Now I'm left a totally open territory.'

'Have you minded?' he asked.

'Minded what?'

'Being, you know, a mistress all this time.'

'You know I haven't. I never do anything I don't want to.'

'Yes, but it can't have been much fun.' He kissed one of my ears. 'Sometimes you must have sat there wondering when the party was going to get going. My God, when we met you were younger than Josh is now! You were so young and you gave everything up!'

'No I didn't.'

'I sincerely hope you did.'

294

'I kept my job,' I protested, 'I kept my friends, I kept all the things I enjoy but, in secret, I gained you.'

'But that's my point exactly,' he said. ' "In secret". No one wants their lover in secret. It isn't natural. The number of times I left here and wanted to be taking you with me to show you off to people!'

'Darling,' I said, and kissed his knee. 'You're so sweet. Do you think of me as the natural type?'

I knew what was coming. I *knew* what was coming. Why were men, even adorable men, so predictable? There was always a chip too little subterfuge in their genes.

'Look at me,' he said. 'This is important.' A little stiff, I slid forward from between his legs then turned round to lean against the sofa beside him.

'What?' I asked, stifling a nervous yawn.

'I'm going to make up to you for the last seventeen years,' he said. 'I want to make an honest woman of you.'

'What a disgusting phrase!' I said. 'I trust that was a joke.'

'The wording was. Not the sentiment.'

'Oh.' I laughed, playing for time. 'Was that a proposal, then? No one's ever asked me that before.'

'Mary, I want you to marry me. I want us to live together.'

'But . . .'

'You wouldn't have to move. Not at first, at least. I'd sell the old house – it's too full of memories anyway and Josh wouldn't mind.'

'Josh would be thrilled.' I stroked his hair but he stopped me, clasping my hand in his. 'You could give him a place of his own.'

'You could keep your job.'

'That's big of you,' I said.

295

'You could even keep your name.'

'Bigger still.'

'Oh Mary, please. I want you with me always.'

'Yes, but why do we have to get *married*?' I pleaded. 'Marriage is so, you know, three-piece-suite.'

'I . . . Well I know it sounds pompous . . . No, it *is* pompous but it's also true,' he said, then hesitated.

'What is?' I asked.

'That I have a position to maintain. Anyway, if we were married you'd have more security.'

'I suppose so.'

'And we could have children. It's not too late.' I let out a small shriek.

'What's wrong?' he asked. He looked quite shocked.

'Tom, darling, one thing at a time. Please?'

'OK.' He reached for his wine and muttered, 'I thought you wanted children.'

'Don't sulk.'

'I'm not sulking. I'm just tired. Tired and depressed and I've spent all day bloody burying Rachel and . . . Are you saying you won't marry me?'

His eyes searched my face. He looked wretched and it was all I could do not to say yes there and then and be done with it. Anything for a quiet life. A quiet, luxurious life. A quiet, luxurious, secure life. No! Rage, rage against the reading of the banns!

'I'm saying, darling Tom, that it's not a decision I can make straight away.'

'Why the hell not? I thought you loved me.'

'Oh Tom, now you're being childish.' I stood. I needed to stalk about. 'Of course I love you. Love and marriage, however, are not necessarily linked. One can make the other shrivel up and die. In some cases the two can even be mutually exclusive. You of all people should know that.' He sighed. I couldn't look at him. 'I'm sorry,' I went on. 'That was cheap. I know you loved her – at first at least. And she loved you. In her way. I'm sorry she died so soon. I really am.'

'For purely selfish reasons.' He was sharper than I thought. I hid behind a flare of anger.

'What the hell do you mean by that?'

'Don't,' he said quietly.

'What?'

'Just don't.'

'OK.'

I continued stalking, clearing away the supper things as I did so. Tom raised himself on to the sofa and arranged the dressing gown chastely over his knees. I returned with coffee. He accepted a cup but left it at his feet, undrunk.

'I don't understand,' he said at last. 'I mean, what did you expect? Did you expect me to keep paying your bills . . .'

'I've told you,' I cut in, 'I'd be more than happy to pay them myself.'

He raised a hand. His tone momentarily icy. 'Just let me finish. Did you expect me to buy you this place, pay your bills and take huge risks to see you . . .'

'Oh huge risks. Death-defying!'

'. . . and not expect to marry you some day?'

'Tom, I hate to say this but in seventeen years you've not once suggested marrying me except in order to explain why it was impossible.'

'It was impossible to divorce Rachel.'

'Because she owned half the stock.'

'For whatever reasons, and that was not the most important

one, it was impossible. But you were always on my mind. It was you I loved, you I wished I'd married and you I want to marry now. I just don't understand.'

He looked tearful. I sat beside him and took his huge hands in mine.

'Tom, listen. Listen to me. I haven't said I won't marry you. If you want a more positive answer I'll say I probably will. How's that?' Tom snorted, and took his hands away.

'It seems all too clear to me,' I pursued, angered in my turn, 'that you *don't* understand. You see the whole case in terms of "making an honest woman" out of me . . .'

'That was a joke.'

'Whatever. As you said, you meant it in spirit. I love you, Tom. I love you very much and I'm thrilled that you want to marry me. But you must see that I haven't been pining away all these years waiting for bloody wedding bells to tinkle. I've had the best of both worlds. Six days a week I've been a busy working woman, enjoying all the social independence of a bachelor. The seventh day, when I've been able to see you, has been important and the joy it's given me has buoyed me up on all the other six but it hasn't been the centre of my life.'

'Hasn't it?'

'No more than it's been the centre of yours.'

'Now wait a minute . . .'

'No, Tom. I'm sorry. You've had your wife, your son, your mistress and your empire. Now quite possibly, if you hadn't had your empire I'd have come before Rachel. But the fact remains that I didn't. At best I came second and in strict terms of calendar time I came third or even fourth. By the same token you've only been taking up one seventh of my time. I'm the first to admit that, in crude terms, you *bought* that seventh with this place. But you have to understand,' – here I tried a smile but he wouldn't catch my eye, damn him – 'if I'm hesitant about surrendering the other six sevenths.'

Tom drained his glass and stood. He came to hug me, his dressing gown coming adrift.

'So,' he said, 'you'll "probably" marry me.'

'Yes,' I said. 'But.'

'But what?'

'But couldn't I just carry on being your mistress? Or are you delivering an ultimatum?'

'Of course I'm not.' He kissed the top of my head and rocked me as though we were dancing. 'Just think,' he said, 'we can go on holiday together.'

'Again.'

'Yes. Again. Properly.'

'We could go back to Lisbon. Or Sintra.'

'We could rent a little palace in the hills there. And think of our life in London! We can go shopping together. We can go to the theatre. We can have friends round. Do what other couples do.'

'Tom?'

'What?'

'We don't have to be married to be like other couples.'

Now he laughed. He was exasperated but believed, deep down, that he had won me over and that I was just being difficult. Poor unsuspecting Tom. We turned out the lights and went back to bed. He was staying the night. Although he was drained of energy, I could tell, he made love to me again. He was whipping himself into a kind of angry vigour, trying to crush my will, and I enjoyed myself, letting him believe that it was thoroughly crushed. When he fell heavily asleep, however, his face in my shoulder, one of his great legs straddling mine, my will had never been more active. Josh would be back at work tomorrow. I would make him cancel any appointments and let me buy him lunch. The Son and the Mistress had urgent plans to lay.

V

The charity whose chair Rachel had filled until her death, provided financial support to the victims of medical incompetence and campaigned on their behalf for legal restitution. She had a sad interest vested in the case. Josh, the only child born to her and Tom, was physically handicapped as a result of a painkiller prescribed to Rachel during pregnancy. His upper half and his brain were untouched but he was born without feet or calves. His thighs were rounded stumps. He was one of a blighted generation. Such were her guilt feelings after his birth that Rachel had herself sterilized.

Josh Spellman's sunny nature, alert mind and seraphic good looks were Nature's compensation for mankind's negligence. By way of shoes, he had a pair of thick leather pads which strapped around his stockinged stumps and buckled to a kind of belt. With these, he could run, play, even climb stairs and join in at football. He was one of the crowd at his nursery school and for some years afterwards, winning over the other children's doubts with his bravery and wit. Trouble arose, however, with the onset of puberty and the desperate wish for conformity that came with it. Although Josh grew no less rapidly than his friends, the difference in their heights became more painfully obvious. As their hormones got to work, other boys isolated him from their smutty conversations and magazine-fingerings, embarrassed – erroneously, it happened – that the Wonderful World of Sex would lie beyond Josh's capabilities or experience. Josh retreated into books and took to a wheelchair. No less patronizing in their assumptions, Rachel and Tom were unaware that this isolation was partly self-imposed. The wise boy had a tenacious survival instinct.

'I'm a *rara avis*,' he joked during our first private conversation, 'a thalidomide fairy. If I were albino too, I'd probably qualify for a generous government subsidy.'

Josh joined the publishers in much the way I had; soon after leaving university, because there was nothing else he wanted to do. He was interviewed by four of us and impressed us immediately with his consuming passion for books. He had read more widely than anyone else we had seen – devouring trash fiction with the same witty appetite he brought to literary biography or the demands of high art. He knew about bindings, about paper, about type-setting. Our only fear was that he might find his first editorial work too limited. We need not have worried. He proved an indefatigable reader of unsolicited manuscripts and unearthed four minor successes in his first year with us. In time, he became our poetry editor.

Tom, of course, was nervous as hell about Josh getting to know me. He rang up in a flap the moment he heard that Josh was coming to us for an interview and for weeks afterwards was convinced that his son would somehow divine our relationship. In the event, Josh needed no intuition. I told him several months after his joining us. I had to. We had become friends. I remember we had been discussing a particularly lurid novel about suburban family life in Beckenham in the sixties, when Josh said,

301

'Of course, I was spared all that hair-raising frankness at home. I honestly don't think my parents have ever had sex with each other in my lifetime.'

'Really?' I asked, pouring more apple juice.

'Really and truly. Separate bedrooms from day one. The official reason was that he tends to be up so late and likes to crash around rather in the morning. But I knew it was actually because she hates sex. She was raised by nuns and the silly woman believed every word they said. Deep down she thinks sex is wrong if it's pursued for anything but bringing lovely babies into the world for christening. You know I was only eight when she told me she had got her tubes tied and why?'

'No!'

'I was rather cross, I remember. I wanted brothers and sisters. Sometimes, in my darker moments – yes Mary, I do have them – sometimes I think that perhaps she had a *stupendous* sex life with him when they first married. I think she did it with him on garage floors and kitchen tables and every which way. I think he was quite a stud when they met – he's quite a bit younger than her, of course – and he sort of woke her up. You can see it sometimes from the way she looks at him when she's had a few too many. And then, when I was born, she reverted to her convent school mentality and decided that I was a punishment for her naughtiness. I think all my lifetime she's been trying to save her soul. No. Not a sexual animal, my Ma. And twisted! If spirits have bones, dear Mary, hers is without a straight one.'

'How does he manage?' I dared.

'Oh I think he manages very well. His own mother died young so Ma's become a sort of mother to him – someone to honour and obey. He's probably got somebody in a well-appointed love-nest somewhere. We'll never know about *her* until his funeral. She'll be the one crying in a veil, who nobody knows. She'll have ostentatiously good legs and will have dressed rather too well in order to cover her nerves.

'But Mary,' he went on, 'what about you?'

'Me?' I fancy I blushed.

'Yes. Everyone here treats you like their maiden aunt but you're not half-way old enough.'

'Thanks.'

'You're not . . .' He searched for a round-edged euphemism. 'You're not a Radcliffe Hall, by any chance?'

'Certainly not.'

'Pity. But I'm not surprised. I suppose you've got a secret lover tucked away in Camberwell or somewhere.' And then Josh grinned at me with the kind of suggestive depravity only angels and small boys can get away with and suddenly the years of telling nobody seemed a tremendous strain.

So I said,

'If I told you, you wouldn't believe me and if I never told you, you'd never guess.'

'Give me three.'

'All right. One.'

'A cabinet minister.'

'Wrong. Two.'

'Your boss and mine.'

'Wrong again,' I crowed. 'Three.'

He thought hard this time and said, 'My father.'

'Wrong three times,' I replied quickly. 'Told you.' But I hadn't fooled him.

At first I thought he was joking when he said, 'It's no problem you know. Your secret's safe as the grave with me.' He said it in such a teasing way. He carried on teasing over the next few days, ringing me at my desk only to ask things like, 'He always wears flannel pyjamas with Ma. Does he keep a spare set at your place – just in case of chills?'

Then one day I snapped – he had teased me at the wrong moment, while I was clawing over a contract with my least favourite agent – and I said, 'Stop it, Josh. All right? Enough's enough. Stop it.' He raised his hands in mute apology. Later on he returned with a punnet of strawberries as a peace offering.

'Mary?'

'What? I'm busy.'

'I do love you, you know.'

'Good. What else?'

'I would never, ever tell him I knew.'

'Good.'

And that was that. We buried the hatchet, shared the strawberries and the subject was never raised again directly. We would merely make fleeting references to whether a Wednesday evening had gone well or not. I think our colleagues began to think Wednesdays were my bridge nights. At least, none of them was sufficiently curious to ask. My only penance for my indiscretion was to allow Josh to call me Ma. He told everyone it was short for Mary-Mother-of-Us-All and soon, for the least flattering but most disguising reasons, the misnomer caught on throughout the office.

Josh disliked restaurants because they so rarely made provision for wheelchairs – although he would occasionally make an exception and walk to one. He used to send his secretary out for pots of take-away food from a vegetarian restaurant in Covent Garden and invite people to lunch at his desk. Insulted at this slapdash way of entertaining, Josh's poets were always won over to it once they discerned they were among the chosen few to enter a charmed circle.

I booked him for a desk-lunch as soon as I came in, the morning after Tom's unwelcome proposal. I sent Kirsty out in a cab to bring us a meal from a Thai restaurant where I brought so much custom that my desire was law. We ate in my office because people tended to drop in at Josh's and I wanted him to myself.

'Still in mourning, as you see,' he said as he wheeled himself in. He indicated the black blanket across the lap. Normally he wore a red or bright blue one. 'Extraordinary how it shuts people up. That ghastly man from accounts – the one with the breath – was in the lift just now and he didn't say a word. I think I should revert to normal by degrees. Perhaps I should wear Black Watch tartan next?'

He put on his brakes then leaned across the desk and kissed me. 'You looked wonderful yesterday,' he went on.

'You saw me.'

'How could I miss you, dressed up like Jackie Onassis in a supermarket? Bad, *bad* woman!'

'I was going to hide myself somewhere but that nice young man insisted on showing me up to the front.'

'Yes. Cousin Martin. Hasn't he grown up *well*!'

'Poor Josh. Was it hell? Well of course it was.'

'Actually, it wasn't too bad. Rather like a wedding but cheaper. Lots of aunts I hadn't seen in ages and won't need to see again for a while. And some people said such sweet things. It was very odd but by the time I left I'd got the feeling that the old witch showed a completely different side of herself to the outside world.'

'Most people do, don't they?'

'Yes but these were people from committees and so on, people

I'd never met, and they gave the honest impression that she'd been a pleasure to know. Mmm! Are those little parcels of duck?'

'Yes.'

He shut his eyes with pleasure as he bit into one. 'No one else in this building could ever get a take-away out of those people,' he teased. 'You wield such power, Madam.'

'Talking of which.'

'Yes?'

'I saw Sir again last night,' I confessed.

'Poor Ma. He was knocking it back at the get-together afterwards. He must have been wrecked by the time he got away. I hope he wasn't, well,' Josh quivered an eyebrow suggestively, 'you know . . . rough.'

I saw no way to break the news tactfully so I came straight out with it. 'He asked me to marry him.'

Josh was far too well brought up to splutter his food but he registered suitable shock. 'How did you reply?' he asked after a moment.

'I said I wasn't sure but that I'd probably accept him. He didn't take it very well.'

'I bet he didn't. "Probably" is not a word he's used to.'

'Do you think I should have said yes?'

'Well of course I'd love you for a mother, Ma, but I think it's up to you.' Josh munched a moment or two, lost in thought. 'Well!' he exclaimed at last.

'What?'

'I never thought he would. I mean. Well. Somehow I got so used to the idea of him just making do with things the way they were. He was so miserable with it the first time around, it seems odd that he wants to get married again so soon.'

'I think he'd wait for a few months. I'd make him. He says he wants to make an honest woman of me.'

'I trust he was joking.'

'He said he was but, Josh, I still think that's how he thinks of it deep down. Oh Josh.'

'What, Ma? Don't look like that. You look miserable.'

'Josh, I don't think I want things to change. I wish your mother hadn't died.'

'Do you really?'

'Really.' Josh picked at some more food, evading grief. 'Of course,' he mumbled, 'you never knew her.'

'I liked things the way they were. I liked being myself, being Ma most of the time and having Tom tucked away waiting for me on Wednesday evenings.'

'Best of both worlds.'

'But if I become the second Mrs Spellman . . .'

'The very idea!'

'Quite. But if I do, I'm worried things will have to change.'

'He'd never make you give up your job!'

'Certainly not. He's already said as much. But. Oh, I dunno. Josh, I don't want to be a *wife*.'

Josh gave me his shrewdest look, the look he used to melt agents into honesty and authors into subjection. 'Is my Ma worried, by any chance, that if she becomes the Wife, someone else will have to become the Mistress?'

'No.'

'Are you sure?'

I hesitated. 'Not really,' I confessed. 'But my main fear is losing my independence. I may be only his mistress but when I fill in forms I can still write single. I like that. And yet . . .'

'You love him.' I nodded, overwhelmed with a not unpleasant wave of sad-spiced exhilaration.

Josh ate on for a while and I drank some hot-and-sour soup. Kirsty came in and left some letters for me to sign. I took a phone call from a literary scout in Amsterdam. Josh was deep in meditation, his sweet brow furrowed.

'Josh, forgive me,' I said after a while. 'I've suddenly realized how monstrous I'm being. This is the last thing you want to talk about. For God's sake, Rachel's funeral was only yesterday.'

'Ssh!' He flapped a handful of parcelled duck to silence me and flicked chilli sauce on my blotter. 'Let me eat for a bit,' he said, with his mouth full. 'I'm getting an idea.' Silenced, I waited for several minutes more. People returned from pubs and sandwich bars to congregate, chattering, by the coffee machine on my landing.

At last Josh wiped his lips and fingers on a paper napkin and sat back.

'Simple,' he said. 'It's ingenious, if a little late Henry James.'

'Tell.'

'You're the only other Ma I ever want,' he explained slowly, 'but to keep you happy, we find Sir another wife.'

'Josh, really!'

'No. I mean it. Don't laugh. It's perfectly feasible. London's crawling with women who'd love to marry him; women past childbearing age, women with careers, who want nothing better than a rich, influential husband to provide for their old age and give them a little extra social mobility. They'd snap him up.'

'I don't want him snapped up. I want him for myself!'

'You'd *have* him for yourself, all except the boring bits that the Late Lamented used to take care of. He'd be "snapped up" like a slightly-worn bargain, for the convenience of it, not for love. We could even find him a society lesbian. There are plenty about.'

'No,' I said, entering into the spirit of things, 'I don't think he'd like that. Not an open marriage – he's so fearfully respectable.'

'The Jewish streak, I'm afraid,' Josh sighed. 'I have it too. Perhaps you're right. And your side of things would be so straightforward whereas the society lesbian's extra-marital attachments could lead to all sorts of messy complications. No. Pass me your address book. What we need, dear Ma, if you'll pardon my sexism, is a good old-fashioned spinster.'

VI

As one who had long spent her days in disguise as one of the breed, my address book yielded bachelor girls in abundance, and spinsters, and 'wimmin', and even the occasional unmodified old maid. Popular as a witty, dependable single man with no visible sex life and no discernible amorous future, Josh was then able to double the list. We pored over it long and hard, like schoolboys over a chess problem or a game of Battleships. Just as bored civil servants ring each other to trade solutions to the same crossword, so, for days, the lines between our flats and desk-tops hummed with proffered names, thumb-nail biographies and character assassinations.

'Ma?'

'Josh.'

'Can we talk?'

'Yes. Your father won't be here for at least another hour. It's

so strange having him come round so often. In the last fortnight I've had what used to be several months'-worth of him.'

'How are you coping?'

'It's lovely,' I said. 'I suppose. He's moved in a suitcaseful of
clothes. I think he's trying to show me how easily we could
become man and wife.'

'Now Ma.' A warning tone entered Josh's voice. 'There's a very
thick line separating man and wife from lover and mistress.'

'I know, Josh. I know.'

I lay down on the bed. I had just stepped out of the bath and
needed to cool down before I dressed again. I used to have two
quite separate wardrobes; a set of clothes to be single in and a
different, noticeably sexier batch for a role as mistress. Now
that Tom had expanded visiting hours beyond my once-sacred
Wednesdays, my dry-cleaners could not keep up. Distinctions
between erotic and motherly were being blurred. The night
before I had greeted him in an ensemble much like something
Rachel would have worn and I sensed the comparison cross his
mind as well. He had undressed me as quickly as possible.

'How are things at your end?' I asked Josh. 'All set?'

'Table's laid, chicken breasts are stuffed, wine's on ice and
my heart's aflame. I've even polished my wheels.'

'His photograph was so good-looking. How did you meet
him?'

'I told you. It's a sort of encounter group.'

'And he's not . . .?'

'No, Ma. He's whole in body and in mind.'

'I know it's silly of me but it just sounds a bit kinky.'

'So? We'll have *beautiful* children. Now listen, Ma. There's
not much time and I've just had another idea for you.'

'Who?'

'Jasmine.'

'Which?'

'Jasmine Wilton.'

'No.'

'Why ever not? She's awfully nice but not too bright. She has a career, she's devoted to her country garden and she needs a man like Sir.'

'Exactly,' I pointed out. 'She needs him much too much. He might be flattered into abandoning me. Dreadful idea.'

'Sorry.'

'I was thinking maybe Pauline Savory,' I countered.

'Now there's an idea.'

'Hmm. She's so cold-blooded, she might not even mind if she found out.'

'She could even draw up a contract to protect your various interests.'

'A little vindictive, though. Remember what she did to the Goddards over the party.'

'Oh yes. She was rather a wicked fairy. It was terribly funny, though.'

'Not for the Goddards.'

'Scratch her off the list then.'

'Who does that leave?' I asked.

'Not a wonderful selection.' On our separate beds we glanced down our heavily edited duplicate lists. Judith Blake, Joan Desmond, Harriet Forbes, Ruky Delgado.

'Not her,' said Josh suddenly. 'Absolutely not her. The Stepmother from Hell.' We scratched Ruky and read on. Joely Lyons. Cathy Hobson. Margaret Creighton-Fermor. I pictured them on isolated chairs around the walls of a party. Proud wallflowers in their neglected prime. It was depressing reading.

'I know they're available', I asked, 'but are they really all in need of a husband?'

'Well, they're none of them society lesbians,' Josh said. 'My research is meticulous. Though I suppose they could always be closet mistresses like you – God knows when they'd fit a lover in. Joely and Margaret are never at home and Cathy gets lonely in anything less than a crowd.'

'No one's in need of a husband,' I told him. 'It's just a neurosis into which we have to persuade them. God but they'd be so insulted if they knew we were doing this!' Josh only chuckled.

'The other problem,' I went on.

'Yes?'

'Is that these are all women we know to have been either married or thoroughly involved at some stage of their lives.'

'They've each got a driving licence. So?'

'Well I know it's sordid but we need someone with no points of erotic comparison. I think we need a virgin.' Josh paused as though I had suggested uprooting mandrake by the light of a full moon.

'How would we tell?' he asked. 'We *can't* have them inspected.'

'Oh, you can always tell!' I scoffed.

'*Can* you? I don't think I know any any more. Even my so-called maiden aunts have one by one confessed to having had their moments. How many virgins do you know, Ma? Besides Patrick Lynton, that is.' I thought for a moment, and then it came to me. The perfect candidate.

'One,' I said. 'Polly Brookes.'

There was an awe-struck silence on the other end of the line. 'We couldn't!' Josh breathed at last. 'Could we? She's so famous nowadays.'

'Exactly. Perfect.'

'Perfect. But how?'

'She has a new novel coming out later in the month.'

'Damn. That'll have her gallivanting all over the country giving readings.'

'Not before I give her a little launch party.'

'You're a bad woman, Ma. A bad, *bad* woman.'

'Well what would you have me do?' I asked him, plaintively. 'Should I just give up and marry him myself?'

'Never!' Josh protested. 'This is far too much fun.'

'Josh,' I pleaded, 'these are people's lives we're manipulating.' Josh turned serious. He was always convincingly grave when defending the indefensible.

'Mary Marlowe, we aren't just looking after Number One. If you married Sir and it didn't work, that would be two lives blighted. Bring Polly into the equation and it could work so well. All three of you could be happy. And if it was a disaster, he'd still have you. The two of you could escape the wreckage unscathed.'

I wondered if I could bring myself to attend Polly's wedding. I pictured myself buying them a present, choosing myself a hat.

'It's too unprofessional,' I decided. 'Polly's one of my longest standing authors. It would be like sleeping with a patient or seducing a witness.'

'Balls, Ma. However it turns out, it will be just what her writing could do with. Look on it as a creative editorial contribution. She'll be grateful to you one day.'

'Josh.'

'Mmm?'

'What do you get out of all this?'

'Two stepmothers for the price of one.'

VII

Polly Brookes and I might have been close had she not been an inveterate liar. Many novelists are given to exaggeration in their conversation – their creative impulse springs, after all, from a need to restructure reality according to their own lights. Polly went too far, however. She would accuse one's answering-machine of being faulty rather than confess to having passed through a harmless antisocial phase.

'I've been ringing and ringing,' she would say. 'I've been trying to contact you for *days*.' She was incapable of answering a simple greeting with a simple formality.

'Hello, Polly. How are you?' was invariably met, not with, 'I'm fine, thanks. And yourself?' but with a catalogue of disasters. These – taxi crashes, dislocated joints, sexual harassment, dead loved ones – were of a kind that were never immediately disprovable and yet aroused one's instinctive disbelief. The maddening thing was that, despite her creative gift, she didn't even lie well. It was as though every plot-twist she thought up for a novel then rejected as too far-fetched, haunted her brain until she gave it verbal release.

A truer friend or a more honest person would have challenged Polly long ago. 'I'm sorry, Polly,' I should have said, 'but I simply don't believe you. Why is it, Polly,' I should have asked, 'that all the appalling things that happen to you, only happen when you're on your own?'

As the years went by her lies grew daring, as though to test my endurance, and came often to involve famous people she might conceivably have met. It became a fantasy of mine, as we sat in my office, or walked, chatting, out to lunch, to trip up her fictive

314

progress with a calm negative. The results, I liked to imagine, would be as extravagant as anything in a medieval exorcism; she would let out a banshee shriek, she would scratch my face, she would turn bright green or even, like another Wicked Witch of the West, melt away leaving only a Chanel suit, a pool of steaming slime and a six-hundred-page manuscript, damp at the edges.

I never did challenge her, though. I lacked the honesty. I didn't like her enough to want to assume the responsibility of rebuilding her after the inevitable collapse. I could have liked her. She was clever, and pretty – in a Bambi fashion – and amusingly acerbic when roused. Her lies kept me at a distance, however, as they did others. Perhaps that was the whole idea and she liked herself in glorious isolation; a Norma Desmond of the literary set.

Typically, once I had set my heart on pinning her down for lunch to broach the subject of Tom, she played hard-to-get. She cancelled me twice, with last-minute excuses about a burst water-main and a mysterious cousin from Toronto. On the third attempt, she arrived so late that I had already picked my way through a salad and was on the point of returning to the office.

'Mary,' she said, hurrying forward to kiss my cheek, 'I'm so *sorry*! You wouldn't believe it. No sooner out of the house than I realized I'd locked the only set of keys inside, so I had to break a window to get in and then, of course, I had to wait until a man could come to replace the glass.'

'Poor Polly,' I said. 'Come on. Sit down.'

'He took an absolute age coming, of course, and when he got there it turned out he was only measuring the window before fetching the glass. I did try to ring you but there didn't seem to be anyone on the switchboard at all. You should have a word with your telephonists. You really should. Oh. Hello.'

315

She turned to the waiter who had slipped to her side. 'A bottle of the Sancerre, please and, oh, yes, a *salade aux lardons*.'

'Anything else, Madame?'

'And some bread.'

Polly dismissed him with a smile then turned her huge green eyes back to me. Why *was* she still single? Could it be only her mythomania? She remained slender. Her wrinkles were small and in all the right places. She always wore her hair in a chignon, a style that had once seemed fuddy-duddy, but which now matched her age to the same perfection as her expensively *vieille fille* clothes. Her below-the-knee suits, silk scarves, low-heels and high necks were all French. Indeed, when she kept her mouth shut, she would have passed for one of those autocratic priestesses of Paris fashion – the kind that used to sit to one side of the cat-walk at a private *défilé*, announcing each creation to *mesdames* as a mannequin brought it on parade. Perhaps it was her manner. Perhaps it was her slightly over-mobile mouth. Perhaps, after all, she kept single through choice.

'Now tell me, Mary. Tell me all,' she asked.

'Well, we've had a confirmation of the serialization offer from the *Observer*, which is good news, and your reading tour's all lined up,' I said. 'I assume Lottie has given you all your dates?'

'Some of them. Nothing for Scotland yet and I think I should go to Dublin.'

'We could drop in on her afterwards, then. If you've got time, that is.'

'Certainly. I only hope I don't get plagued by that dreadful man again.'

'Which man?'

Polly sighed. 'Didn't I tell you? He plagued me. Absolutely

plagued me. He turned up to every single reading and signing –
even in Birmingham – to ask difficult questions. They were very
clever questions – he'd obviously read every book inside out, so I
suppose I should have been flattered – but there was something
sinister about him. Maybe because he knew so much about me
and I knew so little about him. I asked him once how he found
the time to follow me all over the place the way he did and he
just smiled. Like this.' Polly imitated the fanatic's smile. She did
it rather well. I grinned. Her wine and salad arrived. I let the
waiter take the remains of my salad away then I filled both our
glasses.

'The other thing', I said, once it was clear that she had finished, 'is that I want to throw a party for you.'

'For me? How lovely.'

'I know we usually go to a restaurant or have drinks in the
office but I think that's a bit impersonal. I thought it might be
fun to get some caterers into my place. We couldn't fit that
many in there but I think, if we pushed the sofas to the walls,
we could get about forty-five in comfortably. Obviously we
ought to ask some journalists and the usual literary editors but
perhaps you could draw up a list of about thirty friends of
yours you'd like asked.'

'What fun!' said Polly, chasing a chunk of bacon around her
plate. 'I'm not sure I can come up with that many, though.
Does it matter?'

'Of course you can.'

'I don't get around nearly as much as I used to, you know.
I'm getting rather dull in my old age. Most of my old friends
have stopped calling.'

'Nonsense. Anyway,' I went on, watching closely for her
reaction, 'there's definitely someone I want you to meet.'

317

'Who?'

'Darling, he's so sweet but he's rather sad at the moment. His wife had a massive stroke a few weeks ago and dropped dead out in the garden.' Polly's eyes grew larger and sadder. She clicked her tongue sympathetically.

'He'll probably be rather out of his depth, actually. He doesn't read much – he's not literary at all in fact.'

'What a refreshing change! I do get so fed up with our lot. You go out to dinner and all anyone talks about is who's writing what, who attacked whom in which review and how so-and-so is getting their own back. It's so awfully insular. What does your friend do?'

'Well, he's not really *my* friend. I mean, I've only just got to know him myself. He's Josh's father. Tom Spellman.'

'Tom Spellman? But he's a millionaire!'

'Is he? You'd never know it. He's so unaffected. I mean, he dresses very well and so on but he's terribly discreet. I think he's in cars or something.' Was I overdoing it? Polly didn't seem to notice.

'I had no idea poor Josh was his son,' she confided.

'Oh yes.'

Polly clicked her tongue again. She was evidently counting Josh as yet another of that poor Tom Spellman's misfortunes. She munched her lettuce almost greedily, then dabbed some dressing off her chin with a napkin corner. She caught my eye and smirked. 'You are a dark horse, Mary. Is he very keen on you?'

I feigned surprise. 'On me? Oh. Not at all, I shouldn't think. No. Anyway,' I flustered, stroking my necklace, 'you know how it is. I'm not really, well . . . You know.' I waited until she had taken another mouthful before I said, 'No, it's you he wants to meet.'

She gestured towards her breasts, as though to say, 'Me?'

'Yes,' I said. 'Don't worry. He's not a fanatic or anything. And he certainly isn't literary. It was just that when he asked me who my main authors were and I mentioned you he immediately said how much he'd enjoyed the televisation of *A House Built on Sand*.'

'Did you tell him you'd introduce us?'

'Of course not!' Polly pretended relief. 'I simply said, "Oh well, in that case you must meet her some time."'

'And?'

'He looked quite excited. Of course, I wouldn't dream of asking him to your party if you'd rather I didn't.'

'Oh. Well. I think if there really are going to be about forty or so of us, there's no great risk. Let's be daring. Ask him.' We giggled, and changed the subject. It was that simple.

VIII

'Thomas?'

'Mmm?'

'Let's give a party.'

'Why not?' Tom said, then hesitated. 'You don't think it might be a bit soon, though? I mean, with poor Rachel and everything.'

'Maybe you're right.' I lay back on the pillows on my side and laid a hand on his chest, where the grizzled brown hair swirled. He lifted my hand and kissed it then returned it to his chest where he rubbed its palm over one of his nipples.

'Nice idea, though,' he murmured. 'Who would we ask?'

'Well, for a start I don't think we should give it as "us". Not just yet.'

'Oh.'

319

'I do think it's a bit soon to be doing that. But there's no reason why I couldn't throw a party here and just invite you as Josh's father.'

'Oh. I see.'

'It could be the party where we are seen to meet. Officially.'

'Your birthday isn't for ages.'

'Who mentioned birthdays? It can be a book-launch. I know. Polly Brookes has a new novel coming out in a few weeks. It's time the company gave her a proper do – she's made us enough money. I'll get caterers in – there's a firm up the road who are good – and you can come with Josh and pretend that you've never set foot in here in your life. You can have met me just once before, say, at Josh's place. How's that?'

'You *are* a devious creature, Mary.'

'*You're* the one who deceived his wife for seventeen years.'

'Don't.'

'Well you are.'

'I know. Just don't.'

'Sorry. Kiss me?'

He kissed me. His tongue tasted of toothpaste and whisky. He had always drunk whisky at bedtime but the toothpaste was a new ingredient in our lovemaking – part of the gradual domestication process. Before Rachel's death, he never kept a toothbrush in the flat. He saw it as too momentous a step, preferring to borrow mine the morning after. He had also started bringing his work with him. He was pushing through some deal in Germany and the love-nest had become a centre of operations for the duration. It was scattered with brochures and paperwork and an incongruously cheap and ugly briefcase had begun to loiter outside the kitchen door. I kept kicking it over in passing. Its plastic made a satisfying bang when it hit the floorboards.

IX

By an unconscious irony, the florists had decorated the room as though for a wedding. The mirror above the mantelpiece was decked with a garland of mock orange-blossom, white roses and myrtle, as was the linen-smothered table where the caterers had arranged the canapés. Polly saw the resemblance too. She was the first to arrive – it was her party, after all. She walked across the hall, stood between the open double doors and chuckled. 'They've made it look like the last scene of *The Philadelphia Story*.'

'All we need is a harmonium playing "Here Comes the Bride",' I laughed. 'Happy publication day, Polly. Lovely dress.'

'Thank you. I very nearly didn't buy it, you know, because I saw Princess Michael of Kent buying one just like it.'

'Really?'

'Yes. But then I thought, we're hardly likely to go to the same parties and if we did, it would probably say she was coming on the invitation and I'd know to wear something else.'

'Of course. Champagne?'

'Lovely.'

'I've done a little display of the books on a table over here.' I showed her. 'And I've got the petty cash and a box of copies tucked away so perhaps we can mount a signing session at some stage.'

'Good,' she said. 'We can shame the people who got complimentary copies into buying one for their friends.'

The doorbell rang. As I turned to answer it, Polly tapped my arm. 'Is he coming, then?' she asked.

'Is who.. ? Oh, yes,' I said and patted her hand. 'He wouldn't miss it for the world.'

Luckily, the first guests were not Josh and Tom – which would have proved awkward. I had primed Josh that he was to create some wheelchair trouble. This he duly did and managed to delay their arrival by some twenty minutes, by which time the room was already crowded.

'Josh, darling.' I kissed him. 'And you've brought your father. I'm so glad. Hello, Tom.'

'Hello again.' Tom shook my hand, stroking my palm wickedly as he did so.

'Polly's in the corner over there signing copies,' I told them. 'She'll be so glad you both made it.'

'How long do we have to keep this up?' Tom hissed.

'Ruky, have you met Tom? Ruky Delgado, Tom Spellman.' As I left them talking, Ruky was gushing that, of course, she had heard *so* much about him.

I wheeled Josh over to the canapés and handed him a drink. 'Why did you set *her* loose on him?' he asked. 'I thought we'd agreed to keep her clear. She'll monopolize him now.'

'I can handle the Stepmother from Hell,' I said. 'It just struck me that, if he met her first, and then perhaps Joely, then Pretty Polly would make such a striking contrast.'

'Like a diamond against jeweller's velvet.' Josh delicately bit a large prawn in two. 'Ma, I hope you don't mind.'

'What?'

'But I took the liberty of asking Antony.'

'Your new friend?'

'I think he's rather more than that now. The chicken breasts were a great success.'

'Of course I don't mind, Josh. I'm thrilled. Is he here? I don't remember letting him in.'

322

'Well I'll stay put then. If you see him, you'll know which direction to push him in. Go and save poor Sir from Ruky.'

As I walked away, Antony emerged from the crowd. Looking even more than in his photograph like a bright-eyed evangelical, he strode smiling over to Josh and kissed him lingeringly on the lips. The effect was sensational. As he began to wheel Josh through the party, the ranks of guests parted before them with little, frightened smiles.

Tom mouthed 'save me' over Ruky's shoulder as I approached. I winked back. 'Ruky, darling, Tom's had you all to himself for far too long now,' I said. 'Besides, I'm dying for you to meet Josh's new friend.' I steered the politely protesting Ruky over to Antony and Josh then returned to find Tom draining a full glass. He was ready for Polly but I delivered him to Joely for a few minutes, to be on the safe side.

'A toast,' I called out once she had him deep in conversation. 'Ladies and gentlemen, to *Letters Unwritten* – all success.' Glasses were raised across the room to where Polly sat behind a small fortification of books.

'All success!' people cheered, or mumbled, 'Yes' or 'Mmm'. Everyone drank the new book's health.

Ruky shouted, 'Cheers, Polly darling.' Beside her, Josh had swallowed a canapé the wrong way and was spluttering while Antony patted his back for him and held out a glass of water. I went to fetch the lady of the moment.

'How are we doing?' I asked our publicist, Lottie, who sat at Polly's side taking the money for copies.

'Sold out,' she said. 'Nothing left but these ones from the backlist. I think those copies you laid out may have ended up in people's bags.'

'Never mind. Polly, darling, come and mingle.' I wrinkled my nose at Polly to show her it was time. She stepped out from behind her table with a word of thanks to Lottie.

'Enjoying your party?' I asked her.

'Yes.'

'Who do you want to meet?'

'Oh for heaven's sake, Mary. Where is he?'

'There,' I said, indicating with a backward nod of my head for her to look over my shoulder. 'He's talking to Joely.' She craned her neck – she was shorter than me – and widened her eyes.

'Is he the tall one?' she asked. 'With the blond hair turning silver? Famous faces can look so different in the flesh.'

'That's him,' I admitted with a slight pang.

'Well? Introduce us.'

This was wrong. All wrong! She was drawing herself up and turning on her charm like so many headlamps. She was queen of the party. She could not be refused. She would take him from me. I was mad to bring them together. I led her over.

'Joely, angel!' I kissed Joely's cheek. 'I've barely spoken to you. We must have a proper talk before you go. Polly, you know Joely Lyons.'

'Of course I do,' said Polly. 'How are you, Joely?'

'Fine,' Joely said, clasping her hand without exactly shaking it. 'The new book looks wonderful. I've already got it on order.'

'How *sweet* of you.' Polly bared her little teeth.

'And this is Tom Spellman, dear Josh's father. Tom, this is Polly Brookes – the guest of honour.'

'How-do-you-do.' Tom shook her hand warmly. 'You need another drink. Here, let me.' He took her glass and exchanged it for a full one on a passing tray. 'I expect Mary's already told

324

you how much I enjoyed *A House Built on Sand*. Of course, I'm hopeless at reading – I never seem to find the time – but if your TV adaptation was anything to go by, it's a book I should make an exception for.'

'Well, I wouldn't say that exactly,' Polly murmured. Joely had seen someone else she knew and slipped away with a mute wave to Tom. He waved back. I took a tray of sausages from a waiter and, having offered Tom and Polly some, I too re-entered the fray.

Tom talked to no one else all evening. Josh and I could hardly believe it. One or both of us was watching them all the time. I had never seen Polly like this. She was not fluttering her eyelids or gurgling with old-girlish laughter and, to judge from his reactions, she did not seem to be lying excessively either. She was hanging with simplicity, humility even, on his every word. I ached to know what he was talking about. Tom was a darling but no raconteur. As parties draw on and reach that listless, should-we-move-on-to-eat-somewhere period, a conversation of any intensity acts like a social magnet. People would drift over and stand at Polly and Tom's elbows, waiting to be introduced. Polly and Tom (how naturally their names joined hands!) would chat to them but it seemed silently understood that their conversation would continue to take precedence and the interlopers would murmur a farewell and pass on.

When Polly tore herself away at last, it was to say goodbye. 'Mary, darling, thank you so much for a heavenly evening.'

'Are you off?' I asked, glancing at Tom who was leaning on the end of the sofa, muttering something to Joely Lyons. Joely was shaking her silver mane and laughing.

'I'm afraid so.' For a moment, entirely for my benefit, Polly intensified her smile a fraction. 'Tom's sweetly offered to drive me home and buy me dinner somewhere on the way. I know you did say something about you taking me out the way we always do but I honestly think you've done more than enough. I can't get over how lovely this place looks. And the flowers!' She gestured to the fireplace with a chuckle, throwing a glance at Tom who straightened up and left Joely's side. 'Bless you for everything, Mary.'

She kissed my cheek, close to my ear, waved to one or two people then went in search of her coat. Tom walked over and shook my hand.

'Lovely evening,' he said. 'You've made it all look so nice.' I gave him a real smile – *our* smile – to show him that no one was listening and he didn't have to pretend any more but he carried on as though he hadn't noticed.

'I told Polly I'd run her home.'

'Yes. She said. She's very grateful.'

'Bye.'

'Bye, then.'

I watched him leave the room, meet Polly in the hall and steer her out to the porch. Josh saw me watching and wheeled himself over.

'I don't believe it,' he said. 'I really didn't think it would work so well.'

'We don't know for sure,' I replied. 'He might just be driving her home.'

'But Ma, he talked to no one else for the last forty minutes!'

'Maybe she wouldn't let him. Maybe he couldn't escape.' Josh looked at me cynically. I glared back. The beatific Antony walked over and laid large, golden hands on the handles of Josh's wheelchair, silencing us.

'I think we should be off,' he said. 'Mary, it was so good to meet you, finally.'

'And you, Antony. You must come again soon – just you and Josh. It isn't normally as hectic as this.' I kissed him.

'It is in its way,' Josh said, raising an eyebrow. 'Will you be all right, Ma?'

'Of course I will.'

'I'll call you over the weekend.'

Josh caught Antony's questioning glance. 'Ma's short for Mary,' he said. 'My life isn't *that* complicated. Now push me to your car.'

I kissed Josh goodnight, and Joely, and Ruky, and Kirsty, and all the other departing guests who merited it. Then I took myself off to a bistro in the village where there were always some tables laid for one, and stayed there while the caterers tidied the flat. When I returned, nearly two hours later, the empty bottles had gone, the glasses had been washed and packed away for collection. The furniture was back where it should have been and the garlands of flowers had been taken down and dismantled. All that remained to show there had been a party were two vases stuffed with white roses and myrtle, and an acrid smell of smoke, scent and wine. I flung the windows open to the cold night but there was no breeze to clear the air.

X

I had retired to bed and fallen asleep over a new manuscript when the doorbell rang. I let it ring again, to make sure it was not just a trouble-maker. The third ring told me it was Tom. I shivered as I walked across the marble floor of the hall in bare feet. I saw his bulky silhouette through the smoked glass in the front door.

'Tom?'

'Yes.' I let him in. We stood there in the semi-darkness. I tried to make out his features in the wan light from a streetlamp.

'Did I wake you?' he asked.

'No.'

'I did. Didn't I?'

'Yes. What time is it?'

'One, I think. One-thirty.'

'For God's sake come in. My feet are getting cold.' He followed me into the flat and shut the door. I turned on a table lamp then wrapped a rug around my shoulders and curled up on a sofa. The smell of the party had finally drifted out into the night. Tom shuddered and closed the windows.

'You'll catch your death,' he said.

'I was getting rid of the smoke,' I told him. 'Then I fell asleep. Sit down.' He sat on the other sofa, facing me. He looked worn and harassed; one of his most becoming expressions.

'Did you have a good dinner?' I asked.

'Not bad. I took her to Le Paradis.'

'Very nice.' He had promised to take me there but never had. I betrayed no pique.

'Did she tell you many stories?'

'Yes. She lied for about half an hour without drawing breath,' he sighed. 'Odd woman. Very attractive but odd. Then we went back to her place.'

'For coffee.'

'Yes. Coffee. Then she sort of lunged at me and we went to bed.' I froze. He saw me.

'Well what did you expect?' he asked.

'You went to bed?' I echoed.

'Yes.' He stared at me. 'That virginal bit is only a veneer, you know. She's really quite accomplished.'

'How could you!' I spat.

'It really wasn't difficult,' he said. 'As I say, she's a very attractive woman.'

'Shut up!' I shouted, jumping up. 'Shut your bloody mouth and get out.' He jumped up too. I raised my hand to hit him but he hit me first. He slapped me hard across the cheek so that the blood sang in my ears and my neck jarred sickeningly. I stumbled, gasping, to the bathroom, stubbing my toe on the way and locked myself in. He banged on the door.

'Get out!' I repeated, 'Get out get out get out!' Were we drunk? I slumped to the lavatory to nurse my toe then I looked at my face in the mirror, hair tumbling, cheek crimson, lips stiff with rage as though I had been weeping. I did not cry.

Tom stopped banging on the door and started knocking intermittently and muttering, 'Mary? Mary? What are you doing? Let me in.'

'No. What the hell do you *think* I'm doing?' There was a pause.

'I don't know,' he said. 'Let me in.'

'No.' There was a thump and I saw the door press inwards on its hinges and lock as he slumped against it.

'Mary, I didn't sleep with her. Not really.'

'Yes you did.'

'I didn't.'

'You did. You can't lie to me, Tom.'

'Yes,' he admitted after a while. 'So? I went to bed with her. You wanted me to.'

'No I didn't.'

'Yes you did.'

'This is childish.'

'*You* are childish. You throw a party then thrust woman after woman at me in the most suggestive fashion then you fly off the handle . . .'

'Because you slept with one of them.'

'You wanted me to.'

I drew a breath then shouted quite distinctly through the door at him, '*I – did – not.*' I panted. I felt slightly sick. 'I . . .'

'What? What, Mary?'

'I thought you might want to marry her.'

'*Marry* her?'

'Yes, Tom. Marry her. Must you repeat everything I say?'

'What in God's name gave you that idea? It's you I'm marrying.'

'Is it? Since when?'

'You said.'

'I said probably. I didn't say yes.'

'Oh this is stupid. Unlock the door so we can talk properly.'

'No. Go away. You hurt me.' I glowered in the mirror. 'I think,' I added, 'I think you've given me a black eye. How the hell am I expected to go into work tomorrow with a black eye?'

'I'm sorry.'

'Bastard. You absolute bastard. Just go away. I hate you. Go back to Polly fucking Brookes.' He fell silent a moment. I heard his breathing through the door.

'Mary, I don't understand,' he said at last.

'What don't you understand?'

'How could you be so calculating? How could you set her up like that?'

330

'All I did was introduce you,' I laughed bitterly.

'You set her up. I honestly had no thought of going to bed with her. It was an interesting evening and I was fascinated to meet her but. Oh God. Mary, if you'd heard her! I'd just meant to go up and see her to her door – maybe have a quick coffee with her so she wouldn't think I was running away and be hurt.'

'Jesus but you're full of shit.'

'Mary, if you'd heard her! She is so alone, Mary. So alone. I started to leave and I swear she all but fell on her knees.'

'How very flattering to your poor, detumescent ego.'

Tom kicked the door. 'Will you *stop* being so damned superior for once and listen? She begged me not to go. She pleaded. I had to sit on that sofa and listen to this . . . this . . . this catalogue of solitude.'

'Lies. She's a pathological liar, Tom. You must have seen that.'

'Yes, she lies. She lies to make herself more interesting, to keep people beside her. But these weren't lies. Christ, she actually wept. She clawed at me. In that big boring flat with that typewriter at one end of the huge dining-table, and all those wardrobes full of expensive clothes and that –' he groaned, 'that awful *deadness* to it all. It was so pathetic.'

'So you . . . took pity on her.'

'Yes. I suppose I did. I know that makes me sound like some egotistical . . .'

'Tom, what will you do if this world-famous novelist of mine gets pregnant?'

'She won't.'

'You mean you asked her if she's on the pill?'

'Of course not.'

331

'You "took precautions"?'

'No. I . . . I pulled out in time.'

'Oh.' I sat back on the lavatory, noticing for the first time a bottle half-full of flat champagne that someone had left beside the sink. 'Great,' I said. 'Quick thinking but hardly foolproof.'

'Let me in, Mary.'

I thought for a moment. 'Why?'

'Because I'm sorry. Because I promise that if I ever, ever hit you again I'll walk straight out of the door and never come back. Because . . .'

'Well?'

'Because I want to be your husband. I don't want to end up like her.'

'Tom, I scarcely think a man of your wealth and position would ever be reduced to begging for crumbs of sexual consolation. Be realistic.'

'And you be human!' he exclaimed. The last word was distorted and, as I heard him slide to the floor outside, I also heard him quietly sobbing.

I sat in that bathroom for a long, long while. I thought of Polly Brookes and yes, I even imagined myself in her position. I thought of the proud single women I knew, and the pathetic. And I thought of Josh and Antony, of the tender carefulness with which Antony had manoeuvred his lover's wheelchair down the front steps. I did not unlock the door until Tom's sobs had subsided into gentle snores. Then I switched off the light, unlocked the door and stepped out into the corridor. I pushed gently at his shoulder with my hand.

'Tom? Come on,' I said, 'get up and come to bed. It's draughty down there.'

He mumbled something and started to get up, using my arm

as a support. Suddenly he seemed to remember where he was and why. 'Mary?' he asked.

'Yes. It's me.'

'Will you . . . will . . .?'

'Yes, Tom. I'll marry you. I'll marry you after the sales conference at the end of the month. OK? Now come to bed.' He came quietly. I was in bed first. I realized as I pulled the bedding over me that I was chilled to the marrow because the heating had switched itself off hours ago. Tom hung up his suit then slid in behind me. He nuzzled the back of my neck and, as we dozed off, reached a heavy arm around my breasts for comfort.

'Mary?' he asked.

'What?'

'Good.'

XI

I did indeed have a slight black eye the next morning. I cried off work pleading, as a homage to Polly, a flood in the neighbour's flat, then had Kirsty send me a few more manuscripts in a taxi to keep me occupied over the weekend. Tom worked on one sofa, I on the other. He slipped out to a meeting on Saturday and came back with a little box from Burlington Arcade. Brown eyes are hard to match – even when bruised – so he had thought of the colours that best became me and settled for an emerald. The ring didn't fit. It was made early in the last century, for more refined fingers than mine. He offered to hurry back to Piccadilly to have it altered, assuming that such things took no longer than replacing the sole on a shoe. I kissed him and told him not to be silly and said I would take it back on

Monday. It was a beautiful emerald – the first jewel I had ever owned that wasn't a mere industrial chip – but the disparity between Tom's romantic image of my fingers and their thicker, slightly crooked reality, loomed over the rest of the weekend like an ill omen.

On Monday, with the ring safely zipped into a compartment of my briefcase, I returned to the office. My bruise had turned from brown to pale green. I hid it with make-up and wore dark glasses.

'Awful conjunctivitis,' I explained to Kirsty. 'It flared up on Saturday morning and now I look like a bride of Dracula.' In all the better Sunday papers, Polly's new book had received the glowing notices that were now no surprise and I faced the weekly editorial meeting with a light heart.

The firm was based in a fine Bloomsbury town house and the boardroom (also used for occasional lunches) retained the atmosphere of an old-fashioned dining-room. I was one of the last to arrive (which seemed always to be expected of me). Josh was already at the table, as were the other four editors. He gestured at my glasses as I sat down and I repeated the story about conjunctivitis. Coffee and biscuits were passed around and, while we waited for Basil, our managing director, to arrive, we began to discuss an American agent, new to the scene, who was poaching authors from his rivals then demanding extraordinarily high advances for them. After a while, when Basil had still not arrived, one of the junior editors went in search of him and met him on the stairs.

Basil's face was long when he and his secretary took their places, its naturally melancholic folds deepened into profound gloom.

'I represent, as you know, the third generation of my family to have managed this remarkable publishing house,' he said. 'After conversations held on Friday afternoon and earlier this morning, I regret to have to inform you that I shall also have represented the last.' He looked around the table at our surprised faces. 'As you cannot fail to have heard or noticed, our finances have not been of the healthiest in the last two years. The family alas can no longer afford to underwrite our more, how can one put it, *creative* losses to the extent that has always been its pleasure. After due consideration and, needless to say, much heartsearching, I have decided to accept a generous bid. From the Pharos Group.'

Now there were concerned noises. Originally a prestigious literary firm, Pharos had long since been bought out by a press baron and his tabloid editrix wife. They had steadily built up the company's finances on the less than literary reputations of several 'shopping-and-fornication' authoresses and any number of what Josh called sub-genres: book-related board games, 'novelizations' of films and television series, and even adaptations of films which had been adaptations of novels to begin with. Pharos was not a company likely to countenance our publication of new European and South American novels, still less our Egyptian list or the thin works of our stable of contemporary poets.

'I'm not far off my sixtieth birthday,' Basil continued, 'and I shall welcome this opportunity to retire from a field whose changes are becoming a little rapid for me. Frieda and I have long cherished a dream of moving back to Tuscany and now I can make her a happy woman.' A few of us smiled but no one was happy. I stared at Josh who stared back at me.

'Paul and Wanda Yeoward have given me their full assurances that they would not wish to make any changes to the company. Paul says he holds our list in high esteem and will regard us as a prestigious feather for his cap, not merely another firm to be broken up and sold off. The only major changes, which will of course involve the sad necessity of laying off some staff, will be the amalgamation of our accountancy and distribution departments. There is no need to tell you how this will improve efficiency.

'In a few minutes I shall be going from here to Pharos to sign the agreements though I still have a few tasks left to do about the place so I won't be disappearing for good much before the end of the week. Paul will be here this afternoon and for much of tomorrow to do a kind of walkabout and meet the staff. He'll also be wanting meetings with each of you in turn to discuss your authors, deals-in-progress, plans for next year's catalogue and so forth.

'I'm sorry to drop this on you like a bombshell – not least because I know how busy you all are getting ready for the sales conference – but you have to understand that the family's need is urgent, and Paul is not a man to be kept waiting. Thank you.' With that, Basil and his secretary left the room. There was a stunned silence until the door closed behind him and then we all started speaking at once.

I had a frantic morning, having postponed most of Friday's business. I had to claw reprint rights from one agent and take dizzying risks in a telephone auction with another. I had to smooth at least three authors' fevered brows and deal with a fourth's hysterical complaints that his new novel, well-reviewed the week before, was unobtainable anywhere in central London. In the middle of it all, Polly rang to thank me for the party and to say how fascinating but, well dear, really rather philistine Tom Spellman was – she did so agree. Lunch with a gossip-mongering – therefore superbly effective – scout we retained in America was not a welcome diversion.

I missed Paul Yeoward's walkabout – he never made it to my floor. He did however contact me in person, rather than through a secretary, to arrange an appointment for the next day. Josh was the second editor he interviewed. I returned from lunch to find a note asking me to ring him. Guessing it was about his conversation with Yeoward I chose to visit him instead. I found him clearing his desk.

'Josh? What's going on?' I asked, although it was patently obvious.

'I'm off, Ma,' Josh said. 'Or should I say, laid off.'

'*What?*'

'We're to be streamlined.'

'But Basil said . . .'

'Yes. Basil said but Yeoward also said and Yeoward owns us now. He said he was sorry but they're having to "let me go" as the least experienced editor.'

'Briony came after you did. She doesn't even have an English degree.'

'Ah but Briony brought in the money-spinning Mr Wykeham and now she lives with him. So, if she went, Wykeham would, in all probability, go with her.'

'But you're the poetry editor.'

'Quite.' I sat on the edge of his desk watching him sling books into boxes.

'I'm also disabled.'

'Josh, he never gave that as a reason.'

'No. Although I wouldn't be surprised to find that the new offices have no wheelchair access. I'd probably have to come in via the delivery entrance like a lorry and use the service lift.'

'Who said anything about new offices?'

'Haven't you heard?'

'I was out to lunch with Venetia Peake.'

'New offices. The lease is running out here and Pharos won't renew it. It would be more efficient to have us ... to have you under the same roof as them. Think about it, Ma. He had to choose between Briony and me. Not only does she have Wyke-ham, she also has legs, attractive legs at that, which can walk her leggily all over the place, to lunch, to Frankfurt, to launches, to all the places that you've been kind enough to let me avoid going. Don't look like that. I'm not being self-pitying, just real-istic. To the Yeowards of this world, Briony will always represent an opportunity, I will always represent a passenger.'

I stormed up to the boardroom where Paul Yeoward was grilling another of my colleagues but I stopped on the stairs. I had no fears for my job – I was more safely ensconced than Bri-ony and I had more influence – but I suddenly accepted the inevitability of Yeoward's decision. There was no point in storming when he had already made up his mind. It would be wiser to save my rage for questions on which he had less secur-ity; questions, for instance, of literary judgement.

I helped Josh down the few front steps and into a taxi then passed him up his boxes and his folded wheelchair. Several people were leaning out of windows to see him go. As the taxi pulled away across the square we all waved and a slightly angry cheer went up. Genteel revolution was in the air. (It dispersed by this time the next day, however, as surely as the stench of Polly's party had left my flat.)

I returned to my desk only to snatch up my briefcase. Then I walked in a swift, decisive fury all the way across Soho to

Piccadilly and into Burlington Arcade. The name of the jeweller was printed on the silk lining of the box's lid. I was served by a woman. She was discreet, motherly yet efficient – a housekeeper used to these luxuries and their attendant complications. I snapped the box shut again and slid it across the counter.

'Good afternoon,' I said, 'my fiancé gave me this engagement ring on Saturday – I believe that was when he bought it.'

'Ah yes,' said the woman. 'I remember.' She was waiting for a name, to prove I was not a thief.

'Mr Spellman,' I told her.

'That's right. He came in at about three o'clock.' She threw a professional glance at my hands. 'Would Madam like to have it altered?'

'No, thanks. Actually, I want to give it back.'

'Oh.'

'The thing is, it's difficult to give it back to Mr Spellman directly.' She nodded. She understood. 'And I was wondering whether you could perhaps just keep it in your safe or something and contact him to ask what he'd like to do with it. I assume he'll want to sell it back to you but I think it's a decision we should leave up to him.'

'Yes, Madam. That's quite all right.' Relieved, I turned to go.

'If I could just have your name and signature here, Madam.' I turned back. She was holding out a little form.

'It's just a formality, to let the customer know that the item was willingly surrendered.'

'Oh, of course.' I signed, quickly. 'This must happen quite often then?' I asked, with a short laugh. The assistant released a ghost of a smile but said nothing as she tucked the ring and my signature into a drawer beneath the counter.

XII

Tom waited over a week before visiting me again. It was a Wednesday. He mentioned the ring only to say that he had indeed sold it back to the jeweller. We had a meal sent round and slept together but did not make love. Apart from the occasional loving phone call, we then had no contact until the following Wednesday and the Wednesday after that. It was quite like old times. For a while I thought I had won. When he said, 'Of course, you do know there's always a risk of me meeting someone else?' I said, 'Yes. I know. And I know that you might marry them.'

'I might fall in love with them too,' he said. 'I might want to have children by them.'

'That's a risk I have to take,' I replied, and the subject was dropped.

Then he did meet someone else. In fact, he had met her before. I had introduced them. Not Polly – no such Nemesis – and not Josh's Stepmother from Hell. Tom began seeing a lot of Joely Lyons; she of the silver hair and flawless skin. As her first husband had died leaving her the principal shareholder of a major West End department store, the match was an attractive one to the gossip columnists. Handsome widow and handsome widower were seen at restaurants, at the theatre, even, Josh reliably informed me, at a racecourse.

I began to spend a lot of evenings with Josh and Antony. Antony was an architect and was rebuilding his Hackney house for their joint residence. Under Josh's proud eye, he would show me drawings of ramps and wide spaces for a wheelchair and furniture and fittings that Josh could use either from his chair or at his lower standing height. Josh had told his lover nothing about my continuing liaison with Tom.

'It's not just that he's shockable, Ma,' he said, 'although he is, you know, *lipsmackingly* pure! It's more my ingrained cynicism. Telling him would be tantamount to admitting he's family and I can't believe such happiness can last.'

Tom was quite open with me about Joely. Continuing to spend his Wednesday evenings (and some Wednesday nights) with me, he said when he saw her and what they did. He told me things about Joely I had never known nor wished to find out. He asked my permission before proposing marriage to her and even offered to show me the ring – to prove, I imagined, that it was not as superb as the one he had offered me.

They announced a spring wedding. He had the gall to marry her in church. She had the decency to wear something in bluey-green. Josh bought me some red underwear especially and was peeved when I refused to wear it. I had my hair put up and wore devastating grey.

It was a beautiful day and the graveyard banks were bursting with primroses. A lot of the press turned up, of course, as did all Joely's overly-sleek friends. I sat near the back, between Polly and Ruky. When the priest asked if anyone present knew of just cause or impediment and so on why these two should not be joined together, I nearly kept silent. For a moment I thought I could just let them go through with it as planned. I thought how perfect they looked together and how Joely's children would look up to him.

Then I thought, 'Sod this,' and I stood up. Of course everyone was astonished. Nobody ever interrupts, except in films. Ruky pulled on my sleeve to sit down again and Polly chuckled. Tom was the only one in the church not to turn round.

'I do,' I said. 'He bought us a love-nest in Belsize Village seventeen years ago and came to screw me every Wednesday in return for paying all my bills. Well, I'm still in the love-nest and he's still coming every Wednesday.'

For a few seconds you could have heard a pin drop, then Josh shouted, '*Bravissima*!' and I was surrounded by reporters.

XIII

Fantasy, of course. All the pure, idle fantasy of a frustrated will and understimulated mind. Tom *did* sleep with Polly and he *did* give me a black eye and I *did* accept his proposal. I kept the emerald however and, when I let him make the announcement after the autumn sales conference, he gave me a diamond to match. I can't wear them both at once, of course. That would be too ostentatious. I like to alternate them. No one but Josh (and Tom's solicitor) ever knew our secret. Not even Polly. We told people that Josh had introduced us, fond of me and sorrowful for his widowed father. I held my peace and let the world and his wife make the humiliating assumption that Tom had picked me in the charitable nick of time off the shelf of shame. There was some envious murmuring about funeral-baked meats, the marriage to the second wife having come at an unseemly brief interval after the burial of the first, but those who had passed for Rachel's intimates were more charitable and wished us well. I never guessed that wedding presents could be so substantial.

Josh *was* fired by our new bosses (and he *did* give me red underwear for the wedding, which I wore) but he heard no more from Antony after the night of our party. He professed no surprise and little heartache and he continued to gain inventive satisfaction through sources he thought it too indelicate to discuss. I took a week's holiday for the honeymoon (we returned to Sintra) and I never resumed my place in the office. Instead, I persuaded Tom and some of his friends to back a publishing venture Josh and I set up on our own. A family publishers.

One of our first authors, who transferred her allegiances as an act of magnanimous faith and despite promises of fat advertising budgets from Paul Yeoward, was Polly. Within seven months of the launch party thrown so fatefully in her honour at my flat, she was delivered of a novel quite unlike anything she had written before.

'My dear,' said Josh, who read the manuscript first, 'we're on to our first winner. It fairly steams.' Certain passages shocked even me, and I have read the unprintable. It was *The Industrialist*. Polly never told me what had happened between her and my husband. I never told her I knew. The book won a prize and was made into a film by some Italians which did very well on the art-house circuit, for all the least artistic reasons.

The flat, in all its Proustian decadence, we gave to Josh, who had a chair-lift installed on the front steps. In our honour, he threw mysterious parties there on the first Wednesday of every month, to which we were never invited. Tom sold the house in Oxfordshire which Rachel had redecorated so often and bought us a smaller house in Kensington. I have my own study and a dressing-room. Tom is often away on business. There is a largish garden and a conservatory and, abetted by Josh, I have become something of a hostess. Our little company did not stay little for long and I have few hours left for reflection. There are times, however, often on quiet Sunday evenings, or in the silence after Tom has yet again mentioned the possibility of children, or at the end of dinner parties where most of the guests have been guests of his, when I feel less than I was.

GENTLEMAN'S
RELISH

THE LESSON

Jane stepped outside with a basket of washing and her hair was whipped about her face. Even in June, theirs was one of the windiest gardens she had known. Shortly after moving there she had invested in an extra set of pegs; laundry had to be doubly secured if she wasn't to be forever retrieving pillowslips from rosebushes and rewashing shirts the wind had rolled around flowerbeds. It was a miracle there *were* flowerbeds, let alone that she could persuade much to grow in them. Lavender thrived, and rosemary and a kind of low, blue-flowered tree lupin whose seed a cousin had sent up from Cornwall. But the only roses that could cope with the near-constant wind and occasional salt spray were tough, rugosa hybrids, more leaf than flower, and she had abandoned all hope of recreating the lush beds of Stanwell Perpetual and Etoile de Hollande she had relished at Camp Hill and Liverpool.

The sheets cracked like circus whips as she battled to hang them out. She had heard of governors' wives who cheerfully entrusted everything but smalls to the prison laundries but she had never cared to do that; it would have been a step too far into institutional life. Besides, she needed occupation. With both children away in boarding school – at her parents' expense – her days were all too long and solitary.

She had learned by degrees that marriage to a prison governor was not unlike marriage to a priest, only without the flower arranging or the constant invasion of the family home. As with priests, one lived on the job and the job came first. Her husband left her after an early breakfast then remained in the prison until he returned to her, invariably pallid with exhaustion, minutes before supper was ready. And it was a rare weekend when she did not have to share him with the men at least once a day.

He called them that: *The Men*. They only became *prisoners* if they escaped, and there had been no successful breakouts from this prison in years. On one end of a rocky promontory jutting out from the coast, it had started life as a small fortress in Henry VIII's time, and had then been greatly expanded under threat of Napoleonic invasion. The prison dated from the 1840s and made use of the enormously thick fortress walls and the ferocious cliffs on the site's two seaward sides. The Governor's House, also early Victorian, was severely elegant. Both were built from slabs of the local stone – prized by town councils the world over – which the prisoners continued to hew from the quarries that hemmed the prison in on its landward side.

Even more than at Liverpool, and far more than on the Isle of Wight, she felt herself imprisoned there. She no longer had the children as an excuse for excursions. The only other women nearby were officers' wives and, even had she wanted to, it was not done to befriend them and risk showing favouritism. At each of her husband's previous, five-yearly postings, she had socialized with the chaplain's wife – in one case making a cherished friend whose comfortingly spiky conversation she missed acutely – but here the chaplain was acidly single, his house kept by a savage widowed sister Jane encountered as little as good manners would allow.

There was nothing to stop her making day trips but she had yet to acquire the habit of enjoying culture or walks on her own and was inhibited by the brutal landscape that lay between the prison and anything of interest.

Her mother had been a governor's wife too and, like many of her tribe, an army wife before that. She thrived on the predominant maleness of the prison environment, enjoyed the sense of her extravagant femininity in such a setting as her little car was waved through by the guards or her skinny legs were ogled by a working party in her garden.

By contrast Jane had always found that being the lone woman on an island of masculinity made her yearn after invisibility. She had dreams of anonymous city life in which she walked streets so bustling with women, all of them better dressed and longer-legged than her, that she felt herself blissfully eclipsed.

She peered down from one end of the washing line to the heavily supervised road that wound down towards the outer gates. A troop of men was being marched out to work in the quarries. Their voices reached her, noisy with wisecracks and bravado. Her husband claimed they liked the quarry work, which Jane found hard to believe, but certainly they seemed to approach each shift with good spirits. Perhaps it was the sea air they relished and exercise in the sunshine instead of the boarding-school gases of the prison meals her husband insisted on sharing or the medieval stink of the cell blocks at slopping-out time.

One of the men looked up at her then nudged his mate and pointed. She stepped back behind the flapping sheets as the whistling started. The sheets were almost dry already. On some days the washing had become quite stiff by the time she fetched it in.

'Ma'am?'

She turned, startled. An officer was waiting at the garden gate. He had one of the men with him. An older man. Handsome. Respectable-looking.

'Yes?' she asked, unconsciously holding the peg bag to her front as she approached them.

The officer doffed his hat and she recognized him from the Knobbly Knees competition at the Christmas party. 'Governor said you needed some bookshelves making. We thought Glossop, here, could make them for you.'

'Are you a joiner, Glossop?' she asked.

'I trained as a cabinetmaker, ma'am.'

'Excellent. Let me show you what we're after.'

Seen closer to, Glossop was younger than she thought: her husband's age, only prematurely aged by prison. His eyes were the colour of English sea, his dark hair silvered at his temples.

Along with the house and unlimited heating and hot water, one of the perks of the job was the regular availability of trusties – many of them with valuable trades – to help around the place. Over the years she had seen roses pruned, lawns edged, rooms plastered and painted, sash windows repaired, even silk lampshades made by men eager to break the monotony of prison routine by exercising old skills. Apart from the shopkeepers who delivered provisions from what she thought of as *The Mainland*, the only tradesman she ever had to pay herself throughout her marriage was her hairdresser.

Now that her son was away at school and showing every sign of becoming as keen a reader as his father, she wanted to replace his rather babyish painted bookcase with something larger and more adult that would be a pleasant surprise for him on his return.

Glossop took measurements and scribbled them on a pad while the officer stood by.

'Seven shelves, do you reckon?' he asked. 'Or six with a larger one at the bottom?'

'Six with a larger one,' she said.

352

'And how about a nice cornice at the top?'

'A cornice?'

'Like on that lovely bureau bookcase on the landing.'

'Well that would be lovely.' She was startled that he had noticed her antiques and automatically wondered if he had been a burglar.

'And a sort of skirting board to match what you've already got in here?'

'You could do that?'

'I could.' Glossop smiled, at which the officer's expression grew yet more wintry.

'Then yes please.'

'I can't do you mahogany, like out there.'

'No. Of course not. Pine, I suppose.'

'Or oak. We've got plenty of oak at the moment.'

'Have you?'

'Glossop has been making new pews for the chapel, ma'am.'

'I must go and see. Oak would be much better than pine. It ages so nicely. When could you start?'

Glossop glanced at the officer. 'I could measure and cut the shelves and framework this afternoon,' he said cautiously. 'Make the joints. I could bring them in and start fitting them together in here same time tomorrow.'

'That would be lovely. Thank you.'

Invariably she found she was too friendly, even gushing, when talking to the men, which she never was with officers. She supposed she felt sorry for them. Sorry and rather afraid.

'Is that yours?' he asked as they turned to go, pointing at the fishing rod propped in a corner.

'No. It's my boy's. His godmother gave it to him and he never uses it.'

'Shame,' Glossop said. 'That would make a nice little spinning rod.' And the officer led him away.

As she closed the door behind them, she noticed he had left behind him a trace of the prisoner's habitual smell – an entirely male tang; a blend of cheap tobacco, under-washed clothing and confined body. It was a smell she found penetrated her husband's tweed jackets but never his person.

That afternoon she rang her husband on the internal telephone and asked if she could visit the prison chapel to inspect Glossop's handiwork. He was too busy with interviews to take her himself but he sent an officer to escort her.

Most of the pews were just as she had remembered from the last carol service: the worst kind of late nineteenth century pitch pine, dull, dark and penitential, deliberately cut too short in the seat for slouching. Glossop's pews – he had made four – were far paler, made of simply waxed oak. He had felt obliged to echo the silhouette of the others but his furniture was lightened by small details. A fine moulding along the seat edge and the back was just made for one's thumbs to fiddle with during hymns and sermons. On the length of the little retaining shelf designed to hold hymnals and prayer books he had carved a sequence of birds. They were all local ones, clearly identifiable, the sort the more observant men must spot all the time – cormorant, shag, herring gull, jackdaw; toughened, cliff-top birds for a tough, cliff-top prison.

'Aren't they lovely?' she exclaimed, charmed, but the officer would not be drawn beyond a 'Very nice, ma'am.'

'What did he do?' she asked her husband over dinner.

'Glossop? You know it's much better if you don't know. He's a trusty, though. Quite harmless. You'll be perfectly safe.'

'I wasn't worried. Just curious. Cheese or fruit?'

When Glossop returned the following day, bringing his tools and wood with him on a trolley, she encouraged the officer who had escorted him to leave them alone together. 'It's quite all right,' she said, when he hesitated. 'I'll ring when Glossop's ready to leave.'

It was impossible to tell if Glossop appreciated the gesture or not. He simply concentrated on bringing his things up the stairs and carefully spread a spotless dustsheet over the bedroom carpet. She offered him the radio but he gently declined and she realized that if there was any pleasure for him in this assignment, it lay in the brief luxury of peace and quiet, of being amidst muffling surfaces – wood, carpets and curtains – after the cold clangour of metal doors, metal walkways, metal plates and metal mugs. She made them both proper coffee – in a pot – and set a tray with china mugs and a plate with chocolate biscuits and rock cakes on it – far more than she would offer should the acid chaplain come to call.

He didn't seem to mind her watching him work – perhaps he appreciated feminine company, even a middle-aged housewife's – and he answered all her questions, about wood and tools and how he learnt his trade from his father but had taught himself to carve since imprisonment to give his hands occupation.

'Must get lonely for you, living out here,' he said at last, as he was checking the angle of a shelf with his spirit level.

'Sorry,' she said. 'Am I talking too much? Sometimes people visit, real people. Sorry. That sounded awful. But you know what I mean. And I think I gabble at them like a thing possessed . . . Yes,' she admitted at last, when he had let her foolish, rambling answer wither on the air. 'It does get lonely. With the children both away and my husband at . . . at work and no friends nearer than a day's drive away. I like my own company but not here. Not much. It's oppressive.'

'I think it's meant to be,' he said drily. 'Why not go for walks?'

'Oh I used to. But then our dog got old and died and, with the children not here, I didn't have the energy to train another puppy.'

'You should go fishing.'

'Fishing?' The idea was absurd. She pictured herself, mannish in tweeds and waders. 'Oh I'm sure it's terribly complicated and I wouldn't know how and anyway, the nearest rivers are . . .' She realized she had no idea where the nearest angling rivers were and tried to remember where she and the departed dog had last come upon anglers at their intently private business.

'Rod like that and the right sort of float, you wouldn't need a river. You could fish for bass.'

'In the sea?'

'Off a rock.'

She thought of the bass her brother had presented her with last time they stayed with him, of its sweet white flesh, and its skin deliciously crisped with a rubbing of soy sauce before grilling. 'Oh,' she demurred. 'It's my boy's rod . . .'

But her son had barely touched the rod – a present designed to lure his head out of books – and she knew he'd be only relieved to see it get some use.

'I wouldn't know where to begin,' she said, staring at it.

'It's easy,' he said. 'If you're patient and you're not squeamish. It was my mother taught me. You might want gardening gloves, for when you come to handle the scales. The fins can be sharp as any rose thorn.'

Impulsively she took the rod from its corner and held it out to him. 'Show me,' she said.

'Are you left-handed,' he asked, 'or right?'

Standing closer than was probably appropriate, so that she could smell the sweat and wood shavings on him, and guiding her hands with his, he showed her how to hold the rod, how to cast, how the winder thing worked and how to prevent it spinning the line into an impossible tangle at the moment of casting.

While she blushed furiously, he raided her son's little fishing satchel (simultaneous gift of a second godparent carefully briefed by the first) and assembled float, tiny plastic balls and a hook for her and tied them on along with a tiny length of rubber band he called her *stop*. He showed her how to adjust the stop until the float hung vertically in the water. He showed her how she could carefully secure the hook to part of the rod then tighten the line so that she had everything in place for fishing and would need less to carry. He showed her on her Dorset road map how to find the rocks where he had often caught bass when the tide was on the turn and he told her where in Weymouth to buy little packets of sand eels to use as bait. He wrote the name and address in tidy script with his stump of carpenter's pencil.

'Just tell him I sent you,' he said. 'And he'll give you good service. He knows me. We were in the war together.'

At first she had been humouring him, merely being politely curious, but he took the matter so in earnest she found herself swept up in it. And as he described where to park the car on the coast road and how to find the discreet footpath that led to his favoured fishing rocks, she could see what it was costing him to picture a loved place he could no longer visit. She felt shamed into following his instructions to the letter.

357

As Glossop had suggested, she spent an hour practising casting on the windswept lawn, far from any bushes, until she was fairly confident. Then she went fishing. She didn't tell her husband. Eccentricity unsettled him. Besides, he showed little curiosity as to how she spent her days so long as she wasn't spending money.

She felt some doubt about presenting herself at the angling shop as an acquaintance of a criminal in case she was unwittingly passing on a coded message to an accomplice but the name worked like a charm and the weather-beaten man behind the counter was at once all affability and helpfulness, checking over her kit to ensure she had all she needed for the task in hand and adding a ladylike little club called a *priest* to her armoury. When he explained what it was for she realized she had always pictured fish as somehow dying of defeat, in effect, within moments of being landed and the man saw her doubt.

'One quick tap on the back of the head does the trick,' he told her. 'If it's a mackerel, you don't even need the priest – just stick a finger in his mouth and click the head back, like this.' He mimed the swift, deadly gesture and made a soft, crunching noise as he did so.

On her first trip to Glossop's fishing spot she caught nothing, although something took sly bites off the part of her sand eels that dangled free of the hook. She did not mind, though, since there was intense pleasure to be had simply from standing still on a flat rock so near the surface of the sea, where she could admire the acrobatics of seabirds and commune with the doggy faces of the seals that bobbed up to watch her.

She reported back to Glossop in detail as he rubbed beeswax into wood. His questions taxed her powers of recall. What direction was the current moving? Was there much weed? How far from the rock was her float landing? How good was visibility through the water below her? And how far off were the gannets feeding?

Awareness sharpened by his keen questioning, she returned two days later, at the time of morning when much perusal of a tide table told him the water movements would be ideal for bass.

She caught something almost at once. It was big. She could see it fighting the line in the water. In her excitement she forgot which way to wind the winder and which way its little levers should be flicked. She paid line out when she meant to reel it in. She snagged the line on a rock. She was entirely unprepared for the way rod and line seemed to stretch and bend to the point where her frantic winding seemed to take almost no effect. Then, with a lunging and tugging that was surely as incorrect as it was ungraceful, she managed to land the beast.

Even to her eye, trained solely by a lifetime of fishmongers' slabs and a few evenings of poring over *The Observer's Book of Sea Fishes*, she knew it wasn't a bass. But it *was* beautiful, covered in a violent pattern of turquoise and dull gold and with thick, gasping lips of sky-blue. It was hard to believe something so glamorous could come from such unexotically British waters. She was quite unready for the way its eye met hers, rolling, desperate, or for the violence of its thrashing when her hands drew near, or the threatening spikes of its dorsal fin.

She couldn't kill it. Not possibly. She ignored the priest, tugged on the clumsy gardening gloves and, fighting the urge to cry out in distress, held it firmly down while she tried to free the hook from its mouth. This was not a thing she had discussed with Glossop. They'd talked only in terms of hunter and prey, not of captor and release. After what felt like minutes of the poor thing drowning in air, she worked out for herself that the hook's barb meant it had to be drawn through in the direction it was already travelling. She took her little pen knife, fumbled off the gloves to open it, got the gloves back on, almost lost the knife into a rock pool, cut the line, teased the hook out through the creature's jaw – which produced no blood, she thanked God, or she'd have surely given up – then tossed it back into the water.

For a few dreadful seconds she thought she had killed it, as it merely hung in the water and began to turn its pale belly to the sky, a plump offering for gulls. Then it shook itself and flew down into the shadows beneath the rock.

'Sounds like a wrasse,' Glossop told her. 'Corkwing Wrasse. A proper sport fish. You're blooded now. No stopping you!'

She looked *wrasse* up in her cookery books and was relieved to find it described as having watery, rather yellow flesh, fit only for Portuguese stews. Its Latin name, aptly enough it seemed, was *turdus*.

Glossop went on to make shelves for her daughter's room and two bedside tables for her own, then, without warning, was deprived of trusty status halfway through making her a cheese board.

'An act of violence,' was the only explanation her husband offered, and he took against the bedside tables and banished them to the spare room, claiming his had a wobble.

After several more wrasse and a dispiriting quantity of mackerel, which at least taught her how to kill unflinchingly, she landed her first bass later that summer and fed it to him, steamed, *à la Chinoise*. She would have liked to cook it for Glossop but, of course, that was out of the question. Instead she bought him an oceanographic map of the Dorset coast and posted it to him from Weymouth, along with a postcard of swans at Abbotsbury.

Success at last! she wrote. *Only 2½ pounds but delicious and so satisfying. First of many, I hope. Thank you so much.* She hesitated over how to close, aware of rules, aware that a prison cell was all too public and that letters went astray. She used *Yours sincerely, Mrs Whiteley* correctly then defiantly gave him her Christian name, in brackets, and added a ps – *I shall guard your rock for you* – knowing it would mean nothing to anyone else.

Jane became rather an expert at sea angling and bought much and varied tackle from Glossop's army friend in Weymouth but her husband's next posting was a landlocked one. The new house's lush and sheltered rose beds were no compensation.

COOKERY

A favourite piece of broodily autumnal Fauré came on the radio. Perry turned it up and sang along under his breath, still unused to the delight of having the house to himself and being able to make as much noise as he liked. He lifted a saucepan lid to check on the leeks which were sweating in a pool of butter. He prodded them with a wooden spoon then turned off the heat, ground in some pepper and grated in some nutmeg. Nutmeg subtly sweetened the taste and blended nicely with the air of slightly burnt butter. One had to be sparing, however; too much, and the spice overcame the taste of leek rather than merely enhancing it.

He continued singing to himself as he whisked in eggs, cream and some crumbled Wensleydale cheese. Swathing his hands in a towel, he pulled a baking tray from the oven on which two small tart cases had been baking blind under a shroud of silicone parchment weighted with earthenware beans. They were done to perfection; dry without being coloured yet. He allowed the steam to escape from them then, biting his lower lip from the fear of them breaking, tipped each of them gently onto the palm of his hand then slid them, naked, back to the baking tray. He spooned the leek mixture in, sprinkled on a few Parmesan shavings then returned the tray to the oven and set the timer.

The cat, Edie, was clawing at the window and, being on the large side due to a diet of culinary leavings and field mice, threatening to dislodge the herbs that grew on the sill. Perry let her in, kissed her nose in greeting and set her down a saucer of cream. She was the only cat he had known to purr and eat at the same time. The sound was faintly indecent and spoke of appetites beyond the power of man to tame.

'Cookery is power,' his mother told him at an early age. She meant it jokingly. Minutes before, she had taught him how to make a simple chocolate toffee sauce to pour over ice cream (butter, sugar, cocoa, a few grains of instant coffee – he made it occasionally still) and was laughing at how instant a reaction it won with some schoolfriends he brought home to lunch.

He had little sense of humour at that age, even less than he had now, and he asked her, quite solemnly, what she meant.

'I'll tell you when we're alone,' she said, and winked.

He asked her again that night, while he sat on the end of her bed and watched her, fascinated, as she teased out her dancing hair in the breeze from the hair drier. She was taken aback at his earnestness. She had forgotten both sauce and comment. He had thought of little else all day.

'Men have very simple needs,' she said, 'sleep, food, warmth and the other thing. But hunger is the most powerful. When your stomach's turning in on itself, you can't concentrate. When you eat something delicious, you're happy, you're grateful. A griddle's more potent than any gun, Perry.' She laughed. 'Why frighten people into doing what you want when you can win their love with cake? That hubble-bubble stuff in *Macbeth* is a parody of a recipe; a cauldron's just an oversized casserole, after all. If you ask me, those women they burned at the stake were simply cooks who led whole communities by the nose and tongue.'

With the untutored taste buds of childhood, he had favoured sweet recipes at first. Happily these tended to be those involving the most magical transformations. Thus his early cookery lessons carried all the attraction of games with a chemistry set. There was that hot chocolate sauce that, once he had learned to let it boil sufficiently, set into filling-tugging caramel on contact with ice cream. There was the sequence of hot desserts, nicknamed *chemical puddings* by his mother, in which an unpromising sludge would rise up through a watery layer during baking, thickening it into a rich sauce as it formed a puffily cakey crust above it. Victoria sponge taught him pride. Patience he learned through meringue; those wrist-numbing extra minutes of whisking that divided egg whites that were merely stiff from those that were said to be *standing in peaks*, and the slow baking in a cool oven which managed mysteriously to produce a confection so crumbly and dry. It was only with chocolate brownies, however, with which a girlfriend's older brother was so easily persuaded to drop his jeans for a five-minute *scientific* inspection, that Perry learned the extent of his new-found power.

Adult, savoury cookery was taught piecemeal, largely through being asked to help out with occasional tasks. Learning how to brown chicken thighs, roll pieces of steak in seasoned flour, dissect and meticulously de-seed red peppers, he combined his new techniques with what he saw his mother doing and so added *coq au vin*, *boeuf en daube* and *ratatouille* to a still succinct repertoire.

'If you can cook,' she told him, 'you'll never be hungry, but if you can cook *well*, if you can do more than just feed people, you'll be popular too. You'll be able to choose who likes you.'

Thrilled by the potency of such a spell, for he was a scrawny child who had yet to grow into his nose, he hung on her every word. He followed her about the garden absorbing wisdom.

'Parsley,' she pronounced. 'Useful but common. The curly one is only really usable in sauce and soup. And never use the flat-leaved one unthinkingly. Often this plant, chervil, will do much better. Taste it. Go on. See? Now try this. Coriander. Superb stuff. You can use it almost like a vegetable, by the handful, but be careful again. Used in the wrong context it tastes like soap and it sticks to teeth as embarrassingly as spinach.'

In season, she led him around the fields and lanes behind the house introducing him to blackberries, sloes, elder bushes, mushrooms, crab apples, sorrel.

When Perry turned ten, shortly after his creation of a puff-ball and bacon roulade had seduced a new neighbour and demoralized the neighbour's wife, his mother fell ill. For a few weeks, without anyone's appearing to notice, he inherited her apron, and whisked up menu after comforting menu for his father and older brothers, reading cookery books in bed and skiving off afternoon sports sessions at school to race into town on his bicycle before the covered market closed. When she returned, grey and shattered after her operation, she was grateful to have had her wooden spoon usurped, still more to taste his nutritious soups and cunning vegetables after two weeks of hospital pap.

Her gratitude, however, seemed to break the peaceful spell of his father's quiescence. It was as though he were noticing for the first time as Perry stirred his sauces and deftly shredded roots and nuts, swamped in a practical but undeniably floral apron.

'Why don't you play rugby like Geoff?' he asked. 'You'd like rugby. Once you got used to it.'

'Sport bores me. What do you think of this duck? Was the fennel a mistake? Maybe celeriac would work better, or even parsnip. If I could get it to caramelize properly without the skin burning . . .'

Perry was duly banished to a boarding school on the York-shire coast, handpicked for its bracingly sporty philosophy and lack of opportunities for any science more domestic than the use of Ralgex and Universal Embrocation. His mother was brought down from her sickbed and set back to work at the kitchen stove. She collapsed there shortly afterwards and died of an internal haemorrhage halfway through assembling a deceptively humble fish pie. Perry cursed his father for his cruelty but laid on a suitable buffet for her funeral and brought his seduction of the neighbour to an electric conclusion with the aid of some witty yet somehow mournful filo parcels of pigeon, leek and sultana.

He hated school and counted off the passing weeks like a prisoner. His impatience to be free had more to do with the liberty to have access to more inspiring ingredients than with any brutalities visited on him. His growing mastery over food continued to protect him like a hero's winged sandals or magic armour. An ability to dress crab and whip up a mayonnaise won him an entrée to the shielding comforts of the prefects' common room in his second week and the older boys soon set him to baking them cakes instead of forcing him out onto icy playing fields. He even came to look forward to overnight field trips with the cadet corps, given charge as he was of the camp-fire kitchen. Since adolescents have always lurched between the kindred demands of belly and groin, cookery also brought him sporadic tastes of rough-handed romance.

His father and brothers had long dismissed him as effetely artistic and were as surprised as he was when he began to specialize in chemistry. Boarding school had given him a taste for independence. Without his mother there, the family home held little appeal for him and while passing through university and qualifying as a forensic scientist, he went there as little as possible. (He made exceptions for his brothers' successive weddings, miserable occasions where the poor quality of the catering made him more than usually grateful that he had kept cookery as a vice and not pursued it as a livelihood.)

He had only the one live-in lover, first encountered in the meat aisle of a local supermarket. Douglas had come out shopping in tennis clothes, fresh, or rather not, from a match. Perry could not help noticing the way the chilled air from the meat cabinets raised goose bumps on his legs and Douglas noticed him notice. After smiling, smirking then grinning encounters beside toiletries, Kosher and home baking successively, the evening had ended in Perry cooking Douglas lamb noisettes in a pink peppercorn sauce. Smug and yawning twelve hours later, he made them scrambled eggs and bacon. It took only two more dinners for Douglas to move in.

It was a love expressed as Perry knew best, in generous helpings, judiciously seasoned. Over four years, Douglas added running and secret dieting to tennis as he fought in vain the extra poundage that Perry's devotion was heaping on him. Then he fell ill and for three years after that, Perry became an expert in nutritional coaxing as he tried in vain to stave off Douglas's inexorable spells of weight loss, vanished appetite or nausea. The most innocent foods – yoghurt, bread, cheese – would suddenly be branded as enemies. His ingenuity was stretched to the limit. Whenever Douglas was in hospital, Perry would cook a portable supper for them both and make a point of their still sharing an evening meal there, even if Douglas could manage no more than a spoonful before sinking back on the pillows in defeat. Never had the preparation of food carried such an emotional charge for him.

Douglas's was the second funeral feast he had cooked, beating tears into cake batter, anger into cream. He intended it to be his last.

After Douglas there had been men occasionally, but no more lovers. Perry's experience of desire had always been so bound up in the pleasures of the table that he found it hard to surrender for long to any romance that was not essentially domestic. Then the hole in his domestic routine was unexpectedly filled.

A stroke after a hip operation left his father incapacitated. There was a gruesome council of war in which the brothers, abetted by child-worn wives, agreed that residential homes were both soulless and ruinously expensive. Perry had room in his house. Perry had experience of home nursing thanks to his 'lodger's' long illness. They would each pay a nominal monthly sum to their younger brother and he should take their father in. He had never declared his sexuality, assuming it would be taken as read and, as they confronted him with their tidy plan, he sensed it was too late to do so now. He had allowed them to assume he was merely a bachelor, a eunuch with a way with sauces. He had allowed them to assume that, for all their initial doubts, his work for CID meant that he had been vetted as 'sound'. Playing hard to define, he had played into their hands. He could hardly turn around and complain that visiting a speechless, incontinent, not to say unmusical parent on him would starve a love life that was already gasping for sustenance.

At first it seemed like an abominable invasion of his privacy. The old man might have lost control of tongue and bladder but retained his bullying nature and store of indignation. Gradually, however, Perry saw that there was no cause for fear. He was in charge now. He decided what the old man could and could not eat, when he would bathe, when he could watch television and, indeed, what he would watch. To cover the long hours he spent at work in the police laboratories, he took pleasure in hiring just the sort of camp, Irish nurse his father would loathe. Said treasure wore a uniform he described as Doris Blue. He was delighted when Perry confided that his father had been sleeping with men on the sly all his married life and was a wicked old flirt with wandering hands. Perry often came home to find the two of them watching films in which men loved men or women tap-danced and sang their hearts out. The nurse would be watching, at least, and singing along where appropriate. Perry's father would be merely staring, aghast, in the direction in which he had been so mercilessly wedged with scatter cushions.

Perry opened them an account at a specialist video library. In twelve months his father was exposed to the entire output of Crawford, Davis, Stanwyck, Garland, and the Turners Kathleen and Lana. He became a passive expert on the complete weepies of Douglas Sirk – of which the nurse was especially fond – and even the most misbegotten of MGM's musical output. He sat, breathing heavily, through any film that could be remotely described as lesbian or gay, subtitles, Kenneth Anger and all. He watched nothing pornographic, however, at least nothing hard core. Despite Perry's bland assurances, the nurse was sure the excitement would have dire effects on his bladder or even his heart.

It startled Perry to find that he could be so vindictive. Apart from some singularly unhelpful grief counselling after Douglas died, he had never been in therapy and was not given to self-analysis. He had never given voice to the damage his father had done him, so had never given it substance. Even now, he did not immediately seek a retributive justification for what he was doing.

He did not abuse his father physically, although the odd smack might have seemed only the mild repayment of a long-outstanding debt. He dressed him. He undressed him. He bathed him. He changed his incontinence pads. If he spoon-fed him the kind of food his father had always dismissed as foreign or *nancy*, if he occasionally buttoned him into a violet quilted bed jacket that had been his mother's (telling the nurse to humour a camp old man's little ways) it was done in a spirit of domestic spite not unlike that practised between many a cohabiting couple.

As a year went by, then two, during which his father was a powerless, dolled-up guest of honour at several of Perry's more Wildean parties, he came to think of the old man less as a parent than a grouchy partner. As he pecked his father's cheek on leaving for work or retiring for the night, as he amused himself by brushing his still thick, silver hair into a variety of fanciful styles, as he meticulously piped a saucily naked cherub onto his heart-shaped birthday cake, Perry would admit that, while still not exactly fond, he had developed a kind of tender dependence on his father's being there. Bereft of any other outlet, his nurturing energies were making do with the only available man on the horizon. (The nurse was never an option; Perry had old-fashioned views on the healthy inflexibility of sexual roles and had marked the nurse down as a sister from day one.)

Howard caught his eye over the contents of a dead woman's intestinal tract. The corpse had been principal stockholder in a toy manufacturing firm due for flotation. She was found face-down, fully dressed, in her sunken bath. Her family claimed she had drunk too much, fallen in, passed out and drowned. As detective inspector on the case, Howard mistrusted them and ordered an autopsy. The stomach was duly shown to contain

373

precious little bath water, which indicated that she had died before submersion. There was alcohol in her bloodstream but not enough to knock out, let alone kill, such a hardened drinker. Called in by the coroner to analyse the contents of her gut, Perry found beef, onions, red wine, button mushrooms, rice and significant traces of a powerful sedative administered to dogs and horses.

'Her brother's a vet,' Howard murmured. Beneath the crumpled, unshaven look of the overstressed detective, the ghost of a more dynamic person stirred. Leaning against the lab desk, he towered over Perry, who was perched on a stool. 'How specific can you be?'

'Very,' Perry told him, looking up from flicking through the pharmacology files on his computer screen. 'These weren't prescription tranqs. I mean, I can't give you a brand name but I can narrow it to a choice of six or seven and they're only for veterinary use.'

Now Howard smiled, a grin of broad satisfaction that cracked the laughter lines fanning out from his sad, blue eyes. Normally Perry was curt with policemen, judiciously telling them no more than the science they needed. Basking in the big man's approval, however, he would have prattled on for hours if it kept him so close.

'There's something else,' he added.

'What?'

'Well, it's much more concentrated in the gut contents samples than in her blood. Maybe it was injected into the meat they knew she was going to cook? If she ate it rare enough and they stuck enough in, it would still pack a lethal punch. You'll need to check my data with the coroner, but I think he'll bear it out.'

'Thanks,' Howard said. 'Thanks a lot. You've made my

week. This could have turned messy.' He rubbed a big hand across his tired face and over his stubbled chin. 'I owe you a drink.'

'You're on.' Perry saw the wedding ring as he spoke.

From self-protective instinct he spent the rest of the day curbing his interest. When Howard dropped by late in the afternoon, however, changed, shaven and smelling of cheap cologne, he found it impossible to resist his invitation. Howard was a new transfer and unfamiliar with the area. On the pretext of showing him some countryside but actually to avoid running into any colleagues, Perry had him drive them out to a small country pub which served excellent pork and leek sausages. This proved a wise choice for, midway through his second pint, Howard lurched the conversation away from cadavers and poison to his marriage, his teenage daughter and, after much fumbling with a beer-mat, to the reason why his wife had left him. Perry discreetly rang the nurse and persuaded him to tuck his father up in bed and stay late on double time, then they drove up onto the moor and made frantic, bruising and extremely messy love in Howard's car.

Howard cried afterwards, which Perry found utterly bewitching.

They continued to meet regularly back in Howard's rented flat. Howard often cried out during sex or would exclaim, 'I like this. I *do*. This is what I like.' And he often wept after it for sheer relief. He claimed to find Perry overpowering because he could approach sex with another man so matter-of-factly. He had no idea that the very sight of him shyly unbuttoning his drip-dry shirt made Perry want to tap-dance. They always went to Howard's place. Perry found he could not face a meeting between his lover and his father, let alone Howard and the nurse and, when they first discussed their situations, had unthinkingly said that he 'lived with someone'. Howard's assumption that this was a lover and that Perry was risking a relationship to be with him gave Perry an even fizzier sense of power than Howard's grateful tears.

He said nothing to disabuse him. At first he liked the fact that their meetings were secret, snatched, and often in daylight. He liked the anonymity of Howard's drably furnished flat and the sense that it was an arena in which nothing was forbidden them. He soon began to grow hungry for more, however. He yearned for evenings together. He wanted to wake up with him. Most compellingly of all, he wanted to cook him a meal, the more so when he realized that Howard was a stranger to cookery and stocked nothing beyond teabags, cornflakes, butter, milk and a bag of sliced white.

Once he had settled upon fungi, of course, he had to wait a maddening four or five weeks until the most fitting ones were in season. He knew precisely the variety he needed to use. Mercifully rare, they happened to be a speciality of the region, favouring the grassy fringes of beech woods. Remarkably similar, at a glance, to an innocuous variety, the things had often been pointed out to him on walks with his mother. Identifiable only from the way their ghostly flesh bruised blue, they caused paralysis and, in an already weakened victim, heart failure. Taking care to use some kitchen towel to keep the toxic harvest separate from the harmless field mushrooms he had also picked, Perry made a perfect risotto; arborio rice brewed in chicken stock and mushroom juices – with a dash of cream and three threads of saffron – until sticky without being indigestibly glutinous. He went to some trouble. He lit candles and dressed his father in a jacket and tie.

'It could be our anniversary,' he told him as he spooned the fragrant mixture into the old man's eager mouth. 'More wine, dear? It's a good one this – nicely nutty without being sharp. There we go. Greedy! You'll have the end of the spoon off . . .'

He was not foolish. He waited, peacefully holding his father's hand as they listened to Mendelssohn, until it was plain that death had joined them at the table then he went to the telephone and summoned help. When he heard the ambulance approaching, he bravely wolfed down several mouthfuls of the bad risotto on top of the helping he had already eaten of the good. This meant that he was already feeling very cold and strange and barely needed to act when he begged the nice young man in casualty for a stomach pump.

'I don't know how I could have been so stupid,' he told his brothers later, his throat still raw. 'I've been picking mushrooms since we were children. I've never made a mistake before. I'll never forgive myself. Never.'

But he did, naturally. He bade the Irish nurse a tearful farewell, redecorated his father's room, donated two suitcases of old male clothes to Help the Aged and, at last, was in a position to invite Howard to dinner. He made the date for a Friday, intending them to spend the weekend together but had kept this last bit a surprise.

Howard brought flowers as well as wine. The leek tartlets were a triumph, as was the Moroccan chicken with salted lemons. Perry made a mental note, however, never again to serve Howard lemon posset. He liked it almost too much and had a, somehow unromantic, second helping which brought on a nasty attack of heartburn come bedtime.

FOURTH OF JULY, 1862

Alice was beginning to get very tired of sitting by her sister on the bank, and of having nothing to do. Rhoda could sense her ennui just as she could feel the oppressive heat the child was giving off as she lolled heavily against her. Both were breaking her concentration on a peculiarly dry chapter she had just reached on the life cycle of the lobster.

Alice had yet to shake off the last of a heavy summer cold. She breathed through her mouth as she made a show of reading the book too. Rhoda could sense the desire to speak again welling up in the child. It was like the slow, fat bubble Papa used to amuse her with by upending then righting a tin of treacle.

Any minute now, Rhoda told herself.

Sure enough it was only moments later when Alice broke violently away in a bid to distract her further. 'A rabbit!' she shouted, pointing to the other side of the river. 'A white rabbit with pink eyes!'

Rhoda sighed and discreetly turned back a page to begin the chapter afresh. Heat and Alice had reduced it to mental fog. 'Don't be a tease, dear,' she murmured.

'But there was! It ran along the path there and dived through that long grass. It must have a hole there. And it had a waist-coat on and a pocket watch.'

'If only you'd brought your notebook you could have written me a story about it. I said I'd be dull company.'

'Yes, but somebody had to come with you,' said Alice with an unfortunate echo of their parlour maid, 'or people would talk.'

The family's maintenance of respectable behaviour was painfully erratic. Mama still thought nothing of sending Rhoda about town unchaperoned. She had allowed the question of whether Rhoda was *out* or not to slide in a way that left Rhoda known among her more orthodox peers as *Poor Rhoda* and which, she was quite sure, unsettled potential suitors. And, more importantly, their mothers. At Alice's age she had assumed she would one day have a coming-out dance then marry early and well. Young girls blithely assumed the inevitability of suitors as seeds did sunshine. Instead she found herself an old maid of eighteen with a mother more interested in moths than matrimony, doomed to become a governess if nobody would have her soon.

Her dreams of romantic escape to some more regular establishment had been easier to sustain while she was an only child but then she had been left at Miss Bileheart's academy while her parents made a two-year trip to Patagonia in search of some wasp or other and had returned with baby Alice tucked among their less lively specimens. The sisters had recently become fellows in suffering courtesy of a trip to Zanzibar that had produced Eustace. Rhoda felt more than ever the governess-to-be as Nanny was as taken up in the baby as Mama was in her lepidopterology, encouraging Alice to trail after her big sister for amusement.

In Rhoda's nightmares Alice was married off before her, a radiant child-bride in a foam of antique lace with Rhoda her embittered matron of honour in a dark violet silk with black trimmings and horrid jet beads.

'I'm bored,' Alice said, kicking out at a lizard and sending the poor innocent skittering into the long grass. 'Why couldn't we go to the museum to see the dodo?'

'We can't do that every Sunday, dear.'

'Or that garden? The pretty one with the fountains.'

'It's much cooler here,' Rhoda said although she agreed with her. She too loved the public gardens with their elegant benches, gravel walks and wealth of social opportunity. She had only chosen the secluded riverside walk instead in an effort to curb Alice's unseemly showing off by depriving her of a susceptible audience. 'If you keep very still, you might see a frog or a water vole.'

'I hate frogs.'

Rhoda sighed. *I sigh*, she thought, *more often than I laugh. No good can come of it. Soon I shall have a sighing sort of face and a downturned mouth.* 'Have another violet comfit,' she suggested.

Alice shook her head, her face like thunder. There were grass stains on her pinafore and gloves and one stocking was crumpled. She looked less than angelic. 'I'm thirsty,' she announced. A mother little older than herself staggered by under the weight of a large and especially piglike baby. Alice glared at the baby as though to blight it.

Rhoda reached guiltily into her reticule and took out a blue glass bottle. She had stolen it from the nursery cupboard that morning while Nanny was busy with Eustace's bath. She had taken to carrying a supply of her brother's gripe water the way women in the American West were said to carry pistols. It proved effective on her nerves in times of agitation and she hoped its soothing properties might still her sister. She could count on Alice's greed.

Alice snatched the bottle, unstoppered it and took a long, incautious draught before Rhoda could stop her. Then she flopped back on the rug beside her and closed her eyes. Rhoda retrieved what was left of the gripe water and returned to the life cycle of the lobster. But not for long.

'Which is that toadstool? You know, the one that gives you dreams?' Alice asked thoughtfully, eyes still closed.

'The Liberty Cap, psilocybe semilanceata. There were some in the field where we rested earlier.'

'If I ate it, would it make me sick?'

'Alice, you didn't!'

'No,' Alice said uncertainly. 'But if I did?'

'Possibly. You should certainly feel very strange.'

'Oh *good*!'

'But you're never to eat anything you find without showing me first.'

'I wish Dinah were with us.'

'You can't bring a cat on a picnic. It would be both eccentric and cruel. And you would most certainly lose the cat in the process.'

Alice snorted dismissively and shifted so that her head lay in Rhoda's lap. She yawned as might the cat in question, showing small white teeth and a curling tongue and fell asleep as abruptly as a kitten. Even allowing for her occasional snores, she looked, in slumber, as sweet as she appeared to be in company.

Until Alice took her first steps outside the nursery, Rhoda had thought herself fairly attractive, not unchastely witty, an attentive listener, in short, a girl any man might wish to marry. But even before Alice could lisp complete sentences, she had eclipsed her. She was unambiguously beautiful, petulant and given to wild fancies. Men of all ages, Papa included, found her delightful. Were Mama less vague about observing proprieties it would not have mattered but Alice rarely stayed in a room when sent to it and encroached on Rhoda's shrinking territory at all hours. She had only to appear, clutching the dormouse she kept in a straw-lined teapot or begging to recite *'Tis the Voice of the Sluggard* or *Speak Gently, It Is Better Far* for Rhoda to feel herself dull, humourless and overlooked. She lacked charm, she had discovered, and resented those who had failed to instil it in her, which only emphasized the shortcoming.

As if to illustrate the problem, The Mathematician now came by in his rowing boat. Rhoda just had time to slide Alice's hot little head off her lap and onto a cushion before he came ashore.

Two years ago he would not have been her first choice. With his stoop and whiskers he seemed almost as old as Papa and it was hard to picture him as an object of devotion but he remained the most prominent bachelor among her parents' friends and the most regular caller at their house.

'Chaperone asleep on the job?' he asked after they had exchanged hellos.

'Yes and *please* don't wake her. She's been a trial because I dared to thwart her.'

They sat together a little further off in a willow's shifting shade. The air was thick with river scents and the cooing of wood pigeons. Warm from his rowing and apologetically in shirtsleeves, he was far more appealing and youthful than she had ever known him. He smelled of laundry starch and something more manly.

She fed him tarts from the picnic hamper, confessing she had made the mulberry jam herself but not the pastry and, for the first time in their acquaintance, she felt he was noticing her.

'Do you dance?' he asked her and she felt herself blush absurdly as she replied that of course she did.

'When required to,' she added then wished she hadn't because it made it sound as though she danced only under sufferance when, on the contrary, it was one of her chiefest pleasures, second only to reading.

'So do you know a dance called the Lancers' Quadrille?' he asked.

'I love it,' she told him, to correct her earlier cold impression.

'How many pairs does one need to perform it successfully, I wonder?'

Was he planning a dance? The idea was strange, almost comical, but not impossible. He could not give it in his college, of course, but it was not unheard of for bachelor dons to entertain in the assembly rooms or under the aegis of married friends. For a wild moment she imagined him waltzing her through her father's library, her skirts raising a small tornado of disturbed papers and index cards about them.

'It's for a poem,' he explained, abashed. 'However fanciful the destination, I like to embark from a rock of sound fact.'

Discovering he was a poet transformed him almost as much as finding him in shirtsleeves had done.

She answered his strange question and decided she would beg Mama to throw a dance for her, however modest, and see that he was invited. She allowed him to look with curiosity at the book she was reading. Talk of lobsters led to talk of lunch, because he had been served mock turtle soup that day and it seemed she genuinely fascinated him by being able to explain that marine turtles only appeared to be weeping when out of the water because their kidneys could not break down brine so it was constantly discharged from a gland like a tear duct beside each eye.

A puppy loitering behind its walkers threatened to wake

Alice by licking her face and hands. Worried she was coming across as too drily academical, Rhoda seized the chance to reveal her tender potential by shooing the puppy off and sliding Alice's head back onto her lap. Alice mumbled crossly but slept on and Rhoda spread her golden hair across her skirt so that some of Alice's loveliness might reflect up on her.

Of course his eye was now repeatedly drawn to the wretched child and he began to talk so warmly about the poignant brevity of youthful innocence that Rhoda was tempted to rouse her sister at once, Alice having a reliably filthy temper when woken abruptly. Instead she grew cool and formal and must have repelled him because he soon apologized for keeping her from her studies. Despite a rather unseemly, even desperate, late offer of another jam tart, he took his leave and rowed away.

She abandoned her reading and ate the last tart herself. Then, in a sudden access of spite, she roused Alice by shaking leaves into her face from an overhanging branch. Alice woke in such a state of excitement and so full of some vivid dream she had been enjoying that Rhoda feared she had been nibbling hallucinogenic fungus after all.

As Alice finally wandered off and began to amuse herself, Rhoda felt a chill breeze across her heart and suffered an insidious fancy that her life was no more than an unimportant fiction and that any instant an impatient hand would turn the page and she and her crossness and her compendium of facts and her lack of charm would be gone.

She resolved to be a sweeter sister, at least for what remained of the summer.

SAVING SPACE

'Is this place taken?'

'No. Not at all.'

Although the church porch was quite empty, he instinctively rose slightly and slid along on the stone bench to make room for her. Shyness had become a philosophy with him. Throughout their marriage, his wife had always talked to strangers for him, filling the air with words enough for two. Since her death he had developed tactics for evading conversation. On a train or aeroplane or in a dentist's waiting room, he would read or summon up an appearance of such profound concentration as to offer a mute rebuke to any who might think to interrupt his chain of thought. Formalized exchanges with waiters or ticket sellers were easily got through but he had learned to dread the formless conversation of strangers; one never knew where it might lead.

Settling back on the bench, he faced slightly away from her, towards the closed church door. He had not thought to bring a book and clutched only a cushion. His wife had always said that part of the fun of concerts at Trenellion was the lack of seat reservations. Places had to be reserved with cushions, an hour before each festival concert began. This task had always fallen to his wife, who relished the conversations she initiated while queuing and would season each interval in the concert with pinches of information she had gleaned.

'That one there. In the purple. On her second marriage. He's a bone-cracker from St Tudy.'

'See that one? No. Over there by the organ bench. With the funny teeth? Three children in the orchestra this year. Just imagine. Three! Wife not musical at all, apparently. Odd how that happens sometimes. Like vicars with wives who don't do flowers.'

This was his first time back since her death. For four summers in a row he had preferred to let the cottage throughout the season and stay put in Barrowcester, weathering the heat and the tourists. This year, however, his teenage granddaughters had expressed a wish to learn to surf. He had been perfectly willing to let his son and his family have the place to themselves but had been hectored into coming too. His daughter-in-law, who worked as a bereavement counsellor in her spare time, accused him of avoiding memories.

'They're happy memories,' he said. 'Why should I want to avoid them?'

So he had come, clinging at least to the independence his own car afforded, and found his quiet, seaside cottage turned into a kind of purgatory. The bathroom was rarely free when he needed it, the radio had always been tuned away from Radio 3 when he turned it back on, his son kept cornering him with grotesque expressions of hangdog sympathy, his daughter-in-law had a way of ruining perfectly good food by cooking it with fashionable herbs that all smelt more or less of tomcat, and his granddaughters, tall, tanned, muscular creatures like athletes from a Nazi propaganda film, only with less manners, persisted in holding open house to all manner of nouveau-louche youth they attracted on the beach.

The festival's fortnight of nightly concerts was proving his salvation. Playing on the family's aversion to classical music, he bought a fistful of single tickets, cheap at the price, and escaped every afternoon at five-thirty to wait at the front of the queue. He then enjoyed a reassuringly plain, unvarying picnic of boiled eggs, pork pies, tomatoes and red wine before the concert and returned home after it able to face his son's patronage and granddaughters' partying with a measure of equanimity. There were just three concerts to go, three more nights of sanity after which he would make good his escape.

'Excuse me.'

She was a young-old girl, hair in slides, in an ill-fitting floral frock. From its dusty quality and fifties style, it might have come from one of the charity shops he gathered the young now frequented.

'Yes?'

'I know it's an awful cheek but would you mind taking this and bagging a seat for me?' She held out a cushion as faded as her dress, saw his hesitation. 'It's just that I so want a good seat but I ought to be helping in the car park.'

'Oh. Yes. Of course.' He took the cushion and was charmed by her smile. Music student, he thought. Nice, old-fashioned kind of girl. The sort who would play the viola from choice.

He saved her a seat across the aisle from him, so she would not feel bound to make grateful conversation later on. He looked out for her as he ate his solitary picnic but the only car park attendants he saw were girls like his granddaughters, in shorts, sharing a bottle of wine and making fun of drivers who disliked reversing. Perhaps she had chosen to guard the lay-by, a solitary job.

He grew mildly anxious as the church filled and still she failed to appear. When a festival official came to stare at the offending, sought-after space and he explained it was for a car parker, the cushion was briskly whisked away.

'She can stand at the back like the rest of us,' the official said and gave the seat to a tall man with a cough.

Worried, he looked for her in the interval after the first piece, a jubilant Bach motet, but the people standing at the back were unfamiliar. Then he reflected that her face was so quiet he would probably look straight through her if he saw her again. He gave himself over to the pleasures of music and thought nothing more of it.

That night he could not sleep. His room felt airless and seemed haunted by a sweet smell whose source he could not place.

The next concert was chamber music – two string quartets and an obscure Swiss piece involving trombones. The crowd would not be large, therefore, but chamber concerts tended to involve extra competition for a pew with a view, so he came early and once again found himself one of the few people in the porch. He remembered to bring a book as defence, a guide to seventeenth-century bench ends.

'Excuse me?'

A middle-aged woman with a defeated air, she had on an oatmeal-coloured trouser suit of the kind he recalled his wife wearing under Heath. He was irritated at the interruption but no sooner met her eye than he felt oddly protective towards her.

'Yes?'

'I wonder if I could rely on you to save a space for me with this.'

He felt one of the momentary qualms that had become so frequent since he became a widower; did he know her? He had never been good at remembering people, especially women.

This was partly his wife's fault, of course, because she remembered absolutely everyone and, like an ambassador's private secretary, would second-guess when he was at a loss and would discreetly murmur a name in his ear as an unfamiliar face approached. Matters weren't helped by the way Trenellion drew on such a shallow pool socially that concerts were full of men and women of a similar age and type. The women tended to be nicely weather-beaten, gardening, dogwalking sorts with unfussy, undyed hair, many of whom looked remarkably alike to his eyes.

'It's my mother, you see,' the woman continued. 'I can't leave her for long. I mean I can, obviously, for the concert, but the friend who's mummy-sitting won't arrive until half-past.'

'Of course,' he told her and smiled in case he did know her. 'I'll do my best.'

He saw the way other people in the queue glared at him as he took the old cushion off her. *Queue-bargers*, they were thinking, *quislings*, but their glares hardened his resolve. His wife's mother passed her last eight years in their spare room. He knew what it cost to ask for help.

Sure enough, the audience was not large, but the seat he had saved her beside him was put at threat by a lively clutch of people who expressed a wish to sit by their friends.

'Tell you what,' said their ringleader. 'We'll sit and chat till she gets here and then when she comes we can all bunch up.'

He was on the point of saying that the pews only sat four in any comfort when he thought he recognized one of the group as a schoolfriend of his son. Inhibited, he fell to reading programme notes and let them annex the pew. The later the woman was, the wilder his pledges to himself, until he reached the point of being prepared to give up his seat for her. She never returned, however, and her cushion went from being merely squeezed to being sat upon by a stranger. Perhaps the mother had taken a turn for the worse, he thought.

The trombone piece proved surprisingly beguiling.

Driving home, dazzled by headlamps in his rear-view mirror, he could not rid himself of the sense that he was not alone in the car. Even with the window wide, the sweet smell in his room was more powerful than ever. Ridiculously unnerved, he stayed up to party with the granddaughters and their ghastly friends and woke in an armchair in the small hours with a crick in his neck and a strange dog on his lap that showed its teeth when he made to move.

The final concert of the season, a Mozart triple bill, drew a huge crowd, far more than could fit in the church. Many would content themselves with lolling against tombstones near the open doors. Even leaving the cottage at five-thirty he found the end of the queue outside the porch already. He drew up a plastic chair like the others but kept himself aloof from the prevailing Dunkirk spirit with the aid of J.T. Blight's *Churches of West Cornwall*.

'Excuse me.'

One could see at a glance she was frail, with legs like matchsticks and a shakiness to the hand that grasped the cushion. She began to explain that she had promised to collect a friend but he cut her short, taking the cushion from her with a smile, won over by a nostalgic waft of Yardley's English Lavender.

He moved with low cunning and secured two of the best seats in the house. He took the precaution of cutting his picnic short, stinting on the red wine so as to be back at their cushions in good time. He defended her place from all comers. When, at the eleventh hour, the chorus and orchestra already in place, an imperious woman in black satin said, 'I really must ask you to give up that seat. Seven-thirty is the absolute cut-off point for reservations and we still have a queue,' his reaction took him by surprise.

'It's my wife,' he told her. 'She is coming, she's desperate to, but she's very ill you see and can't queue for long. She'll be here any second, I'm certain of it.'

To his amazement the woman melted and was almost placatory. 'Of *course* she will,' she said. 'That's quite all right.'

He realized to his horror that she had been a friend, if not quite an intimate, of his late wife and plainly thought he had lost his reason to grief. Shamefaced, he turned swiftly to face the front again, praying no one else had overheard his words who knew the truth of the matter and might report the story back to his son.

As the conductor swept through the applause to his podium and still the old woman had not appeared, he noticed her cushion for the first time. It was a sun-bleached affair in dog-worn chintz. An honourable, holiday cottage sort of cushion, that spoke of long afternoons and sweet, familiar pleasures. The same cushion he had taken from strange, female hands the night before and the night before that.

Instinctively he withdrew his hand from it and sat to one side, giving it space.

'As some of you may realize,' the conductor was saying, 'tonight's performance is dedicated to Betty Pearson, who cheerfully dubbed herself *spinster of this parish* and was for four decades a crucial, modest, background figure in keeping the festival ticking over. She died last week. Dear Betty, we know you're listening. This one's for you.'

As the overture to *Così* bubbled around them, he became

aware of the smell again, the sweet smell that had twice invaded his bedroom. He heard the unmistakable rustle of cellophane and the muffled clunk of happily sucked boiled sweet bumping tooth. No one else seemed to be bothered by it and before long the music had cleared all other thoughts and sensations from his head. Hours later, however, rinsing out his picnic things, he was so startled that he stumbled back and sat on the kitchen stool, tap still running.

In the small Tupperware box where he had left no more than an uneaten tomato and some salt in a small twist of foil, someone had tucked an unopened bag of barley sugars.

PETALS ON A POOL

Edith was only at the festival because of an administrative error. It was the *other* Edith Chalmers they'd wanted. She knew it, her agent knew it and so – rapidly – did the festival organizers but two decades of such slights at last gave rise to a small demonstration of bloody-mindedness and she affected not to have understood, which duly shamed everyone else into saying nothing.

She was the first Edith Chalmers. She wrote quietly devastating studies of a quiet sort of English character: thwarted people too well bred to fight, people who numbered priests among their friends, people who not only noticed split infinitives but found them morally troubling. The other Edith Chalmers, who had no such qualms, wrote bestsellers about illegitimate girls of no account who rose to positions of tediously itemized wealth and high status. She only bothered to call herself Edith P. Chalmers for her first offering, *To Boldly Sin*. The sales of this eclipsed all those of her namesake in less than two weeks and the P. was dropped from the second edition. It was the kind of effrontery that she celebrated in her heroines.

The first Edith naïvely thought her publishers might sue but they merely resorted to a suitably quiet sort of branding, thereafter announcing her as Edith Chalmers (Author of *Sad Cypresses*) or Edith Chalmers (Author of *A Corner Table*).

'You've been invited to the Bali Book Festival,' her agent said warily. 'All expenses paid. They want you for a spotlight session and then a panel on romantic fiction. Shall I let them down gently?'

Edith would usually have sighed and said yes but she thought of her late best friend Margaret, who had written whodunnits about a dog breeder and said yes to everything. Margaret was a tireless attendee of readers' days and book festivals and regarded each and every train ticket, hotel bed and feast of mini-bar chocolate as just compensation for the failure of her publishers to see that her lengthy backlist took fire. Margaret remained a shameless freeloader until her recent death. Edith missed her keenly.

'No,' she told her agent. 'Say yes for a change. Tell them I'd be delighted.'

She assumed the organizers would find a way to cancel once they'd seen their mistake but perhaps, being oriental, they were too strenuously polite. They e-mailed gushingly to say how wonderful, what fans they were and so on. Then they e-mailed again, rather more coolly, to say how unexpectedly difficult they were finding it to gather sufficient stock of her titles for the festival bookshop. They sent her aeroplane ticket with nothing more enthusiastic attached than a compliment slip. It was only an economy ticket – the other Edith lived in a tax haven and passed much of her life in first class – but this Edith was slight and would be perfectly comfortable. It would be a free holiday with only a little work attached, it would be interesting and it would offer some correction to the disparity in her and her namesake's fortunes.

As she fought through the airport crowds into the stifling evening air of Denpasar, Edith faced humiliation by taxi driver. Ranged along a crowd barrier was a three-deep line of drivers, all holding cards with the names of the passengers they were there to collect. She could see her name nowhere but some of the writing was small. She unearthed her glasses then walked along the line squinting at the names, a process made no easier by the way each driver waggled his card as she drew close, blurring its lettering. She walked up and down four times, melting in the heat, bitterly regretting her decision to come, and was at last reduced to perching on her sagging suitcase, in full view of all the drivers, to wait.

Her name appeared at last, wildly misspelt, behind all the others, waggled by a driver who explained, entirely without apology, that they had still to wait for someone else.

'Might I sit in the car at least?' she asked but he only smiled and repeated,

'We have to wait, lady. Very important guest.'

This proved to be a formidable journalist from Hong Kong, Lucinda Yeung. Lent height by heels, soignée to the point of agelessness, she made Edith conscious of the crumpled hours she had just passed in travelling. She had a set of immaculate suitcases, of a shade that toned with her cream suit, and left their driver to cope with them while she consulted her little kid-bound agenda and quizzed Edith. As soon as she'd ascertained that she wasn't the other Edith Chalmers, she relaxed and confessed to having 'stitched her up once'. She broke off to grill the driver in quickfire Bahasa then turned back with a feline smile. 'Turns out we're staying in the island's best hotel,' she said. 'You're very lucky. The drive will take around thirty-five minutes. Do you mind if I conduct a little business? I'm chairing several events and I'm way behind as always.'

Edith said that would be quite understandable and Ms Yeung spent the rest of their blissfully air-conditioned journey on her telephone, greeting a succession of authors with virtually identical praise for their latest books and the bluntly delivered instruction that they were not to turn up for their events with prepared speeches.

'The public comes to see you interact, not reading your homework. And they don't want readings either; they can read your book themselves once you've convinced them to buy it.'

The end of each call was softened by some variant of the praise that had opened it and some regally personal touch, an enquiry about a garden or husband or pet made after a rapid glance at the notes she had made alongside the names and addresses in her agenda. A call completed, a name was scratched off a list. Ms Yeung's professionalism was so astonishing it did not occur to Edith to be offended or to make any effort not to listen in.

The last author was dealt with as they finished passing through Ubud, roughly five minutes before their arrival at the hotel. Ms Yeung put away her agenda and gave Edith her full, interested attention.

'Don't worry that we're so far out from all the action,' she told her. 'There'll be a free car to take you into Ubud whenever you need and the compensations are terrific. The nights are cooler and quieter out here. You won't be troubled by barking dogs or woken by cockerels and the rooms and service are perfection.'

The car paused at a gatehouse for security men to check beneath it for bombs then they were waved through. They approached a brightly-lit pavilion, where staff were lined up in expectation.

'Now don't go racing off with your famous friends tomorrow. I'll want to catch up with you,' Ms Yeung said as a young man in a version of traditional dress came to open their door.

Female staff met them with namastes and draped them with

scented white garlands of welcome. Then, before Edith could say goodnight, they were deftly separated and whisked in different directions into the lantern-lit grounds.

It was like no hotel she had ever visited. There was none of the usual sordid business of credit-card swipes or checking who was paying for what. Edith's guide introduced herself as Ayu.

'I'm your personal assistant for the duration of your stay. Anything you need, anything you don't like, just dial one and I'll answer,' she said. 'I'll stop by each morning after breakfast to file your requests for the day. Your room is this way. Watch your step here, it's a little uneven.'

She led the way past a bewildering succession of pavilions and pools, gardens and terraces. She pointed out various restaurants and spa centres in passing which Edith was sure she would never rediscover by daylight. Edith could hear rushing water somewhere far below and, through the trees, a music like nothing she had heard before, at once frenetic and calmly circular, as though moving at two speeds at once. It seemed to be made by gongs or tuned drums of some kind.

'It's a temple ceremony,' Ayu told her, seeing she had paused to listen. 'There's a full moon this week ... So. Here we are. This is your room and your own pool is just there across the terrace. Beyond that grille you'll find a library with a computer and broadband access.'

She unlocked and slid open a huge glazed door into a suite of rooms easily the size of Edith's little flat in Tufnell Park. She demonstrated shower, fridge, television, lighting, remote control, air conditioning, mosquito nets and only then, on the point of bidding goodnight and as though she sensed it was deeply distasteful, she asked for Edith's passport and took a swipe of her credit card on a tiny electronic reader she produced from a pocket.

After a dreamy night haunted by the sound of distant gongs and the perfume of aromatic oil in the lanterns on her terrace, Edith woke to find herself in a kind of paradise. The hotel was a series of tastefully converted antique buildings spread across an old estate or plantation on the steeply folded sides of a river valley. Through the trees came virid glimpses of deserted rice fields but no other buildings.

Edith had been trained by Margaret never to have a hotel breakfast delivered for fear of extra charges and a reduction in choice. Besides, breakfast in a pretty pavilion built over a cascade was part of the treat. Deciding not to fret after English marmalade and her usual toast and strong coffee, she elected to embrace, with a good child's passivity, whatever this adventure threw at her. She thus found herself sipping a lawn-green concoction made of melon and parsley and eating some kind of pancakes stuffed with nuts and berries.

It was impossible to sense how many guests there were since they were housed far apart and many, like Ms Yeung, might have elected to take breakfast on their terraces. The restaurant was almost deserted. There was a severe Japanese woman glaring into her tea in a corner and an Australian couple were leaving, softly arguing, as she arrived. At the table next to her a wan young man was poring over the festival programme. He smiled fleetingly and mouthed a hello at her as she sat so it didn't seem too forward to speak back once she had finished the last of her surprisingly filling pancakes.

'Are you here for the festival too?'

'Looks like it,' he said quietly.

'Are you Irish?'

'American,' he said. 'But my mother was from Limerick.' He looked back at the programme. 'My event seems to have been left off this.'

'How terrible! Is it too late to complain?'

'Oh I'm used to it. A voice in the wilderness, that's me.'

'I'm Edith Chalmers,' she said brightly, in an effort to head him off from gloom.

He brightened at once. 'No!'

'The other one. The one no one's heard of.'

'Ah. Well no one's heard of me either so we're quits. I'm Peter John.' He leant across to shake her proffered hand. His grasp was so cool and weak she wondered if he were unwell. 'You see? You've forgotten it already. I always told my mother it was a mistake to marry a man with no proper surname; two first names give the mind no anchor.'

'I'll think of you as Prester John,' she said. 'Then it'll stick. Sorry. What do you write?'

'I'm a poet,' he said. 'So my case is hopeless really. Still, we're in the very best hotel and I intend to make the most of it. Although even the staff seem to have forgotten I'm here.'

As if on cue, the waitress ignored his pleading look as she came to clear Edith's place. Edith offered him a roll and nut butter as he looked famished but he waved her little basket aside.

'No thanks,' he said. 'I've a massage at ten and it's best on an empty stomach. They're going to pound me with sea salt then dribble me all over with stimulating oils. But show me your event so I can circle it.'

She flicked through his programme and shyly pointed out her two events, feeling she ought really to give him one of them. He circled them both with a tiny pen worthy of Ms Yeung. It was ivory with a little skull carved on its cap.

'If I hear no one else,' he said, 'I shall come into town to hear you, the other, the *real* Edith Chalmers!'

Although her events were not until the third day, she felt honour bound to attend as much of the festival as possible because someone else had paid for her to be there and she had been nicely brought up. Besides, the hotel's luxury – a part of which plainly lay in its keeping the vulgar question of prices aired as rarely as possible – made her nervous. It might have been different had someone from the festival welcomed her and made it quite clear what she was and wasn't going to be paying for at the adventure's end . . .

So for two days she fought jet-lag and lived like a nun among sybarites, eating minimal breakfasts, catching her free ride into Ubud in the morning and dining in the evening off the treats in her lavishly restocked fruit bowl, which Ayu had expressly pointed out were free of charge. By day she heard novelists and translators and historians and poets. She sat through discussions of adultery in young adult fiction, the gender politics of far eastern folklore and Does Post Colonialism Exist. She winced at one woman's account of her daughter's circumcision and laughed at another's sonnet to her neurotic Abyssinian. It was all very lively and interesting but she felt lonely in a way she never felt at home, where she saw far fewer people. She longed to escape and explore the island, which clearly had a unique and fascinating culture, but she was intimidated by her lack of language and the vast denominations of the local currency. She felt she shouldn't go touring during festival hours yet when the last event finished it was nearly dark and she was nervous of missing her free ride home.

She spotted Lucinda Yeung repeatedly, either on stage or in the middle of an animated crowd, but Ms Yeung's glance seemed to slide over her in a myopic way that discouraged friendly approaches. The other writers all seemed to know each other and wandered off to socialize in merry groups but nobody thought to ask Edith along, perhaps because she had removed her author's badge when she tired of explaining why she couldn't sign the other Edith Chalmers' books.

Massage, she was startled to gather, seemed to be playing a greater part in the festival for most writers than literature. Whenever she listened in on an offstage conversation, writers seemed to be comparing notes on which kind of pummelling, stretching or kneading had worked best for them so far, which day spa offered the best value and which the most handsome or beautiful practitioners.

Her lifeline, on the second day, was Peter John. He seemed to have been as overlooked as she was. Not only was he not in the programme but no badge had been made up for him and the shop had stocked none of his books. He seemed quite unabashed. He fashioned his own author badge which read *Peter John: Neglected Poet*!

Whenever he saw her he came to sit by her to gossip for a while or simply make her feel less unattached in the crowds. Madame Yeung, he assured her, was far too grand to chat to either of them now that her column was so widely syndicated around the Pacific rim and her cable show had taken off. 'Consider yourself honoured she gave you five minutes in the taxi from the airport,' he said. 'She stood up Seamus Heaney and they say she once made Peggy Atwood cry, which must take some doing.'

Undaunted at being left off the programme, he made regular use of the open mike sessions during the lunch hour, reciting his poetry by heart to the near-empty auditorium in his whispery voice until jostled off the stage by someone else who acted as though he wasn't there. Edith was not a poetry-reader by habit but she liked his. His verses were dry and witty and desperately sad and she couldn't think why he wasn't famous, especially as he was so pale and interesting.

'I don't care,' he assured her, as though reading her mind. 'Really I don't. I'm here. That's what matters. And my poems are all out there. Somewhere.' He glared towards the bookshop. 'Frankly I'm really more interested in the pursuit of deep relaxation. I'm running up a vast bill on massages at the hotel. Heaven knows how I'll pay for it. I suppose I'll just have to watch my card go into meltdown. The deep tissue man is a genius. And there's a Javanese woman, unexpectedly stout, who does incredible things with jets of warm water. You should try it, Edith. Give yourself a lift before your big day.'

But she doubted him. She watched him when he didn't know she was watching, scanning the poetry shelves to look at the fat, signed piles of his rivals' work or reciting his poems while three Australian women loudly disagreed with one another about Sufism, oblivious to him. She believed he was slighted at every turn. When they caught the car back to the hotel, she had to stop the driver from leaving without giving him time to climb aboard. And, for all his talk of the wonderful massages he was getting, the hotel staff seemed to pay him as little heed as they did the geckos which chuckled so startlingly from the restaurant eaves.

She felt their interest in her slacken too, once Ayu realized she wasn't going to book a chakra realignment or a colonic irrigation. Ayu was still there to greet her each morning as she emerged for breakfast, but by the third day she did so with a singsong slackness that hinted at mockery.

Edith's events were both, in their way, disasters. Her

spotlight session had a tiny, restless audience because she was programmed, in the smallest auditorium, at the same time as the latest Indian prize-winner was packing out the big one. As for her panel discussion on romantic fiction, her attempt to take the subject seriously, although she was by no means a romantic novelist, went for naught because one of her fellow panellists had broken the agreement and written a lengthily tedious speech, not remotely on the topic, which she insisted she had to read as she had been up half the night writing it. After which there were only fifteen minutes left for their moderator – not alas the implacable Ms Yeung – to ask the rest of them one question each.

But Peter came to both sessions and so, astonishingly, did Lucinda Yeung, although she did not sit rapt as he did but took such repeated notes in her agenda that Edith suspected she was merely claiming the nearest convenient chair while she prepared for her next session with someone more newsworthy.

'I feel I've seen nothing of Bali,' Edith confided in Peter, once she had explained to the only audience member to ask that no, the bookshop had only managed to stock one of her earliest books, not the latest and that all the others were by a quite different Edith Chalmers. 'And it's my last night. It seemed criminal doing nothing but coming to festival events and walking in the hotel grounds.'

He convinced her to stay on in Ubud as night fell and the streets began to buzz with scooters. 'But I've left all my cash at the hotel so you'll have to be Sugar Mother,' he said with an unexpected wink.

That was fine by her. When she last counted her rupiahs on her bed she seemed to have over a million still.

He said he wasn't hungry since that morning's particularly

411

strenuous massage seemed to have wiped out his appetite, but he encouraged her to take a table in the Café Lotus to drink a delicious cocktail of lemongrass, lime juice and pressed ginger then he led her off down some lively side streets to a little restaurant, where they seemed to be the only big-boned Westerners, and chose for her a sequence of small dishes of fish and chicken that seemed the very essence of exotic travel after her lonely plunderings of her fruit bowl.

Finally he led her to a neighbourhood temple. A full moon ceremony was building up to some kind of climax or at least was in full flow. The steps were busy with worshippers coming and going, the air bright with the jangling melodies of the percussion orchestra he explained was called a gamelan. It would have felt quite wrong to go inside as they weren't Hindus but he found a comfortably low wall outside where they sat for a happy hour smelling incense and frangipani, listening to the music and hubbub and marvelling at the elegance with which local women could ride side-saddle on their husbands' scooters while balancing little towers of fruit or rice cakes on their heads to offer at the altars within.

'I think this is why I became a writer,' she found herself saying suddenly. 'For the excuse it gives simply to sit quietly and watch.' And, sitting and watching, she spotted several writers from the festival walking by and she felt gratifyingly less of a tourist than they were, simply by virtue of sitting still. 'Thank you,' she said at last. 'Thank you for that.' Lent courage by having a pale and interesting young poet at her side, she had no trouble in hailing them a taxi back to the hotel.

They rode in silence but there was no awkwardness because the driver's radio was serenading them with flute music. When she caught Peter's eye occasionally, as they bumped around a

412

corner or swerved to avoid a precariously laden scooter, he smiled at her before looking back at the passing night scenes.

'Can you really not pay your bill?' she asked at last as they were walking back through the grounds.

'Oh. Probably not. But it couldn't matter less. I'll plead ignorance, say I thought it was all covered by the festival. It couldn't matter less, honestly, Edith. I have been here before.'

She realized they had observed none of the usual literary festival etiquette of exchanging addresses or cards or assurances to review one another favourably but he had cast a kind of spell on the evening's end so they merely shook hands and he melted peaceably into the scented night. The scent, she had discovered by now, was nothing more exotic than citronella oil burning in the little lanterns on every surface to discourage mosquitoes, but she was still enchanted by it and by the elegance with which the lanterns had been used instead of banal electric light to outline flights of steps around the grounds.

She packed everything but the clothes she would be travelling in and the unwieldy Norwegian novel she had yet to finish. Then she sat out on her terrace, feasting shamelessly on fruit she couldn't name and listening to the gentle plashing of water in her infinity pool and the distant flutes and drums coming from a temple that had been silent every night until now.

What, she wondered, would her friend Margaret have done differently had she been there? Struck up useful friendships, certainly. Left with invitations to festivals in Kuala Lumpur and Shanghai all but confirmed. Eaten more. Drunk more. But Edith doubted she would have befriended Peter John. At heart, like most crime writers, Margaret was a social conservative and his pale and interesting qualities, his lack of vim, would have repelled her.

Edith ate the last rambutan in the bowl, dabbed her chin with a napkin and decided that when she got home she would institute some changes. She might even do what her agent had been suggesting for years and write something wildly different under a pseudonym. Something with sex and risk. Something with a plot.

She woke very early, as she always did the night before a long journey. Once she'd dressed and thrown back the curtains, she saw Ayu had not yet taken up her usual patient position on one of the terrace chairs. But perhaps that was because it was her last day and there could be no question of her suddenly requiring excursions or treatments.

Despite the terrific heat, she had not once swum in her pool because it had not occurred to her to bring a swimming costume to a book festival. She appreciated the pool as a thing of beauty, though, lined with slate tiles and reflecting the canopy of great trees overhead. The wind must have risen a little overnight for each morning the pool's surface had been thinly carpeted with leaves which a groundsman would patiently extract with a rake while she was at breakfast.

This morning there were petals as well as leaves, as though some crimson shrub had shed all its blossom in the night. And, inches beneath them, Peter John was floating, open eyes to the morning sky, dressed in his habitual linen trousers and baggy white shirt. He looked paler than ever, as though the moonlit water had chilled him from merely pale to a silvery kind of blue.

She knelt at once and, dropping her book and spectacle case, tried to grasp his trailing shirt tails. He was floating just beyond her reach however and she was fearful of falling in herself. Growing breathless, she stood, glancing about her, and called out, 'Hello?' Her voice sounded especially feeble and blood-lessly English against the exotic birdsong and rustling of leaves. Usually the grounds were discreetly busy with staff by this hour. There always seemed to be a gardener raking up fallen leaves or one of the smarter-dressed personal assistants ferry-ing a guest in a buggy, but for once there was nobody in view. Edith hurried back inside, fumbling to fit her key into the lock with shaking fingers, and dialled 1.

'There's a man in my pool, Ayu. A fellow guest. I . . . I think he's drowned,' she said.

The sofa was immensely deep and comfortable and she found she had no power to leave it now she had sat. Perhaps she had not slept as well as she'd thought. Feeling her sixty-nine years, sweating despite the air conditioning, she waited and ate a grape or two abstractedly. Then she heard voices by the pool: a man's and a woman's, Ayu's. Ayu sounded almost angry but then she appeared at Edith's door, utterly composed, and tapped lightly on the glass.

'Miss Chalmers? Are you all right?'

'Yes. I'm fine,' Edith said, forcing herself to rise. 'It was a bit of a shock, that's all.'

'Er. There is no one in the pool, Miss Chalmers. Here. Come and see.'

One of the groundsmen, his skin far darker than Ayu's, was raking the leaves and petals off the water and heaping them in a shallow, woven basket. Peter was no longer there. The grounds-man saw her staring and said something in Bahasa. Ayu snapped back at him but he smiled at Edith and she felt stupid.

'I'm so sorry to have alarmed you all,' she said.

'That's all right. There were a lot of flowers on the water. Perhaps it was a trick of the light?'

415

'Yes. Of course. Yes. I'm sure that's all it was. I'm so very sorry.'

'I've had them bring your breakfast to the terrace,' Ayu added. 'In case you were . . .' She sought the correct word and, as always, her cautious use of an idiom highlit its strangeness. 'In case you were *not quite yourself*.'

'How kind.'

'Your flight for Singapore leaves at twelve forty-five so I'll bring the buggy for you at a quarter to ten.'

'Thank you. And will you bring my bill then?'

'Your bill? Oh. Please, Miss Chalmers, there is nothing for you to pay.'

'Nothing? But I had several breakfasts. And snacks.'

'Nothing. Enjoy your breakfast.'

Ayu performed a tidy namaste and withdrew via the poolside where she dropped her courteous tone to deliver another clattering rebuke to the groundsman.

There were several altars about the place, lapped in the black and white checked cloth Peter had explained symbolized the perfectly maintained balance of good and evil. Every morning someone left fresh offerings on them, Lilliputian arrangements of flowers and fruit on a leaf, usually with a smouldering incense stick in their midst. One saw these everywhere in Ubud, not just on altars but on the pavements and thresholds, protecting a house from unhappy spirits presumably. Edith had assumed that the hotel altars were purely decorative, like the faux-antique Buddhist or Hindu statues she had seen tourists showing off to one another at the festival. But perhaps not? Perhaps they were ancient sites of worship that long predated this artificial, impeccably staffed Eden.

As Edith obediently sipped her Juice of the Day – carrot,

papaya and lime, a little card informed her – she saw an old woman, surely too roughly dressed to be a member of staff, placing a fresh offering at the altar that lay between her terrace and the point where the hotel grounds gave way to the dazzling green of the rice fields.

Edith forced herself to eat her pancakes, as they were probably the last wholesome food that would be set before her for twenty-four hours. She watched the old woman finish her interesting combination of prayers and housekeeping at the altar and make her way up towards the pool, via one of the bush-screened paths that criss-crossed the grounds' jungly planting. Edith saw her exchange a few words with the groundsman – who seemed as respectful of her as Ayu had been haughty with him – before kneeling at the poolside just where Edith had knelt earlier, to leave a little offering there too. The old woman began to talk again but the groundsman waved her away and completed his clearing. He respected her offering however, even making a small, private gesture as he passed it. It reminded her of the rapid, barely conscious gesture she had seen Sicilians make against the evil eye.

The scent of incense began to reach Edith's seat and when she had finished her breakfast and drained the last of her astringent green tea she went, fortified, to examine the offering. The groundsman smiled at her defensively as he lifted his basket of sodden foliage and petals.

'*Bhuta Kala*,' he told her. 'For the spirit,' he told her. '*Hantu*.' Then he turned swiftly away as though he had said too much.

The only thing she couldn't pack was the garland of sweetly scented flowers with which she had been welcomed. She had kept it on her dressing table and it had not yet begun to turn brown. Throwing it away would have felt wrong so, before she followed her suitcase up to Ayu and the waiting buggy, she

417

walked back to the pool and coiled the flowers neatly about the old woman's offering.

To lighten her luggage she inscribed her nearly-new copy of her latest novel, *A Respectable Sufficiency*, to Peter.

'Would you give this to my friend who is staying here?' she asked Ayu when they'd arrived at the entrance pavilion where her car was waiting.

'Of course,' Ayu said. 'What is their name?'

'Mr John. Peter John.'

'Oh but,' Ayu began, then she faltered. Glancing to one of her occupied colleagues, she bit her lip, a bit like a reluctant child, but took the novel from Edith. Then she smiled as defensively as the groundsman had. 'I'll give it to him, Miss Chalmers. Have a good flight now. And come back soon!'

She stood on the pavilion steps to wave the car off, as she had surely been trained to do so that each visitor could glance back at a parting tableau of delicate Balinese courtesy. However Edith saw her calling something over her shoulder whereupon two of her colleagues hurried over and stared at Edith as the car pulled away.

The driver was not her usual one and seemed to have almost no English and no desire to exercise the little he had, which was a kind of mercy. He said only, *'Berhantu!'* gesturing back at the hotel. When he saw she couldn't understand he merely shrugged and asked, 'Airport?' to which she nodded.

As they neared the top of the drive they had to slow down to allow the passage of a guest out jogging with her personal trainer. To her surprise, the guest was Lucinda Yeung, barely recognizable with her hair tied back and no make-up on but infinitely more approachable. Ms Yeung spotted her and gestured excitedly for her to lower her window.

'I'm writing a piece about you for my column, Edith,' she said. 'I wish we could have spoken more. I think your novel is very interesting. Unique, in fact. I'll see you're sent an invitation to the Hong Kong festival and get you on my cable show. You're original. So unlike all the others of your generation. I think I could really make something of you.'

'Oh. Well thank you,' Edith said.

'You'll come?'

'Of course.'

'Good.' And Ms Yeung was off again, apparently outrunning her trainer.

Hong Kong, along with Adelaide, was one of the festivals to which Margaret had always longed in vain for an invitation. Edith knew she ought to go but now that she was embarked on her journey home, to her silent flat, her books and the notes for a still unwritten novel, an ageing weariness began to steal over her. With every dusty mile placed between her and the ambiguous paradise she was leaving, she framed fresh excuses and grew in certainty that exotic travel did not suit her.

OBEDIENCE

Perran was slightly late arriving because the puppy was still unused to car travel and first vomited then shat in the Land Rover on the way over. Classes took place in a barn on a remote farm a few miles inland from Zennor. Evidently used for pony classes at other times, the old building was deeply carpeted with sawdust and its inside walls were marked out with white-washed numbers at intervals.

As always, Chris greeted the dog not the owner.

'Evening, Toffee.'

Perran pulled Toffee to heel and joined the other pupils walking in a large clockwise circle around her. The dogs varied from a ball of fluff, too young yet to do much more than follow its owner in a childish panic, to a magnificent Belgian Shepherd, forty times its size. There was a handful of clever mongrels, a Border Collie rejected for sheep training on account of an 'hysterical tail', an ancient, unexpectedly spiteful Labrador and two white lapdogs he could not place but suspected were French. The owners were as varied as the breeds. There were children dutifully attending with bewildered Christmas presents and two women, well into their sixties, who always wore gaudy fleeces and hats as though to suggest they were warmer than their wintry expressions suggested. These two had dogs who were exceptionally obedient, clearly veterans of many classes, so perhaps they only attended as a favour to Chris, to inspire and encourage.

'Toffee, heel. Good boy,' he said, remembering to keep his tone light and playful because apparently that was what puppies responded to best.

Toffee did not look like a puppy any more. Although only five months old, he was already well over twenty-five kilos and tall enough to rest his head on the kitchen table. He was a source of some guilt. Perran had always wanted a deerhound, had been fascinated by them ever since he was old enough to pore over guides to different breeds, doubly fascinated because there seemed to be none in the county, only lurchers of all shapes and coats and the occasional greyhound, retired from racing and rescued by a charity. He had watched them on the television – at Cruft's or in period dramas – and had once been allowed to pet one as it waited obediently outside the beer tent at the Royal Cornwall Show. But owning one of his own had never been possible. First his father vetoed it, buying the family a golden retriever instead, precisely, bewilderingly, because that was what other people had. Then there was Val, his wife. Val liked dogs well enough, she maintained, but they should get children out of the way first because a farmhouse was cluttered enough without both. But then children had never come along, first because money was too short and then because of his technical difficulty.

When he saw deerhound puppies advertised in *Farmer's Weekly*, he became like a man possessed. He twice found pretexts to drive out to Dartmoor to view the litter, each time feeling as guilty as he imagined a man must feel meeting a mistress. The third time he was unable to resist buying one. It cost a crazy amount, enough to pay a broccoli cutter's wages for over twenty days, but he had some cash put by in a building society from when he got lucky on a horse, money Val knew nothing about. He introduced the puppy as a charming mongrel bought for a tenner from a man at the slaughterhouse, somewhere Val never went.

'Ten quid, for *that*?' she complained.

'He says it's nearly a deerhound,' he told her. 'At least half. Maybe more. You only have to look at him. We can call him Toffee, 'cause he's so soft.'

She fought it for a while but softened when Toffee licked her hand and fell heavily asleep against her feet, exhausted by the terrors of a first car journey. She was adamant, however, that the dog eat nothing more expensive than scraps, that it come no further into the house than the kitchen, that clearing up after it until it was housetrained was entirely his responsibility and that should it fail to be housetrained in six weeks, it was to live in the old milking parlour.

He agreed readily to all conditions in his excitement; the greatest triumph was still his, after all. He hid the pedigree documentation when it arrived from the Kennel Club (Toffee's real name, his secret name, was Glencoe McTavish, of which Toffee had seemed a reasonable and plausible diminutive) and took care to lose his various pocket dog encyclopaedias in a bale of things for the parish jumble sale, to lower the chances of Val's making comparisons between the breed ideal illustrated and the dramatically emerging lines of their so-called mongrel. Toffee was like a disguised prince in a fairytale; sooner or later his breeding would out.

The deadline for housetraining was two weeks gone. Perran always woke first anyway, trained to farming hours since boyhood, so it was easy enough to slip down to the kitchen, mop up any accidents, plead with Toffee to try to be good next time then slip back upstairs with a large enough mug of tea to keep

Val sweet and in bed while the tell-tale taint of disinfectant floor cleaner had time to disperse. Obedience classes met with no objection; he knew she was glad to have one night a week to herself.

'And halt.' All the owners halted. Half the dogs sat obediently. The other half had to be pushed down. A puppy yelped. You could always spot the puppies who would be a handful if they grew up unchecked, the monsters-in-making. It was the same with children. Everyone watched Chris expectantly. Half the fun of these classes was that you never knew what she would have you do next; jump little pony jumps, weave your dog in and out of poles, have it sit and stay while you walked to the fullest extent of the lead or even let go of the lead altogether and crossed the room, if you were showing off and your dog could do it.

He knew she was a lesbian, that she lived with a driving instructor who had cornered the market in teaching car-shy wives and widows, but that didn't mean he couldn't admire her. She was a good-looking woman, very neat, not like Val who dressed for warmth and had a horror of revealing herself. Chris showed off her trim figure by wearing jodhpurs and a tailored suede jacket. She carried a little riding crop for pointing with and tapped it against her thigh when they were performing tasks with a pattern to them.

'And weave,' tap, 'and through the tunnel,' tap, 'and halt,' tap. He liked that. She did this for love, since the tiny fee charged could barely cover costs of barn-hire and training treats, but there was a nice mystery to her because although she plainly loved dogs, she was here without one and you had no way of knowing what breed she favoured.

'So ask her,' Val said, typically, Val who could ask anyone

426

anything. It took a woman without mystery to assume another had nothing to keep to herself.

Chris waited until she had everyone's attention and a rescue greyhound called Misty had stopped yodelling.

'Now,' she said. 'Now that we're all here . . .' That was meant for him and Perran looked suitably crestfallen, only no one was laughing. 'I think you'll all agree,' Chris went on, 'it's only right we should have a minute's silence to think about Janice.' He looked around. Everyone was hanging their heads. One of the children was even dutifully mouthing what could have been a prayer. He hung his head too, so that Toffee looked up at him and produced one of his curious cries of uncertainty and impatience that was half yawn, half whimper.

He wanted to crouch down and give him a hug only Chris was always telling off the men in the class for leaning over their dogs too much. He supposed it was love he felt for him. Because of the lack of speech, love for animals was an odd affair, doomed to frustration. You couldn't hug them as hard as you wanted or they'd be frightened. What you really wanted, he supposed, was to *become* them. You wanted to see out of their eyes and have them see out of yours. There was a bit of particularly soft fur, just behind Toffee's huge black ears, that gave out a marvellous scent, a warm, brown biscuity smell, a bit like horse sweat, which brought on this feeling in a rush. He had heard Val talk with friends about babies often enough, heard, with an alien's fascination, how often women were filled with a hot desire to eat them, had once even seen a woman thrust one of her baby's feet entirely into her mouth and suck it. Perhaps this love of dogs and love of babies were not so dissimilar?

'So long, Janice,' Chris said at last. 'We'll miss you, girl.' Someone blew their nose. 'Now,' Chris went on, having cleared her throat. 'The police have asked if they can have a brief word with each of us afterwards. Don't worry if you'll be in a hurry. The sergeant can just take your details and pay a house call tomorrow or whatever. Otherwise they'll want statements tonight.'

'But I thought she was on holiday,' one of the elderly fleece ladies said.

'Were we the last to see her alive, then?' asked her friend.

'Looks like it.'

The greyhound yodelled again, breaking the gloomy spell.

'Right,' said Chris. 'Dogs are getting bored. Let's practise our downs. In a big circle now. That's it. You first, Bessie. Off you go. Not too slow. That's it. I'll tell you when. Now.'

'Down!' said Bessie's owner and Bessie dropped from her trot to flatten herself most impressively in the sawdust. It looked impressive but somehow insincere and you sensed she'd never do it so well without an audience.

So Janice was dead. Unthinkable. Janice Thomas. Haulage princess. *The Broccoli Tsarina* they had called her in *The Cornishman* once. Her father had begun the business in a small way, running three lorries that collected produce from the farms and took it to a wholesaler in the east. But Janice, hard-faced Janice, who nobody liked much in school, had been away to business college and made some changes when she came home. She wasn't proud. She drove one of the lorries herself for a while until she got to know all the growers, however small. Then she used her knowledge of them to persuade them to sell through her instead of merely using her as haulier, so Proveg was born, sprawling across an industrial estate outside Camborne. She was no fool. She chose the site because there was high unemployment thanks to all the closed mines and retrenching china-clay works and labour was cheap. Soon everyone had a son or daughter or wife who had done time on the packing lines or in the quality control shed. The pay wasn't brilliant but she was still regarded as something of a saviour. 'She doesn't *have* to do it,' people said. 'She could have worked anywhere. She could have worked in London for big money.'

Then she began to show her sharper side, bailing out farmers and truck owners in trouble so that she seemed their rescuer until their fortunes took enough of an upturn for them to realize that she now owned their truck or most of their farm. Or rather, that Proveg did. Janice always played a clever game of making out she was just one of the workers and speaking of Proveg as though it owned her too and she was merely another employee, paid just enough to stay loyal but never quite enough to break away.

She put her father in a home when he went peculiar – a home substantially refurbished by Proveg's charity. She drove several growers to the wall. There was a suicide or two, nothing compared to what BSE caused, but enough to register as a local outrage. Women in their cups joked that some lucky bloke would get his hands on the money soon enough but no man tamed Janice in matrimony. No woman either, for all the mutinous gossip. She lived alone in the hacienda-style estate that had sprouted from the paternal bungalow. She went to church; her pretence of worker solidarity didn't extend to attending Chapel. She smoked with defiant satisfaction. She took one holiday a year – in the brief interval between the end of the winter cauliflowers and the start of the early potatoes – always somewhere fiercely hot from where she would return with a leathery tan that showed off the gold chains that were her only visible finery. She kept a horse and bred Dobermans. She had been bringing the latest puppy to classes for several weeks now. She favoured the lean, houndlike ones rather than the over-weight thugs.

When he had mentioned this, Val said, 'Lean or no, she'll never get a husband with those around the house. Devil dogs, they are.'

'Maybe she doesn't want one,' he said. 'A husband, I mean. Maybe she's happy as she is.'

'Happy? Her?' Val asked and snorted in the way she did when she wanted to imply that there were some things only a woman could understand.

'Toffee, heel. Good boy. That's it. Down. *Down!*'

'Don't repeat your order,' Chris said, as he knew she would. 'He'll just learn to ignore you.' But Toffee went down after a fashion, largely because he was tired.

'Good boy,' Perran said, then tugged him back onto his feet. 'Toffee, heel. Good boy.'

Val set great store by marriage. She thought he couldn't understand or wasn't interested, but he could tell. He saw how she divided women into sheep and goats with marriage the fiery divide between them. Women who lived with a man without marrying him first she thought not loose but foolish. She did not despise spinsters or think them sad, not out loud at least, but it was plain she thought of them as lesser beings. Childless-ness, her childlessness, was thus a great wound in her self-esteem. He could tell from the way she huffed and puffed over the young mothers in the village who sometimes blocked its one stretch of pavement with their double-occupancy pushchairs.

'As if they're something really special,' she snorted but her glare would have a kind of hunger to it.

He did not mind staying on to give a statement. He was

collecting Val from the First and Last and she wouldn't thank him for appearing early and cramping her style. He gave his name and recognized the sergeant from schooldays. Garth Tre-sawle. A mate's younger brother, forever trailing behind them as they skived off, whining wait for me. And they'd had to wait because even then he had a tendency to take notes and bear witness.

'And when did you last see Ms Thomas?'

'Here,' Perran said. 'Last time we had a class. We talked a bit about boarding kennels because she was about to go on holiday to Morocco. The next day, she said.'

'You drove straight home afterwards?'

'Not exactly. I stopped off at the pub to pick up my wife.'

'What time was that?'

'Nearly closing time. Only she wasn't there. Found out later some friends had taken her on to theirs. Someone's birthday. I went back on my own.'

'Talk to anyone at the pub?'

'Er . . .' He cast his mind back to smoke, music, turned backs around the television. 'No.'

'Did anyone see you get back?'

'No. There's just the two of us and I was asleep when Val got back.' He remembered her drunken curses as she stubbed a toe on one of the bed's sticking-out legs.

'What time was that?'

'I was asleep. Past midnight.'

'How well did you know Ms Thomas?'

'We were at school together. You remember that, Garth. You were there too.'

'Sorry, Perran,' Garth sighed. 'We have to do this by the book.'

'Okay. Sorry.' Toffee whined and Perran settled him back on the sawdust. The wind was rising again, whistling round the barn roof and flapping a loosened tab of corrugated steel. 'I was at school with her so you could say I'd known her all my life, but we weren't friends. Of course I had dealings with her later, through Proveg. She buys ... I mean she bought our broccoli and crispers. Pushed a hard bargain. Did with everyone. She won't have many friends, I reckon.'

'You harvest your own broccoli?'

'Yeah.'

'What with?'

'Knives. Same as everyone else.'

'Stainless steel?'

'No. Proveg have been on at us to change. New rules. Supermarkets don't want rust on their precious broccoli stalks. But there's nothing wrong with the old ones if you look after them. Dry and oil them. Keep them sharp with an angle grinder. And they're not brittle. The stainless ones get chipped on all the stones.'

He had been cutting broccoli since he was twelve, and in that time had seen the move from boxing them up in hessian-lined wooden crates that were taken to Penzance Station on a trailer to bagging them individually and arranging them in supermarket crates on the spot. There were health and safety regulations now. Knives had to be signed out and in by the cutters and so did any (regulation blue) sticking plasters, for fear someone get a nasty shock of finding a bloody bandage in their cauliflower cheese. Other Proveg rules forbidding smoking, eating or dogs and insisting that *in the absence of a chemical toilet, allowable where teams number five or less, antiseptic wet wipes are to be handed out to workers needing to relieve themselves in the field* he and Val blithely ignored. They had even discovered that, once the tractor had driven down a row once or twice so that tracks were well cut into the mud, it was possible to send the tractor slowly through the field without a driver, thus freeing up an extra pair of hands to cut while Val rode in the makeshift rig at the back trimming, bagging and packing. Health and safety regs would surely have outlawed this but Val kept a weather eye open and if she saw a Proveg four-wheel-drive in the distance could tip him the wink to down knife and drive for a while.

Garth Tresawle made an extra note and underlined it. He looked up.

'How many do you have?' he asked.

'Four.'

'Where d'you keep them?'

'In a shed. And no. It isn't locked.'

'How many men work for you?'

'On the broccoli?' Garth nodded. 'Two. Ernest Penrose and Peter Newson.' He gave their addresses, as best as he could remember them, and his own, and that was all.

They would have a hard time pinning charges on the mere basis of a knife. West Penwith was bristling with knives at this time of year. The daffodil and broccoli harvests brought crowds of itinerant workers into the area in search of hard labour and tax-free bundles of earthy notes. There was some resentment among the local hands, jobs being scarce, but Eastern Europeans would always be prepared to work for that little bit less than Cornishmen, especially with the threat of deportation hanging over them. Every winter there was a flurry of lightning raids by customs officers and police, tipped off about the latest troupe of illegal immigrants slaving in the eerily weedless bulb fields or in stinking acres of vegetable but every spring brought fresh vanloads. Many of them slept rough in barns and hedges to save money. Perran had found them in his sheds occasionally, or evidence of their passing through.

It was said that many of the home-grown cutters were fresh out of prison or dodging parole. He had seen the way Val discreetly clicked down the locks on the car doors when she rounded a corner at dusk to find a gang spilling across a lane, their shapes bulked out with extra clothing, their muddy knives flashing as the headlamps swept across them. There was no lack of suspicious and appropriately armed strangers to pin a local murder on.

As always, Toffee was too exhausted by the class even to remember to be carsick on the way home. Perran left him in the Land Rover while he went inside the pub.

It was a ladies' darts match night – Val played on the pub team – so there was a scattering of unfamiliar faces, though not half as many as during the tourist season. Then everyone staying on the windswept campsite would take refuge in here until closing time forced them back to caravan and canvas. There was, however, an unmistakable holiday atmosphere tonight. He would have expected to find the women in one room, garrulous around a table, the men hunched, wordless, around Sky Sports in the other. Instead, he found the outsize television neglected and almost everyone squeezed around two long tables beside the fire, a jumble of glasses, exploded crisp packets and overflowing ashtrays in their midst. The landlady was with them, sure sign of a rare celebration, like the occasions – cup finals, the occasional wake – when she locked the doors and declared the gathering a perfectly legal private party. Ordinarily sat amongst her cronies, women she had known since childhood, Val would only have acknowledged him to demand he bought the next round or a packet of cigarettes. She certainly would not have asked him to join them but would expect him to wait with the men until she was ready to leave.

Tonight was quite different. She spotted him at once and called out, 'Here he is,' with something like eagerness. A drink was bought him and space made on the settle beside her. It was quite as though they had all been waiting for him. Someone asked how the puppy classes were going and he told her but quickly realized no one was really interested.

Then Val said, 'Well?' and it transpired that they had heard the police were questioning everyone at the class because Garth and a couple of detectives had been in the pub at the beginning of the evening and one of the detectives, the younger one with the funny eye, was a cousin by marriage of the landlady. It was not like on television, where the facts of a murder were kept under wraps so as not to influence key witnesses. Correct police procedure was near impossible in a community this small and inter-related. They might have thought they were withholding crucial details but the women who had found the body, or most of it, Proveg employees on the night shift, were cousins of a woman on the visiting darts team and, in any case, had been far too traumatized by their discovery not to phone at least two people each before the police arrived on the scene.

Janice had been stabbed in the stomach repeatedly with a cauliflower knife. This last detail was a fair guess, given the width of the wounds the less squeamish of the witnesses had glimpsed on lifting Janice's shirt. There was no blood on the floor, so presumably she had been killed elsewhere. Her mouth had been stuffed to overflowing with cauliflower florets and a Proveg Cornish Giant Cauliflower bag strapped over her head.

Her hands and arms had been hacked off. The girls could find no trace of them but, hours later, there were horrified phone calls from branches of Tesco's, Sainsbury's, Safeway's and the Co-Op where they had arrived, neatly tucked into trays of Proveg quality assured produce. And the body was said not to be *fresh* so the landlady, something of an expert on serial murder, was backing the theory that Janice had never been on holiday at all. No one knew what had become of the Dobermans or the horse but Perran asking that gave rise to a small wave of horror-struck and morbidly inventive suggestions.

'Still,' Val put in, barely keeping the relish from her voice. 'At least it looks as though they didn't suffocate her. She must have been dead already when they put the stuff in her mouth because there was no sign of a struggle. Judy said the florets weren't broken at all. Still fit to cook, she said. So what did they ask you, love?'

'Oh.' Perran shrugged. 'How long I'd known her. If we talked at the class that night – which we did, of course. What time I got home. What kind of knives we use.'

'Reckon Garth thinks you did it, boy,' someone put in. Laughter faded quickly into uneasiness.

'Well,' Perran admitted. 'I don't have a whatsit. An alibi.'

'You do!' Val insisted.

'Hardly,' he told her. 'You were out when I got home and drunk when you finally made it in.'

There was uproarious laughter at that then one of the women said, 'Maybe Val did it. She always had it in for that bitch.'

'Val had an alibi. She was with us.'

'Not like Perran. Who'd have thought it!'

'Ooh, Perran! Here, Val. You sure you're safe going home with him and everything?'

'Good on you, boy. She had it coming.'

There was teasing and laughter and, amazingly, Val clutched his thigh under the table as she laughed back and faked girlish terror. Perran felt an unfamiliar sensation as the teasing and backslapping continued and the conversation turned to Proveg and how the growers might now join forces to buy it and run it as a co-operative, which is what they should have done all along. It took a minute or two for him to identify it as pride. He had not felt like this since their wedding day.

'She'll stop,' he thought, 'once we're alone. Once we're back outside.'

And certainly Val seemed sobered by the night chill and the silence in the Land Rover. But as he drove her back to the farm, she slipped her hand over his where it rested on the gear stick.

'Poor Janice, though,' she said. 'I mean, I know she was a cow but the thought of her all alone . . . Things like that don't happen to married women. Not so often, anyway. I'm glad there's you. You too, Muttface,' she added because Toffee had woken and was leaning over from the back, sniffing the smoke in her hair. 'I'm glad there's you too. You'll keep us safe, won't you, boy?'

'Reckon he'd just wag his tail and lick the blood off the mad axeman's fingers,' he said.

'Don't!' she squeaked and shuddered.

They drove the few minutes home in silence but when he pulled up inside the garage and cut the engine she turned to him in the darkness and asked, 'You didn't do it. Did you?' And from something in her voice he sensed the distinct possibility of sex.

IN THE CAMP

Lara could normally spot the new children a mile off because they tended to cling either to their parents or to some token articles of clothing – swimming trunks, typically, but one new arrival had memorably retained long socks and sandals. But he approached them directly, as unencumbered by textiles or relatives as any regular in their little gang. Lara had not noticed until then that that summer they were all black- or brown-haired; they tended to become so muddy and stuck with leaves and twigs that such physical niceties could be hard to distinguish. He strode confidently into their midst in the forest clearing and they instinctively formed a respectful circle about him.

He was blond – real, golden blond – and his skin had the even tan of a committed naturist. Lara guessed he was twelve or even thirteen. He was just starting to grow pubic hair – she was eleven so pubic hair had begun to fascinate her – which was as golden as the hair on his head, but he still had the leanness and thin arms of a boy. He looked like the illustration of Narcissus in her book of Greek myths, only Narcissus wore a skimpy sky-blue tunic with a Greek key design and carried a bow and arrows. This boy was beautiful, she decided, and rather frightening.

'Hello,' he told them. 'I'm Wolf.' He pronounced it Volff but otherwise his English was excellent. 'What are you doing?'

'We were playing rounders,' Lara told him.

'You were pitching the ball wrong,' he told her. 'If you throw

441

the ball underarm like that it's too easy to hit. Let me show you how to pitch properly.' He held out his hand for the tennis ball.

'I'm Lara,' she said as she handed it to him.

'Hello Lara,' he said and enslaved her with a quick, dazzling smile. 'Now watch me,' and he pitched the ball with such ferocious speed that Chubby Eric jumped aside to avoid it and tripped, which made everyone laugh. It was a bloodless coup. They had been a muddy democracy of sorts but from that moment Wolf was in charge.

He showed them how to pitch and how to strike and the game became fiercer and more exciting and a couple of children, including Chubby Eric, didn't want to play any more and slipped away, unlamented, to find their parents. Then Wolf taught them Ball He and they chased each other back and forth between the trees, scratching their skin and bruising themselves as they slipped on the mossy patches. In fact they played He often – it was one of the best ways of keeping warm when naked as, unlike some games, it kept everybody in motion. But Ball He had an edge to it since whoever was He didn't have to get close enough to their prey to touch them but simply had to hit them with the ball. Now that Wolf had taught them how to throw, to make even a fluffy tennis ball like a bullet from a gun, their throws were more accurate and quite painful, more to be feared than a playful tap from a friend's fingers.

Lara dreaded being hit. The ball had become wet and muddy and she saw how it was leaving splatter marks on its targets that made the game more than ever like shooting. She was a swift runner and as nimble as a whippet at changing direction on her summer-toughened feet. She dodged several attacks, including one from Wolf, who shouted something in his own language when he missed her and had to retrieve the ball from the undergrowth.

At the same time she found she longed to be He, longed to be at once victim and aggressor, so she lingered on purpose, taunting him, skipping from side to side then ran in a straight line precisely so he would hit her at last. The blow stung and she felt a great spatter of cold mud it sent across her back, but now she was He and had the power she found she was laughing so hard she could barely run. She'd chased Wolf for a while but then crossed the path of Eileen, an older girl she had never much liked, and threw the ball hard at her head and darted away laughing with Wolf and the others, as Eileen cursed and slithered after the ball in the mud.

Eileen was a bad throw and, possibly on purpose, threw one of her next attempts so that the ball flew out into the lake. People moaned and said she was a spaz but, as it happened, retrieving the ball gave them all a chance to let the furious game dissolve in a leisurely swim out to the pontoon where they all flopped, panting in the sun like so many pink and brown seals.

Families dressed in the evening. It would have been too cold to stay naked but Lara suspected it also had to do with hot gravy and knives and forks. Supper was served in a big chalet beside the lake and they all sat apart with their respective families. Then there was dancing to records or a lecture but Lara usually pretended to be tired so she could go to bed with a book instead. Her parents quizzed her about the new family and seemed reassured to hear Wolf had said they were from Zurich.

'Swiss,' her mother said. 'I was sure they must be.'

Wolf's parents were just as blond as he was. They must have been the same age as her parents nearly but they seemed far fitter.

Her parents were both academics, grave and pale, helpless without spectacles whereas Wolf's parents had muscles and looked like an advertisement for something to do with health and the outdoors.

The next day her parents played them at badminton and, after dark, at bridge, so her mother must have decided they were *All Right*. Without clothes on one had to be more circumspect, apparently.

Lara knew he was a bit older than her but had thought Wolf would take his cue from their parents and become her new friend. Something about the way he had touched her arms when showing her how to pitch and caught her eye and laughed when she hit Eileen on the head made her wake fully prepared to insult or cold-shoulder whatever playmates she needed in order to cement an alliance with him. But, after two days of childish company, he suddenly seemed more interested in Mr Johnson, or Johnson, as he called him imperiously.

The Johnsons were the youngest couple in the camp. She was expecting a baby so wasn't available for games so Mr Johnson, who was dark and handsome and worked as a PE instructor in a minor public school, was much in demand.

Wolf needed to challenge him, for some reason, or at least to win his notice.

'Race me across the lake, Johnson!' he shouted at him. 'Watch me dive, Johnson!' 'Johnson, how is my serve?'

Mr Johnson was polite and obliging. He raced Wolf and Lara across the lake, easily beating them but complimenting them on their strokes all the same and showing Wolf how to splash less with his legs. He patiently watched Wolf's repeated dives off the high board and spent some time helping him improve his tennis serve too but Lara could see he was uncomfortable, embarrassed even, at the Swiss boy's bids for attention and she wasn't surprised when he rowed his wife out to the Island after lunch. This was the one place children weren't allowed and heavy with lurid mythology as a result.

Wolf took control of the afternoon games as he had on the first two days. They played Masters and Slaves on the obstacle course and Vampires on the old tyres that dangled on ropes across the stream, but she could see, from the edge of spite that came into his commands, that he was unhappy. She still thought he was beautiful and she easily stayed on the right side of him by doing his every bidding faster and more tidily than the others so that he started calling her Tiger Cub, which she liked and hoped was a name that might stick. She had not forgotten, however, his odd foolishness in the morning and held back a part of herself in watchfulness.

She fought genuine sleepiness after supper because there were charades that night. The Johnsons shone unexpectedly at the game, even pregnant Mrs Johnson, who was inclined to laugh too hard and get sweaty. Wolf's family proved hopeless, either through insufficient informal English or a failure to understand that the game was meant to be amusing. Her parents were neither good nor bad, which was a relief.

The next day it poured with rain. Several families donned clothes and drove off on *cultural excursions*, which would almost certainly involve the cinema, an entertainment the camp owners were far too principled to provide. Lara's parents both retreated into books. She had almost finished her last one and needed to eke it out over several more nights so she joined a raggle-taggle band of children in the games chalet for ping-pong. Interestingly most had opted to stay naked though one or two, Lara included, appeared in clothes because of the cold but soon discarded them on the chalet's old sofas and chairs so as to fit in. One boy retained just a Pacamac. More fancy dress than proper clothing, it whirled about him as he ran and began to stick weirdly to his skin where he got hot.

Sitting out a game or two with Wolf, she found he was no less interested in Mr Johnson still but that now his thoughts had turned dark with obscure disappointment.

'That Johnson is a bad sort,' he pronounced.

'How do you mean?' she asked.

'He's a pervert.'

'No!' Lara liked Mr Johnson and his funny, pink wife.

'He stares too much. He was watching you girls in the water yesterday and he touched himself when he thought no one could see him. But I saw and that's why he's avoiding me.'

'No he didn't. I expect he just had an itch. I've had itches. There are water fleas in the lake sometimes.'

'You're too young, Tiger Cub. You don't understand. He's bad. You should be careful around him.' Wolf looked less attractive when he frowned and she looked away and picked an oak leaf from between her toes.

She had said hello to Mr Johnson on her way over from her parents' cabin. He was defying the rain, heading for the woods with his binoculars slung around his neck and his bird book protected by a plastic bag. Perhaps he and his wife had *had words* and she wanted to be alone because of her heavy pregnancy. He looked a little sad, she thought, venturing off on his own and she would have offered to join him on his expedition only she had stupidly put clothes on and they were rapidly getting wet. When she grew up, she decided, a man like Mr Johnson would make a better companion than one like Wolf or his advertisement-shiny father.

Bored of sitting out, Wolf initiated a game of Round the Table. Lara enjoyed this because she was fairly hopeless at ping-pong but deft at snatching up and slamming down the bat when it was her turn to hit the ball. She liked the permitted violence of it.

The mood became wilder and wilder as more and more players were eliminated. Chubby Eric's spectacles steamed up so much he had to beg for a pause while he rubbed them on someone's discarded shirt and Eileen cracked a fingernail painfully when slamming down the racket and said fuck which induced near-hysteria. Lara was soon out too but didn't mind because another round would soon be starting.

Then Wolf, who had made it into the last four, was run out and he protested ridiculously. Everyone remembered how odd and silly he had been with all his showing off to Mr Johnson that morning and the older ones turned on him.

'Well go if you're going,' Eileen said and everybody laughed because her fuck had earned her new popularity. Even Lara laughed, because it was quite funny even though she didn't care for Eileen, and Wolf saw as he left and his eyes slid over her in a dismissive way that stopped the laughter in her throat.

When they all gathered for supper that night, Lara discovered the Johnsons had left suddenly. Spirits were high on account of the way the weather had shaken up camp routines so there was skittish socializing between tables and word soon got around that they had been *asked to go*. *Asked to go* was the phrase always used when there had been a complaint – invariably against a man – involving staring, cameras or what Lara's mother tantalizingly called *unwonted attentions*.

Wolf ate with his parents at their usual table near the door. Nobody was gossiping with them and they were talking little to each other. Lara guessed Wolf had said something to his family during the spite-hungry tedium of the long, wet afternoon, which led to an official complaint. She was shocked to the core that he could do something so wicked and wondered if he was regretting it. Nobody liked a tell-tale.

There was a lecture that night – a woman with an unfortunately high voice talking about Birds of the Cevennes – and only scant attention was paid. Lara stayed up for once and could sense a barely suppressed excitement among the adults. Sure enough, as soon as it was seen Wolf's family had left the chalet, a kind of unofficial party broke out, with dancing and drinks, and she was hurried off to bed. Her parents returned in unusually high spirits much later than they normally did. Her mother was actually giggling and Lara enjoyed lying in her bed and eavesdropping through the curtain while they thought she slept.

When he tried to join them the next day, the children ignored Wolf entirely, by common, unspoken consent. The first girl he addressed directly was the newly popular Eileen, who dared to look right through him and acted as though no one had spoken. At once this became the first of the day's games and everyone followed suit. He was swiftly maddened by it, as they sensed he would be, and punched Chubby Eric hard on the shoulder. When even Chubby Eric heroically contrived to ignore his presence, he stalked off, shouting at them in his own language.

The sun returned with full heat at last and they spent the day swimming and basking, enjoying the woods and water with none of their recent savagery.

Wolf and his parents were asked to leave too. Perhaps because it involved a child their own children had been playing with, this news was kept back by most of the parents for much of the evening but inevitably it leaked out because there was nothing more interesting to discuss over supper.

In a thrilling development like something out of John Buchan,

Mr Johnson had cleared his name by returning with an old army friend who was now in the Dorset constabulary. He had him challenge and question Wolf and his family before the camp owners. Wolf had refused to admit he was lying but in his ever-wilder accusations had let slip something about his father's cameras.

Bringing a camera to the camp was as strictly against the rules as men without wives. It transpired Wolf's father had not only been busy taking surreptitious snaps of them all but that his wife had been carrying a concealed cine camera in her cunningly modified knitting bag. All film was confiscated and exposed and, in a final, glorious flourish, the policeman friend had insisted on inspecting their passports before the family was escorted off the grounds.

'Germans after all,' Lara's mother said when she thought Lara wasn't listening. 'I told you I didn't really care for her.'

THE DARK CUTTER

He crossed two fields, opening the gates wide as he went, then clambered onto a hedge, cupped his hands on either side of his mouth and called.

They each had a slightly different cattle call. His older brother produced a low, booming sound midway between a moo and a foghorn. Their father's call had two notes, the second lower than the first, and usually had a trace of words to it, a sort of weary 'come 'long'. His own tended to emerge as a sort of falsely cheery *Hey-oop!* with a rising note at the end. He hated raising his voice or trying in any way to seem different but, try as he might to imitate the others, his call always came out the same way.

Fog had come in off the sea soon after dawn and was drifting inland as a succession of clammy curtains. The steers were Charolais crosses so in these conditions became almost invisible, their buff and off-white flanks barely distinguishable from the pale granite of the hedges and pearly grey of the fog. There was a distant low-lying field where they spent the night sometimes, grouped together out of the wind like so many companionable boulders. He was about to jump off the hedge to go in search of them there when he heard them – one crazily high-pitched moo first and then a chorus of baritone answers – and stayed put to call them again. There was another moo, closer at hand, before their great forms lumbered out of the surrounding grey.

They were following one of their leaders, a burly, round-shouldered animal, whose lopsided horns had been sawn off a few months back when one threatened to grow into its cheek.

He slid down off the hedge and, calling them again, waited until a few had come close enough to sniff and recognize him then began to lead them back the way he had come, across the fields to the lower yard. The trick was to walk slowly enough to hold their interest but with enough speed to keep them from merely falling to graze on a different acre. Luckily the herd had been in this run of fields for ten days now and was eager for change.

As he walked, he heard their snorting breaths and felt the ground shake whenever one of them gambolled up a yard or two to his side. Occasionally, driven by an overflow of energy perhaps, one would mount another and ride it for a yard or two or a couple would suddenly pair off for a quick trial of strength, thumping their huge skulls together, eyeball to eyeball, fringe to fringe, then pushing until one yielded to the other. All about him now, they gave off what he thought of as their smell of contentment – a yeasty mixture of the sharp-sweetness of chewed grass with the sweaty tang of their pelts.

He slipped back to close a gate behind them as the last stragglers passed through then hurried forward with a shout to encourage the herd to keep up its momentum. Seven times out of ten they came like this when called, not from obedience – he knew better than to credit them with that – but from hunger, curiosity or boredom. The other times, when they refused to come but simply ran in maddening circles or, worse, lay unbudgeably munching, tended to arise when the field they were in was still fairly new to them.

Who was he kidding? There was no order or method to

these creatures; sometimes they were cussed or flighty, some-times they weren't.

Inspired, perhaps, by the dawning realization that they were nearing the farmyard, where they were fed barley in season, and the familiar Dutch barn where they were bedded down in the coldest, wettest weeks of winter, one of the steers suddenly kicked up its heels and broke into an ungainly, farting run, tak-ing the others with it. They surged through the second gate and he raced to shut it after them. As he secured it with a length of old barbed wire he grazed the inside of his wrist and swore softly.

The herd was swallowed by a fresh veil of fog as it rounded the awkward corner above the farmyard. The hope was that his father and brother were ready for it with open gates and an open pen so the steers could pass straight to their destination. Sometimes some small thing, a laughing child, a darting cat, a fertilizer bag caught and flapping on the gorse, would panic them at the crucial moment and send them skittering back in a way that would be comical if it weren't so irritating. An angry half-hour or more could follow in which they attempted to round the herd back towards the yards in an L-shaped field with all too many awkward corners where they could baulk and hud-dle. He wished at such times that they possessed a cattle dog. Not a spooky border collie, with those staring eyes, but a proper cattle dog, reliable and sturdy, like the ones Australians used, to help round the beasts back towards the yard. But his father hated dogs, having been mauled on the hand as a boy, so the wish was futile, at least while the old man lived.

This morning they were lucky and the beasts ran, unstar-tled, into the main yard and down to the lower one where they could be sorted. The lower yard gate, a far heavier one than those they had passed in the fields and with proper fastenings, was clanged shut behind them. He then had to join his father and brother in trying to persuade the herd into the big pen.

Like many parts of the farm, the lower yard had evolved by a subtle interplay of accident and necessity in which design had played little part. It was an L-shape, or a V, even, with gates top and bottom and pen and crush off at the farthest end. There was also a marked change in level where the yard turned a corner.

As usual his brother had parked one of the tractors to block off one angle and placed a line of feeding troughs behind it so as to steer the animals towards the pen's open gate. As usual the steers ignored the hint and surged down to the other, closed, gate, pressing their faces to it to peer out at the tantalizing fresh pasture beyond. When shouted at and chased, they simply ran back uphill the way they had come. They ran back and forth a couple of times, from the top of the slope to the bottom. Growing increasingly nervous and with one or two of them slipping and falling in the rush, until enough of them led the way into the pens for the others to be fairly readily chased and whipped into following suit.

He hated whipping them. He and his brother had stiff lengths of blue plastic water pipe which extended their reach when trying to head the animals off but which were inevitably used to prod and beat as well. Their father preferred the riding crop from his hunting days, which was shorter but had a little tassel of leather on its end 'to pack a good sting', as he liked to say.

He knew this soft distaste in him was shameful and unmanly, that directing the animals firmly, with shouts and even kicks, was the only and the safest way. Yet he winced inside at the sound of whip on hide. He never whipped the face of a turning animal the way the others did and only used his hose when he was frustrated at some beast's stupidity. They all talked to the animals as they worked, saying things like, 'Get in, would you?' and 'Oh, you bloody thing!' but he suspected he was the only one of them who, in his mind at least, muttered apologies too.

As always he was the one to jump into the pen with the steers to direct them, four at a time, into the smaller pen and on to the crush. His brother would work the crush gates and neck-clamp and his father would peer into twitching ears and tick off herd and animal numbers in a muddy notebook. Being inside the pen was, he knew, the most dangerous job next to lassoing a steer's swollen foot in the crush, one where you were likely to be kicked or crushed against the bars, but he was quite unafraid so knew he could do the job without hitting them. He liked to think he could calm the animals by talking to them in a kind, low voice as he waved them through the gate between the pens or out into the crush but knew they were basically wild at heart and wanted no man near them however kind-hearted. They hated this abrupt interruption of their freedom and the replacement of grass with shitty concrete and the clamour of cold steel. The crush weighed them as they passed through it and made a terrible oily clanking. Even briefly held in place in it by the neck, they invariably shat themselves soupily with the shock of it. The sharply grassy smell of the herd in the pasture was soon replaced all about him by the sourer stench of fear.

Thirteen steers were needed for collection by the cattle lorry the next morning. The law had relaxed since the BSE crisis but they were still effectively obliged to have every animal slaughtered before it was thirty months old. One or two were obviously finished, weighing in at six hundred and fifty kilos or more and with properly beefy flanks and thighs. Others of the

457

same age were not such good feeders and needed a few weeks more. So there was much arguing about which of the border-line cases should go. Then one of the ready ones was found to have lost his metal ear tag which won it a stay of execution because it was illegal to send them to slaughter without two tags in place, and another Hansel and Gretel discussion ensued as to who was fat enough to take the lucky animal's place.

The twelve already picked had been ushered in twos and threes to the cattleshed on release from the crush. The remaining animals now milled nervously around as they were inspected, snorting, ducking their heads, and seeking comfort in the closest possible proximity to each other. Some even thrust their heads shoulder deep between their neighbours' legs. Others pressed, head first, in tight huddles in the inner corners of the pens as if affecting an interest in the weeds on the high walls, all unaware that it was their rumps, not their faces, that were being assessed.

At last a choice was made, a stocky two-year-old that, though still giving the impression of youth because he was so much shorter than his companions, had filled out his frame as far as he was likely to do. He joined the others in the shed with something like relief, kicking up his heels as he felt himself on deep straw and out of scrutiny. The rest were turned out from the yard's lower gate into new pasture and soon broke into a run and were lost to view in the fog.

How soon did they forget? It was a question he had last dared ask thirty or forty years ago, when he was a boy and it was still profitable for their father to run a dairy herd alongside the beef one. Some calves had just been separated from their mothers and the despondent, regular lowing had kept waking him in the night.

'They're animals,' his father said. 'They don't remember. They don't understand time. They get worried sometimes but that's just instinct, not feeling. Don't let it bother you.'

But it did bother him. Frequently. And he envied friends at school whose fathers produced only daffodils and broccoli on their land, or potatoes and anemones. Growing up, he had hoped for but never acquired, the hard outer layer that had come so naturally to his brother. He mastered all the tasks that were set him. He had been on courses on chemical spraying and hedgerow management and conservation headlands. He learned how to fill out the complex paperwork that would prove they had complied with new regulations and qualified for various EU subsidies. He had even done quite well in ploughing matches over the years. He had proved he was a good judge of calves at auction. But still this inner softness, weakness even, persisted and made him feel an impostor among his family and peers.

Looking at advertisements in *Farmer's Weekly* sometimes, at the sentimental picture plates of wet-eyed calves and contented sows with titles like *Little Mischief* or *A Mother's Pride*, he wondered if he were not mistaken. Perhaps all farmers felt the way he did and were simply masking their occasional discomfort from one another, the way men liked to pretend to each other that they had neither respect for women nor emotional need of them.

Once, when a steer they had only had a week sickened and died, racked by seizures thought to be caused by lead paint poisoning from some shed on the farm where he was reared, his father seemed upset for a few minutes but that might simply have been because he had not put the animal down himself with a gun instead of incurring hefty vet's bills in the hope of pulling the wretched thing through.

Another time a cattle lorry had come driven by a man who started using an electric prod as they herded the steers on board and his brother had sent him away indignantly and complained to the haulier who had hired him. But that hadn't been concern for the animals' welfare so much as worry the animals would not fetch a fair price. If an animal was frightened before slaughter, he claimed, it could tense up so badly its muscles held too much blood in a way that would spoil the meat. He had simply feared that a cattle prod would tense them up more than a simple whip or stick would do. The slaughtermen called such a blood-heavy carcass a *dark cutter*, his brother told him, a term that now came back to him whenever he passed a butcher's shop window or was chopping meat for a stew.

He had topping to do all that afternoon so he could listen to the radio in the tractor as he drove up and down the grass fields for a few hours, dreaming of other places, other lives. But that evening, just before sunset, he slipped down to the shed where the cattle were waiting. If his brother had challenged him, he'd have said he was heaping up the silage for them but he also came down to exercise his guilt and wonder.

It was amazing how swiftly the mud and shit crumbled off their coats when they were bedded down in a good depth of clean straw. He stood a while, leaning on his pitchfork, watching their eyes on him as they chewed or rubbed their noses on the silage heap in a kind of ecstasy of greed. They looked healthy, content again, and, of course, entirely unsuspecting, and this cheered him. He wanted them to have as good a last night as possible and was disgusted at himself. Faced as they must have been with an occasional lovely face or particularly endearing child, had concentration camp guards indulged in a similar sick sentimentality? Had they given their charges pet names and convinced themselves their arbitrary instances of kindness counted for anything?

They had toad-in-the-hole for supper. He ate too much and slept badly, tormented by indigestion and dreams in which he must answer for himself to his father and accusing friends but could muster only bovine bellows.

They had an extra-early start, before sunrise, to be ready for the lorry. Guiding steers from their shed into a cattle truck was even harder – given their arrangement of buildings – than persuading them around the yard and into the pens. Cattle lorries were so long they would only fit into the main farmyard one way and had to be parked hard up against the cattleshed's outside wall. The animals had to make a u-turn, out of their shed, in through a smaller one that might once have been a piggery, and out through its other side where a narrow door opened directly opposite the lorry's rear. To steer them from the large shed into the smaller one, the two tractors were parked tightly, nose to tail, with a couple of pallets lashed on either end, blocking off any other route. An old galvanized steel gate was leant against the side of the lorry's tailgate to prevent escapes and help channel the animals up and in and the tailgate was thickly spread with old straw from within the small shed to mask any alien smells like pig which might have lingered from previous loads.

Cattle lorries had barriers which folded out from the walls and subdivided their interiors to stop animals falling and hurting themselves. Six or so steers at a time could be driven in and the barrier folded out and bolted shut behind them. But persuading even six animals to pass through the small door on the other side of the little shed and up into a lorry – something they had only been in once before, when they were far smaller and more biddable – could rarely be accomplished at the first attempt.

Steers had a maddening way of bunching up inside the little shed, forming a bottleneck just inside the door or allowing the inevitable curses and thwacks to panic them. As often as not one, placed just out of range by his brothers, would take one suspicious look at the lorry then turn around to face the wrong way, obstinately blocking the route for his fellows. Once one of them took fright and decided to run back the way they had come it was impossible to stop the others following and the shed was so low and small it would have been crazily danger-ous for a man to push in there with them in an effort to head them off. All one could do was try to block the route back to the bigger shed, lashing out and cursing when the steers tried to turn back and cooing desperate encouragement at the least sign of an animal daring to pass on into the lorry. Sometimes just one or two would comply and stagger up the tailgate and in only to be spooked and thunder back down when their brothers failed to join them quickly enough.

Of all the stages of his interaction with a steer, the day of its departure was the one when his determination to treat it humanely was most likely to crumble. If only they would trot peaceably on board the way they entered a new field, it would have been possible to treat them well until the last. But they never went peaceably, or very rarely. His guilt at sending them for slaughter fed his frustration at their wilfulness and stupid-ity and he would lash out as fiercely as his brother then feel himself diminished for it.

The sun rose on a steady, penetrating drizzle and the lorry arrived so soon afterwards that it might have spent the night in a lay-by in the village and been waiting there for dawn. The driver was new and not local. Masking his nerves in trucu-lence, he complained about the smallness of the yard.

'Nobody told me,' he said, although his lorry was no longer than usual, and he made a great performance of having to nose up into Home Field then execute a multiple-point turn in order to be able to back up to the position where they needed him.

No one was like this when their father was around, as he had one of those stern countenances that commanded respect, but he had driven up-country for a cousin's funeral the night before.

'I don't do rounding up,' the driver said flatly, hearing a steer bellow inside the cattleshed as he climbed down. 'No insurance.'

The farm was insured against third-party claims, it had to be. But no one told him that as it was not a thing one wanted known. The usual driver always helped a bit. He liked to. But he was a farmer's son and knew what he was about; a novice in such a situation offered more risk than assistance. This man was an outsider and an unknown quantity. He was older than most drivers and had a terse bitterness to him that spoke of failures and bad solitude.

'Just stand and hold the gate firm against the tailgate,' they told him. 'We'll do the rest.'

They could manage with just the two of them so long as the driver held his ground at least and had the sense not to start shouting and hissing at the animals as they approached.

Watched suspiciously by him, they made the last few arrangements, scattering straw and securing the barrier for him to stand behind. Then they walked in through the small shed and counted out the first six cattle.

These milled around a little at first, mooing mistrustfully and driving him and his brother back into the space between tractors and cattleshed a couple of times. Then their leader showed the way, heading up the tailgate with a few clattering steps. The rest followed him with little resistance until they felt the safety barriers being swung across and bolted behind them, by which time it was too late.

The next seven included an especially strong, wild specimen his brother had nicknamed Shakin Stevens on account of his quiff, that had once actually jumped out of the crush when being wormed, and they proved far less tractable. They surged in and out of the little shed several times, only panicked further by the stinging from the hosepipes. They wedged themselves in there the wrong way round, backs to the exit, blinking as the blows and curses rained down on their faces. They squirted diarrhoea across each other and rained down piss by the gallon. They answered the mooing from their brothers in the lorry with bellows and snorts. The stupid driver made matters worse by trying to encourage them as if he were on a rugby touchline and their curses at the cattle became as much curses at him, not that he would have noticed above the din and churning back and forth. Then one of them, who had spent several minutes blocking the exit for the others while he stared out at the lorry, finally took a step or two back and the rest began to leave. First two tried to go through at once and threatened to become wedged, then they went out in quick succession.

He and his brother pressed on into the shed hissing, shouting, waving their arms and lashing out so as to be sure the others followed before the leaders changed their minds and doubled back. The driver shouted again, even louder this time, and they cursed the bugger for his stupidity that might cost them another ten minutes of torment. Then there was a bright ding of hoof on metal and the clang of a falling gate and suddenly there was mooing coming from quite the wrong direction.

All at once the other four animals surged out.

Damning the idiot for not having even the nous to hold a leaning barrier in place, his brother stamped out after them and immediately swore and shouted for him to follow and quickly.

The last seven cattle were loose in the farmyard. Two were tasting the willows in the hedge. The rest were merely standing, nonplussed by their unexpected release.

The driver lay on his back, hands flung up above his head as though he were falling down a pit. The gate he had been holding in place lay across his hips. There were muddy hoof prints up the front of his overalls, as in some cartoon. The kick that had felled him had caused his nose and a part of his forehead to cave in so that his face was now a kind of bowl where vivid blood was pooling.

He ran to the back door to ring for an ambulance, although he was fairly sure the man was dead, and to call the abattoir. Another driver could not be freed up until that afternoon at least, so they had to move the tractors then let out the steers that were already loaded and herd all thirteen animals back into the cattleshed. If one of them had blood on its hoof, it was impossible to tell which by now. He forked up the silage for them and they fell to eating at once, swiftly calmed by food.

It did not seem right to move the body until the ambulance arrived but they lifted the gate off it and laid the man's hands at his sides.

'We should cover it,' he said. 'Shouldn't we?' But his brother couldn't answer because he was slumped in the filthy straw on the tailgate and had buried his face in his palms, shoulders heaving.

He was fetching clean potato sacks from the mill shed to make a sort of shroud when a family of walkers arrived on the footpath from the cliffs, thinking to cross the farmyard, and he felt he had to wave his arms and warn them off as they had children with them. As he shouted instructions that came out more abruptly than he'd intended because of his nerves, and sent them the long way round the farm, down the lane instead of across the fields, he saw fear in the husband's eyes and, in the wife's, something like disgust.

MAKING HAY

The children burst in full of the pleasure they assumed the young, by their very youth, gave to the old. While they were signing the visitors' book, Maudie exchanged a look with Prue then reached into the baby jacket she had been pretending to knit for some weeks. She took out a crib she kept hidden on a piece of card and scanned it expertly. *Grandchildren*, she read. *James, nine, vehicles, football, bananas. Effie, seven, ponies, death, Jaffa Cakes*. There was a number after every entry on the card, be they friend or relative, to indicate how much she currently loved them. Neither child was scoring highly.

'Look who's come to see their old granny!' she exclaimed, catching sight of her daughter-in-law's pick-up speeding away.

James and Effie kissed her dutifully. Effie sat in one of the specially high-seated armchairs and bounced self-consciously. James mooched, staring at Maudie's bandage.

'Wave hello to your grandfather.'

They waved uncertainly. Maudie's husband sat apart with the few male residents. The cramped back sitting room, where smoking was allowed, was the men's territory. They congregated, taciturn, around the sports channel for the long stretches between meals, leaving the ladies the run, so to speak, of the more spacious and sociable day room. Grandpa stared at the children blankly but two of his companions waved back and Herbert Boskenna did that clicky thing with his dentures which was his equivalent.

'Can I watch too?' James asked. 'The Grand Prix's on.'

'No, dear. The men don't like to be disturbed. Maybe when you're older.'

'How about in here, then?'

'Miss Tregenza's waiting for Gary Cooper.'

'She's asleep,' put in Effie and they all looked briefly at Miss Tregenza, a thin, pale thing with little hair and no conversation.

'No, dear,' Maudie observed. 'She always looks that way when she's waiting.'

'Nurse'll be in in a moment,' said Prue, 'to turn Gary Cooper on, then she'll perk up. You'll see. She likes Gary Cooper. We all do.' Prue gave one of the coarse chuckles which reminded Maudie why they had never been friends until now.

'There's a banana in that fruit bowl with your name on it,' she told James but the boy sulked, unused to denial. 'Do you want a Jaffa Cake, Effie?'

Effie pulled a long face. 'I'm on a diet,' she said. 'Mum says I mustn't eat between meals.'

'Well teatime's a meal.'

Effie pulled the face again. 'Better not,' she said.

'How long have you got?' Maudie asked them both.

James sighed with a characteristic want of tact. 'Quarter of an hour,' he said, as though that were a small eternity. 'She's gone to Cornwall Farmers to fetch Dad more wrapper for the silage.'

'Is he doing that this afternoon, then? I wouldn't have thought it was dry enough . . .'

'Yup,' James said absently, staring as Nurse clicked in a Gary Cooper DVD. Miss Tregenza's reanimation was nothing startling but she opened her eyes, shut her mouth and assumed a look of complacent serenity. She began to croon the introductory music, slightly in advance of the orchestra.

'Knows all the tunes,' Prue said as the titles rolled up the screen. 'Ooh, *The Fountainhead*. I think I like this one. Patricia Neal always had such lovely, crisp-looking hair.'

'Wouldn't you rather be helping your dad?' Maudie asked, ignoring her.

'Not really,' James said. 'It's all tractor work really. Mum won't let me load new rolls of plastic on the bale-wrapper in case I get my hands stuck.'

'Well that's the trouble with silage, isn't it Prue? All done by machine. Wrapped in plastic. No art to it at all, really.'

'Lazy, I call it,' Prue said.

'And it stinks,' said Effie. 'It's nice enough now but when you cut it open in the autumn it's like sick with mould on.'

'In our day,' Maudie told them, 'everyone round here still made hay and that doesn't stink. Good hay smells sweet.'

'What's hay?' Effie asked.

'Dried grass, stupid,' James said, watching the film.

'It's more than that,' Maudie told him. 'Hay's a craft. It's a mystery. You have to cut it just at the right time. The ears can be forming but leave it too late and there's no goodness left. And it has to be dry. You need four clear, dry days at least. You can't cut it wet 'cause it won't dry right lying down. It has to be cut dry then tedded – that's turned to you – twice daily. It has to dry fast so the goodness doesn't leach out. If you're slow drying it, respiration carries on and the sugars turn to gas and water.'

'And heat,' Prue put in. 'Hay gets hot. Put it in a rick too soon and the whole thing could go up. Every few years someone would have an almighty fire. When we were younger, the whole family lent a hand, cousins and all. If you were old enough to walk, you were old enough to turn hay. And there were competitions.'

'There still are, for silage,' James put in. 'Dad says there's no point.'

'Nothing wrong with competitions if you've a chance of winning,' Maudie said to shut him up. 'Your grandfather, in his time, was the most competitive haymaker on this peninsula. He wasn't like the others, though, watching weather vanes and looking how high the birds were feeding; he went out and got the science. Knew all about balancing his herbage dry matter and how he had to get the moisture content down by a third.'

'A quarter,' Prue put in sharply. 'They reckon you should aim for a hundred and fifty grams per kilo nowadays.'

'If you say so,' said Maudie, who maintained a stout disapproval of metrication. 'He knew about amino-acid leaching and stomata closure and the rest. He was obsessed with raising his yields. He was sure if you prepared the grass in the right way back in the early spring, you could produce a hay that took up the same amount of space in the barn but fed the animals twice as well.'

'Didn't he have a muck spreader?'

'Of course he did but that wasn't enough.'

'What about fertilizer?'

'We couldn't afford chemicals. We had to make do with what nature gave us.'

'What, then?'

Maudie edged forward in her chair slightly, aware that she was competing for their attention with Gary Cooper. 'Blood,' she pronounced.

'Dried blood?' asked James.

'No.' She was scornful. 'That's no use. When Mother Eddy went peculiar and danced off a cliff and they cleared out her cottage, he found an old book which spelled it out for him. You needed fresh blood. There was plenty of blood when we killed a pig but we used all that for puddings. But he got chickens.'

'Not much blood in a chicken,' Prue sighed.

'It was quality that mattered. Quality and freshness. And then there were the kittens.'

'No!' Effie was deeply shocked.

'Of course. Barn cats have kittens all the time. It's a fact of life. And the mothers'd die of hunger and exhaustion if you let them raise them all. My dad always used to drown them. Put them in a sack, nice and quick, and into that old cattle trough at the top of the yard. Don't be silly, Effie. It was a natural kindness. He had to do it. But then your grandfather there started taking the kittens himself. He thought I didn't know but I'd see him keeping an eye on the litter instead of drowning it straight away.'

'Wanted them plump and juicy,' Prue said with just the right hint of relish.

'That's right. One day he'd be out there in the barn, weighing them in his hands and the next night he'd take longer than usual shutting the yard gate and walking the dog. And I'd know what he'd been up to because he'd spend an age washing his hands. I even heard the little click as he slipped the fruit knife back into that rack by the bread crock.'

There was a pause filled only by a startled cough from Miss Tregenza as Gary Cooper's astonishing profile caught the light. Effie breathed through her mouth. The child needed her adenoids out. Maudie briefly summoned up the gratifyingly intense image, glimpsed through a slyly lifted floorboard, of her sister, Bridie, gassed and splayed on the kitchen table, having hers removed by Dr Wadsworth.

'Did it work?' James asked suddenly and his voice pulled her back from reverie.

She looked at him hard; the image of his father. In that, at least, he did not disappoint. 'Do you know, it *did*,' she said. 'At least, he took the Grassland Association's cup two years in a row. But winning wasn't enough. He'd set himself a challenge to beat.

'The third year it was a horse. I even remember his name. Destry. As in *Destry Rides Again*. He was the last of the horses. We had the first tractor west of Penzance but that wasn't until 1938. Anyway, poor Destry hadn't been put out to pasture for two months when his heart gave out. The vet said he'd had a murmur but I think it was sorrow. He missed the labour. Anyway, horses were usually shot by the knacker when their time came. He'd come out and finish them off kindly then buy what was left for dog meat. Don't look like that, James. During the war, people ate horse, too.'

'Tasty,' Prue said nostalgically. 'Red wine. Bit of juniper to take off the muskiness.'

'Horse meat, Prudence. Not dog.' Maudie shook her head to the children, as though to explain that Prue wasn't all there.

'But your grandfather said no. After all Destry had done for the farm and seeing he was the last of the line, he should do the deed himself and call the knacker out afterwards. Well, I thought. We're moving on from kittens now. And sure enough he didn't finish him off until after dark. Told Mum it was because he couldn't bear Destry to see the shotgun but I knew it was the blood. He needed to shed the blood at night so it would have plenty of time to soak into the soil before the sun rose and dried it up. And he must have known a shot to the head wouldn't reach a big enough artery so he wanted to use a knife afterwards and be able to rinse his boots and hands off under cover of darkness.' She sighed. 'Funny, though. I'd

474

forgotten all about it when they called us all out to get the hay in that summer. But then I breathed it in.'

'Was it . . .' James was all attention. 'Was it disgusting like silage?'

She paused for effect. 'It was the sweetest hay I had ever smelled. Like fresh baked bread in a ripe orchard. I took one sniff and I caught your grandfather's eye – he was a very handsome man in those days – and he smiled, ever so slightly. So I knew I was right. And it didn't just win him the cup again, it was like miracle food. The cattle were so sleek and muscly on it and the meat, when it came, was so well marbled with fat, someone started a rumour we'd been doctoring them with some chemical. Which we hadn't, of course. Nothing but grass, our own milled barley and our own sweet hay.'

'Cream and roses,' sighed Miss Tregenza so suddenly even Maudie was startled.

'What's that?' Prue asked her.

'How you can tell a good bit of meat.' Miss Tregenza's eyes were momentarily freed to roam as Gary Cooper had left the scene to less principled and therefore less handsome characters. The tip of her tongue crept out to moisten thin lips. 'Puts you in mind of cream and roses.'

The sad falling off in meat quality with the rise in low-fat cookery was a pet topic of Maudie's but she had a professional eye on the clock and her fifteen minutes were nearly up. 'Anyway,' she continued, 'I thought to myself that'll be it now. He can't get another horse. He can't make sweeter hay than this. He can rest on his laurels. Sure enough he went back to letting my dad drown the barn kittens and our hay was good but no better than anyone else's who knew to watch the weather and judge the season.

'But then the War came and all the evacuees. Hundreds of grubby, rowdy little town children on the trains from Paddington and Bristol. Some of them had never seen the sea before, never mind a cow. We had six – four boys and two girls – *and* those saucy Land Girls. But one of the six children went missing. A little tyke, he was. Red hair, crusty knees, hated washing. About your size and age,' she said, carefully assessing James. 'Jacky. Jacky Porter. No one was surprised when he vanished. He was forever wandering, always skiving off when they were walking to school. So we just supposed he'd run off back to London. We did all we could. The sad thing was that he went just too early to find out he'd nowhere to run *to*. Mother and aunt dead in a flattened house. Terrible really. And he had no father who'd claim him.'

'Shame,' Prue sighed and shook her head at the fecklessness of men. The children only stared. Maudie pretended an interest in the progress of the baby jacket.

'That summer,' she said, 'when your grandfather had cut the hay and the girls and I were out tedding it, I came across a Fair Isle cardigan. Well I knew it had belonged to the Porter boy but I thought nothing of it. He was a tearaway who left clothes all over the place and, as often as not, had a sock missing or couldn't find his tie before church. But I gave it to your granddad to hand in to the police, just in case. And there was something in his face as I passed it to him. A sadness. A kind of . . . dignified regret.

'I've often wondered what he did with the body. Down one of the old mineshafts? Or perhaps he ploughed it into a barley field.'

'What about the hay?' Effie asked impatiently.

'Hang on a second, dear. Knit two, purl two, cast one onto

t'other, knit two, purl two . . . The hay? The hay had no smell at all. Looked fine enough. Dried quick enough. But it was a dead thing. Characterless. And I swear to God the cattle didn't like it and we actually had to buy in bales from Zack Hosking. And if the story ended there, I'd have said it was divine punishment, plain and simple and that he saw the error of his ways.'

'Why?' James asked. 'Did the grass die?'

'Lord, no. It takes more than a bit of blood to kill off a whole field of grass. It was stranger than that. We let the cattle in the field for a few weeks that autumn before the rains started in earnest and I went up there one morning to check they had enough water. And they were nosing at something. You know how inquisitive steers get? They were nosing and dragging their hooves. So I walked through them to take a look and there was a sort of mound. Like a big molehill. Well we don't get any moles, as you know. Only rabbits. So I thought it was a bit queer and I scraped a bit at the earth with my toe, the way the cattle had started to. And they were all nosing around me and snorting and sneezing.' Maudie mustered a shudder. 'I remember it so clearly. I crouched to feel and my fingers found a sort of . . . well *skin*, really. Greyish, where the earth had been on it, but pink inside and quite warm. Well, I dug more aside and realized it was a sort of . . . a sort of *bag*. Full of liquid and . . . and something else. I was just going to run and fetch your grandfather or one of the Land Girls – they were only a few fields away – when it kicked. Or something inside it kicked.

'Prudence, it's no good. You're going to have to finish this matinée jacket for me – I can't make head or tail of this blinking pattern.

'You know how sometimes you go into a house or into a

room and, although you can't say exactly what's wrong, you get a bad feeling?'

Both children nodded although it was certain neither had the slightest psychic ability. Even Prue had fallen quiet. The only sound was Nurse using the rotary iron in the hall, the murmur of sports commentary from the smoking room and subdued, manly conversation from Gary Cooper and a colleague.

'Well that's how I felt and I sensed that whatever it was, I had to destroy it. I ran to the hedge and fetched the biggest bit of granite I could carry and heaved it back. I thought I'd just shut my eyes and drop it on the thing, the way you would on a rabbit with myxomatosis. I wasn't thinking beyond that, of the mess or having to explain it or anything. I was just about to let go when I heard a strange sucking, whiny sound, a bit like a very new kitten now I think of it. And I opened my eyes, looked down and almost dropped the rock.

'The skin of the bag, or whatever it was, had sort of split apart and there, all wet and shiny like a little seal was a baby. A perfect, black-haired boy baby. The skin had shrunk up like a burst balloon but the last of it was sticking to his head and, as I bent to scrape it off him, he opened his soft blue eyes, emptied the stuff out of his mouth and claimed me with his cry as surely as if he had called me Mother.'

Maudie glimpsed her daughter-in-law's returning Jeep. 'And that,' she said, 'was the baby that grew into your father.'

There was a stunned silence.

'I don't believe it,' James said at last.

'*I* don't care,' Maudie told him. 'He'd deny it, of course, because it's only human to want to be like everyone else. I just thought you ought to know. That's why his middle name is Fielding.'

'The mark,' Effie said softly, remembering something. 'There's a red mark on his head where his hair's falling out. Is that . . .?'

'Yes, dear. Where the bag was stuck to him. His birthmark, if you like. Now here's your dear mum to take you home.'

They were curiously reluctant to leave but more reluctant still to do as their mother bid them and hurry next door to give Grandpa a fond goodbye kiss. Herbert Boskenna clicked his teeth at Effie while she was waiting her turn and the child truly turned pale with fear.

'She ought to eat more,' Maudie told her daughter-in-law, 'and he needs to watch less television – it's giving him nightmares. Bye all. Come back soon.'

'The trick,' she confided in Prue as Nurse wheeled in the tea things and wheeled out Miss Tregenza, 'is to spike the narrative with just a seasoning of solid, agricultural fact.'

BRAHMS AND MOONSHINE

The clouds had drifted away during the concert and people exclaimed, as they emerged from the church, at the unexpected brightness of the moon and stars. A comet was making a centennial appearance in the western sky that Easter. Gretel wanted to linger with the others to admire the clarity of its tail but Corey was keen to be off. The Requiem had barely begun when he realized each of them had supposed the other had shut the chickens in their coop before leaving. He had been fretting about foxes ever since.

'Isn't it beautiful?' she said, meaning the comet. Her heart was still brimming with Brahms and she wanted to make the rare sensation last.

'Yes, come on,' he said. 'If we get a move on we can get out of there before we get stuck in a queue with this lot.'

She followed him obediently, feeling in her wallet for the key to the van. There was a retiring collection after the concert to assist the fine old church's restoration. Still blissed-out on music, Gretel had reached for her money as they left their pew, generosity welling up within her, only to find he had raided her funds to buy oil for the chainsaw. She could offer nothing to the pretty girl with the begging bowl but twenty pence and a worthless, craven smile.

The concert-goers' cars were crammed into a field across from the church. It had been drizzling all week. She felt cold mud on her toes as she hurried after him and cursed the foolish impulse which had prompted her to wear pretty shoes and her least ancient dress. No one else had dressed up; forewarned, they thought only of warm practicality. The exceptions were the musicians, glimpsed here and there, incongruous in backless dresses or dinner jackets amid the mud and four-wheel-drives.

The van was not a four-wheel-drive but an old, much-patched Commer converted to a mobile home, built for unhurried journeys and long, recuperative rests. When they arrived, she had taken one despairing glance at the mud and pleaded with the young musician waving them in to let her park on the thin island of firmer ground near the entrance. But he was bound by regulations and insisted, smiling, that she park with the other large vehicles, most of them shamingly new and all of them surely better equipped for such conditions.

'Well go on, then.'

'We're skidding.' She felt the sickening lack of grip.

'Slowly,' Corey said, 'or you'll make it worse. Ease her out. Steady!'

She drove because he had lost his licence before he met her. Some terrible tale involving a child, a bicycle and worn brake shoes. Told her in the flush of new love, the story had demanded and won her sympathy but increasingly its lack of details came to rankle and her mind framed the questions she could never ask. What was the child's name? How old? Just how badly disabled had the accident left it? And why did Corey only voice indignation, not remorse?

'Here. Let me. There's a tarp back there. Stick it under the wheels with that old blanket and I'll try.'

While he shifted across to the driving seat, she slipped out, stuffed blanket and tarpaulin between mud and wheel then stood back.

484

'Okay,' she called.

'Push!' he shouted back.

She braced a foot against the stone gatepost behind her and placed both hands squarely on the van's rear. She felt rust beneath her fingers and imagined her fists bursting straight through bodywork that was little more than filler and cheerful paint.

'Okay,' she called again.

He revved. The wheels churned uselessly, burying the blanket and chewing up the tarpaulin.

'Stop,' she called. 'Stop! I can feel her sinking.'

All about them glossy four-wheel-drives were pulling away. She thought of asking for help but she knew what the swinging headlamps revealed; an ageing New Age couple and an even older van. She imagined women taking in the mud caked round her inappropriate shoes and sprayed up her faded Indian cotton, heard their hastily mouthed commands to their husbands to pay no heed and hurry on by. She knew she and Corey presented the very image of fecklessness, of thankless time-wasting.

Corey was losing his temper. He had a child's inability to deal with stress and so had designed his life along lines of dull simplicity. His back-to-basics philosophy masked a fear of confrontation and unexpected challenges. He had made a big effort, she knew, coming out tonight, sitting restlessly through a concert of what he called *her* music but the effort was worthless for being so paraded. An evening of his reluctantly given was small recompense for the tedious hours she had spent driving him back and forth from the lay-by where he peddled the crude wooden mushrooms he 'carved' with a chainsaw. Even so, he was going to make her pay.

'Why'd you stop pushing?' he asked.

'I told you,' she said. 'It's sinking. You'll only make it worse.'

'This was a stupid idea, parking in here.'

'There was nowhere else to park.'

'You knew we'd get stuck. If those chickens are dead . . .'

'I'll buy you some new ones.'

'Oh yes. Money solves everything. Wave your wand and spend your father's precious money.'

'Excuse me?' Gretel turned her back to flag down the last four-wheel-drive as it began to pull out. Grinning, actually grinning, the driver wound down his window.

'Sorry,' he said. 'Daren't stop or we'll get stuck too.'

'Good luck,' the woman beside him called and they purred away.

As Gretel stood aside to let them pass, the mud sucked off one of her inappropriate shoes. She groped in the dark for it but her fingers found only ooze and she nearly lost her balance.

'Oh. God, I'm so sorry.'

It was the young man in the dinner jacket who had waved them in. She had spotted him later, in the chorus, cheeks pink with effort, eyes shining with emotion. His white shirtfront glowed bluish in the light of the moon. He shone a torch across them then politely dropped its beam.

'Can I help push?'

'Better not,' she said. 'We might sink even further.'

'I should never have let you park here. Come on. I'll shove too.'

So they pushed again while Corey revved again and the van sank up to its rear axle. Uncomplaining, the young man now wore mud on his shirtfront like a penance.

'I could ring the A A or something,' he suggested, shining a torch into the liquefied mire.

'We're not members,' she said and it felt as though she were confessing to not being members of society. 'I normally fix the van myself.'

'Oh. Well, I'd offer to pull you out myself but I've only got a 2CV. Erm. Tell you what, the chairwoman's got a Land Rover.'

'Oh goodie,' Corey said, mimicking his accent. 'And where's she?'

'She'll be up at the pub, I expect. I'll drive up there now and see if I can find her. If I do, I'll send her right back with a tow-rope. Or I'll send someone else. It won't be more than half an hour max.'

'Oh brill,' Corey said and swore.

'I feel awful about this,' the young man went on. 'You'll never want to come again.'

'No no,' Gretel said.

'Quite right,' said Corey.

'There'll be two free seats for you on the last night. I'll have them left on the door for you. I'm sorry there's not much more I can do.'

'It's not your fault. Honestly,' she said. 'Thanks for every-thing.'

He found her missing shoe before he left and handed it over with further apologies then he disappeared into the lane. Moments later they heard his 2CV gunning uncertainly and pulling away. There was no one left besides them. The night enveloped them, as did Corey's filthy mood.

Gretel tried turning on the radio to lighten the atmosphere but he told her not to waste the battery. She said she wished she'd known to bring a picnic like everyone else, then they might have had leftover sandwiches to enjoy. Which of course made things worse because now he was hungry as well as stranded.

Suddenly he was getting out.

'Where are you going?' she asked.

'Home,' he said.

'But he said it would only be half an hour.'

'So? They could all be dead by now. Anyway, what makes you think he was telling the truth? He'll be in the pub with his mates. He'll be drinking. No one'll come. I'm off.'

'But how . . .?'

'I'll hitch,' he said. 'Your van. Your mess. You wait.'

'Don't go,' she said. 'Don't be like that. This is silly. You'll never find a lift.'

But he did, almost immediately. A Beetle stopped, a new one, and when the light came on inside she saw the young woman driving it, blonde, sporty-looking, a surfing type. She heard him say, quite distinctly as he got in, 'Oh, she'll be all right,' and he sped away without a backward glance.

Alone at last, unhurried and with no headlamps to spoil the clarity, she found herself in the perfect situation to admire the comet. It was the first she had seen. Until now she had always assumed they were swift blazes in the night sky, like shooting stars. Or perhaps shooting stars were simply other planets' comets? Her grasp of astronomy was vague but she had always wondered how the superstitious, the Three Wise Men, the invaded Saxons on the Bayeux Tapestry, could have built such significance on something one might blink and miss. Instead, she now saw, comets were like frozen things, speeding, maybe, but at such a distance they barely seemed to move.

She'll be all right. She repeated his words in her head like a mantra. The Brahms had stirred her up, brought her repeatedly close to tears with its grand talk of death, of mourning, of last things and grass-like flesh. It left her exposed and childlike, in need of the kind of hugs Corey only offered when drunk and unhelpfully sentimental but the comet at once belittled and calmed her. *Nothing matters*, it said and *Everything is possible*.

Gretel removed her second shoe, so as not to lose it, then walked barefoot to the back of the van. The squelching mattered less without shoes on. It was only mud. It would wash off. She turned on the light and closed the door behind her. There was water in the flask and gas in the canister. She set the kettle on to boil. There were some Garibaldi biscuits in the tin beside the teabag jar, softened with age but still quite palatable. Munching while she waited for her tea, she checked the cupboards. The tools were there, naturally, and the jack – one drove a van this old nowhere without them – but so were the van's original picnic set, the road atlas, her duffel coat and a good thick jersey she had given up for lost. The mud would not have done anything to the blanket a launderette could not undo. Her wallet was empty of notes but it held the card only she could use, *the Card of Power* as she thought of it. Her driving licence, stowed behind the sun visor, seemed suddenly the official recognition of some much deeper ability than mere self-transport. She dunked her teabag and made a mental list of all she would be leaving behind if she failed to follow Corey. A heap of old clothes, old paperbacks, her clumsy attempts at pottery and an attractive, straggle-haired hitch-hiker she had once rescued from a downpour on Salisbury Plain. Nothing she could not replace, should the need arise.

The festival chairwoman arrived with Land Rover, tow-rope and a tactful lack of expressed surprise at finding one person where she had been led to expect two. She pulled the van back out to tarmac then paused, after unhitching the rope which, miraculously, had not pulled off its bumper. Her manner was bracing in a good, old-fashioned way that instilled confidence rather than terror.

'Are you positive you'll be all right?' she asked as though on the verge of offering a warming mustard bath and a serviceable change of clothes.

Gretel felt the mud crack on her cheek so she must have been smiling.

'I'll be fine,' she said. 'Honestly.'

THE EXCURSION

The idea was to make a full day of it rather than have the demonstration as the be-all and end-all. The minibus collected them from outside the church at ten-thirty. Gwen and Bernie bagged three seats at the back so she could sit with them.

They were like that, Eileen had realized. Forceful.

People who escaped from inside aeroplanes seconds before they turned to fireballs did so because for a few moments something in their genetic makeup enabled them to override all inculcated sense of decency to trample on the hands and faces of other passengers in a single-minded rush for life. Afterwards they would say how guilty they felt and people assumed this reflected a becoming sense of unworthiness at being spared. Actually what they spoke of was uncomplicated guilt at their memories of elbowing an air steward in the face or punching a dithering child aside from the escape chute.

Gwen and Bernie were such people and Eileen was not. They bagged her a seat because they wanted her with them but if the minibus were balanced on a cliff, they'd jump out without a backward glance at her.

They were big-boned, wet-lipped, hot-palmed meat-eaters; more like brother and sister than husband and wife. She preferred not to imagine them naked.

It was not far. A forty-minute run on the motorway then half that again dawdling in queues through the city's outskirts and system of roundabouts. Someone had a daughter-in-law in the police who had tipped them off so they knew exactly where to meet up and when. There were two hours to kill so they tried on shoes in Marks – Gwen was a martyr to corns, apparently – before enjoying a sort of package-deal OAP lunch in the café at the top of Dingles.

She had not known them long. They had met through church. Eileen had attended the same church most of her life. She believed in Father and Son and – if not pressed for specifics – Holy Ghost. She accepted the probable truth of much of the Bible and found a recital of the Lord's Prayer a great comfort at times of stress. She disengaged her intellect when joining in the Creed but she would unhesitatingly have ticked any box marked Christian. She worshipped at the church her mother had preferred, which embraced an undemonstrative, tasteful brand of Anglicanism, a church for women like herself who were happy enough to lend a hand at a fundraising bazaar but preferred their religion undiscussed and uninvolving.

At least she thought that was the sort of woman she was. Then Gwen and Bernie turned up in the congregation one Sunday – the numbers were never spectacular so one could always spot new faces – and sat beside her. It was one of the few churches in the diocese that persisted in holding out against doing the Peace but they startled her by clasping her hands in theirs at the moment in the service where other priests might have intoned *let us offer one another a sign of peace* and murmuring, 'Peace be with you,' with such urgency she spent the rest of the service worried that hers was not so tranquil a soul as she had thought.

They sought her out during coffee and biscuits afterwards and introduced themselves.

'We can tell you're not happy here,' Gwen said. 'Can't we,

Bernie? I mean, it's not right. Not right for you. I'm sure he's a lovely man but you have to go back to first principles, sometimes.'

'I'm sorry?' Eileen said, confused.

By way of explanation, Bernie nodded towards Reverend Girouard, who had not long been with them. '*Homosexual,*' he hissed.

'Shame,' said Gwen. 'It's a lovely church otherwise. Old.'

'He even wants to bless their unions,' Bernie added. 'He asked the bishop.'

Eileen had already gathered from the flower arrangers that there was no likelihood of a Mrs Girouard and that Mr Clancy, who had been giving organ recitals for a while now, was possibly rather more than a lodger at the vicarage. The two men were exceptionally polite and good-looking and, after her initial surprise, she had begun to decide that their domestic arrangement made a pleasant change from the previous incumbent who had one of those resentful, difficult wives who seemed almost standard C of E issue these days and played Divide and Rule with the ladies on the flower rota. She had not analysed her response very deeply but a small part of her pleasure stemmed from the sense that she was not reacting as her parents would have done. Her unvoiced welcome of the two men was a timid rebellion against the norm. Now she found she lacked the courage to give it voice, however, and felt shamed into agreeing with Gwen and Bernie.

'I know,' she heard herself sigh. 'It probably isn't right. I mean, not ideal. But what can one do? We're lucky to have a priest at all, as far as I can see.'

'One that's white, you mean,' sighed Bernie.

'That's not what I . . .' Eileen began.

'Vote with your feet,' Gwen cut in. 'Next week you're coming to us at St Mungo's.'

She could have laid low, perhaps, pleaded sickness or lain out of sight on the kitchen floor when Gwen came tapping on the window with her wedding ring. She had gone with them, however, meek as a lamb.

St Mungo's was not at all the sort of church her mother would have liked, so initially there was a tacit satisfaction in changing allegiances. The hymns were happy and unfamiliar, their words projected onto a big screen so that everyone's hands were left unencumbered for waving in the air or clapping. The priest was a muscular, short-haired man – like a soldier or PE instructor – who wore a plain suit instead of robes and kept walking among them and making eye contact so that every-thing in the service felt tremendously personal. The Peace was no mere embarrassed handshake but a heartfelt festival of greeting in which people actually left their pews to meet stran-gers across the aisle. The priest tracked her down. There was no escaping him. Offset by his short silver hair, his eyes were chips of sapphire.

'I'm Paul,' he said, offering a hand both large and warm.

'Eileen,' she told him. 'I'm Eileen Roberts.'

'Peace be with you, Eileen,' he said, bringing his other hand into play so that both of hers were trapped. 'Welcome to St Mungo's. I mean that. Truly.'

And she felt so hot behind her eyes she thought she might faint.

His handshake was so firm and his welcome so compelling that she proved unswervingly disloyal and came back to St Mun-go's week after week. Reverend Girouard was undoubtedly better bred but there was no denying that his twinkly charm was effete by comparison, weak even, and she reminded herself – and her mother's disapproving shade – that some of the disciples had been rough-edged working men, men her father would have dismissed as *common*.

Gwen and Bernie did not come every week. She soon realized this was because they worked as covert missionaries, targeting churches where the priests were unmarried or unorthodox, to lure away to St Mungo's discontented worshippers who might otherwise have left the church entirely.

'I suppose it's all the same God, though,' Eileen let slip in a weak moment and Bernie corrected her.

'Yes, but some vessels are unworthy, Eileen. You wouldn't serve your guest on unclean china.'

She had since seen Reverend Girouard's good-looking friend Mr Clancy on the High Street a couple of times and crossed the street quickly to avoid any awkwardness. Reverend Girouard himself had come round once and actually called her name through the letterbox when she failed to answer the bell. She hid from him in the broom cupboard in case he peered through a window and saw her. She felt ill afterwards from the excitement and had to lie down.

There was already a small crowd outside the law courts but, tipped off by the policewoman daughter-in-law, they knew to stand in a less obvious position down a side street where the authorities thought the van could emerge unimpeded.

They had all enjoyed a glass of wine with lunch and, as they waited, Gwen expounded on the accused's crimes with something approaching relish. Eileen did not take a newspaper as a rule because the photographs upset and haunted her. She preferred the radio, whose rare horrors one could always switch off. But Gwen talked horrors now, how the victims had been young men, little more than boys really, how they had been drugged and sexually preyed upon, how there were signs for those who knew how to read them that his purposes had been Satanic. He had shown no remorse and had even laughed to himself as the judge read out the charges.

What they told her fired her up with disgusted indignation but still she was not the sort of woman to make a spectacle of herself in public. As the time grew ever nearer she became increasingly tense, not wanting to be singled out for holding back, but not wanting either to behave in a way that was extreme. But just as the gate was swinging open and the unmarked van emerging, Gwen thrust a box of eggs into her hand from the collection she had picked up cheaply in Poundstretcher.

'He laughed to himself as the judge read out the charges,' she said. 'Just think of that. He laughed, Eileen!'

The crowd surged out into the road and Eileen was swept along with it. She knew she'd have to join in, she knew she'd have to throw an egg at least if only to do what was expected of her. But as the van drew near and the people around her started to shout, 'Filth! Filth!', and to throw things she shouted the first thing that came into her head.

'Satan!' she shouted. 'Murdering Satan!'

A sort of heat rose up behind her eyes, as rapidly as boiling-over milk, and her head was suddenly full of the poor boys, of lads she had known who might have been the killer's victims.

The rear of the van was blanked out, of course, and she found she directed all her uprush of hate at the startled man who was driving, not quite hidden by the grilles over the van's windows. She fancied there was fear in the look he gave her before the police came to his rescue and made the crowd stand back to let him pass.

It was over in seconds. She felt her cheeks on fire and found she was laughing, almost hysterical with embarrassment, by the time the van was rounding the corner. Bernie looked at her with respect.

'It's the Spirit,' he said. 'The Spirit is on you!'

But it wasn't, she knew. Gwen knew it too, glancing at her with a woman's sharper instinct. Eileen had tasted something more like ecstasy and her flesh was alight in a way that made her want to hide herself. She was disgusted with herself too. She had only meant to join in a little. It was quite unlike her to be so carried away and hatred was an emotion of which she had little experience.

On the minibus home everyone was chattering and excited, as though they had been abseiling or done a bungee jump at an age when no one would have expected it of them. Eileen pretended to join in but she was thoughtful, disturbed at the emotional roiling their messy little demonstration had set off in her.

By the time they were being dropped outside the church again, her old mute passivity had fallen on her however and she was easily persuaded back to Gwen and Bernie's for a restorative cup of tea.

It was an unremarkable house, over-furnished with unremarkable things; a house in a gravy advertisement. She donated a box of fondant fancies she had bought in Marks and was saving for later. Gwen sliced up a Battenberg and passed it round. The pieces were far bigger than Eileen would have allowed herself. She normally made a Battenberg feed eight, not three. She broke her slice into more manageable blocks of sponge and icing.

'Hey,' Gwen said. 'Show Eileen the tape.'

'Are you sure?' Bernie asked.

'Oh, she's one of us, now,' Gwen said, dabbing a pink crumb from the corner of her lips. 'Aren't you, Eileen?' She had not finished her mouthful properly. Eileen saw mashed cake on her tongue. 'After this afternoon's display,' Gwen chuckled. 'Eh, Eileen, who'd have thought you had it in you!'

So Eileen sat on in a vast Parker Knoll recliner like an imprisoning dentist's chair – Bernie had yanked up the footrest because they knew she had vein trouble – and watched a video with them.

It was a home-made affair, crudely shot by their son who worked in the Middle East as an engineer with an oil company. Because of the crowds, the passing cars, the glimpses of women, children, people on mobile phones, it took her a while to decipher what she was supposed to be focusing on. Then she saw the diminutive figures beyond the bustling foreground, figures in a clearing of bloodstained sand. It was, she understood as Gwen began her fascinated commentary, footage of punishments and executions, shot by the son with a hidden camera. It was not all shot on the same occasion or even in the same place. He was an ever-ready collector, like a trainspotter; a connoisseur of extreme justice.

She glanced away from the screen long enough to take in again the photograph on the mantelpiece her eyes had skated over earlier in a restless search for something beautiful. There he was. A mixture of Gwen and Bernie. Big-boned. Cheerful. Smirking in his mortarboard. Her eyes were drawn back to the screen.

There were floggings for adultery and lechery and removal of hands for theft. There were stonings and, astonishingly, beheadings. The shootings were shockingly banal by comparison, because they were so familiar from films yet quieter and less dramatic than anything faked. (Gwen and Bernie afforded these their slightest respect and talked across them, ordinary talk about food plans, neighbours, fish-food pellets.) Then there was a scene so specific yet so odd that she could not quite believe what she was seeing and, reading her mind, Bernie rewound the tape to show her again.

Two men were pushed to their knees then tied to a stake. Then everyone backed away to allow a bulldozer to cause a sizeable wall to topple onto them, hiding them from view in dust and rubble. There was a cheer from the crowd on the video and an answering murmur of assent from Bernie.

'Homosexuals,' Gwen said. 'They used to stone them apparently until someone decided that was spiritually unclean for the executioners.'

'Splashes,' Bernie explained.

'So they topple a wall,' Gwen said. 'Go on, Bernie. Show her again.'

Somehow Eileen found the lever to lower the footrest and made it out of the chair and onto her feet. Somehow she found excuses and even thanks to stammer before finding her way out without actually seeming to flee.

Back at her house she locked the front door behind her, ran to the bathroom and brought up everything, OAP lunch, fondant fancies, Battenberg. She rid herself of everything of the afternoon but the stains in her memory, the fear in the driver's eyes, the admiration of ingenuity in Gwen's voice. She heard the woman's placid suburban tone, that would have been no different if she had been explaining a cunning technique for building a rockery or installing a water feature.

The spasms were so violent she had to wrap her arms about the lavatory bowl, and left her so weak that she rested her cheek against its cold porcelain for minutes afterwards, still hearing Gwen and seeing atrocities.

'We missed you,' Reverend Girouard said as he shook her hand after the next Sunday's service. His grasp was so coolly reassuring she found herself imagining how it might feel to hold his hand across her face. 'Daniel – Mr Clancy – thought you might have forsaken us for St Mungo's.'

Mr Clancy passed them, dunking a custard cream in his coffee. 'The dark side,' he murmured flirtatiously.

'I tried it out,' she admitted. 'Because they asked and it seemed rude not to. But it wasn't for me. They do the Peace, you know and it's all a bit much.'

'Well, welcome back,' he said and Eileen saw how it was possible to feel at once judged and forgiven by a smile.

HUSHÈD CASKET

They found it quite by chance. There was nothing on the map or in the guidebooks. Sons of hysterical women addicted to spontaneity, they were both methodical men, keen and meticulous planners. They had spent half the morning at Beverley Minster and had calculated on squeezing in the churches at Patrington and Hedon before they stopped for a late, wintry picnic. An unscheduled diversion was no more in character than trusting in fate to provide a palatable provincial lunch.

Hugo nearly didn't stop. He was a fast but inhibited driver and hated ever having to swerve onto a verge or lay-by to execute a three-point turn.

'Stop!' Chris told him, flapping a hand against Hugo's forearm. 'Please. Something really interesting . . .' And he made Hugo pull over and park so they could walk back, armed as ever with camera and sketch pad. 'Through here!' he called, hurrying ahead.

They had entered what passed for a valley in Yorkshire's seaward south-east. There was a press of overgrown trees beside the lane. What might once have been a lych gate had been smothered in ivy and neglect and all but lost beneath bird-sown elder and holly.

'There's nothing there,' Hugo insisted, glancing between the map and photocopies he had taken of the relevant pages of *England's 1000 Best Churches*. 'Probably just a barn or . . .'

But Chris pressed on, ducking under the holly. He had

glimpsed a buttress as they flew past and was anticipating a little Gothic Revival jewel or at least one of those architectural riddles that made church-crawling such an addictive pleasure. The guidebooks had missed things before. Only two days into their honeymoon they had found a magnificent Saxon font, which alone was worth three stars, in an unlisted church they had only visited to track down the key-holder for one that was in all the books. Besides, he was the pretty one in the partnership, used to a fairly generous wilfulness allowance.

There was little left of the original building – a foreshortened nave, badly patched up with some decidedly agricultural breeze-block masonry. The old chancel and apse had been left to collapse, cut off by a new east wall and a crude, inappropriate window. What might once have been an avenue of clipped yew from lych gate to porch now formed a forbidding canopy, chilling the sunless air beneath it. But it was still a church where the map marked nothing, so Chris waited in the porch in triumph for Hugo to catch up.

'Well spotted,' Hugo said, picking a yew berry off Chris's shoulder, and Chris felt a flush of pathetic pride. The significance of his having at last found a lover whose preferred bedtime treats were lives of the likes of Ninian Comper or monographs on East Anglian corbels and whose top ten was not of dance tracks but bell towers passed him by in his happiness at having finally found the right match. It was his mother, waving them off on this eccentrically unsensuous honeymoon, who slyly observed that he had married his father. And she should know. Hugo wasn't conventionally sexy or notably rich so perhaps his main attraction for Chris were these small, heart-bumping instances – when he correctly dated a clerestory or found them some five-star Norman in a deeply unpromising suburb – of fatherly approval.

The porch displayed none of the usual vital signs of even remote parish business: no flower rota, no service list, no contact number for longsuffering key-holders, not even a notice about closing the door behind one so as to stop birds becoming trapped. There was no noticeboard, even, just plaster-work mapped with bright patches of green. Another curiosity was that the door was fastened from the outside, with two stout bolts so rusted and unused that Hugo had to take off a boot and wallop them with its heel to persuade them to shift.

By rights the hinges should have let out an echoing whine and skeins of cobweb sprung down from around the lintel. Such touches of Gothic might have offered camp comfort. Instead the door opened soundlessly onto a space where one felt not even a spider would have lived for long. There were no pews, or pulpit, no altar even. There was only a tomb, grey with dust, a large cardboard box and a font. There were none of the usual accretions a church gathered about itself with age – no memorials to virtuous wives or to sons lost in cruelly distant colonies, no antiquated cast-iron radiators, no mildewed hymnbooks, no stoutly tapestried kneelers and no electricity. Were it not for the font, it would hardly have seemed like a church at all. The interior had been scraped and replastered in the late 1800s, to judge from the tell-tale use of treacly wood stain on the undistinguished roof timbers. The windows – nonrepresentational stained glass, a fiery red margin around that peculiarly gloomy Victorian green – must have been replaced at around the same date, possibly following whichever fire or disaster had wrecked the original east end and left the place so stripped and truncated.

'Hardly feels like a church at all,' Chris said then wished he hadn't because the words gave the place permission to feel sinister. Hugo only let out a preoccupied *huh* for answer. He was already busy photographing. That was what they did usually: he photographed the whole while Chris executed quick water-colours or sketches of telling details, gargoyles, carvings and so on, the two elements to be combined eventually in an album.

By their usual standards the building was not even second rate, but the tomb and font were arresting. The tomb was ancient. Whatever inscription it had borne had long since worn away but it was of a type with one they had seen in St Martin's, Lowthorpe, where the sculptor had demonstrated considerable bravura in portraying the corpse as so many mounds and dips beneath a shroud. The Lowthorpe monument was of a married couple, however, its shrouded bier a grim parody of a wedding bed. This showed just one body, a man's, uncomforted by pomp at its head or pets at its feet. It had been defaced, an angry cavity chipped away where the genitals had perhaps been too generously suggested for later sensibilities.

Chris sketched rapidly, his mind half on the need to press on if they were to do justice to Patrington before dusk. He used charcoal, as it was apt for conveying the sweeps and shadows of carved cloth. Hurrying on to choose the best angle from which to sketch the font in pencil, he felt again the sense of dread that had pricked him when he dared to imagine the place was *not quite a church*. The font was carved from a basalt so black and so smoothed with age it might have been lead. It could have been pre-Christian, of course, and simply adopted for baptismal rites; he had seen such things before. It had fig-ures on it, crudely carved, which appeared to be engaged in a dance or procession around its base, led by a taller figure dan-cing backwards with arms outstretched.

He jumped at the sound of the door thumping closed and glanced round to find he was alone. Hugo would be circling the outside, hunting for clues to the age the interior's shoddy restoration had masked. One of the crucial differences in their approaches to church-crawling was that whereas Chris required something attractive or at least amusing to hold his attention, Hugo could become entranced by a dull piece of lead detailing or some sidelined and anonymous lump of wood he was convinced might once have been a Golgotha.

Chris had glanced at his watch, shut his pad and been all set to follow him when his eye was drawn to the cardboard box. Had the church, or whatever the building now was, been even half as cluttered as they usually were, his gaze would have slid straight over it. The lack of clutter, however, the absence of the usual flower-arranging junk, stall of unloved books or garishly inappropriate Sunday school art projects, lent it a peculiar resonance. As did its placing. For, quite accidentally of course, it had been left on the floor at just the point where one would have expected to find an altar.

Hearing Hugo's whistling, he snapped charcoal and pencils back into his cunningly adapted spectacles case and made for the door ... then stopped with the chilled handle under his fingers. There was no one here to laugh at him so he darted back to indulge his instincts and tidy the box off to one side where it wouldn't be the first thing visitors saw on entering. The place was depressing enough without litter.

The cardboard was damp, almost soaked through. He'd picked it up firmly and his grasp was enough to make it give way. Something fell onto his shoes. He tossed aside the cardboard, revolted, and looked down. It was a battered nylon sports bag of the sort carried by youths selling poor quality tea towels and nail brushes door-to-door. Or by burglars.

He crouched down to unzip it, half-expecting a cache of

silver candlesticks and picture frames. The light in the building was so dim and the bag so dark that at first he thought it must be empty, then his questing hand found wood.

It was a tea caddy. George II, he'd have said, of an elegant sarcophagus design with little ball feet. Damp had left the wood blue with mildew, which made him sneeze. It was hard to judge its condition on the spot but he felt at once the unquestioning urge to acquire that often possessed him in junk shops and auction houses. He could tell at once how good it would look lovingly restored to its former lustre, with the other bibelots on the half-moon table behind his study sofa. He wanted it. He had to have it. Leaving it behind to moulder still further would be an act of cruelty and that was that.

Hugo coughed impatiently. Chris zipped the caddy back in the repellent bag, virtuously scrumpled up the mass of sodden card along with it for safe disposal in a proper place and hurried out to him.

Hugo was predictably horrified. 'You can't just *take* it!'

'Someone else did. It was obviously stashed here by some kid who nicked it and then didn't know what to do with it,' he suggested. 'Got shot of the iPods and jewellery then panicked and dumped it. It's nothing to do with the church. If it *is* a church still. I mean, it's an abandoned building, for Christ's sake. Look at it!'

As a sop to both their consciences, he wrote a quick note on a pad from the car and pinned it to the door. *Found here: antique wooden tea caddy.* By an instinct born of long years of bad dating, he made one of the zeroes in his mobile number look deliberately like a six. The note was fluttering in the wind as he left it; he had every hope it would not last the night.

The base Hugo had rented from the Landmark Trust for their

honeymoon grandly described itself as a castle. It was actually just the surviving gatehouse and banqueting chamber of a medieval bishop's country residence, still fantastically atmospheric for all that it was only a fragment. Both main rooms were magnificently vaulted. There was a tremendous spiral staircase to a roof terrace with unnervingly low crenellations around its edge. Even the bathroom had an oriel window.

While Hugo fricasséed chicken and sang along to a Barbara Cook CD, Chris found dusters and beeswax furniture cream in the housekeeping cupboard and set to work on the caddy. It was every bit as good as his instincts had told him. The condition was perfect. It was made of mahogany or rosewood – or something more exotic as it was oddly weighty – and there was a lozenge of ivory inlaid about the keyhole. His determination to keep it grew as he made the wood shine once more. By the time Hugo was calling him to the supper table he had made up his mind that if anyone did ring up about it, he would pretend they had a wrong number, even if Hugo was in the room.

Hugo could be shamingly honest. It was one of the things Chris cherished about him, along with his not smoking. When obliged now to put the correct money for postcards into a church's honesty box instead of the usual deceptively clattering collection of coppers, he would soothe his irritation by telling himself, *I married a Man of Principle*. He thought of it like that, with capitals, like the title of an Edwardian novel.

But perhaps the principles were weakening. As Chris set the caddy down without comment on the candlelit dining table, Hugo murmured, 'Oh. That *is* nice, isn't it? I expect you were right. Someone stole it then lost interest when they couldn't get it open. Either that or they didn't like to try selling it without a key. Odd, though, that they didn't try to force the lock. Hope this is okay. I forgot tarragon vinegar so it might be a bit rich with all this cream.'

It hadn't even occurred to Chris that the caddy was locked until Hugo mentioned it. Now it irritated him throughout supper. Beneath their roving conversation, his mind kept returning to the subject like a tongue to a chipped tooth.

There was no television or radio to lull them into somnolence and the small fire had little effect on the warmth of so vast a room, so they retired far earlier than usual. Chris read an M.R. James ghost story and Hugo, who had no patience with fiction, read James's essay on the Lady Chapel sculptures at Ely. Then they made clumsily perfunctory love, possibly because they were both so wide awake, which sort of petered out. Rather than slip into blissful oblivion, they lay there fidgeting for a while then Hugo apologetically turned his bedside lamp back on and returned to his abbeys while Chris, thus released, slipped back downstairs on the muttered pretext of thirst.

He ransacked the chest of drawers where games and jigsaws and the accumulated detritus of many holidays were stashed. It was even colder downstairs now that the fire had gone out and his dressing gown was only of silk. He was shivering and on the verge of giving up when he found what he needed: a couple of grimy paperclips adrift in a leaking Monopoly box.

One of his earlier, less judiciously chosen lovers had taught him how to give better blowjobs, how to break into a car with a wire coat hanger and how to use two partially uncoiled paperclips to pick small scale Georgian and Victorian warded locks.

He worked on the caddy at the dining table. It took him longer than usual because his hands were sweating with nerves for some reason, and he had to break off repeatedly to wipe them so as not to lose his grip on the wires.

The lock gave suddenly, startling him. The hinge turned on an unusually powerful concealed spring, which caused the lid to fly open with a bang as soon as the little lock's levers gave under pressure. There must have been a gust of wind down the chimney or up the stair at the same moment for a kind of shudder passed through the building, fluttering curtains and causing two of the doors to slam.

Chris held the caddy to the light and was surprised to find it quite bare inside; in the second that it opened, he thought he had caught a glimpse of something like ash inside it. He saw it was lined, most atypically, with lead, hence his having thought the wood so unusually dense. It couldn't have been for tea after all. A tiny sarcophagus for a small pet, perhaps? A tamed starling or tiny marmoset whose mourning owner wanted them kept beside her but not so close as to have body fluids leaking through the joinery onto her writing desk.

But the need for a spring was a mystery. He tried pressing the lid closed again and found there was no catch to keep it shut so it flew wide again immediately. By instinct, he raised the casket to his face and sniffed its insides. There was none of the normal antique smell – no ghost of bergamot or lavender dust. There was only the unmistakably frank musk of warm, male groin. It cut through the honeyed overlay of the polish he'd applied earlier like a dirty laugh in a silent order.

Shocked, amused and, for all the chill and their recent fumblings, turned on, Chris pressed his nose in deeper to breathe it in again then flicked out the light and hurried back upstairs to show Hugo.

'I got it open at last,' he called up as he rounded the stair's spiral. 'And I think I can see why someone locked it, because of these sprung hinges. But get a whiff of –'

He was startled to find Hugo not curled up half-asleep with M.R. James but standing naked in the doorway, waiting for him. Usually fairly slow to get started, he already had a pornographic hard-on and his eyes were glittering like splintered coal.

'On your knees, Boy,' he said in a voice he had never used before. 'And worship.' He snatched the casket and tossed it aside then pushed Chris roughly down to the icy stone threshold.

As was explained earlier, their recently registered partnership was founded on the principle that Chris was the pretty, Hugo, the lucky one. The dynamic seemed to work for them both and Chris had never analysed it beyond noting occasional pangs for the craving he had felt with the picklock or some of the other Unpresentables.

Overnight it was as though their polarities had changed. In the days that followed, Hugo looked at him with nothing warmer than amusement and he found himself desiring without dignity or control. Hugo hadn't suddenly changed shape. His legs were still sturdy, still slightly out of proportion to his long trunk and wiry arms. He had not suddenly developed a rippling six-pack or a swimmer's shoulders but Chris had only to look at him to want to press his face into his belly or feel Hugo's forearm hairy against his lips. At a glimpse of Hugo's teeth or the way his hair grew in forks down the back of his (shortish) neck, something gave way within him and he felt no feeble sense of shame or decency could stop his wanting to possess or be possessed by him. Seeming to sense this, Hugo would give his newly characteristic smirk and murmur, 'Insatiable!' in a way that only made the hunger for abasement more intense.

As the holiday progressed, the casket went ignored, as did their stash of maps and guides and careful itineraries. Instead, Chris fell in with whatever whim seized Hugo – be it an afternoon lost to a seaside amusement arcade, an extravagant quest for new, frankly rather common clothes or an evening wasted on a terrible horror film full of lingering torture scenes – in the hope that his meekness or subservience, or whatever this was, would be rewarded by more sex and as soon as possible.

They had never been a couple that touched in public. Chris was perfectly happy, if not quite proud, to be gay but he disliked public displays of affection in anyone, had always thought them ill-mannered. Yet suddenly he was groping Hugo whenever he could, seizing his arse, his hand, his thigh – whatever Hugo would allow – immune to the angry or uncomfortable looks this provoked in others. Aside from a very few attempts in the first days of their courtship, they had only ever made love under cover of darkness. Now they were having sex in broad daylight, even in the open air, even in a corner of an otherwise unremarkable church.

It was in many ways the very thing one would hope for, but hardly dare expect, from a honeymoon, only it was so unlike who they were.

Chris made no connection between what was happening and the stolen casket until his phone rang on the fourth day.

Hugo had horrified him by going out on his own soon after breakfast, returning after two agonizing hours with a burly, donkey-jacketed road worker who was evidently as deeply under his spell as Chris. He had the road worker strenuously service them both in a kind of frenzy – hands and boots leaving tarry prints on the sheets – until the man seemed to come to his senses and announced in a broken undertone that his wife would be expecting him. Hugo had fallen into a deeply sated sleep so Chris pulled on a dressing gown and saw their visitor politely out.

The phone had gone unused for so long he had trouble tracking its ringing down to a pocket of the tweed coat he hadn't worn since Hugo called it *maidenly*, a few days before.

It was a woman. Fifty-something. Maybe younger, but she sounded careworn. 'I found your note,' she said at once.

'Oh God,' Chris said. 'Is the caddy yours? I was so sure someone had stolen and dumped it and it was getting ruined by the damp. Where are you? I can jump in the car and bring it –'

She laughed, cutting him off. 'We don't want it *back*! I wish you all joy of it. Just tell me . . . have you *opened* it?'

'Well, I have to say I was a bit cheeky and I picked the lock with a couple of paperclips. The spring in the hinge was a bit of a surpr—'

There was a clatter.

'Hello?' he called out.

She had just dropped her phone on the nearest surface. Her voice grew rapidly fainter. She was calling to someone and laughing. Laughing almost wildly. 'Dee? Dee! He opened it! Oh my God! At last! Dee?' Her tone changed. 'Dee!' There was silence for a minute then footsteps coming closer and her rapid, asthmatic breathing. Then came the sound of three digits being dialled and then her voice again, frantic now. 'Bloody hell. Hang up, will you? I need to –'

Then it went dead as she succeeded in breaking the connection. Chris checked his phone's record of incoming calls but the display logged her simply as Unknown.

Shaken, feeling a little bruised after the morning's unexpected extra exertions, he pulled his dressing gown more tightly about him and poured two tumblers of restorative Barolo – they had slipped into a holiday habit of daytime drinking – and bore them upstairs.

516

Their grandly vaulted bedroom reeked of sex in a way it had surely never done in the bishop's day. Hugo was still fast asleep, with just a sheet to cover him. His arms and legs were flung out in childlike abandon, as though sleep had caught him un-awares. For all the room's iodine reek and the tarry fingerprints on his cheek and neck, he had an air of innocence about him. Chris set the wine on the bedside table as silently as he could and gently drew the blankets over the sheet to keep him warm. He realized he was looking down at him fondly, hungry for nothing but the quiet pleasure of gazing unchecked. He saw that he was thinking of Hugo's innocence as something *lost*.

As if by association, he glanced about them for the casket. For an instant he thought Hugo could have thrown it out in one of his new fits of temper, then he spotted it on its side beneath the chair where he had tossed his clothes earlier. It was still gaping open but when he picked it up he found its lid closed quite easily and stayed closed. Whatever had the woman been making such a fuss about? He set it on the dressing table, open-ing and shutting it a few times to see if there were some hidden catch he had missed. The spring must have broken when the casket fell to the floor. In the looking glass he saw Hugo stir, wake and stare at him from the mass of pillows.

'What are you up to?'

He whipped around guiltily. 'Playing with the box,' he said.

Then Hugo's eyes took on that glinting blackness again and Chris felt compelled to go to the bedside and offer him his glass of wine. If he looked even half as shattered as he felt, he must look half-dead, he thought. He longed for nothing and nobody but a long, inactive sleep followed, perhaps, by a gentle day of church-crawling across the Humber in northern Lincolnshire but, probed by Hugo's gaze, he found he was getting hard again.

'So. How did we compare?' Hugo asked. 'Was he man enough for you? Hmm?'

Chris tugged back the sheet to press one of Hugo's feet to his face and take its big toe deep into his mouth. He heard the unmistakable clack of the casket's lid flying open again.

There were only two days of honeymoon left. The ever-shrinking part of his mind that was still alert to things like time, diaries, responsibility and the need to return to his primary-school job the following week, struggled to form a plan and hold it in mental place long enough for its execution. A fox's yelping woke him in the depths of that night, while Hugo was still asleep, and he was able to slip across the room and close the box again. But when sunlight returned and Hugo had finished with him for the moment and gone to take a much-needed bath, he found the box open again and again as hard to close and keep closed, as if some unseen force were holding it wide. He knew he could only think or act freely when Hugo was asleep or out of the room. He hurried downstairs, past the mercifully closed bathroom door, found the bent paperclips in one of the plates Hugo had been using as an ashtray for his new cigar habit, and hid them in his dressing gown pocket. Then he hung the gown on the back of his bedroom chair and left the box close by it, oh so naturally positioned on the dressing table.

He knew minutes later he would neither know nor care about any of this but sensed, with a shred of survivor's instinct, that if he woke again in the night he would have exact comprehension of where they were and why. Having so plotted, it was with a mix of regret and sweet, quasi-suicidal abandon that he gave up halfway through the attempt to dress and went to tap on the bathroom door to ask if Master wanted his back scrubbed.

The day that followed was especially draining. Hugo fetched no more what he called *takeaways* but he insisted they drive all the way to a windswept funfair near Bridlington where he made Chris ride every sickening ride with him although he knew – or always *used* to know – that they brought on his labyrinthitis. And everywhere he flirted – with men, women and children alike. Everyone caught in that glinting stare responded like a dog to roasting chicken. Hugo seemed to feed off their eagerness to please, as if their quick devotion were a kind of fuel to him, but there was always a trace of mockery in his expression as they fawned on him.

'He despises us,' Chris thought, briefly freed by Hugo's taking a long, lascivious lick from a small boy's cheerfully proffered ice cream. 'He despises us for being merely human.' But then Hugo flicked his eyes back to him and smirked in a way that made Chris breathless with jealousy. He would have brained the child had its mother not arrived to snatch it away with a hot-cheeked apology.

After the possibilities of crude sensation had been exhausted in the funfair, Hugo made them gorge on seafood then he drove them at maniacal speed out to a car park near the bleak tip of Spurn Head where he pleasured a sequence of birdwatchers in their cars while Chris looked helplessly on through the misting car windows, half-wishing a policeman would intervene.

After such quantities of sea air and exercise and the wine Hugo encouraged him to drink over supper, they slept profoundly and it was not the fox yelping but an urgent need to piss that woke Chris shortly after dawn. Returning from the bathroom he saw Hugo's sleeping face, blameless and benign, and remembered the casket. He hurried over to it, all but slammed it shut then frantically worked the paperclips in its lock, his fingers cramped from tension in his hurry to work the mechanism before his clattering woke Hugo.

It locked and held fast. He tugged at the lid to test it then bundled the thing into a bag of dirty laundry that lay ready for their departure. He slipped back to the bed.

'Hugo? Hugs?' Hugo stirred at his touch and mumbled grouchily. The second he opened his eyes Chris could see he was himself again. They no longer looked coal-black but had resumed their old watery grey. They were even a little bloodshot. And his voice was his own once more: soft-edged, slightly peevish.

'What time is it?' he muttered.

'It's early. Sorry. I couldn't sleep. I thought I'd slip into town and bring back papers and croissants for our last breakfast. Before we start packing up, I mean.' He kissed him on the forehead. 'Go back to sleep.'

There was really no need to hide the casket but he left it in the laundry bag just to be safe and carried it down the winding stair with a heap of books, as though starting to load up the car.

He found a locksmith after driving around Selby's one-way system a few times. He was clearly the first customer of the day. A small, sharp-featured woman in a nylon housecoat unbolted the door to let him in.

'He's in the back finishing his breakfast,' she said shyly. 'I'll send him out,' and she darted through a curtain at the back of the shop. Chris could smell toast and bacon. It felt curiously intimate, as if he were sharing their kitchen. The man, pinker, larger, brought his mug of tea out with him. He seemed friendlier than the wife, the sort of man who kept a lurcher and would murmur tendernesses to it when away from the house. Chris felt a pang of guilt and half thought to leave the box under his arm and make something up, buy a padlock instead.

But then he saw himself in the mirrored back of a key ring display, saw how exhaustion had aged him by years in a matter of days, and he resumed his ruthless purpose.

'I need a key making for this,' he said. 'And the lock freeing up.'

The man took the box. 'Oh yes?' he said. 'Ooh. Heavy, ain't it?'

'Er. Yes. Don't shake it, though. It's . . . it's quite valuable.'

'Well that shouldn't be a problem. I can do it while you wait, if you like. I've a stash of old keys out back. One of them's bound to fit.'

The wife reappeared briefly, to cast an appraising glance over the man's shoulder at the casket. She must have been listening in from the breakfast table.

'No hurry,' Chris stammered. 'Honestly. I've got a few other things to do in town. You finish your tea. I'll take one of your cards, if I may.'

'Right you are, then.'

As he left, the bell on the door jangled behind him in tinny accusation.

He drove off, bought a paper, found an old-fashioned baker's and bought them rolls for breakfast still warm from the oven and, from a shop nearby, local butter and honey. Instead of returning to the locksmith's, he drove back out towards Cawood and stopped by an ancient phone box on the edge of the village. He glanced at his watch. They'd surely had long enough. He took out the locksmith's cheap little card and rang the number on it.

The woman answered. A woman. Her voice was transformed and husky, somehow lubricated. 'Hello?'

'Oh. Yes. I brought the little tea caddy in for your husband

521

about forty minutes ago. I wondered if he'd managed to get it open.'

'Oh yes,' she said. 'He got it open all right. Didn't you?' Her voice hardened suggestively. 'I said didn't you!'

Somebody mumbled something then cried out as if struck.

When she came back on the phone, her voice was so close he imagined he felt her breath, hot at his ear. 'That was very clever,' she purred. 'And rather nasty. Christopher.'

His hand shook so violently as he hung up that the receiver bounced off its bracket and swung with a clunk against the wall. He lurched out to the car and sped back to find Hugo.

The gatehouse was still quite silent. There were no signs of life from upstairs yet but neither was there that sense of all-seeing malignancy, he realized. They were free. They had been spared. He walked to the kitchen to put on the kettle and toss the rolls in the oven to keep warm. He poured an orange juice and downed it in three greedy draughts, its taste as fresh and clean as the reassertion of order. Then he filled a second glass and carried it upstairs.

Hugo didn't stir as he came in. He lay there with a hand thrown across his face as though to ward off a blow from an unseen assailant. It was such a pleasure to see him simply lie there, homely again, even vulnerable. Chris wouldn't wake him straight away.

DREAM LOVER

'What do you mean?' she said, fingers twined in his hair as he continued to nuzzle her awake. 'Of *course* you do. Everyone does.'

'Not me.'

'You must. If you didn't you'd . . .'

'Die?' He looked up from the breast to which he was paying sleepy homage. He grinned. 'I don't think so.'

'But everyone dreams. You must simply forget them.'

He shrugged. It could not have mattered less to him. She loved that in a man; that guileless, unquestioning confidence in his own normality.

'So how about you?' he asked. 'How'd you sleep?'

'Fine,' she said, thoughtfully.

'Did you . . .?'

'Well yes,' she said, remembering. 'I did. It was rather amazing. You took me to a huge hotel and I was so excited but when they gave me the key to our room it was just a sort of drawer with a mattress in it. Not a room at all.'

'What happened then?'

'Well, I wasn't angry at all. It was rather cosy. You showed how you could lock me away and I'd be quite safe until you got back.'

'That turn you on?'

'Well yes. Yes it did. And then I . . . No. Don't stop. That's good.'

525

How could he not dream? Recalling and recounting her dreams was one of her earliest, deepest pleasures. The reality was probably scrappier, an impatient affair of hurried bowls of cereal and egg-stained school blouses, but when she recalled girlhood breakfasts, they came back as leisurely, sunlit affairs with her mother, all attention, asking her how she slept and whether she dreamed then listening, truly listening. If asked, she could date quite precisely the moment, aged nine, when she first understood the importance of escaping the family into marriage. The unpalatable insight came on the morning her baby sister first felt old enough to assert herself and interrupted the recounting of a dream with a weary sigh of, 'Boring!' The interruption was allowed to pass unrebuked by their mother. A terrible moment, that. A truly terrible one.

She had tried several men on for size until she found this perfect fit. Healthy. Handsome. Good (e.g. not too extensive) fidelity record. Dead mother not overly mourned. Steady job. Own place. No unpresentable neuroses. An excellent lay. But now this. It was no more than a minor irritant. At first she actually liked the idea that he never dreamed but would listen intently while she recounted her night-narratives. It seemed all of a part with his uncomplicated maleness, like bristles or travelling light or having nothing in his bathroom cabinet but aspirin and a bottle of muscle rub. She began to boast of it in front of him.

'He doesn't *dream*!' she would exclaim. 'Isn't that so like a man?'

Friends would mock her, saying he must be keeping things from her, smutty fantasies, not-quite-forgotten girlfriends.

'Ask him,' she'd say and would delight in watching him shrug and tell them, 'What? So I don't dream. Is it a crime?'

and she would cast him a proprietorial smile as he fended off her friends' inquisition.

She liked the difference between them because in many ways he was her superior – better paid, better educated, a lifetime non-smoker, a dumper not a victimized dumpee – but in this one sphere she could hold the upper hand. Compared to him, she entered sleep like a priestess into a tabernacle and emerged, her face shining with vision.

Then a business trip to Australia left her so badly jet-lagged that her sleep patterns were jangled for several days. She lay there beside him rejecting first one elbow then the other for sleeping on, holding him until she became unpleasantly hot, backing off from him until it seemed he was invading her space, even risking waking him by sitting up to read.

Waking him? Fat chance. He simply lay there, a secretive smile dimpling his stubbled cheeks, deep in self-sufficient slumbers. And not dreaming. And it began to disturb her that in sleep he could become such a blank, however pornographic; it reflected badly on her. Any fool could dream.

So why couldn't he?

There was a woman in the office called Magda, an older woman, who had been in therapy of one kind or another for so long she was something of an expert.

'I've got this friend,' she told Magda, 'who's desperate because she wants to keep a dream diary but she can't seem to remember her dreams long enough to write them down.'

The colleague smiled in a way that was not entirely friendly and shook her head with the worldly, self-satisfied air of one who has experienced everything and for whom life holds no more nasty surprises.

'I was just the same,' she said. 'We all are, tell her. You wake up and all these other thoughts start crowding in and the dream sort of crumbles. All she needs to do is write a little card saying any dreams question mark and stick it on her bedside table or her headboard or wherever she'll first look when she wakes up. If she does that and keeps a pad and pen handy too she'll soon find she stops forgetting. It'll become second nature. Did you want that last Cherry Bakewell or can I?'

So she tried it.

'Humour me,' she told him as she stuck a little, prettily lettered card to the edge of his bedside table.

'It won't work,' he said. 'I told you I don't dream. I never have.'

She hesitated a moment, tempted by simplicity, then remembered that his dreamlessness was a kind of insult because it meant he never dreamed of her.

'We'll see about that,' she said. 'Relax. Go to sleep. Forget the card's there.'

And at first nothing happened. For three mornings in a row they woke to the confidential murmur of the clock radio and he read the card that asked him any dreams question mark and answered nope and turned to her with an I told you so air.

On the fourth morning, however, although he still said nope he did so with a minute hesitation and he couldn't meet her eye afterwards.

'There *was* something!' she said, pouncing. 'Wasn't there?'

'No?'

'You dreamed. I could tell!'

'No.' He frowned. 'Well. Yes. Do you know, I think I may have done.' He laughed uneasily. 'But it sort of slipped away.'

'Never mind,' she said and kissed him, triumph warming her from within.

'I . . . I think it was a good one,' he said and frowned again. 'Damn.'

'Relax,' she said. 'Don't fret. Plenty more where that came from. Do you want your tea in bed this morning?'

They both drank heavily that night so their respective sleeps were a comatose blank, but the night after that he woke her up in his excitement.

'I dreamed,' he said.

'Wha—?' She was still half asleep.

'I dreamed. I really dreamed.'

'Great.' She sat up, rubbing sleep from her eyes. 'What happened?'

'I was in a field,' he began.

'Yes?' she prompted him at last. 'And?'

'That's it. I was in a field.'

'Is that all? What did you do there?'

'Nothing. Just stood, I suppose. But it was a big field, huge, and so green and the sky was this incredible blue. It was like one of those Renaissance paintings you like, like the background of a Piero. You know? How he sort of paints the silence?'

'Just you,' she repeated. 'In a field. Nothing else. No one else.'

'No. But I had this wonderful feeling. Something amazing was going to happen!'

'It was just a dream,' she said, indulging her need to flatten his spirits in her disappointment.

'Yeah,' he said, slumping beside her as he turned out the light. 'I guess.'

The next night they ate old French cheese which, cliché or no, had always produced spectacular results for her. Sure enough it seemed she had barely closed her eyes before she was living through an entire Barbara Stanwyck film, with her in the steamy lead role, fighting her way to the head office of a vast corporation by sleeping with a succession of ever more powerful and ugly, suited men. Only she didn't sleep with them because it was enough to know they wanted her and how badly. All she had to do was press them in the middle of the chest so their eyes narrowed with lust and she seemed fairly to light up with gratification. It was all superbly art directed, with restrained nineteen-forties details everywhere, flattering lighting, a great wardrobe and even tracking shots. And there was a magnificently bizarre climax in which she left the top of the building on a sort of flying desk, leaving all the pleading suits behind and below her.

But when the alarm woke them he was in there first, eyes bright with the need to relate a boyish extravaganza involving jungles, horses, treasure and a powerfully erotic encounter with the Foreign Secretary.

'But that's wonderful,' she managed. 'You dreamed. You really did this time.' She was about to cut in with her dream but found that somehow, in the effort of picturing his, she had lost all but a few greying rags of it.

'How about you?' he asked, touching her cheek with one finger in a way that had always faintly irritated her.

'What about me?'

'What did you dream about, Pumpkin?' He snuggled up to her which lessened the pain somewhat.

'Oh,' she said lightly. 'You know. Girl stuff.'

That night some rather pushy friends served them Cornish hen lobster for dinner. For her as for many, lobster was next only to mescalin and magic mushrooms in its ability to induce frightening dreams if eaten soon enough before sleep. She took off her make-up and climbed beneath the duvet with the same, not unpleasant queasy anticipation of a teenager taken to a slasher movie by a boy she wants to kiss.

Only the lobster affected him before it could take hold on her and she passed a shattering seven hours, repeatedly kicked or jolted awake as he became acquainted with his unconscious terrors. She returned to the office so grey-faced and lacking in concentration that two clients asked if she were unwell.

Making up the bed with fresh Egyptian cotton that evening, she accidentally knocked the *any dreams?* card out of sight into the mess of out-of-favour shoes, old magazines and dust bunnies that lurked under the mattress. She did not retrieve it.

Now that there was no stopping him, however, he needed no encouragement. The dreams came thick and fast and, as he became adept at remembering them in ever-greater detail, he sometimes had as many as three a night to tell her, often beginning his urgent reports before it was even light. A lot of his dreams were about food, vehicles or thinly veiled desire for world domination. They rarely featured her and when she did appear it was never in a starring role but as a sort of cute younger sister (and she projected the cute part) gamely watching his exploits from a safe distance.

In the mornings, she began to slip out of bed before he woke sufficiently to start talking. She began to grow painfully tense between the shoulderblades if dinner-party conversation strayed from coffee offers to talk of sleeplessness. She began to take more notice of Brian from Accounts, a tantalizingly self-contained, rather handsome bachelor, who played squash every evening after work and had always struck her as an eminently sensible, feet-on-the-ground sort of man. Brian, she felt sure, was not a dreamer.

SLEEP TIGHT

The child's cry cut through the Schumann quintet Desmond was playing as he enjoyed a whisky after supper. He tried ignoring it at first and turned back to the article his brother had just published in a journal. *The Global Village*, he read, *Towards a Dialectic.* But the cry came again, more urgently, jangling his nerves and sending his glance skittering across the text. He swore under his breath, knowing he was being quite unreasonable, set down his book and glass and climbed the stairs.

'Coming,' he called out as cheerfully as he could.

The boy, Hamish, cried, 'Quickly! Please!'

'I'm here,' Desmond said, turning on the landing light and letting himself into the smaller spare room, his boyhood room, where he had thought to make the child at home among books and kites and ancient toy bears. 'Whatever is it? I thought to find you murdered after such a row.'

Hamish was sitting stiffly upright against the headboard, his eyes wet in the moonlight. 'It was the Moth Lady,' he said softly.

Desmond sighed, 'Her again,' and turned on the boy's bed-side light, thinking it would comfort him.

'No!' Hamish cried out. 'No light! It makes her worse. It's the light that brings her.'

Desmond duly flicked off the light again, startled by the glimpse it had afforded of the boy's drawn, tear-stained face.

535

'Okay,' he said and sat on the edge of the bed. 'Hamish, I thought we'd discussed this. There's no Moth Lady.'

'But there *is*!'

'Well. There is in your dreams but in real life you're quite safe from her. There are moths because it's a warm summer night and they follow the lights and come in at the open windows. But there are none in here. They're all downstairs with me and my reading light.'

This rash stab at levity brought on another whimper.

'Look,' he said. 'I'll close your window. How's that? You'll still get fresh air from the open door. Better?'

There was a sniff and he could tell the child was nodding.

'Good boy. No more dreams now. Sleep tight.'

He returned, via a much needed top-up, to his brother's supremely tedious article. His brother worked for a charity and was forever implying that this was a nobler pursuit than Desmond's picture restoration, although he earned three times as much. His salary had done little to leaven his prose style.

Desmond disliked children as a rule, his brother's in particular. He found them tedious and unrestrained. He associated them with noise, mess and primary-coloured plastic and regarded any friend embarked on parenthood as lost to a hostile power until further notice.

Hamish was an exception. Wary, thoughtful, bookish and apparently without friends, he reminded Desmond of himself in boyhood and it was a happy accident that he had acquired him, and not one of the more typical specimens, as a godson.

Hamish's unmarried mother, a curator and old friend, had often brought him to stay – cautiously at first, then with more confidence once she saw how he and Desmond warmed to one another, but this was his first visit on his own. She was away at a conference for two nights in the nearest university town and had dropped Hamish off en route.

'I shan't ring,' she said. 'It would only get him all churned up. But of course you can call me if there are any problems. There shouldn't be, though.'

For a seven-year-old he was, indeed, a remarkably easy guest. While Desmond worked in his shed, he spent contented hours either curled in the shade reading a book or wandering the paths around the marshes and reed beds that surrounded the cottage, armed with a little magnifying jar and a pocket guide to insects. He had no allergies or irritating dietary fads but politely ate whatever food Desmond set before him.

An unobtrusive boy, he repeatedly put Desmond in mind of a characteristically mordant phrase of his mother's: *too good to live*. Desmond would miss him when he was gone and wondered if it would be thought sinister if he invited him back at the tired end of the summer holidays. Unmarried men had to be so careful around children these days and the precautions had a way of arousing, unbidden, thoughts of the very deeds they were designed to prevent. Hamish's mother could always be invited too, of course, but, being an adult, she required active hospitality whereas the boy required as little attention as a demurely self-contained whippet. Until now, that was.

The music had come to an end and there was no sound but the usual soughing of the night breeze in the reed beds and the persistent tapping of insects against the windowpane nearest to his lamp. Hamish's slightly hoarse, unbroken voice was so unexpected in the studious gloom that Desmond sloshed his drink on the upholstery in surprise.

'She's back,' Hamish told him. 'She wants to take me with her.'

'Jesus!' Desmond shouted. The child's mother had not breathed a word of this neurotic fear of his. Perhaps it was put on? A piece of manipulation born of resentment at her self-absorbed absence?

Hamish lingered on the edge of the pool of light and Desmond remembered his fear of the bedside light upstairs. Curious child! The boy's plump lower lip was trembling and he shivered. He had come down without his dressing gown and slippers and even in July the house was prone to draughts.

'Come on,' Desmond told him. 'Come and sit on the sofa and tell me all about the bloody woman.'

Hamish climbed obediently onto the chaise longue, tucking his legs up beside him as though afraid of what might lurk underneath.

Feeling a great upswell of emotion, an unfamiliar mix of ordinary compassion and intense, heart-warming awareness of himself as a fatherly protector, Desmond unfurled an antique patchwork quilt he kept on one of the sofa arms for the bitterest nights and tucked it around him. 'There!' he said. 'That's better.'

The boy nodded, still wretchedly wan.

'Cup of cocoa? I can make some for us both.'

'No!' Hamish almost shouted, adding softly with tragic politeness, 'Please don't leave me, Desmond.'

'I won't. Good Lord! We didn't eat *so* much cheese with supper, did we?' Desmond sat back in his armchair, abandoning *The Global Village* for the time being. Perhaps the child felt the lack of a father. 'Tell me about it,' he said. 'Sometimes you have to talk about bad dreams to make them stay away.'

'She's not a dream.'

'But . . . Very well. If you say so. Who is she?'

'I *told* you. The Moth Lady. She's very thin and sort of . . . *whispery*. She's naked and she has compound eyes and antennae like brown feathers. She doesn't speak but she just uncoils her proboscis and touches me and I sort of *feel* her words. She wants to take me and I don't want to go.'

'Well you won't. You'll stay right here with me.'

'Please don't laugh at me.'

'Sorry. I wouldn't dream of it. Why does she want you?'

'I can't tell. But she wants to wrap me in a leathery cocoon so I can't move.'

'So you'll become a moth too?'

'No. For . . . I think it's for food.'

Desmond sighed. The boy had obviously spent far too long hunting dragonfly in the glare of noon. Perhaps he even had a touch of sunstroke. Desmond put a hand to Hamish's forehead but it was cool and slightly clammy. 'No one is taking you for food or for anything else,' he assured him. 'You curl up there and go to sleep. You're quite safe. If the Moth Lady or anyone else comes for you, I'll spray them with poison and stick them with a pin for you to admire in the morning. There there. Only joking. Don't take on. You're sure no cocoa?'

'No, thank you. Desmond I . . . I think I'll be safe here. Won't I?'

'Absolutely.'

'Are all the windows closed?'

They weren't, of course, because it was July and the house would have swiftly become stuffy. His practice was to leave the dining room's window open and its door closed so that cooler air could be drawn in but no insects could see his reading light to be drawn in too.

'You know,' Desmond began, making one last appeal to

539

reason. 'Moths do no harm to anything. It's only their caterpillars that eat wool or plants. I've given up planting verbascums because of the verbascum moth caterpillars and I never waste money on cashmere in case a clothes moth lays eggs on it, but I couldn't say I'd ever been *hurt* by one. Wasps and hornets, now, they're another matter. And there's a spider you find on compost heaps – the woodlouse spider – that can give you a painful nip . . .'

'I didn't say she was a moth. She's just *like* one.'

'Ah.'

Hamish was unconvinced but he was also exhausted, worn out by fear, and he yawned heavily as he spoke and pulled the quilt more snugly about him.

Relieved, imagining he would carry him back to bed when he himself retired, Desmond took a sip of what remained unspilled of his whisky and picked up the journal again. He found his brother's article once more. *The Global Village*, he read, *Towards a Dialectic*, but his concentration strayed within seconds and he soon realized he had read the same dull sentence several times over without even grasping the sense within its woolly construction.

He glanced up. The Schumann had ended and Hamish was sound asleep. Desmond discarded the journal again and reached instead for the little insect book that had inspired the boy's imagination so drastically. *232 Species in Colour*, it promised. He flicked past pages of beetles and flies of improbable size and came to a halt at a page devoted to the Goat Moth. Its body was elegantly striped in shades of grey and cream, it had, indeed, a certain dustily feminine elegance, but it was scarcely threatening even when reproduced to seem the size of his thumb. *Evil-looking caterpillar*, he read. *Has a pungent odour. Not easy to find as they feed on dead willow trees but a large tree will sometimes have hundreds of larvae boring in it.'*

There were several dead or dying willows across the way on the marsh's edge. He had a clear image of them as he too fell asleep; he pictured the unnerving way they had of seeming to rot and die, only to spring up again from where a broken limb had rooted in the mud.

He woke at the sound of his whisky glass smashing on the floor. He opened his eyes. There was a filthy smell coming from nearby, far more pungent than the smell of whisky. He traced it in seconds to the lamp where he saw, to his disgust, that some kind of fly or moth was cremating itself against the bulb. He turned the lamp off instinctively then cried out as broken glass pierced his sock. He limped across to the hall in the moonlight and turned on the light out there.

Hamish had taken himself off to bed. The quilt was discarded on the floor, with uncharacteristic carelessness.

Desmond tutted, folded it back onto the sofa arm, then swept the broken glass into a dustpan. He opened the back door to tip the shards directly into the rubbish bin and was briefly transfixed by the beauty of the night and took a few steps away from the door in his socks.

The breeze that had been stirring the reeds earlier was now quite gone so the air was full of suggestive scents – river mud, grass mowings, lavender from the bushes that defined the path to the garden gate and something else, something sweet. The full moon was still up, reflected in the water and silvering the reeds and willows.

Then he saw the moths. He saw only a few at first, which were apparently crossing the garden from the marsh, but, tracing their flight, he saw that there were scores of them, maybe more than a hundred, dancing in the moonlight and seeming to gather about Hamish's unlit, reopened window.

He ran back through the house, ignoring the pain in his cut foot, shouting the boy's name.

The bed was empty, the sheets quite cold. An old, long-forgotten fear told him, as he ran from room to empty room, that his search would be fruitless.

He had waded, gasping, around the marsh's fringes for half an hour, muddying his boots and trousers, before he thought to ring the police and the boy's mother.

He knew what people would say. He knew how it would look.

FREEDOM

Lorna's formidable sister-in-law went caravanning every summer and was a keen member of the Caravan Club and observer of its clannish codes. She and her husband always stayed in well-populated camp-sites, usually by prior arrangement with fellow members. They would arrange their caravans in a tight formation – pioneer style – to keep the rougher, tented element at bay, and would recreate a suburb on wheels, visiting one another's caravans for drinks and bridge and ingenious one-pot suppers.

If Lorna had not sensed this was not for her, the sister-in-law confirmed it by never once urging her and her family to follow suit and join in the fun. She handed round photographs of the holidays and explained the features of each restlessly upgraded caravan with the patronizing air of a displaced urbanite explaining running water and regular bath-times to a barefoot family in a mud hut: expecting wide-eyed admiration, not company amidst the bubbles.

Lorna and her husband preferred to rent remote cottages for their holidays. These were invariably more basically equipped than the sister-in-law's latest caravan and were found in the trustworthy back pages of *The Lady*. Holidays were exhausting for Lorna because she had to pack most of her kitchen equipment and larder as well as pillows and bedding, cats and dogs, maps and library books, but it was precisely because each holiday was a bit like moving house that it was so stimulating. Lumpy beds, idiosyncratic plumbing and other people's taste were half the adventure. Adapting to new surroundings stirred one up and refreshed one's appreciation of home. Then there was the matter of space. The sister-in-law had just two very good if unenquiring children who were easily pleased whereas it was a point of re-assurance for Lorna that her three boys and a baby were restless and inquisitive and not easily to be contained in a mobile home, however well equipped.

But that morning she was detained at the village garage while Mr Boorman topped up the oil and water for her and, idly inspecting the huddle of second-hand cars on his little forecourt, she came across the caravan. It was eight years old, so must have been made in nineteen fifty-something and was called The Sprite, which charmed her. It was powder-blue and cream on the outside and seemed to have more character than the new, white things the sister-in-law favoured. She opened the narrow door and stepped up inside.

It was tiny but ingenious. There were two beds, both dou-bling as seats, a little Formica-topped table, a cold-box, a sink and a two-ring gas cooker. There were curtains whose gay fabric reminded her of a favourite skirt she had worn out before her marriage and the cushions were covered with a sensible sort of orangey bouclé. She sat at the table, gazing around her and out of the little windows, and was won over.

One could be sure Mr Boorman had maintained it well – he was quite misty-eyed about selling it – and the price he was asking was not much more than two months' rent on their usual sort of cottage. She impulsively wrote a cheque for a deposit then set about persuading her husband over Irish stew that evening.

He was unsettled at first and seemed doubtful of the taste of her suggestion – he had never approved of his brother's marriage or his subsequent caravanning – but she won him over by appealing to his frugality. This would be like a cottage where two months' rent lasted for years! They could travel far further than usual, she suggested, by being able to spend a night here and a night there. They could journey the length of the country. They could show the children castles and cathedrals and Hadrian's Wall. They didn't even have to stay in horrid campsites every night if they didn't mind washing with a flannel or making do with the sea. They could buy a tent as an overflow dorm for the older boys. It would be fun. It would be an adventure.

And since he had always trusted her to arrange everything and was too busy to be bothered with it himself, he agreed.

What she didn't realize and certainly didn't admit to herself until years later, was that what had charmed her about The Sprite was its suggestion of precious freedom. It had reminded her, she saw too late, of Wendy Houses where she had made pretend tea and raised pretend families as a girl. The escape she had pictured in it, beside a dreamy loch or overlooking a romantic ruin, was made on her own.

Her husband was a clumsily erratic driver – he had learnt on a tank during the war – and had no more training than she did in how to reverse a trailer still less a view-obscuring caravan. Following religiously a circular itinerary supplied by the AA, they journeyed all the way to Northumberland and back but it was a white-knuckle ride. He kept forgetting the caravan was there, so it was forever mounting pavements and scattering pedestrians. They were twice cautioned by ashen-faced policemen and had a very nasty row with a woman who claimed they had scraped the paintwork on her roadside bungalow. It was a miracle nobody was killed.

The children loved the caravan at first but never mastered their disappointment at not being allowed to ride in it. They saw castles and abbeys galore and completed well-stuffed holiday diaries but the weather was filthy, the boys never got the hang of putting up their tent unassisted, the baby cried for England, they all caught nastily productive colds and the one night they stayed in a camp-site smart enough to have passed muster with the sister-in-law, the Jack Russell disgraced them all by proudly rounding up a flock of sheep and driving it among the furious campers. Lorna was a cook who needed space, she discovered, and cooking family-sized meals on a doll-sized stove proved such a strain they repeatedly dined on fish and chips or even pork pies.

The only one who really enjoyed the experience was her husband, who was a natural Spartan and never happier than when doing without or making do. When Lorna's camera film was posted back from the developer's in its distinctive yellow envelope, she found that he was smiling in every photograph, pipe clenched in chattering teeth.

A few weeks after their return, with the excuse that it took up too much room in their drive, Lorna hitched up The Sprite one more time and drove it to her parents' house on the Isle of Wight.

'Easy enough to collect when we need it again,' she said but somehow the occasion never arose.

Shown the holiday photographs, in particular one with the baby parked morosely on its potty and Lorna furiously frying sausages beneath a line of flapping nappies, the sister-in-law pronounced them the sort of people who gave caravanning a bad name.

*

They had a field beyond the garden wall, Lily's field, bought with Lily's money to stop anyone building on it and where she kept a pair of retired donkeys to hold the thistles in check. What with the cost of maintaining fences and paying vet's bills – donkeys not being as hardy as they looked – the field had become her folly. So there was a certain irony in parking the daughter's folly within the mother's.

Lily cursed the caravan at first, thinking it a senseless, common creation, unable to imagine why Lorna had bought the thing or why, having seen sense, she kept it. Then weeds grew about its wheels and she began to overlook it.

Influenced by advertising, she had always looked forward to her husband's retirement, picturing it as one long summer weekend. She should have realized that weekends were only a pleasure because they were short and exceptional. There was a limit to how often he could clip the hedges or mow the lawn. His hobby had always been bonsai and that was scarcely time-consuming. Now that he was home all the time, he was bored, and now he was no longer earning, he was niggardly.

She loved him dearly, of course, but theirs had always been a combative love founded, she now saw, on her clawing back in the course of the working week the territory she conceded at weekends. Now that he no longer had work, he began to take an invasive interest in hers, finding ways of cooking and cleaning that were somehow superior. Their garden was large but the house wasn't and with him home all the time she found his temper and restless energy left less and less space for her.

One autumn afternoon, when he elected to make large quantities of admirably cheap jam from the bullaces that thrived along a nearby bridleway, she realized she was on the verge of losing her temper and saying something she might regret. So she stalked out to commune with the donkeys in the drizzle. Their stoicism, and the meaty sensation of their ears beneath her hands, were usually calming but that day they were being wilfully unsociable. Then the drizzle turned without warning to a downpour so she claimed the nearest available shelter.

It was musty but it was dry and, she perceived as she sat on one of the squashy little banquettes, miraculously peaceful compared to the house. The drizzle turned to full throttle rain and Lily was startled by the noise it made on the skylight. Stranded but curious, she investigated further. Lorna was a reliably bad housekeeper and, sure enough, had not thought to empty the cupboards entirely. Lily found a packet of gypsy creams, Lapsang tea and a bag of sultanas. She experimented with the little stove and found there was still gas in the canister and water in the whistling kettle. Hunting for matches, she found some overdue library books, including a smutty American crime novel. She set the kettle to boil, discovered that a tug of a leather strap turned the larger banquette into a fairly comfortable double bed with a charming view of her donkeys sheltered under distant trees and settled down with a lapful of sultanas and the biscuit packet tucked in the crook of her arm and began to read.

This might have remained an isolated incident had bullace pickle not become the next day's project and the stench of spice and vinegar not driven her outside again.

She finished the crime novel and started another. She brought out fresh water and better biscuits, secretly purchased. By stealthy degrees the caravan became hers. She bought second-hand paperbacks for its bookshelf, a little radio, a cheery pelargonium, a doormat. Claiming her GP had told her to exercise more, she took to embarking on daily walks which led circuitously to its door and an hour or two of cherished, feminine peace. She didn't care that it was a little shabby and dated: the Doris Day décor was a reminder of happier, earlier years in her marriage. She didn't care that her husband took advantage of her absences to drink. When they met up again at teatime, each was as sweet as pie.

*

Leo inherited the field from his mother who in turn had inherited it from hers. It was months before he visited in person, then he drove over with a bossy boyfriend who was determined they should build eco-friendly holiday chalets on it. No one had mentioned the caravan, which had been broken into and vandalized as much by time and weather as by disaffected local youth. While the bossy boyfriend measured and photographed the site and took notes, Leo let himself in and sat, astonished, on the only surviving cushion.

He had no memories of his holiday in it as a baby but had spent days and nights in there as a child because his grandfather couldn't bear small boys in the house and banished Leo and his brothers to the field on visits. His grandparents' marriage was not happy – his grandfather drank and his grandmother probably did too in order to cope with his temper. Looking back, he suspected she used to hide in the caravan when they weren't visiting. Quite possibly she resented their visits for depriving her of a bolt-hole, but perhaps she sheltered behind the business of entertaining guests as effectively as she could in a field at the bottom of a long garden.

Being noisily insecure, Leo's brothers had forever found excuses to cross the field and garden to visit the adults at nights but Leo had loved the caravan, loved the sensation it offered of playing house and the feral, male air it acquired after a few days of their presence in it.

The same fifties curtains swung in the breeze now, sun-bleached but intact. The bumpy fabric his fingers remembered still covered the cushion and on the shelf, dog-eared and buckled by alternating damp and heat, he found the collection of unsuitable novels he had learned to decipher and relish over a succession of half-terms.

He took up *Death Becomes Her*, flicked the mouse droppings off it, opened it at random then thrust his nose between the pages and took a luxurious sniff from its spine. The strangely mixed bouquet was unchanged and unmistakable: glue, camping gas, sunshine. Freedom.

He looked up to find the boyfriend staring from the doorway. 'You wouldn't understand,' he told him. 'It's a caravan thing.'

GENTLEMAN'S RELISH

In his more desolate periods, Frank told himself the boys had grown up without him. He saw them on Sundays if they had no other plans and on holidays but otherwise his sons were shadowy presences in his life. They were largely represented to him by things: clothes discarded on chair backs, boots tumbled on the doormat, the detritus of midnight snacks encountered as he snatched his breakfast.

On weekdays he left the house before they appeared, so as to catch an early commuter train into town to his job in the City. When they were younger he used to walk around the bedrooms waking them before he left. He had treasured this brief, one-sided contact, the glimpses of them still capable of childish vulnerability in sleep. However a casually cruel hint was dropped that a clock radio was a less startling way to start the day so now he made do with taking his wife up her breakfast tray, deprived of precious contact with the others.

The eldest was at university now, the middle one, the rebel, had left school early to take a well-paid, unsuitable job and had developed a mysterious social life and with it, an aversion to eating any meal with his parents. The youngest, at fourteen, was effectively a bed and breakfast guest, for he ate his supper with the boarders at school. He was required to stay on there for prep, which took until nine, and often elected to stay on longer to play with his house string quartet. He was rarely home before ten-thirty, by which time Frank had invariably fallen asleep in front of the television, so missed him.

The weekends were thus a rare chance to encounter one another. Conditioned as he was to waking early, it was small hardship to take only one extra hour in bed so as to come downstairs in time to see a bit of his youngest over breakfast.

An only child of a widowed father, Frank had been raised by people paid to raise him. Looking about him as a teenager he had been led to assume that marriage was life's great pleasure, fatherhood its dutiful cost and so was overwhelmed to find that in reality the emphases were reversed. He loved his wife well enough but it was his children he adored. Bathing them, playing with them, teaching them to read, catch a ball, build a sandcastle, gave him more pleasure than a man was expected to reveal. In the long hours in which he was forced out of his sons' company, he worried about them and dreamed of the simple, physical pleasure of their presence with the mind-addling intensity of new love.

It was a shock to realize that with each boy in turn, the cruel necessity of Frank's day-long absences in town weighed against their mother's constant surveillance to make him almost a stranger to them, an orderly intruder on their raucous nursery joys. Made to feel shy among his own, he found he could show less and less of what he felt.

The onset of puberty rendered each boy in turn a stranger to his father. The first two morphed from child to young adult in a kind of frenzy of bad temper, worse skin and withering – if inarticulate – contempt. The youngest should by now have embarked on this necessarily painful phase, burning off his sweetness to acquire strength, but seemed to be holding the process at bay. His voice had broken and he was shaving occasionally: there was nothing wrong hormonally. As the family's Benjamin he was the one they least wanted to see leave boyhood behind. At times he seemed to share this reluctance. At others it was as though the habitual dreaminess of his childhood had subtly turned to a sly watchfulness. Thanks to his brothers he had twice watched at first hand the process by which boy turned man; he was an expert.

They didn't talk much at these Saturday breakfasts. Like his mother, the boy usually ate with his nose in a book. Frank refused to be put off, however, and would make a point of asking him how he was progressing at school, how the house teams were doing, that sort of thing. An inoffensive line of enquiry. He would like to have heard answers to real questions, of course. *Are you as happy as you seem? Do you think about sex all the time? Or love, even? Is anything worrying you?* All the questions his own father never asked him. But to get such answers one had to elicit them and precisely because his father had never asked him such things he had neither language nor courage to ask them of the boy. So they would speak instead in the traditional coded idiom of fathers and sons wherein safe questions of sport and work stood in for more risky ones of happiness and affection.

Once she was up and dressed, his wife talked almost incessantly, maintaining the sort of amiable flow she had been raised to believe was required of women to fill the awkward silences left by males. When she was present, all conversation passed through her as though she alone could bridge the linguistic gulfs between man and man or generation and generation. But all they heard of her on these early Saturday mornings were the murmur of her bedside radio and the occasional clink of her breakfast china.

Today was not as other Saturdays. Today Frank would have to speak to the boy without code because yesterday he had received a rare phone call at the office from his housemaster. Startled from the pleasant afternoon trance brought on by crossword defeat, an excess of dull memos, and a fulsome retirement lunch in the boardroom, Frank's immediate reaction was nauseous fear. The only possible reason for such a call was a clumsy, accidental death. In the seconds it took his secretary to put the call through, he had pictured the boy with his neck broken on the gym's parquet floor or floating in a crimson bloom beneath a diving board. Then he heard embarrassment rather than fear in the other man's tone and relaxed a little. The crisis was of a stealthier kind than he had first imagined.

With similar backgrounds – Classics, army, early motherlessness – the two men shared a difficulty in approaching emotive subjects head on but, with a few minutes of coughing, nervous chuckles and sucking on pipes, had established that the boy had written an inappropriate communication to one of the younger French teachers who, luckily, had panicked and passed it on to the housemaster. The words *love letter* had not been spoken but Frank had deciphered them in the man's pained, unfinished sentences and slightly wild references to *hothouse emotions* and the need to encourage more healthy interaction with the local girls' school. There was talk of a mixed-sex debating society or drama club.

'Of course, it's entirely up to you,' the housemaster had said. 'If you'd rather we left this in your hands we can. Or I can pass it on to the chaplain. Good man. Experienced at dealing with this sort of thing. Discreet. Queerly enough, he has a background in industrial relations.'

Ashamed that it should be assumed he would pass the buck

at once, Frank startled himself by saying that no, he would handle the matter himself and attempt a fatherly conversation. The thought of this had stayed with him through the afternoon, as insistent as indigestion. The need for honourable secrecy had introduced an unpleasant whiff of deceit to the evening's conversation with his wife. The air needed clearing.

'Morning.'

'Morning, Dad.'

The boy was eating muesli and chopped banana, nose deep in a small book of French poetry. It took Frank a while to fetch his habitual breakfast things from kitchen to breakfast room. He half hoped he would take too long over it and let the boy slip away.

'Coffee?' he called through.

'It's okay, Dad. I've got a cup. Thanks.'

During the week, Frank knew, the boy and the middle brother had established a touchingly manly routine whereby they took their breakfast on either side of the wall, one at the breakfast room table, one in the kitchen, so that, while forced to rise at the same hour, neither needed actually to speak.

At last he sat across from him, a reassuring library thriller wedged open beside him with a pot of Gentleman's Relish, and began to butter toast. The boy sighed and turned a page. His nails were too neat and too clean, as was his hair. This was a different breed of rebelliousness to the more usual sort shown by his brothers at this age and correspondingly harder to meet with equanimity. Frank suffered vivid nightmares sometimes, in which the boy developed a bright-eyed religious mania and took to paying evangelical calls on all their friends in a suit and tie or took to entertaining middle-aged women to tea and petits fours. Lank hair or a filthy leather jacket would have been almost reassuring.

At moments like this, aware that he was imposing himself on the periphery of the boy's small circle of wordless restraint, Frank remembered the profound physical disgust his own father engendered in him at this age, particularly in the queasy early hours of the day. The muffled clicking of his false teeth as he chewed bacon, the sickly spiced smell of the lotion on his hair or merely the inoffensive sound of him folding his newspaper had made Frank want to flee the room to an untainted atmosphere. Usually he recalled this at the worst moments, as he was crunching cold toast or gulping coffee and nearly choked in his effort to be as unrepulsive as possible. Even as he checked himself, he knew it was hopeless; the werewolf-sharp senses of adolescence would pick out a patch of bristles his razor had missed or latch on with revulsion to the pinging sound his teaspoon made on his mug.

'Heavy day today?' he asked, refusing to let the slim volume of Rimbaud put him off.

The boy sighed again, pushed aside his cereal bowl and tore into a tangerine. His eyes retained their sleepy focus on the pages of his book. 'Not really. The usual. Double Latin with a prose. French. History.'

'But it's a half day, yes?'

'Saturdays always are, Dad.'

'Of course.'

'Fives match this afternoon, then *Elijah* at Glee Club then supper then prep then Compline then home.' The boy was humouring him as one might a tedious aunt.

A small, feminine cough came from upstairs. It was as though, even at long range, his wife could tell their conversation lacked sparkle.

'No cello tonight, then? No quartet?'

'Not on a Saturday.'

Desperate, Frank glanced at his son's book for a cue and asked without thinking, 'So who's your French master this year?'

'Mr Lawrence. Tony Lawrence.' The boy cleared his throat and fiddled with the tangerine peel. He shut the book, dared to meet his father's eye. 'He's just come down from Oxford. I think he's only passing through. The other boys tease him a bit.' Running out of words to mumble, he blushed intensely and dropped his gaze back to the book.

Frank was appalled. He had not meant to be so direct. He had planned a circuitous approach with questions about friends in general and then on to friendly teachers and the folly of favouritism. 'But you get on with French, don't you?' he asked. 'You want to carry on with it for your As, your mother said.'

'Yeah, Dad. Look. I should go and brush my teeth.'

He slipped away, leaving the poetry book behind in his confusion. Rimbaud's photograph stared out from the cover. He looked petulant, probably unwashed, full of churning, filthy thoughts epigrammatically expressed; a toxic Peter Pan.

Frank stared back as he ate his toast. Out of the blue he remembered the fuss when his father caught him reading the charlady's copy of *Forever Amber*. Confirmation classes had been brought forward by several months and there had been a sequence of enforced excursions with hearty boys who were not quite friends.

He heard taps turned on and off, a lavatory flush. There was a brief flurry of easy chat as the boy called in to sit at the foot of his mother's bed then the thunder of his feet on the stairs.

'You forgot this,' Frank called out.

The boy glanced into the breakfast room, his pallor restored, bringing with him a faint whiff of the blue chemical he used to keep spots at bay. He glanced at the book carelessly.

561

'Oh, that. I'm just reading that for fun. Have a good day. See you later.'

'Bye.'

And he was gone. There came a crunch of cycle wheels on gravel, the desolate clang of the iron garden gate.

Frank rang the housemaster quickly, closing an intervening door so his wife should not hear.

'I think, on reflection, perhaps a chat with the chaplain's our best option,' he told him. 'Unless you think . . .?'

'Er no. Quite,' the housemaster said. 'I'll have a word this morning. He's a good man.'

'Discreet, you said. Not sure my wife should . . .'

'Absolutely.'

Hanging up, he felt the relief of a burden lifted and soon after, the less familiar sensation of guilt at a responsibility shirked.

He washed the last traces of Gentleman's Relish off his knife then climbed the stairs to fetch his wife's tray. He would spend the morning sterilizing seed trays and scrubbing flower pots in icy water as a penance.

You are invited to join us behind the scenes at Tinder Press

TINDER PRESS

To meet our authors, browse our books
and discover exclusive content on our
blog visit us at

www.tinderpress.co.uk

For the latest news and views from the team
Follow us on Twitter

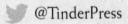 @TinderPress